WE LAST SAW JANE

STACY M. JONES

ISBN: 978-0-578-76146-6
Imprint: Stacy M. Jones
First printing edition: 2020

Any references to historical events, real people, or real places are used fictitiously. Names, characters, and places are products of the author's imagination.

Book design by Sharon Aponte, Chick & a Mouse Graphic Design.

For more information and to contact the author:
www.stacymjones.com

DEDICATION

For Troy Friends
lifelong friendships & wonderful memories

ACKNOWLEDGMENTS

Special thanks to my family and friends who are always a source of support and encouragement. Thank you to my early readers whose feedback was invaluable. Sharon Aponte, a wonderfully-skilled graphic designer, thank you for bringing my stories to life with amazing covers. Thank you to Dj Hendrickson for your insightful editing. To the detectives who I call for fact-checking - thank you always for answering my countless questions so patiently with your expert knowledge.

Thanks to my readers who have been with me since the first in the series and new readers just finding my books – I hope you enjoy reading these stories as much as I enjoy writing them.

WE LAST SAW JANE

CHAPTER 1

"Mom!" I yelled from the top of the stairs in my mother's house. My yellow Labrador, Dusty, who stayed permanently with my mom, sat at my feet. "What time is my dress fitting?"

My mother, Karen, appeared at the bottom of the stairs. She had grown her straight blonde hair to her shoulders and wore more makeup lately, highlighting her navy-blue eyes. She pursed her rose-colored lips at me. "Please, don't be so loud. It's at two. You have plenty of time. Liv is coming with us."

My mother and sister, Olivia, who went by Liv, were helping me plan my wedding. The date had been chosen for the end of the month in Lake Placid, New York. I had always wanted an October wedding, but that had only given us three months to pull together the entire event. To plan it efficiently, I had driven from the house I share with my fiancé, Det. Lucas Morgan, in Little Rock, Arkansas to my hometown of Troy, New York.

Luke was back in Little Rock wrapping up work before he drove up to meet me. He was finally taking a few weeks of vacation time he'd accrued over the last two years. Luke rarely took time off. It seemed whenever he tried, a murder would inevitably garner all of his attention.

"Is Liv on her way?" My sister was notoriously late for everything. I had no time to spare.

"Text and remind her," my mother said dismissively as she walked away from the stairs and out of sight.

I grabbed my phone from my pocket as I walked back into my bedroom. Even well into my thirties, my mother kept my room pretty much as I had when I left for college. There was a fresh coat of paint and a new chair and bed, but otherwise, it was the same. I plopped down on the bed and texted my sister a quick message I knew she wouldn't respond to. Getting her to text back took about the same effort as it did for her to show up on time.

I snuggled into bed and closed my eyes. Nearly everything was planned for the wedding. Luke and I opted for a small and intimate ceremony and reception with only our immediate families and closest friends. I had chosen the Whiteface Lodge and Spa in Lake Placid. Their wedding coordinator had taken care of everything on their end. I only had to worry about my dress, flowers, and a photographer. My last dress fitting today was the only thing left. I had about thirty minutes before we had to leave and I was ready. More than ready.

Just as I closed my eyes to take what Luke called a power nap, sirens wailed close by. Dusty's head perked up, and he shot off my bed into the hallway and down the stairs, his nails clicking on each step.

"It's the police, not the fire department," my mother called out.

I roused myself from bed. By the time I made my way down the stairs, my mother and the dog were nowhere in sight, but the front door was open. I stepped out onto the front porch to check out the action. The sirens had drawn out the whole neighborhood. My mother, with Dusty sitting at her feet, stood at the corner with several other neighbors. I stepped off the porch as two more cop cars came barreling towards the end of the block and made a right onto Pawling Avenue.

As I reached my mother, I asked, "What's going on?"

"I'm not sure exactly. The cops turned up a side street. There might be something going on at the school."

My mother, Dusty, and I walked up two blocks. Sure enough, cop cars sat on the campus of the Austen Academy for Girls, which was an all-girls boarding school developed in the 1890s. Its Collegiate Gothic style stone buildings sat behind a wrought iron fence that bordered the entire 130-acre campus. The campus had more than thirty buildings including dormitories and faculty residences. Girls came from across the globe to attend high school there.

When I was young, my mother often threatened to enroll me. My co-ed Catholic school was enough. I knew a few local girls who went to Austen, as it was known. Most of them were a tad too pretentious for me, but that was the vibe of the whole place. Looking back, I don't think my mother's nurse's salary could have afforded the tuition even if she wanted to follow through on the threat.

Not having attended there, however, didn't mean I didn't know the campus. When I was young, I was friends with a girl whose parents taught there. I often spent weekends playing on the campus. We'd swim in the pool, run around the grounds, and even ate in the dining hall. During those weekends, I also explored the incredibly creepy underground tunnels that ran through the campus from building to building. Students and faculty used those tunnels, especially in the winter.

Not much crime happened in our neighborhood and almost none at the school that I could recall. I stood watching for a few more minutes as cops, staff, and students milled about.

"Any idea what's happening?" my mother asked one of the neighbors, but they didn't know any more than we did.

I checked my phone for the time and nudged her. "We should go so we aren't late." I waited a few more minutes and then tugged on her shirt until she followed me back to the house. I knew she hated to miss the action. As we turned back onto Locust Avenue and were a few feet from the driveway, my sister came speeding down the street. She pulled her car to a screeching halt along the curb in front of the house and got out making apologies.

"Sorry, sorry, I'm here." Liv waved at us as she got out of her car and pulled herself together. She fluffed her blonde hair and pulled down her shirt over her flat belly. Liv was built like my mother – thin, blue-eyed, blonde, and buxom. I was the opposite in nearly every regard. I was taller than both, curves for miles, and my naturally auburn hair and dark eyes were from my father. I didn't look like I was related to either of them.

We went back into the house with the dog, grabbed our things, and headed out. My mother let me drive so we piled in my SUV and left for the dress shop a few miles away.

"When is Luke getting here?" Liv asked from the backseat.

"In a few days. He's going to drive up. I told him to fly, but he insisted he wanted to drive."

"Have you made sure they have enough rooms at the hotel?" my mother asked for the seventh time since I had arrived back in New York.

"I think if I called them again and asked, they'd hang up on me and cancel the wedding. Everything is planned. No need to worry. It's all under control." I navigated the streets into downtown Troy like the back of my hand. The dress shop was on 2nd Street in an old brownstone.

After finding a spot on the street and parallel parking with ease, we went into the shop. Within twenty minutes, the woman working had me in my dress and standing in front of a mirror. I had chosen a straight ivory-colored gown with a sweetheart neckline, three-quarter length sleeve, and an all-over overlay of lace. I had found the design in a vintage 1920s shop and searched until I found a similar dress. It fit me perfectly, coming in at my waist and accentuating my generous hips.

Turning around to my mother and sister, I held my arms out. "What do you think?"

Liv gushed over how good I looked, claiming it was the most beautiful dress I'd ever worn. My mother was quiet, which generally wasn't good. I held my breath while she assessed.

Finally, she broke out into a wide grin. "When you described it, I was concerned about how a straight dress would look, but this is beautiful." She kissed me on the cheek.

The woman in the shop approached, but the calm and pleasant look she had on her face when she dressed me was gone. I ran my hands down the dress thinking there must be a tear in the lace.

My mother noticed her, too. "You looked worried. Is everything okay?"

The woman held a hand up to her chest. "I heard on the news there is a student missing from Austen Academy for Girls."

My mother and I shared a look. That's what had been happening with all the cops at the school.

"Do they know what happened?" I asked, wanting to get out of the dress quickly so I could check my phone for any news.

"I have a friend who works with the police department," she said, wringing her hands. "They have no idea, but it's going to be big news. The student is a senator's daughter."

CHAPTER 2

Luke clicked away on his laptop, typing a report that was due to Captain Meadows within an hour. His mind was everywhere but on the report. The wedding and the drive to New York hung over his head. There was still so much to do.

Det. Bill Tyler wheeled his chair over in front of Luke's desk. He tapped on it twice with a pen. "What time are we all going out tonight?"

Luke's best friend and best man, Cooper Deagnan, had planned a bachelor party for later that evening. "I think we're meeting for dinner at seven. I'm not sure what else Cooper has planned. You still coming?"

"As long as there are no strippers, I'm there."

Luke laughed. "That's not on the agenda. I think we are getting dinner and then going back to Cooper's place to play some cards. I told him I wanted something low-key. I'm fairly certain after the few months Cooper has had, he wants the same."

"Being accused of murder will do that to a guy. My wife would kill me if there were strippers."

Det. Tyler had been married for as long as Luke knew him. He was probably the best husband, outside of his own father, Luke had ever known. If his marriage to Riley was half as happy as Tyler's marriage, Luke would count himself lucky.

Luke shook his head. "I don't think Riley would be happy either. What are you going to do without me for six weeks?"

"I'm not sure," Det. Tyler said, laughing. "I'm waiting to see who is going to be the first to try to take your job while you're gone."

"They can try, but they won't succeed." Luke had been made head of the homicide division more than a year ago. He had the best closure rate of any detective. He had earned the spot. It didn't mean that more senior detectives had been happy with the choice, but for the most part, Luke was well-respected. He never shied away from the tough cases. In fact, he relished them. But six weeks of vacation time was calling his name, and nothing was going to stand in the way this time.

Luke had taken time before the wedding and after for their honeymoon. Riley had left that up to Luke to plan. He clicked open another browser on his laptop and pulled up their itinerary. They were flying from New York to London and then onto Paris. There were some smaller stops along the way in both England and France. Luke didn't care where they went as long as they had the chance to enjoy their time together.

He closed the browser for the trip and finished typing his report without interruption. He dropped it off on Captain Meadows' desk. His boss had left earlier in the day without explanation, but Luke assumed he'd see him tonight at Cooper's. Luke went back to his desk, closed down his laptop, and gathered his things. He took one last look around his desk to make sure he had everything and breathed a sigh of relief. Luke had closed his final case three days earlier. He had nothing pending and no cases had to be reassigned to other officers. One homicide that had dragged on without even so much as a hint at a suspect was now fully in the hands of Det. Tyler. There was nothing left for Luke to do.

He waved to a few people and headed out the door, hoping to avoid the inside of the police station for the full six weeks. Before heading home, Luke drove to his parents' house in Hillcrest. His parents, Spencer and Lucia, lived in the same house Luke had grown up in. They were flying up to New York a few days before the wedding. His mother had never been to Lake Placid and couldn't wait to enjoy the town. For weeks now, she had been calling Luke talking about all the places she wanted to see and asking a million questions about the wedding. He loved that she was so excited. Riley had even gone out of her way to include his mom in decisions about the wedding.

Arriving, Luke parked in the driveway and walked into the side entrance. He stepped into the kitchen expecting his parents' normal chatter, but the house was unusually quiet. "Anyone here?" Luke called out as he made his way through the house.

"In the living room," Spencer responded. "Come see this, Luke. Senator Thomas Crandall's daughter is missing."

Senator Crandall was a long-time senator from California and now Senate Majority Leader. He wielded immense power. Luke didn't follow politics much, but he heard the man's name mentioned from time to time. Luke knew nearly nothing of the man's family though.

Luke went into the living room, gave his mother a quick hug and kiss on the cheek, and took a seat next to his father on the couch. "What happened?"

Spencer lowered the volume on the television. "His daughter, Jane, is at a boarding school in New York. It seems she wasn't in her dorm this morning."

"Is that so unusual with kids from boarding school?" Luke didn't have too favorable an impression about boarding school kids, and he wasn't even sure why. He didn't know any.

"I wondered the same thing, but it sounds like there might be more to the story," Spencer said absently, his eyes still focused on the news.

Lucia sniffled back a tear. "I know how that poor momma feels. When Lily went missing, it was like the world stopped."

Luke's younger sister went missing her freshman year of college and was murdered by a serial killer who had targeted young girls at colleges across the country. Luke solved the case years after his sister's disappearance. While Luke had done his best to make peace with the situation, he didn't think it would ever get easier for his parents. The last thing Luke wanted was for his mother to be sad.

"Why don't you change the channel and watch something else," he suggested.

Spencer reached his hand over and patted Luke's arm. "We live with it every day. There's no point running from it."

"Is Riley all set with the planning? She said things were coming along when I spoke to her yesterday," Lucia said, a smile finally appearing on her face for the first time since Luke arrived. "We can't wait to see you two married, and it's a wonderful vacation for us."

"Riley said everything is going well. She has her last dress fitting today. I'm itching to get up there and relax."

The three of them grew quiet when the news resumed. The national news anchor detailed the disappearance and showed a photo of a smiling girl with curly light brown hair. Jane Crandall was a sixteen-year-old junior at Austen Academy for Girls. By all accounts, she went missing some time Friday evening. Reports indicated Jane's friends grew worried when Jane missed breakfast and their run earlier this morning. When Jane didn't show up at the dining hall for Saturday afternoon lunch either and couldn't be found in her room, her friends became concerned and contacted Jane's housemother. The woman reported Jane had been in her room at the nine-thirty check-in the night before. Jane's roommate was out of town for the weekend. Right now, that was the last anyone had seen Jane.

When the program took a commercial break, Spencer asked, "How does a student go missing from a school like that? Isn't there security?"

Luke sat back on the couch. "I don't know, Dad. Luckily, this case is far away from me."

"Not so far," Lucia said, giving her son a look that only mothers can give.

"What do you mean?"

Spencer clicked off the television. "The school is located in Troy, New York. You're headed right where the national news is descending. Good thing you're not getting married locally. They said in an earlier report, the senator and his wife are on their way there."

Luke pulled out his phone from his pocket and did a quick search for the school's address. His stomach dropped when he realized Austen Academy was a mere two blocks from Riley's mom's house.

"I'm not leaving for a few days. I'm sure by the time I get up there, it will be all sorted out," Luke said, hoping it was true.

Luke spent another hour with his parents, talking over the wedding and details for their trip. After Luke was assured they had everything under control and confirmed again his father would rent a car upon his arrival in New York, Luke kissed his mother goodbye and left.

As Luke drove back to his house in the Heights neighborhood of Little Rock, a niggling feeling crept up his spine. He hoped that Riley stayed focused on the wedding planning and kept herself out of trouble.

CHAPTER 3

"I think Anderson Cooper is standing in front of our house," Liv squealed with her nose pressed against a front living room window. The sheer white curtains wrapped around her like a full-body veil. I sat glued to the television and had been in the same spot since we got back home.

By the time we arrived back in our neighborhood after leaving the dress shop, news vans had already lined up and down our narrow side street. After pulling in the driveway, I walked to the end of the block to see news media had swarmed Pawling Avenue on both sides of the street and were now taking up side streets as well. The media grabbed any spot they could find.

Most had their camera lights on and their respective reporters were interviewing residents of our community. My mother and sister made a beeline to the house to avoid the crowd. I had to brush off two reporters as I walked to the end of the block and back home.

Troy only had a population of about fifty-thousand people. We had two prestigious colleges – Russel Sage and Rensselaer Polytechnic Institute – as well as Hudson Valley Community College, all tucked into eleven square miles. You couldn't go anywhere without tripping over a college student. The din of rumors and chatter about Luke's capture of a serial killer, the man responsible for his sister's murder, living in our community, had only recently died down. The city had made national news then. Now it seems they were back.

"Riley, did you hear me? Anderson Cooper's out front," Liv said annoyed with me for not listening.

"I don't think it's Anderson Cooper," I started to say, but then changed the channel from a local news station to CNN. Sure enough, Anderson Cooper was standing on the sidewalk with my mother's house in the background. Liv peeking through the blinds was in the live on-air shot.

"Forget what I just said. Anderson Cooper and your eyeballs are on the national news, looking like a creeper spying on him."

"I've never been on television before," Liv said, fluffing her hair.

I threw a couch pillow at her back. "Seriously, get out of the window or go out and give an interview."

Liv turned to me. "Jack just pulled up. I'm waiting to see if he gives an interview."

Jack Malone was my mother's boyfriend. They had gone to grade school and high school together and then later married and divorced other people. While they'd seen each other at our Catholic church from time to time, it was Jack's help on the serial killer case last year that reconnected them. They had been inseparable since.

Jack had been a homicide detective for the Troy Police Department until his retirement. Last year, after helping me solve a local cold case and bringing a serial killer to justice, Jack got the investigative bug again. He had applied for his private investigator license and had been taking some cases. Given how well known he was in the city and his stellar reputation, Jack didn't even advertise his services but had more work than he could handle.

Liv left her post at the window and sat down next to me on the couch. "Jack dodged the news. He's on his way in. What has the news said?"

I hit the mute button. "The same thing they have been saying all afternoon. They believe Jane Crandall went missing some time Friday night. There is some speculation she ran away, but they haven't confirmed anything."

"They won't," Jack said, his voice deep and strong behind us. He kissed me on the top of my head and did the same to my sister. "They are keeping this all close to the vest, considering whose kid she is." Jack stopped talking when he saw my mother and went over to give her a hug and a kiss.

"Dinner will be ready soon," she said. "Girls, why don't you go wash up for dinner."

Liv and I shared a look and laughed under our breath. We were both in our thirties and hadn't been told to wash up for dinner since we were in our teens. Even at that, my mother, a registered nurse, worked the evening shift at the hospital, and more times than not, either she'd have dinner ready we could reheat or I'd cook. When we were much younger, we had a sitter who only cared that we went to bed on time so she didn't have to deal with us.

Liv got up and I followed her to the kitchen. We sat down at the table side by side across from my mother and Jack. We each served ourselves meatloaf, mashed potatoes, and carrots. I wasn't a huge fan of meatloaf, but certainly wasn't going to complain.

"Do you think they will find the girl, Jack?" my mother asked, taking a bite of her dinner.

"They better, or they are going to have a very public debacle on their hands." Jack looked over at my mom. "I talked to one of the detectives, and while they are working to rule out kidnapping, they also think Jane might have run away. I don't know much about the missing girl, but all kinds of rumors are flying that she might have been in trouble before, which is why she was sent to boarding school. Nothing has been confirmed though."

"Drugs?" my mother asked with her eyebrows raised.

"Not that anyone said yet, but you never know."

With annoyance in her voice, my mother added, "I hope they find her soon. The media outside my door is going to get old quickly."

Liv leaned her arms on the table. "Mom, the media should be the least of our worries. A girl is missing. The media is a minor inconvenience."

My mother waved her fork at my sister. "Olivia, don't scold me. You know very well I want the girl found safe. I'm just saying that if she's one of these rich kids who took off and is causing a big ruckus for nothing, it's a waste of our police department's time and energy."

"You sound cold though," Liv said frowning.

"Just eat your dinner."

A cellphone rang, but I knew it wasn't mine. Mine was upstairs. I glanced at my sister and then my mother. Both shook their heads.

Jack stuffed the meatloaf on his fork into his mouth. "Sorry. It's mine." He reached in his pocket and pulled it out, moving the screen farther away so he could read the number. "Don't know who that is." He silenced the phone and set it on the table. Not even thirty seconds later, it rang again. "It's the same number. I better grab it."

Jack stepped away from the table, and we continued eating. My mother asked my sister about her new job as a receptionist for a doctor's office, which Liv seemed to enjoy. Liv had been dating and living with my ex-husband until about a month ago. I think the idea they were both doing something slightly forbidden had been the draw. When that wore off, so did the relationship. Although my mother had told her repeatedly that she could come back home and live, my sister opted for an apartment a few streets over. I was just about to ask Liv when I was going to get the tour of her new place when Jack came back. His brow furrowed and he seemed agitated.

"Everything okay?" My mother patted Jack's arm as he sat down.

His eyes flashed around the table. Jack seemed to be a bit lost for words. He took a sip of his drink and then dropped his news. "That was Senator Thomas Crandall. Apparently, he is not getting the response from the police he hoped so he's looking to hire me to help locate his daughter. He'd like to meet me as soon as he lands this evening."

"Well that's a big win for your business," I said.

"It is," Jack said hesitantly. "It just puts me in an awkward position with the police department. Crandall is coming to me because he's not getting what he wants from them."

"What does he want that he's not getting?" Liv asked, finishing the last of the mashed potatoes on her plate.

"There has only been one detective assigned to the case, and Crandall is a bit put off by that. All the speculation about Jane running away has put him off. The senator feels they aren't taking it seriously, and I can't blame him. If it were my kid, I'd be doing everything possible to find her." Jack dug into his meatloaf while it was still warm.

"It's not out of the question to think she ran away," my mother said between bites. "I think they've already made too big of a deal about this, the media included. They don't even know anything yet."

I wasn't sure why my mother was being so dismissive. If one of us was missing, she'd tear the whole country apart looking for us. I didn't feel like getting into an argument with her though. "Did you say you'd take the job?" I asked Jack.

"I did," Jack said, putting down his fork. He raised his eyebrows at me. "What do you think? You want to come to the initial meeting with me?"

"She absolutely does not!" my mother yelled, dropping her fork to her plate.

Of course, my interest was piqued, but the last thing I needed right now was an investigation. Still, though, this could be big for my private investigation firm. Not to mention, I probably knew the Austen Academy campus better than Jack. "I'd be happy to go for an initial meeting and give some insight if I have it, but my mother is right, I can't get too involved."

My mother glared at me across the table. As the saying goes, if looks could kill, I'd be dead.

CHAPTER 4

"Cooper, what time is everyone getting here?" Adele called from the bathroom.

Cooper got up from the couch and walked down the short hall to the door and opened it. Adele stood in front of the mirror wrapped only in a towel applying her makeup. He explained, "I'm meeting everyone at the restaurant, so you have plenty of time. I feel bad we're making you leave for the night."

Adele laughed and leaned into him. "You aren't making me leave. I volunteered so you boys can do your guy thing for the night. Besides, being here and playing cards is far tamer than most bachelor parties."

Cooper tipped Adele's face towards him and kissed her passionately. "Those days are far behind me."

Cooper wasn't exaggerating. After waking several months ago to find a dead woman in his bed and no memory of the night before, his days of bars and drinking were over for good. Not that he missed it. Cooper was head over heels in love with Adele, and he wasn't going to let anything mess it up. Adele had stood graciously by his side until the real killer was caught, and then she moved in with Cooper, into the very condo where the murder had happened. At first, Cooper thought the idea was out of the question, but after painting and getting new furniture and Adele moving in, there were days Cooper didn't even think about the murder. His condo was his again.

Adele kissed Cooper and slid a hand down his chest. "I'll be right down the road at the Marriott if you need anything. Have you talked to Riley since she got to New York?"

Cooper and Riley had been in business together for a few years. She was also one of his best friends. "She called me shortly after she arrived, but I haven't heard from her since. I'm sure she's busy getting things ready."

Adele ran a hand across his belly. "I was wondering what you'd think about driving up with Luke. We can grab a rental car and hotel and spend some time up there before the wedding. I don't have any court cases pending."

Cooper was glad Adele's cases were slowing down. She had launched her new criminal defense firm when she moved to Little Rock months earlier, and work had been busy from the start. "I don't have any investigations pending. I testified on that custody case last week. Let me ask Luke tonight. I'm sure he wouldn't mind." Cooper left Adele to finish getting ready. He had to change his shirt anyway before he left to meet Luke and the rest of the guys.

About an hour later, Adele left, and Cooper was right behind her. They gave each other a quick peck and a hug before walking in opposite directions. Cooper walked the few blocks to the restaurant and found Luke waiting for him.

"They have the reservation under your name."

Luke hitched his jaw towards the dining room. "I figured that out. They are just getting our table set up for us. There's just five of us, right?"

"Yeah, for dinner. I figured I'd keep that just a few of us. The rest of the guys are meeting us for cards and drinks at my place later," Cooper said, hoping for the large round table they usually had in the back of the dining room. He had hoped they'd sit them far away from the others to give them some space. "Before everyone gets here, Adele asked if you'd mind if we drove up to New York with you. She wants to take some vacation time before the wedding."

"Fine by me. It's a long drive, and the company would be nice. I can check with Riley if you want to stay at the house. I'm sure there's enough room."

"That's what I was thinking, too. I'll ask Riley. Let me send her a text right now."

Luke waved him off. "Wait until morning. Riley told me she was going to spend time with her sister tonight."

The hostess came over and escorted Luke and Cooper to the round table in the back of the dining room where Cooper hoped they'd sit. They each ordered a beer as they waited for the others. "Are you nervous about getting married?" Cooper asked.

Luke shook his head. "Sometimes I'm nervous Riley will be a runaway bride but other than that, not a worry in my head. We are great together. I can't wait to start a family."

The server dropped off their drinks. Cooper took a sip of his beer. "You know it's funny. Last year, I would have thought you were crazy, but since meeting Adele, I feel the same."

Luke raised his eyebrows. "You're ready for marriage?"

"Not yet, but soon."

Within a few minutes, the rest of Luke and Cooper's friends arrived. Det. Bill Tyler was first and Captain Meadows followed. Joe, who was Luke's neighbor and the husband of Riley's best friend, Emma, was last.

"Sorry guys, getting out of the house was a chore," Joe said as he sat. "Emma was glued to the news and feeding the baby, so I had Sophie to get into bed. Dealing with a three-year-old is like wrestling an alligator."

"What's on the news that's so important?" Cooper asked.

Joe informed them all about the case playing out in New York. He didn't know much, only what Emma had yelled to him from the other room. Luke knew about the case and added what Joe left out.

Luke took a sip of his beer and finished by saying, "I have my fingers crossed Riley doesn't worm her way into the investigation. The school is not even two blocks away from her mother's house, and you know how she is. Trouble seems to find her even when she's not looking for it."

The server came by again and took the rest of their drink and food order. When she was gone, Captain Meadows said, "You know without a doubt Riley will find a way to be involved. She'll be interviewing a witness as she walks down the aisle."

That got a laugh out of all of them because it was true, but Cooper caught the worry in Luke's eyes. Luke may have been laughing with the rest of them, but it was obvious to Cooper he was concerned. In truth, so was Cooper. His phone buzzed in his pocket but he didn't answer. He let it go to voicemail. A few seconds later, the familiar buzz of a text vibrated against his hip.

"Excuse me for a minute," Cooper said, checking his phone. He held it up. "Adele has called me twice, and I want to see if anything is wrong." That was a complete lie. It was Riley who had called twice.

Cooper navigated out of the restaurant to the sidewalk. He called Riley back. "This better be important," he said when she answered. "I'm with Luke at dinner for his bachelor party, and this is a no girls allowed kind of deal."

"Sorry to interrupt. It is important. Otherwise, I wouldn't have called," Riley explained. "Are you with Luke right now or did you step away?"

"I stepped away."

"Good. Do you know about the case of the senator's missing kid?"

"At the girl's school. Joe and Luke were just talking about it," Cooper said dryly. He had assumed this is what Riley had been calling about. There was no way a huge case was happening feet from her, and she wouldn't be involved. "I hope you haven't gotten involved with that."

"I'm not…really," Riley said with hesitation in her voice. "Jack got a call at dinner from Senator Thomas Crandall. He wants Jack to help find his daughter."

"Okay, well, Jack is more than qualified to handle it. He was a detective after all. Why are you calling me?" Cooper had tried to sound stern, but it came across angry and it wasn't the tone he meant to strike.

"Jack asked me to sit in on the initial meeting with him—"

Cooper interrupted. "You are supposed to be up there planning your wedding. That's a terrible idea. I know for a fact it would upset Luke."

"Right, Cooper, calm down. I'm not being stupid. If you'd just let me talk, I'll tell you."

Cooper didn't say anything.

Riley continued, "Jack wants me to go to the initial meeting with him and walk him around the Austen Academy grounds. I had a friend who went to school there so I know the campus well. It's just a basic consult. I might give Jack some insight here or there, but I won't get involved. Besides, I'm busy. You're my business partner so I wanted to run it by you. It can't hurt to have our business in front of the Senate Majority Leader. I'm also calling because there is an opportunity for you to help Jack if you'd like. He told me he can't handle the case alone. It's too much for him. I suggested since you were coming up here anyway maybe you'd come up earlier and give him a hand."

Cooper hadn't been expecting that. "I was going to see if you minded if Adele and I came early with Luke anyway so tell Jack I'd be happy to help."

"Perfect, and you and Adele can stay here at the house. I'll get the spare room ready for you."

Cooper ended the call and went back to the table.

"Everything okay?" Joe asked.

"All is good. She forgot something back at the condo and wanted to make sure we weren't back yet," Cooper said, sipping his beer. Luke caught his eye though, and they both knew Cooper was lying.

CHAPTER 5

Jack and I left the house shortly after I hung up with Cooper. I was glad he had agreed to come to New York earlier than planned and help out. Jack was too. It was a big case, and Jack needed a sounding board at least. As much as the case interested me, my mother was right. I had more important things to focus on.

We walked to the Austen Academy campus. There was no point driving given how close it was. As we walked the two blocks, we were stopped every few feet by a reporter. Neither Jack nor I had anything to say. They'd be clamoring for an interview once they found out Jack had been hired by Senator Crandall. We could avoid it for now.

We walked to the side entrance of the school, but the driveway was blocked by cops. Surprisingly, we were waved through after Jack and I showed some identification. Not all the local beat cops knew Jack on sight, but they certainly knew his name. We continued down the road until we entered the main part of the campus.

Sidewalks cut a path between gray stone gothic buildings and an expansive lawn. Black light poles dotted along the path. The landscaping was understated but in keeping with the feel of the campus.

I took Jack to the right, straight to the administration building where we were meeting with Senator Crandall. Jack pulled open the heavy wood door and was met with a stern-faced woman.

"Roseline," she said, putting her hand out to Jack. "I'm Headmistress Marybeth Winslow's administrative assistant. I assume you're Jack Malone, the detective Senator Crandall called. We've been expecting you."

She gave me a once over and offered me her hand. Her grip was stronger than any man's I've ever felt and didn't match her petite frame. I don't know why, but the image of her wringing a chicken's neck with her bare hands popped into my head.

"I didn't know Mr. Malone would be bringing someone else," Roseline said. It was more question than a statement.

I introduced myself and explained who I was and why I was there, adding that I was familiar with the school's grounds and could be of some basic assistance to Jack. All in all, I felt a bit out of place.

"You didn't go to school here though, correct?" Roseline asked, looking down her nose at me.

"No, I live in the neighborhood and went to a different high school."

"I see," she said curtly, turning around and giving me her back. "Follow me."

"Will we be meeting with Headmistress Winslow?" Jack asked.

Not bothering to even look at him, she said, "No, she's left for the day."

Jack and I shared a look and followed Roseline into the building, down a long corridor, and then up a flight of stairs. We walked halfway down the dimly lit hallway, and she held the door open to a conference room. After Jack and I stepped through, Roseline shut the door and left without saying another word.

"I wasn't expecting a party, but that was a fairly cold reception," I said.

"She's probably worried we are going to find them at fault for something. A kid is missing from their school. Most likely the school is closing ranks worried about their liability. They have a hefty endowment and a board of trustees with deep pockets. Their reputation is on the line."

"You'd think Headmistress Winslow would be here then…" I trailed off as the door opened.

"I don't care anything about their reputation. I only care about finding my daughter," Senator Thomas Crandall said from the doorway. The man stood about six-four, had a head full of dark hair and piercing blue eyes.

I had seen the man on television, but nothing could have prepared me for his confident, no-nonsense demeanor. Jack wasn't an easy man to intimidate, but even he looked uneasy.

Jack stepped forward with his hand outstretched and introduced both of us. He explained, "Certainly, Senator. I was just explaining to Riley why the school staff gave us such an icy welcome. The main goal, as you said, is to find your daughter."

"At any cost," Crandall said, raising his eyebrows. "If it destroys the reputation of the school, you do it. If it angers your former police department, you do it. I don't care if it angers the governor of New York, you do it. Can you handle that?"

"Sir, I'm just here to find your daughter. I'm retired. It doesn't matter who I anger at this point. I don't owe anyone anything," Jack explained.

"And you?" Crandall asked, looking in my direction.

"The same," I said. "I run my own business. Nothing gets in my way of finding the truth."

"Very good. My wife, Lynn, is in Jane's room right now. I thought you might want to speak to me first. Then we can join Lynn at the last place my daughter was seen."

The three of us sat down at the table. Crandall pulled out a hefty roll of cash and handed it to Jack. He slipped it in his pocket. They must have discussed money over the phone because neither of them said a word about it or barely acknowledged the exchange. This was Jack's investigation, so I was hesitant to jump in and start even though I had several questions.

"When was the last time you spoke to Jane?" Jack asked.

"Jane's mother spoke to her Friday morning before classes. It's been several days since I spoke to her. We normally video chat over a weekend, but I've been in D.C. and quite busy with work, as you may be aware."

There was pending legislation for healthcare and infrastructure I knew was in debate in the Senate. Crandall's schedule had to be packed right now. The fact he was sitting in front of us instead of just sending his wife or a staffer was a testament to his relationship with his daughter or his reputation. I wasn't sure which at the moment.

"Was there anything odd or unusual about either of your interactions with Jane?" Jack pressed.

"Not when I spoke to her, but Lynn said Friday morning Jane seemed a bit melancholy. That's the word she used. Jane had taken a history test and didn't do as well as she wanted. She was also having some disagreements with some girls here on campus. I don't know what that was about. You'll have to ask Lynn."

Jack looked at me. I took it as my cue to ask anything I wanted to know. "Senator, was Jane dating anyone?"

Crandall's face hardened. "Jane is only sixteen. She wasn't allowed to date. Besides the stellar education, that's why we sent her to an all-girls school. She didn't need to be around boys. I know there have been some rumors about Jane having some behavior issues. Nothing could be further from the truth. Jane has always been well-behaved."

Not being allowed to date wasn't an answer, but I was hesitant to push more right now. "Did Jane get along with all of her teachers?"

"As far as I know."

Jack and I took turns running down a full gauntlet of questions typical for a missing person's case — assessing where Jane might have gone if she were upset. We asked if there was any other family she might be visiting, friends back home she might have turned to, what kind of access to money Jane had, and so forth. Crandall answered each question. I didn't get the sense he had anything to hide.

Jane has access to a good sum of money in her bank account, but Crandall was watching those. Jane hadn't touched any money since last weekend when she went with friends on a shopping trip with a houseparent. Jane didn't need money at school so the last account activity wasn't surprising.

Jack pushed his seat back and leaned forward on the table. "Did your daughter have issues with anyone at the school?"

Crandall shook his head. "Not that I'm aware of. As I said, everything has seemed fine."

Jack looked to me and back at the Senator. "I don't have any more questions for now. Let's go join your wife, and we can get a look through Jane's room."

Crandall stood. "I think that's probably best. To be honest, while I was active in my daughter's life, my wife would know more of the day-to-day."

We followed Crandall back out of the administration building the same way we had arrived. Once outside we followed the sidewalk across the campus until we reached the dormitory and academic buildings. If my memory was correct, most buildings were a mix of both. Classrooms were on lower floors while girls' bedrooms were on the upper two floors of each building. Each building had common rooms in the basement. Two dining halls were shared by all.

Jack nodded to cops as we found our way into Jane's building. We went up four flights of stairs and made our way down the hall to Jane's bedroom. There we found Lynn sitting on Jane's bed reading from a journal.

As we entered, she held the book toward her husband. "How could we not know this, Thomas? Jane was pledging some secret society. That's why she's been so upset lately. She was being hazed."

CHAPTER 6

"Hazed?" Crandall asked confused, taking the journal from his wife. He didn't read it but handed it to Jack who in turn handed it to me. Crandall then introduced Jack and me to Lynn.

Lynn was a petite woman, probably no more than five-foot-two and thin. She had shoulder-length blonde hair and a pretty face. It was clear she had been crying. Pointing to the journal, she cast her eyes toward me, pleading, "Will you read it please and tell me what you think?"

I sat down at the desk nearest the door and started to read. While I did that, Jack asked Lynn similar questions to what we had asked Crandall. The answers were the same. There were no leads to go on. I focused on adolescent print in front of me. Jane's handwriting was neat, sharp, and precise. She didn't doodle as other girls did in journals. There were no hearts or bubble letters. The letters were straight and crisp.

Jane started the journal at the beginning of the school year just after Labor Day. Many of the first journal entries were about her classes and a guy named Liam who Jane had met the last school term. They had talked through text most of the summer. Jane hoped she'd see him soon. There was little mention though of where they had met or where Liam went to school. There wasn't even a last name to go on, but it all seemed fairly harmless and typical for sixteen. I kept reading.

In late September, a few weeks into the school term, Jane's entries had turned darker. She had written about being chosen for a secret society called the Clovers. From Jane's writing, it seemed the society invited juniors to join, and they were put through what most would call pledging from October through December. When school resumed after the holiday break, the girls who had done well would be provisionally sworn into the society. If they succeeded during this time, their senior year, they'd be full members.

Jane was excited at first to have been selected. As Jane noted, only twelve girls with good grades, athletic ability, and who had a good standing on campus with teachers and other students were selected into the Clovers each year. It was an exclusive and secret club.

Jane didn't detail what membership into the Clovers meant, but as the weeks wore on, her journal entries detailed the stress and strain of pledging. There was one senior in particular who Jane referred to simply with the letter N. All that could be discerned from the journal entries was that N had it out for Jane. Every chance N had it seemed she belittled Jane. The two girls seemed at odds with each other.

In one entry, Jane even thought about quitting, but she indicated there was no way out. She had to finish. I found that hard to believe, but Jane believed it. While Jane spoke at length about how she felt about the pledging process, she didn't detail the activities. Nothing was spelled out. I wanted to know if it was similar to pledging a sorority in college or if it was something more sinister. Lynn said Jane had been hazed, but I wasn't seeing that in the journal. I saw bullying for sure but not hazing.

I finished reading and set the book down on the desk. When there was a break in the conversation, I said as much. "It seems Jane was invited to join a secret society and one of the girls, a senior, was bullying Jane quite a bit. The pledging process to get into this group seemed to be causing Jane quite a bit of distress."

Senator Crandall turned to me. "My wife said Jane was being hazed. What specifically happened to her?"

"It doesn't say," I said, standing. "This is one avenue we definitely should explore. Is there any chance at all Jane ran away? She said in her journal she wanted to quit this society called the

Clovers, but she couldn't. Could Jane have seen running away as her only way out?"

Senator Crandall's face fell. "I didn't even know about this at all. Maybe I didn't know what was happening in my daughter's life as much as I thought I did." He looked to his wife and asked seriously, "Lynn, could Jane have run away?"

Lynn dropped her head. "Jane would have just come home. I'm sure of it. She would have called me or her sister at least."

I recalled Jane being the youngest of three children, but neither Jack nor I had asked about her siblings. "Is there a way I can speak to Jane's sister?"

Lynn wrote down a name and number for me. I checked my watch. It was getting close to nine. "Is it too late to call?"

"No, Abby goes to Princeton. She's aware Jane is missing," Lynn explained. She teared up again. "I knew we shouldn't have let Jane go this far to school. Abby and her brother stayed close to home for high school. She was too young to be so far from us."

I didn't know what to say. Lynn's guilt was written all over her face, and no matter what I said, it wouldn't take it away. I took the slip of paper and stepped out into the hallway for privacy. I turned to the left and then to the right looking for a seat where I could make the call. There was a bench at the far end of the hall. I walked down as I punched in Abby's phone number.

"Hello," a young woman said tentatively after a few rings.

I introduced myself and explained her mother had given me her number. "I just need to ask a few questions about Jane if that's okay."

"That's fine," Abby said. She loudly exhaled a breath. "I hadn't talked to Jane all week though. I've had mid-terms, and I've been focused on schoolwork. I'm not sure how much help I can be. The police didn't seem to think anything I said was important."

"I'm not the cops," I reiterated. "I think everything is important. Sometimes it's the smallest details pieced together that give the full story. Do you have any idea where your sister might be?"

"I wish I did," Abby said softly. "Jane is a good kid. She never got in trouble much when she was younger. That was all my brother. He's the middle wild child. Jane and I were both overachievers. You might be thinking because she's at boarding school, Jane was either a bad kid my parents sent away or she's some spoiled rich kid. She's neither."

I assured her, "I don't make judgments about people. It would close me off to information if I walked into situations assuming I knew things I didn't." It was the truth. I didn't know why Jane was at Austen Academy. The girls who typically went to Austen Academy were like Abby had described, but I didn't know Jane. I asked, "Did Jane tell you anything about being invited to join a secret society called the Clovers?"

"No," Abby said, confusion in her voice. "I've never heard anything about that, but it would surprise me if Jane joined. My sister is outgoing and likable, but she's not easily swayed. When I told her last year that I was pledging a sorority, she thought it was stupid. She asked me why I'd put myself through humiliation just to be able to call some girls sisters. I can't see her joining a group like that."

"Jane did join," I explained. "She wrote about her experience in her journal. She was being bullied. But it struck me as odd that Jane said she wanted to quit but couldn't. Does that sound like your sister?"

"Not at all. If Jane put herself through something like that, it was for a good reason. That's all I can tell you."

"Did Jane ever tell you about a boy named Liam?"

Abby said the name a few times aloud as if searching her memory. "No, I can't say that's a name I recall. It wouldn't surprise me if Jane had a boyfriend or at least someone who liked her. As I said, she was friendly and outgoing and pretty, but she was level-headed, too."

"You said earlier your sister isn't like most boarding school kids. Your mother said neither you nor your brother went away for high school. Why is Jane across the country at Austen Academy?"

"Jane's best friend Maddie went there," Abby explained. "Jane and Maddie went through grade school and middle school together. Maddie had a scholarship for Austen Academy, and Jane didn't want her to go alone. My parents can afford it. Austen has amazing academics so after a good deal of begging, they allowed Jane to attend."

This was the first I had heard about Maddie. There was no mention of her in Jane's journal either. "Do you know how I can reach Maddie?"

"You can't," Abby said, matter-of-factly. "Maddie killed herself last year at the end of the school term. Jane never believed Maddie killed herself though. If anything was troubling Jane, that was it."

"I had never heard about a suicide at the school. I have family in the area who never mentioned anything either," I said, wondering why it never made the news. If my mother knew, she would have told me.

"You wouldn't. Austen Academy has a long history of keeping scandal quiet. If my father wasn't a senator, you probably wouldn't have even known Jane was missing." Abby got quiet for several seconds. Expelling a breath, she added, "Jane said there is a lot that goes on at the school no one knows about. Jane never elaborated, but she said I wouldn't believe half of it. I don't know what happened to Jane. I couldn't even venture a guess, but I haven't heard from her. But please tell me anything I can do to bring my sister home, and I'll do it."

CHAPTER 7

Luke's bare thigh stuck to Cooper's leather sofa as he stretched his legs the morning after his bachelor party. He ran a hand down his chest and then rubbed his eyes. Sunlight shot through the blinds, alerting Luke it was well into the morning. Glancing down at the floor, Luke's clothes were in a heap next to him.

Luke hadn't had that much to drink – a few beers with dinner, a few more at Cooper's while they played cards and a celebratory shot of whiskey. He had no idea how Riley drank the stuff. It burned going down and sat like a brick in his stomach.

"You awake?" Cooper said quietly from the kitchen.

Luke sat up, wearing just his boxers and a tee-shirt. "Yeah, that was a late night. I'm not so much hungover as I am tired." Luke yawned and stretched. "What time is it?"

"Just after nine. Adele's coming back at noon so there's time if you want to go back to sleep."

"No, I'm good. I have to get home. That was a great night."

Cooper poured a cup of coffee and carried it in to him. Handing Luke the mug, Cooper said, "I'm glad you had a good time. I have some news though." Cooper sat down in the recliner across from the couch.

Luke took a sip and savored it. It was just what he needed. He gave Cooper a half-hearted grin. "I know. Riley is involved in the case up there."

"How'd you know?"

Luke laughed. "I've known you half your life. You don't lie well. I assumed last night at the restaurant when you said it was Adele, it was Riley who texted you. Call it a gut feeling."

Cooper cocked his head to the side. "Jack got a call from Senator Crandall asking him to find his missing daughter. Riley explained Jack asked her to go to the initial meeting with him. If it makes you feel better, Riley asked me if I wanted to help him instead of her. She knows she can't get involved."

Luke took another sip of coffee. He appreciated Cooper trying to cover for Riley. "When has Riley ever done what she knows she's supposed to do? The case will pull her in. She'll meet the mom or some best friend and attach like she does. Then she will be all over it. We both know her."

Cooper sat back more in the chair and took a sip of coffee. "I told her I'd help Jack. This way I can keep her at bay. I can tell her what's going on so she still feels like she's a part of it, and I'll let her tell me her opinion of what we need to do without her having to be directly involved."

"You think that's going to work?" Luke asked skeptically.

"I think it's better than nothing."

Luke considered it. He realized last night that it was a forgone conclusion Riley would get involved in the case. He hadn't known she had asked for Cooper's help though. Maybe Cooper was right, and with his help, it might get her to back off and focus on the wedding.

"Riley said Adele and I should stay at the house. When do you want to start the drive up? It takes twenty-two hours, right?"

Luke nodded. "I was going to do it in two days, but if you want to take turns driving, we can just do it overnight. Will that work for Adele?"

"She won't care. She will throw in her earbuds and stream something on her iPad."

"Let's leave in the morning then. I have everything ready."

"Fine by me," Cooper said standing. "It will be okay, Luke. I promise. With all of us there, we can redirect Riley's attention back to where it needs to be. It's just exciting right now, and she doesn't have anyone to distract her." Cooper paused for a beat, but he looked like he wanted to say more.

"Is there something else?" Luke said, folding the blanket he had used and setting it on the corner of the couch.

"I was going to say this is a bigger issue than just this one case, but I didn't want to overstep."

Luke reached out and squeezed Cooper's shoulder. "Riley and I started talking about her work before I proposed, and the conversation will continue. Riley and I have to find some middle ground with this."

Cooper raised his eyebrows. "If you aren't happy with Riley's work as an investigator, don't you think that's something you should talk about before the wedding? She's not going to give it up. Riley loves what she does."

"I know. I think it's me who is going to have to compromise on this. Riley is passionate about her work. I'd never ask her to give it up. I have to get accustomed to her putting herself in harm's way."

Cooper nodded. "Riley had to do the same with you, Luke. You're probably in far more danger than Riley is with child custody cases, cheating spouses, and the majority of the work we handle. There is the occasional murder investigation, but for the most part, the day to day of what we do is fairly safe." Cooper went to the kitchen and poured himself more coffee. He held the pot up to Luke. "Want more?"

"I'm good," Luke said as he pulled on his jeans. "Keep reminding me I'm in more danger when Riley does crazy things. I have a feeling as much as I try to sort this out in my head, it's going to be a struggle for me. I'm officially telling you to keep me in check."

That was one of the best things about his friendship with Cooper. They knew each other's strengths and weaknesses. They weren't afraid to say the hard things that needed to be said to each other from time to time. Luke knew Riley's work would continue to be a sticking point for him only because he wanted her safe. He had no choice but to adjust. It didn't mean it was going to be easy.

Luke left Cooper's condo, and once he got to his SUV, he called Riley. "I'm just leaving Cooper's now," he said as Riley answered.

"Did you have fun last night?"

"Yes, it was a great night, low-key like I wanted." Luke buckled his seatbelt and put the car in drive. He navigated out of the parking garage and onto downtown streets, heading back home.

"I'm glad you had fun. Listen, Luke, I don't want you to be mad..."

Luke stopped her. "Riley, I know all about the case and your involvement. Cooper told me this morning. I saw the case on the news last night. I'm not angry or anything. I'm glad Cooper will be there to help Jack."

Riley didn't say anything for a few seconds, and Luke wasn't sure why. He asked, "Was there something else?"

"No, I prepared an entire speech about why I needed to help Jack. I assumed you'd argue with me. You've rendered me speechless." Riley laughed. "When are you coming up?"

Luke smiled. The last thing he needed right before the wedding was a fight. "Cooper, Adele and I are leaving in the morning and driving straight through. I'm hoping to get in early Tuesday morning. We'll be tired though and probably sleep for a while after we get in."

"Fine by me. I'll have the spare room ready."

"How is the case going?" Luke asked. He couldn't lie, he was curious about it. Luke had worked some high-profile cases before but not one with a senator or anyone high up in government.

"Jack and I are meeting this morning to go over a few things as follow up from our meeting with Senator Crandall last night. I don't know what to think yet."

"Got a gut feeling on it?" Luke asked absently as he navigated the roads with ease. He was less than ten minutes from home. He had told Cooper he was ready to leave for New York, but in truth, he hadn't even packed yet.

"I don't. There's a possible boyfriend, some secret society Jane was pledging, and her best friend killed herself at the end of the last school term. There's a lot to explore."

It sounded like Riley had a handle on it already. Luke said, "Cooper will be there soon. I'm sure he will be a big help to Jack."

"I'll be happy when you're here," Riley said sweetly.

It was exactly what Luke wanted to hear. "How was your dress fitting yesterday?"

"It was perfect. My mom didn't even give me a hard time. I assumed she would have thought it hugged my curves too much or was too straight or something. You know how she is."

"Call me if you need to tonight. I'm going home to pack and go to bed early so we can get an early start tomorrow." With that, they said their goodbyes. Luke headed home, hoping Cooper could keep Riley out of the case and saying an extra prayer she didn't get too involved before they got to New York.

CHAPTER 8

I sat in the chair in my bedroom with Dusty at my feet while I clicked through Maddie's social media profiles for any clues as to why she might have killed herself. After I finished speaking with Abby last night, I had gone back into Jane's room and followed up with her parents. Senator Crandall didn't see what Maddie's suicide had to do with anything, and Lynn got wide-eyed and angry with herself for not thinking about it sooner. They were at opposite ends of the spectrum.

Lynn had explained Jane struggled all summer with the death of her friend. She was worried about Jane coming back to campus and had even suggested setting up a local counselor. But Jane had said no. Jane told her mother if she needed to talk to someone, the school counselor would be good enough. Lynn said that Jane seemed to settle back into school, so she didn't think about it too much after that.

I didn't know if Maddie's suicide had anything to do with Jane's disappearance, but it couldn't be ruled out. I scrolled through Maddie's Facebook profile, but there wasn't much on there. I didn't know if her parents had deleted posts or if she just didn't post much at all. Twitter and Instagram were the same. There were a few photos of Maddie and Jane together happy and smiling for the camera from last year. It was haunting knowing that within a year one would be dead and the other missing.

"Riley, are you up there?" Jack called from downstairs.

"I'll be right down." I knew Jack was going to ask me what I thought as Luke had, but I had no instinct about the case at all. I nudged Dusty with my foot, but he seemed content to stay exactly where he was. I assumed that once I left the room, he would jump up on my bed where he knew he didn't belong. My mother said he often slept there.

I went downstairs and found Jack sitting at the kitchen table with my mother nowhere in sight. "Where's Mom?" I asked and then felt a bit foolish. Jack wasn't my father, but I noticed my sister and I tended to treat him as such when he was here.

Jack didn't seem to mind though. "She ran to the store to get a few things for dinner tonight. She mentioned Luke and your friends will be here in the next day or so."

"They are leaving tomorrow morning and should get in the next day. Cooper is eager to help." I opened the fridge and grabbed a can of Coke. "Do you want anything?"

Jack shook his head. "I want to talk about Jane now that we've both had time to digest what we heard last night. First impressions?"

I flipped open the tab and the soda hissed back at me. I took one long gulp, feeling slightly guilty knowing I should be drinking water instead of soda. "I think Senator Crandall wanted us to think he pays more attention to his kids than he does. Lynn runs the household with him gone, but they both seem slightly out of touch with Jane. The fact that Lynn would assume Jane was okay with her friend's suicide, especially coming back to campus that quickly, tells me Lynn wanted things to be better than maybe they were. The whole secret society pledging thing has me stumped."

Jack nodded and jotted down some notes. "You're perceptive on Jane's parents. I had similar feelings, but tell me what you mean about the Clovers."

I took another sip. "Jane's sister, Abby, told me Jane wasn't a joiner. Jane had given Abby a hard time about pledging a sorority. Jane had friends and was athletic and a good student. I can see why the Clovers would want her. What I don't know is why Jane joined and kept it up, especially given how much she was bullied throughout the process. Something doesn't feel right for me."

"Fair points. Do you think they had anything to do with her disappearance?"

I shrugged. "I can't say for sure. Someone could have kidnapped her or Jane could have run away. For all we know, she could have taken off with her boyfriend. We need to talk to more people."

"We?" Jack asked with raised eyebrows. He set down his pen and stared at me. "Your mother gave me a hard time about asking you to get involved. You said Cooper was coming to help me. Don't you think you should let me handle it until Cooper gets here?"

I pursed my lips in annoyance. "Do you not want my help?"

"Of course, I want your help, but I also don't want to argue with your mother and get you in trouble with Luke." Jack sat back.

He was right, but I had two days before Cooper would even get here. All the wedding planning was done. There wasn't anything else for me to do except sit around and look pretty and that wasn't in my skill set. I hit Jack with some logic I hoped he couldn't refute. "Isn't the first forty-eight hours after someone goes missing the most critical? That window will be closed by the time Cooper gets up here. The least I can do is lay some ground for him. Talk to a few witnesses."

Jack held his hands up in defeat. "It's your choice, kid. But if your mother asks, I'm going to tell her that you strong-armed me and didn't give me a choice."

I laughed. "You're afraid of my mother?"

"She's a tough woman. I want to keep her happy and her kid safe."

It's been a long time since I was called a kid. Truth be told, I kind of liked it. I never had a father around. He and my mother divorced when I was young. He went back to Ireland and only came back long enough to get my mother pregnant again with my sister. Then he was off again rarely to be seen. Outside of blurred childhood memories I can sometimes piece together like a jagged puzzle, I couldn't remember one time my parents were in the same room together. It was nice having Jack around.

"Where do you want to start?" I asked, finishing off my soda.

"Let's go back to the school. It's Sunday so I don't know who will be around, but I'm hoping given everything happening on campus, we can get access and start talking to people."

It sounded like a plan. "You asked me what I thought, Jack, but you didn't say. Do you think Jane ran away or something happened to her?"

Jack shook his head. "I don't know. It's too early to tell, but Jane's parents are convinced she didn't run away so we are going to have to walk a fine line with them. We need to stay open to all possibilities."

I ran upstairs to grab my keys and cellphone and then locked the door behind us as we left. The news vans still lined the streets, and Jack was pestered for even more interviews than before. Senator Crandall had put out a statement earlier that morning that he had hired well-known local retired detective Jack Malone to help find his daughter. A few reporters shouted at me asking who I was and how I was involved, but I ignored them just as Jack did.

As we approached the still-blocked off entrance to the school, a detective, with a gun on his hip and a badge dangling from a chain around his neck, approached. He had a ruffle of dark messy hair, three-day-old stubble, and grayish eyes any woman not engaged could get lost in.

He reached out a hand to Jack. "I heard Senator Crandall brought in their own investigator. I was worried until I heard it was you."

Jack introduced me to Miles Ward, the detective who had been assigned to Jane's disappearance. Jack explained he had trained Miles when he was still on the police force.

Miles hitched his strong square jaw at me. "You look familiar."

I introduced myself and explained my investigative background, giving him the highlights. "I'm from Troy. I grew up here and was a private investigator here for a while, but I live in Little Rock now. I think you might have met my fiancé, Det. Luke Morgan. Last year, he brought down the serial killer known as The Professor."

Miles stepped back and appraised me a little more seriously. "Is Det. Morgan here?"

"He will be in town on Tuesday."

"I didn't get a chance to meet him before, but I'd like to." Miles pointed between Jack and me. "What's the plan? I can't stop you from investigating, but I don't want to work at cross-purposes either."

Jack looked at me and back at Miles. He leaned in and quietly suggested, "How about a meeting where we share some info and set a game plan. I'd rather be working together than against you."

CHAPTER 9

Jack, Miles, and I found a quiet spot in the middle of the campus on a bench near some trees. Miles didn't want to go into any of the buildings to talk because he didn't trust the staff. He wanted to keep information close to the vest. Headmistress Winslow had already told him that she was worried about protecting the school's reputation and so he didn't trust anyone. I understood completely and felt the same. Besides, it was a nice fall day. I was happy to be outside.

As we sat down on the bench with Jack in the middle, Miles asked, "What are you hoping to do here?"

"I was hired by Senator Crandall to find Jane so that's what we will do," Jack said matter-of-factly. "The senator hired me because he said the police department felt like Jane ran away. He is concerned Jane won't be a priority."

Miles clapped his hands together. "I do think Jane ran away. All indications from her journal indicate Jane was having trouble here. There is a boyfriend too, but with no last name, we don't have a lead on him. Jane's friends are unwilling to talk. More to the point, her friends' parents are unwilling to let them talk to the police. I've had more lawyers call me than I can even respond to. They don't want their daughters involved in any kind of scandal. The school has closed ranks, too. I don't even see how I can go about investigating."

"You're willing to dismiss this so easily?" I asked, trying to hide the annoyance in my voice and failing.

Miles screwed up his face in anger. "What exactly would you like me to do about it? I have no idea where Jane is, a school that won't provide me information, and kids who won't talk. I have no indication of foul play, no crime scene that looks like a kidnapping, and no body to indicate anything other than Jane left on her own accord. The only thing I find strange is that no security camera picked up Jane leaving the building. It's like she just vanished."

"I looked for cameras inside last night but didn't notice any." Jack turned to me with his eyebrows raised in a question.

"I didn't see any either," I said, looking up at the buildings near us.

Miles explained, "The only cameras they have are in the parking lots, positioned at the front driveway of the campus, and on the side entrance near the administration building. You have a few in the back, too, near the athletic center and track, but none otherwise. There are no cameras inside the buildings, in the back at the teachers' residences, or here in the quad."

"You don't find that strange?" Jack asked.

Miles shook his head. "This is an old campus that doesn't have much crime. We are in a section of the city that doesn't have much crime. Some of the board of trustees and parents balked at putting young girls under surveillance, especially inside of their dormitories and classrooms. The cameras are positioned to catch people coming and going from the campus but not focused on activities once on the campus."

"When you reviewed the surveillance footage, you didn't see anyone suspicious coming or going around the time Jane disappeared?" Jack asked.

"Nope," Miles said, clearly annoyed. "All this leaves me with is a girl who seemingly vanished from her dorm. The housemother was the last to see Jane around nine-thirty. There is nothing on surveillance indicating Jane left campus. I'm a bit stumped how she managed it, but I still believe Jane left on her own accord."

It occurred to me Miles hadn't been told about the tunnels. It wasn't a design of the school that was widely known. "There are tunnels below us under this whole campus, Miles. Students can go from one building to the next without coming above ground. If Jane ran away, I'm sure she planned how to get off the campus without being seen. I don't think it would be that hard to do."

"Tunnels?" he asked, clearly hearing the information for the first time. "Did you go to school here?"

"No, but I live right down the road. I had friends who went to school here. Jane could have used a tunnel, or if someone took her, they could have lured her out through the tunnels."

Miles seemed to consider the information, but he didn't offer anything further on the subject. Instead, he shocked us completely. "This isn't public yet, but in our search for Jane, we found a teacher's body."

Jack furrowed his brow. "On campus?"

Miles pointed off toward the back of the campus. "Way in the back in the teachers' cottages. He lived here on campus. I was just coming up from there when you saw me. The medical examiner just removed his body."

"How did he die?" I asked, lost for words of what it all meant.

"Gunshot wound to the head," Miles said evenly.

"Suicide?" Jack asked.

Miles shook his head. "Looks suspicious to me."

"Murder?" Jack asked, surprised. He kicked his long legs out in front of him on the bench and leaned back.

Miles swiveled around on the bench, checking out all directions. When he was sure we were alone, he leaned in. "This is not something we are telling the school right now. I don't think it's suicide. I think it was meant to look like a suicide. The victim was right-handed. We found the gun in his left hand. Most people don't risk an unsteady hand when shooting themselves."

Jack ran a hand down his face and exhaled. "Got any leads?"

Miles shook his head. "Not a one."

"Didn't anyone hear the shot?" The campus was big but not that big. A shot would have been heard.

Miles stood. "Let's go for a walk."

Jack stood and walked right next to Miles. I lagged behind as we walked down the sidewalk, moving across the quad toward the back of campus. We walked past the athletic building that didn't fit with the design of the older buildings. The athletic center housed the pool, basketball court, gym, and other amenities. The track sat beside the building. From there the campus opened up to a hilly wide-open grassy area and woods on both sides. Following the path to the far back of campus, there was a row of four small cottages used as on-campus teachers' residences. There were police personnel milling around at the last of the four cottages, farthest from where we were.

"I didn't even realize these were back here," Jack said, appraising the structures.

"The campus is much bigger than it appears from the front," I explained. "From what I know, these have been on the campus since it was first built. Many of the teachers lived right here with the girls. Now only a handful of teachers live on campus."

Miles pointed to the one on the end. "That's where Erik Yates was found. He was a history teacher and just two months shy of his fortieth birthday."

"This still doesn't explain why the shot wasn't heard." We were far from the main buildings but not that far. A killer might have remained out of sight back here, but the shot definitely would have been heard.

Miles pointed to the cottages. "There are only two teachers who live back here. Erik and another teacher who was away for the weekend. The other two cottages are empty. Erik was alone back here with his killer." Miles looked down at me. "What else do you see?"

I wasn't sure what he was driving at.

Miles opened his arms wide. "There's nothing but woods and land back here. Beyond campus is just farmland. We found the body about two hours ago. We are just getting started. Some locals heard a shot, but it's not the first time a gunshot has been heard around here, and it won't be the last. No one thought anything of it."

Miles was exactly right. The school's property this far back was nothing but woods until it hit Pinewoods Avenue, which was a mix of farmland, woods, and a few homes. A single shot would be easily dismissed. I asked, "What time was the shot heard?"

"Just after eight Friday evening." Miles put his hands in his pockets and rocked on the balls of his feet. "Follow me. I'll show you what else I found."

Jack and I followed Miles to where the sidewalk met the grass. Miles looked back at us to make sure we were following. "It's not far."

I knew where we were headed, but it had been a long time since I had wandered back this far on campus. The grass gave way to a dirt grooved path. It was one of the original roads into the school. We walked until we reached the farthest section of the school property. Tall maple trees with their bright red leaves had been stationed around the area providing a blanket of shade. The same iron fencing that ran around the perimeter of the school property also lined the back. All I could see were the pointed ends at the top of the fence posts. Thick shrubs as tall as Jack stood in front of the fencing blocking the view and the street on the other side of it.

The path ended at a simple iron gate that had been long-ago padlocked shut. Thick leafy vines snaked through the iron bars doing far more than the padlock ever could. It would take a few hours of work to cut through the foliage to get the gates open.

"Doesn't look like anyone has come through this way in several decades," Jack said, reaching out and tugging on the vines. "Looks like mother nature has reclaimed this area."

"You would think." Miles jerked his head to the right, and we followed the shrub line to where the back and side fencing met. Miles got down on his knees and parted the shrubs like a doorway. Jack and I hunched over and watched as Miles crawled through the shrubs, easily snapped out a section of fencing, and made his way to the other side.

Jack rested a hand on my shoulder. "Looks like the girls found a creative way in and out of here."

The hidden way out of campus didn't impress me much. High school kids have been finding a way to sneak out for as long as there have been high school kids. I glanced back at the cottage. Erik Yates was killed around eight and Jane was last seen at nine-thirty. I had no idea if they were connected, but it seemed like a stretch to think they weren't. It was the first time I had any real sense Jane might be in danger.

CHAPTER 10

Cooper stacked several shirts in his black suitcase and then added in pants next to them. He looked down at the clothing and frowned. Adele had already packed, and Cooper was jealous of how organized she was for the trip and the way her clothes had made neat piles in her suitcase. Cooper didn't fold as well. He was close to giving up and throwing everything in a mish-mash heap when his phone chimed, alerting him that he had a text.

Thankful for the distraction, he pawed through socks and boxers on the top of his dresser until he found his phone. He read the text from Riley, asking for his help on the case already. Cooper was more than up for it. He sent Riley a quick text back and asked what she needed.

Cooper sat down on his bed next to his suitcase and waited for her response. Adele's sweet singing voice echoed in the hallway from the kitchen where she was making them dinner. It didn't escape him how lucky he was. Cooper's mother had passed when he was young. His father had remarried more times than he could count and then passed away a couple of years ago. He had no siblings, that he knew of anyway. Riley and Luke were the closest family Cooper had, but now he had Adele, too.

The phone chimed in his hands. Cooper read Riley's words, but he wasn't sure what she was asking of him. It didn't seem to have anything to do with the missing girl. He texted back and asked her. A few minutes later Riley connected the dots for him.

"Dinner's ready!" Adele called from the kitchen.

Cooper closed the lid on his suitcase and joined Adele in the kitchen. "Riley just asked me to look into a suicide at Austen Academy. It seems Jane's best friend killed herself last year. Riley is wondering if there is any tie to the missing girl and why the friend killed herself."

Adele put a pat of butter and dropped a little brown sugar on her sweet potato. "Do they ever really know why someone kills themselves?"

"I don't know, but Riley is trying to figure out if it might have something to do with Jane's disappearance."

Adele dug into her food. "Does Riley think the senator's kid ran away?"

"It sounded that way, but Riley also said all options are still on the table." Cooper took a bite of his steak. Adele had cooked it in the cast iron skillet they had bought together. It was their first moved-in together purchase. She had seared the steak to perfection and he told her as much.

After a few bites, Cooper lamented, "I'm not all that comfortable calling this girl's parents to ask why their daughter killed herself."

"I can make the call if you'd like." Adele offered. "As a criminal defense attorney, I'm forced to have uncomfortable conversations all the time. It might be easier coming from a woman anyway. You're not always the most empathetic."

Cooper narrowed his eyes at her ready to defend himself but then he smiled. Adele was right. He empathized easily, but he rarely expressed it well. "I'm a terrible packer and have no empathy. Why do you love me again?"

"You're great in bed."

Cooper nearly choked but knew Adele was joking. She loved him for more than that. He winked at her. "On a more serious subject, can you help me pack? I'm terrible."

Adele pointed her fork at him. "If you wash the dishes."

Cooper held his hands up in surrender. "I can do that." That's how easy their relationship was. Cooper never knew it could be like that. It wasn't what he saw at home growing up. There were constant fights over the pettiest of issues. It was the biggest reason Cooper had avoided long-term commitments until now. More than anything, he needed peace at home.

They finished their dinner, and Cooper did the dishes as Adele rearranged his suitcase and packed the last of his clothes. As Cooper finished drying the dishes, he thought better of Adele making the call for him. He'd need to report back to Riley, which meant she'd have endless questions about how the girl's parents sounded and what exactly they said. If Adele made the call, he would only have the information secondhand. Cooper explained that to Adele when she met him back in the kitchen.

"You can put the call on speakerphone, and I can help if needed. This way you lead, and I'll pitch in when needed. Would that work?" Adele asked.

It was the perfect solution. Cooper punched in the number Riley had given him. The girl's name was Maddie Collins. Her parents were Gary and Teresa. When a woman answered, Cooper confirmed he was speaking with Teresa. He explained he was a private investigator looking into Jane's disappearance and asked if it would be okay to ask her some questions about Maddie's death. The woman was more than willing. She was almost excited, which took Cooper by surprise.

Teresa explained, "Gary and I have been so worried about Jane. The girls had been friends for years. Jane is like a daughter to me. Anything I can do to help, I'm willing. But I have to tell you, I don't believe Maddie killed herself."

Cooper asked if it would be okay to put her on speakerphone so Adele could also be on the call. Teresa readily agreed. He set the phone down on the table between them. "Maybe we should start there. Why don't you think Maddie committed suicide?"

Teresa exhaled like she had been waiting to answer this question since it happened. "Maddie wasn't depressed. She had a great school term, made straight As, and was looking forward to her summer vacation. We had just spoken two nights before they found her. She and Jane had all sorts of adventures planned as soon as they got back here to California. Maddie was also enrolled in a painting class, and she was ecstatic about developing her passion more. Maddie had no history of mental health issues. No depression or anxiety that we were aware of. There was absolutely nothing that indicated to me or anyone else that Maddie was at risk of suicide."

Cooper wasn't surprised by what Teresa said. He just wasn't sure if it was her guilt or if what she was saying were true. Riley hadn't indicated to Cooper there might be questions surrounding Maddie's death, but she might not have known. Just like Teresa might not have known if Maddie was depressed.

Noticing the confusion on Cooper's face, Adele asked, "Teresa, we weren't given a lot of detail about Maddie's death. We don't want to upset you, but if you could, would you be willing to tell us the circumstances?"

Teresa grew quiet for a moment, but when she spoke next, her voice was strong and clear. "Maddie was found on Saturday afternoon in one of the school's tunnels. The police said that she used a rope around a pipe to hang herself. The medical examiner labeled it a suicide and put the time of death on Friday evening around midnight. Maddie's roommate said when she woke up around one that morning Maddie wasn't in her bed. She assumed she had gone to the bathroom. When she woke on Saturday morning, Maddie was gone still. There was some lag time between her roommate knowing Maddie wasn't in her room and the school being aware something might have happened. Those girls cover for one another."

"Did you come to the school after Maddie was found?"

"We left as soon as we were told. I spoke to the detective who had been briefly assigned to the case and to the medical examiner. All the school administration cared about was keeping it quiet. My husband was ashamed and believed we had missed something, so he did what they asked. It was not the way I wanted it handled. If it were up to me, I would have had a new detective assigned and had the media there until I got some satisfactory answers. For my husband's sake, I kept quiet."

Adele pressed. "You said there are still questions. I know you said you believe your daughter wasn't in the psychological state to kill herself but did anything else raise a concern?"

"There were more things than I could count that raised concern," Teresa said angrily. "It's rare for young girls to commit suicide by hanging first off. Secondly, the knot that held the rope to the pipe wasn't something my daughter knew how to tie. I was finally able to get a photo of the scene and when Gary saw it, he knew, too. Maddie didn't kill herself. The knot was a clove hitch knot and a good one at that. Maddie didn't tie that."

Cooper motioned for Adele to do an internet search for a clove hitch knot because he had absolutely no idea. Adele handed him her phone and he read quickly. It was a common knot used in sailing. "Teresa, did you ever go back to the police with your concerns?"

"I did, but the medical examiner had ruled it a suicide. Unless we were able to convince the medical examiner to rule it a homicide, there was nothing they were willing to do. He wasn't willing to change his ruling, so I took Maddie's autopsy report to a well-known forensic pathologist. He told us based on the marks on Maddie's neck, it looked like manual strangulation. When someone is hung from the position my daughter's body was in, it would leave different marks than she had. Maddie's hyoid bone was also broken, which wouldn't have happened in a hanging."

"Did the medical examiner change his ruling?" Cooper asked.

"No, they didn't. The police and the school have let someone get away with murder."

Adele asked probably the most important question of all. "Did Jane know?"

"She did. We talked this summer and Jane was determined to find out what happened to Maddie. I'm afraid now it might have cost Jane her life," Teresa said sadly with resolve.

CHAPTER 11

I sat at my mother's kitchen table staring at my phone while listening to Cooper tell me about his call with Maddie's mother. When Cooper was done, I explained my meeting with Miles and told him about the teacher who was murdered, although the cops still weren't calling it that. It somehow hadn't even been reported on the news yet either.

Cooper exhaled. "What you're telling me then is that we could be looking at two murders at the school in less than five months?"

"I guess that's exactly what I'm saying." This was far more than a missing girl from school now.

When I initially heard about Maddie's death, I had been expecting a tragic story about teen suicide, but now I was faced with another murder that no one other than the girl's parents and possibly Jane thought happened. I wasn't even sure what to ask, but starting with the basics seemed like a good idea.

"Did you feel like the mother was credible?"

"Very," Cooper said adamantly. "I think the most convincing thing for me was the forensic pathologist report and their findings. It wasn't suicide. I have the report and photos Teresa sent me that I'll send you when we're done."

"Teresa knows we are just trying to find Jane, right? We don't have the resources to open a full investigation on Maddie, even though her case certainly deserves it." We could easily fall down a rabbit hole and lose track of keeping Jane the priority. I needed to make sure that didn't happen.

"She knows, but I'm inclined to agree with her when she said she believes Jane's disappearance is connected to Maddie's death. Now whether Jane started poking around and has met the same fate or she got spooked and ran, who knows."

I rubbed my forehead and stretched my legs out under the table. "It's also possible Jane was overwhelmed with grief and she took off."

"Riley, I think anything is possible, but the person who killed Maddie could be connected to the school. Teresa said the girls cover for each other. If anyone is going to know what's happening there, it's other students. I don't think you'll get very far with the administration."

"I know this is more complicated than we initially thought. If you want out of this, I'll tell Jack. He will completely understand. He's been trying to convince me to walk away because of the wedding."

"No, I'm in," Cooper reassured. "There's always more than we bargained for. Tuesday will pretty much be a wash for us because we will need to sleep once we get in, but count me in for Tuesday night. I can always stick around after the wedding to help Jack if needed." Cooper paused for a beat and then issued a warning. "Don't get too involved, Riley, or you won't be able to let it go. I won't tell Luke how far you're already in, but you better get your head right by the time he's up there."

I knew Cooper was right. Luke and I were supposed to finally be enjoying some downtime. Investigations ruined his last two vacation chances. I couldn't do that to him again.

"I won't," I lied, knowing I was already too far in. "Once you get up here, I'll fully hand this over to you, and Luke and I can start our vacation. As soon as you send the email from Teresa, I'll send it to Jack."

Cooper and I hung up. I thought about calling Jack with the information, but he had taken my mother to dinner. My mother hadn't been sure when we'd get back from Austen Academy, so she hadn't cooked anything. I was on my own. I poked my head in the fridge and moved a few things around, but I didn't see much. I was hungry but nothing appealed to me. I craved something. I just didn't know what.

As I was standing with the refrigerator door open, Dusty wandered into the kitchen and stood by my side. "Do you need to go outside?"

He didn't run to the back door the way he normally did when he wanted to be let out. He must be hungry, too. I grabbed his bowls and gave him some water in one and poured his dry food into the other. He moved over to them and took a drink of water but then turned his head back to look at me.

"What?" I shrugged not knowing what he wanted. Dusty came back and stared up at the fridge. I patted him on the head. "Is there something in here you want?"

I pulled the door back open and fished around until I found the fresh sliced chicken. I held some in my hand and Dusty bounced from one foot to the other. My mother spoiled him, but he deserved it. I pulled a few slices off the platter and dropped them in his bowl as my phone rang. Dusty dug in.

I grabbed for my phone before it went to voicemail. "Hello."

"Riley, its Det. Miles Ward from the Troy police department. Got a second?"

"Sure," I responded somewhat hesitantly. I hadn't given him my phone number, so I had no idea what he wanted.

"Actually, on second thought. Are you free to come back to the school right now? I know it's almost dark, but I called Jack and he wasn't available. I thought I'd call you."

I told Miles I could be there in about ten minutes. We planned to meet back at the same bench in the middle of the campus where we had met earlier in the day. I grabbed my phone and keys and ran up to my bedroom to grab a sweater. The temperature had dropped. Fall settled in and with it came colder nights. The walk to the school was quick and uneventful. It looked like the media had taken the night off as the streets were empty other than residents' cars.

As I made my way across the campus, I passed by groups of students coming out of the dining hall, and I assumed, heading back to their dorms. They said hello, and I nodded in return. Either they had been prepped to expect visitors to campus, or because I was a woman, they assumed I didn't pose a threat. It reinforced how easy it was to access the campus. Right now, with the police presence, they had more security than they normally had. The front gates were usually open and the side entrance, too. My mother had on more than one occasion used their track to walk. Others in the neighborhood had as well. I knew the buildings were locked at night, but I had a question about the tunnels that I made a mental note to ask later.

Det. Ward sat on the bench staring off into the distance.

"I didn't think I'd be hearing from you again," I said as I approached.

Det. Ward turned around to look at me and then stood. "I guess you do live close."

I pointed towards home. "My mother lives right on Locust. Did you want to discuss something?"

Miles sat back down and patted the bench next to him. "Sit and we can talk."

Sitting down, I took in the expansive quad in front of me. Dusk had settled and the tall iron lamps illuminated the walkways. The campus had a creepier vibe in the evening. The vibrant attractive campus in daylight became somewhat ominous as the darkness settled.

Turning to Miles, I asked, "What is it you need?"

He wasn't paying attention to me though. His eyes seemed transfixed on the quad.

"It's creepier at night, right?" I asked.

Miles glanced over at me. "It is. I never realized that until now."

I told Miles about my walk onto the campus that evening and that no one seemed to care that I was an outsider. "I wonder if that happens all the time. Not one of the girls even questioned who I was."

"Where did you go to high school?" Miles asked suddenly.

The question took me aback. "Catholic Central High School. Why?"

"I went to Troy High. I thought maybe we went to school together. I can't figure out how I know you."

I smiled. "Maybe you just remember me from parties in the woods."

"Probably," Miles said, his voice quiet.

He seemed melancholy to me. Maybe the cases were overwhelming him like they were for me. Luke often had the same face when he was smack in the middle of a frustrating case with no leads.

"Can I help you with something?" I asked.

"The tunnels. You mentioned them earlier today. For some reason, no one here bothered to mention them to me. I feel a bit foolish I hadn't known about them before. I was hoping you could tell me more."

If Miles didn't know about the tunnels, it meant he hadn't been the detective involved in Maddie Collins' suicide case. It was curious though how he had missed that. I reminded him, "A student killed herself earlier this year in the tunnels. That didn't make the news or was talked about among the detectives?"

"No," Miles said, confusion on his face. "All anyone said about the case was that it happened on campus. I assumed it was in her dorm. I never questioned it and never had a reason to. How do you know where it happened if it wasn't made public?"

Repeating the words that he had said to me earlier in the day, I nudged him, "Let's take a walk."

CHAPTER 12

Together Miles and I walked to Jane's dormitory building and found the door unlocked. We entered and only made it a few feet before a woman approached.

"You can't be in here," she said.

Miles flashed a badge. "Can you show me how to access the tunnels?"

The woman hesitated at first, and Miles shoved his badge towards her again for emphasis. She turned on her heels, and we followed down a corridor and then another to a door that led to stairs.

"Just follow the stairs and you'll see the girls' lounge area. There is a door on the left which takes you to the tunnels. The girls can show you if you get lost." With that, she walked away without saying another word.

"Not exactly friendly." Miles stepped back so I could walk down the stairs first.

The stairs were wide and well-lit and led directly into a wide-open area where girls were chatting, watching television and some were studying. When they saw us, every eye turned our direction, and they stopped talking.

Miles stepped in front of me and flashed his badge again. "We are looking for the entrance to the tunnels."

A few of the girls simply pointed to a door in the far corner of the room. Two of the girls shared a worried look I wasn't sure how to interpret. I didn't have time to question it though because Miles made a beeline to the door. He found the door unlocked and opened it. Miles stepped inside first and then closed the door behind me.

"We have questioned most of those girls and either they claimed not to know anything about Jane's disappearance or refused to talk to me. I didn't feel a need to stick around and chat with them." Miles took a few steps and then turned to me. "I have no idea where I'm going so maybe I should follow you."

The tunnel was exactly as I remembered it. The narrow space was wide enough only for the two of us to walk side by side. The white walls needed a fresh coat of paint, and the overhead lighting flickered. The concrete floor was gray with distinct scuff marks from use. I knew the tunnels were like a maze to the unfamiliar. I didn't know where I was going but continued forward as if I did.

We kept walking until the corridor forked to the left and right. I stood for a moment orienting myself in direction, trying to remember the campus above me and my orientation to it underground. I turned right and got no argument from Miles. A few feet later, we came upon U-shaped piping that was similar to what Cooper had described earlier. "Let's stop for a minute."

I pulled my phone from my pocket and scanned my email. The photos Cooper promised to send were there. I swiped through until I found a photo of interest. The photo showed a close-up shot of the pipe with the rope knotted in the middle. I held out my phone to Miles. "This is the spot where Maddie Collins killed herself in May. See the intricate knot? Teresa, Maddie's mother, called it a clove hitch knot and said that there is no way Maddie knew how to make that."

Miles stared down at the photo and then assessed the spot in front of us. He shook his head. "This wasn't my case, but I would have been suspicious. I can't imagine one of the girls coming down here to kill herself."

"I didn't want to say it before, but you might have two murders and a missing girl on your hands."

Miles shook his head in disgust, but he didn't comment. It was a quality that drove me a little bit crazy. He was a hard man to read. I was used to working with Cooper and Luke who gave me everything I needed to know right on their faces. Miles wasn't like that. He was controlled and didn't let things slip until he was ready. It was maddening.

I paused for another second to see if Miles would comment on Maddie, but he didn't. I put my phone away and continued down the tunnel. Every so often we'd reach a door. Some were open and others locked. We found entrances to other residence halls with the same type of common rooms we had just been in, academic buildings, and we finally came to the door that led into the ground floor of the athletic center.

"I think this is as far back as the tunnels go," I said, opening the door into the small space. There were cleaning supplies and boxes and off to the right stairs to the main floor. The smell of chlorine hit my nose.

"Didn't you say this building was new?" Miles asked, looking around the small space.

"Yeah, fairly new. It wasn't here when I was in high school."

Miles nodded. "I wonder why the tunnels went back this far if this is new."

I shrugged. "I believe there was another building here that they tore down. They must have kept the tunnel in the design." I went to step back out of the room into the tunnel again, thinking we'd head back the way we came, but Miles was frozen in place looking at a spot on the far wall.

"Is something wrong?" I asked, trying to figure out what he was looking at.

Miles took a few steps and moved some boxes out of the way. "There's another door back here. Look at the dust on the floor and how it's swept back in this spot."

"Maybe it's just a closet." I inched closer to his back and caught a whiff of his cologne. It was woodsy and masculine.

"I don't think so. These boxes are empty." Miles stopped picking them up one by one and instead gave them a swift kick to the side. As he pulled open the door, a rush of cooler air hit us both. "It looks like it's another tunnel."

Miles was right, but it wasn't one I had been down before. I didn't even know this was here.

Miles looked back at me. "You want to check this out with me or wait here?"

I stepped into the tunnel right behind him. I slid my hand down the wall, searching for a light switch but couldn't find one. There was no overhead light to illuminate the path like in the previous tunnel. Miles pulled a small flashlight from his pocket and pointed it down the tunnel. The walls had the grimy appearance of fifty years of dirt and decay that even a good coat of paint probably wouldn't cover.

My biggest concern other than walking into the unknown was the cobwebs that hung from the ceiling above us. I shivered at the thought of it. I wasn't even afraid of spiders, but I was fairly certain I was walking into their lair.

"Where do you think this goes?" Miles asked, taking tentative steps forward.

"I have no idea. I've never been in this tunnel before. I didn't even know it was here." The light from his flashlight bounced around in front of us. I reached out and grabbed the back of his shirt to steady myself.

"You could have stayed back if you're scared," he said softly.

"Why are you whispering? Afraid the ghosts will hear you?" I laughed when he didn't answer. "I just don't want to fall. What direction do you think this is heading? I'm a bit turned around."

Miles stopped. He pointed the light in each direction as if he were thinking through our location. "I'm not sure either, but it feels like we are heading towards the back of the school."

"Maybe it brings us right to the back gate."

"Well, that could certainly be how Jane got out of here without being seen." Miles continued forward. He'd walk a few feet and then stop and assess. Sometimes it felt like we were walking uphill, and other times, the ground was flat. I had no idea how far we had gone when Miles flashed the light up ahead.

"There are stairs up there." Miles approached and put his foot down gently on the step. He applied a little weight and then stood on it. The stairs reminded me of the old basement steps in my mother's house – narrow and made of planks of wood.

"Let's hope this holds up." I stepped up with him and we ascended the stairs.

At the top, two doors met in the middle. There was a wooden latch that came down to lock them from the inside, but it was unlocked. Miles handed me the flashlight and pushed both sides of the door open and we came up out of the ground.

I expected to see black iron fencing and tall shrubs. Instead, we were in the woods, but not too far off the beaten path. We both turned and realized at the same time we were several yards behind the teachers' cottages. The police had gone for the night and the cottages were all dark.

Miles started to walk forward but stopped abruptly. "Be careful walking. I don't think anyone has searched this far back in the woods yet." We walked a few more feet and then Miles pointed. "Look, you can see right into the back windows of these cottages."

I got my bearings and said, "I bet this was used as an old teachers' tunnel so they could walk back and forth to the main school buildings and their residences, especially in the cold snowy winters."

"That's what I was thinking, but the entrance in the athletic building wasn't locked and neither was this other door," Miles said. "That means anyone from the outside could sneak into this tunnel from the woods and go to any building on campus. It also means the girls had a way out unseen."

CHAPTER 13

"Are you hungry?" Miles asked, glancing over at me.

My stomach growled loudly in response. "I guess you can take that as a yes. Did you hear my stomach growling before?"

"No." He laughed. "I think we should get some dinner and talk this out. How about the diner?"

Miles didn't have to tell me what diner he meant. I knew he was talking about Alexis Diner. My mom went there frequently. It was open late, even on a Sunday. "Sure, we can do that."

"I'll drive and drop you off later." Miles continued our walk out of the woods.

I only made it a few feet from Erik Yates' cottage when something mixed up in the leaves caught my eye. I called to him. "Wait. Let me look at this."

There on the ground was a bright purple winter scarf. I waved Miles over, and we both stood there looking down at my find.

"Don't touch it," Miles said. "This could be evidence."

"Wouldn't you have searched this area when the teacher's body was found?"

Miles looked away. "Our crime scene techs searched the inside of the cottage, but I guess they missed this back here. I have crime scene techs coming out tomorrow to go through the place again. I know officers did perimeter search, but I'm not sure now if anyone came back here."

I wasn't judging. I was just trying to figure out how long the scarf could have been there, but I guess given the facts, we couldn't be sure. I told Miles what I thought. "You know it might not even have anything to do with this. Girls are clearly using that tunnel to sneak in and out. Who knows what else they have been doing in these woods?"

Miles told me to wait while he ran back to his car. He said he had a camera and an evidence bag. I didn't particularly like standing in the woods on the edge of the campus with no one occupying the cottages, but I didn't have much of a choice. I shivered against the cold. I shoved my hands in my pockets and looked up at the sky. At least it wasn't pitch black. The moon was nearly full and the sky was a blanket of stars.

Every twig snap and rustle of leaves sent me over the edge. At each sound, I jumped and spun around ready to protect myself. When there was nothing, I was left feeling foolish. I chided myself for my irrational behavior and focused all of my attention towards the front of campus hoping to see Miles walking toward me. A few minutes later, a tap on my shoulder had me jumping out of my skin. I spun around ready for a fight but just ended up startling the young woman standing behind me. We both screamed.

"Who are you?" I asked, as my heart beat rapidly.

"Who are you?" she shot back at me.

I tried to explain, but stammered over my words. After a few deep breaths, I explained who I was and that Det. Ward had run back to his police car. "We found what might be evidence."

"How did you get back here?" the woman asked.

"Miles Ward is a detective. We were conducting a search. Who are you?"

The woman glanced at the cottage and back to me. She hadn't looked down, so I don't think she saw the scarf. "I'm Heidi Sykes. I'm a teacher here."

She had her blonde hair twisted up in a bun on the top of her head, a scarf wrapped around her neck, and a sweatshirt and jeans on. Her sneakers looked worn and muddy.

"What are you doing out here this time of night?" I asked not able to hide the suspicion in my voice.

Heidi pointed to a cottage. "Irene Hodge lives there. We are both English teachers. I hoped she was back from her weekend trip. I wanted to ask to see her lesson plan for this week. We had discussed doing a joint project. I saw you standing back here and was going to call security, but decided to check it out myself."

"That's dangerous for you to do given everything that's happened on the campus this weekend."

She eyed me. "Are you saying you're dangerous?"

"No, but you had no idea who I was when you approached."

Heidi shook her head at me. "This is a safe campus. I walk around at night alone often. It's peaceful on the back lawn at night."

"A teacher is dead and a student is missing. I'd hardly call that safe," I argued.

She raised her eyebrows at me. "Suicide and runaway. That doesn't mean the rest of us are in danger."

I was going to argue but thought better of it.

Heidi shrugged. "Well anyway, I'll leave you be. I can see Irene isn't back yet. Have a good night." With that, Heidi cut between two cottages and disappeared into the night.

A few minutes later, Miles was back. He got a look at my face. "You seem paler than I remember. You okay?"

I told him about Heidi. "What she said didn't make any sense. If she went to the front door of the cottage as she said, she wouldn't have seen me standing back here this time of night."

"Maybe she heard a noise and walked back to check it out."

Miles didn't seem to think it was a big deal, so I dropped it. He took a few photos of the area and the scarf before slipping on gloves and putting it in the evidence bag. We made our way across campus to his police car which was parked at the side entrance near the administration building. The campus was too quiet this time of night, and I couldn't wait to be off the grounds.

About fifteen minutes later, at the diner, Miles asked for a booth far away from any other customers. We were seated and ordered quickly. When the server left, Miles peered at me across the table and asked, "What are your impressions about the case so far?"

I rested my hands on the table in front of me and chose my words carefully. "I don't know much about the teacher's death other than what you said about it being suspicious. As far as Jane goes, I haven't interviewed anyone yet. Given the teacher's suspicious death, don't you think the two could be connected?"

"I wouldn't think so, but I go where the evidence leads me." Miles took a sip of soda as soon as the server set it down.

"The problem is there is no evidence that confirms anything for me either way." I paused because that wasn't necessarily true. There hadn't been a struggle at Jane's dorm because someone would have heard. The only thing I could say with certainty was that Jane left her room willingly. I wasn't sure if I could say the same for the campus at large.

I tapped on the table with my index finger. "Let me back up from what I just said. If Jane was taken, she went with the person willingly, which means it was someone she knew and felt safe enough to go with, or she was on campus someplace other than her dorm and taken from there."

Miles seemed to consider that. Meeting my eyes, he said, "I can agree with that. It's still more likely Jane ran away."

I smiled. "We are going to have to agree to disagree for now. There are still too many unknowns for me to make that call." I took a sip of my water, and my stomach growled again. Hopefully, my grilled cheese and fries would arrive soon.

"What do you think about Maddie's suicide?" Miles asked, toying with his fork.

The question caught me a bit off guard. I thought that was a closed subject. "The knots on the rope and the forensic pathologist's report tell me it wasn't a suicide. I think you have another murder. I think it's too much of a coincidence to say all of these cases aren't connected."

Miles leaned in. "I can agree with your first point, but not your second. That's partly why I asked you to dinner. I can't dig around in the Maddie Collins case. There was a determination made by our medical examiner and a very seasoned detective who already doesn't like me much. I think you should pursue it though if you feel strongly it wasn't a suicide."

"I can't pursue anything. I was only temporarily helping Jack. I'm getting married," I reminded him.

"That means what?" Miles said, giving me a grin I'm sure most women would find it hard to say no to.

"It means I'm supposed to be taking a break. Once Luke gets here Tuesday, he's not going to want me digging around in any of these cases."

"Oh, so it's that kind of relationship? You should have said that. I thought you were a different kind of woman." Miles took another sip of his drink.

I couldn't tell if he was teasing or being serious. "What does that mean?"

Miles leaned back in the booth with a broad smile plastered across his face. "I didn't take you for the kind of woman who let a man decide what you do. You come across with a sass I like. I guess I was wrong."

I tipped my head back in a laugh. "You can't goad me into looking into the case. Luke isn't like that either. We just decided to finally take a break together. My partner, Cooper, will be helping Jack. I can pass off the info to him."

"I don't want to work with Cooper or Jack. I want to work with you," Miles said evenly. Then he winked at me.

Suddenly, I didn't feel like this was all about work, but I was so bad at reading the signs. It felt like Miles was flirting with me. I spun my engagement ring around and around on my finger and tried to avoid his gaze for the rest of dinner. I didn't need a mirror to know my face was apple red.

CHAPTER 14

Luke packed the SUV efficiently and picked up Cooper and Adele before seven. They stopped briefly for breakfast and hit the road. Luke drove for about two hours in near silence, enjoying the open road. Cooper had eaten his breakfast sandwich and promptly fell asleep in the passenger seat. Adele was in the back with headphones on and had barely picked her eyes up from her iPad.

Luke punched in Riley's number and waited as the phone rang. "Good morning, beautiful. How's my soon-to-be bride?" he asked as Riley answered. Luke could tell by her groggy voice she had still been asleep.

"I'm sleepy. Are you on the road already?"

"It's nearing nine-thirty. We are just passing Memphis now." Luke carefully changed lanes and followed the signs to stay on I-40. "Why are you so tired? You're supposed to be relaxing." Riley sighed loudly, and Luke knew immediately it was the wrong thing to say. He backtracked. "I just meant you said you were going to relax."

A rustling of covers echoed through the phone. Riley explained the teacher's suspicious death. She yawned loudly. "I was out late with the detective on the case. Jack was with my mom and couldn't help him, so he asked for me to meet him at the campus and walk the tunnels with him. I know the landscape on the campus better than Miles."

"Did this detective work with Jack?"

"Not with him, no. Jack trained him before he retired. Miles is my age."

Luke tried to keep his focus on the road and manage a weird feeling of unease that spread through his gut. Before he could say anything, Riley surprised him.

"Miles was impressed with your work taking down The Professor. He said he'd like to meet you when you arrive." Riley yelled to her mother that she'd be down to breakfast soon. Back on the phone, she said, "I'd like to tell you a little about the cases, but I know that you don't want to be involved and will probably be annoyed I'm as involved as I am. I want your opinion but don't want to start an argument."

The weird feeling evaporated as quickly as it came. "I'd be happy to meet him if we have time. I have nothing but open road in front of me. Go ahead and tell me about the cases."

Riley spent the next half-hour going over details of the three cases. It was a bit hard for Luke to follow so occasionally he'd stop her and ask a question, and she'd respond with more information. When Riley was done, she asked, "Do you think all three cases could be connected?"

"What was Jane's relationship with Erik Yates? That would be my first question. You have two deaths that appear to be murders and a missing girl connected to at least one of the victims. What's her connection to the other?"

"I don't know that yet. I'm hoping to talk to a few people today. This way I can give the info to Cooper. Jack is doing some other interviews, but we felt Jane's friends might be more receptive talking to me."

Luke had to interview high school and college-aged girls for previous cases. He'd rather talk to hardened criminals. Riley would have better luck talking to them than Cooper. "Good luck with the interviews. You know interviewing adolescent girls is completely frustrating for me, but you have a way with people. Does Miles think the cases are connected?"

"No." Riley exhaled loudly. "But he said he is inclined to believe Maddie didn't kill herself. He said he couldn't step on any toes at the department though so he couldn't look into it. He asked me to, but I'm going to talk to Jack about it today."

"Did you consider maybe Jane was looking into Maddie's death and stumbled onto something that got her killed?" Luke changed lanes again and refocused on the road in front of him.

Riley didn't say anything for several moments. Finally, she said, "I hadn't considered Jane might be dead. I've been hoping she ran away or had been taken and there would be ransom or something."

"If there's a call for ransom, it usually happens by now. It doesn't mean it won't still happen, but generally, you know fairly early on that it's a kidnapping. Besides, Jane was last seen in her room. How would kidnappers remove her from campus without anyone noticing?"

Riley explained more about the tunnels, especially the one leading from campus to the teachers' cottages that was completely unsecured. "Security seems pretty lax on campus. More so than I would have thought, but I still can't see someone kidnapping Jane from her dorm. No one heard any disturbances that night."

"Did the senator seem at all concerned his daughter might have been kidnapped for ransom?" Luke glanced over and noticed Cooper waking up. Luke nudged him and said quietly, "Riley is on the phone talking about the case. You might want to listen in."

Cooper nodded, rubbed his eyes, and pulled himself to an upright position. He told Riley he was on the call, too.

"Now that you mention it, Luke, Senator Crandall didn't seem concerned about ransom or anything like that at all. Her parents were concerned because the police assumed right away Jane ran away, which is why he hired Jack. The senator never brought up kidnapping and ransom. Jack didn't either."

"The senator might be trying to stay calm for show," Cooper said. "He has a hard-nosed reputation to keep. He might not be comfortable showing emotion in front of people."

Luke nodded. "If Senator Crandall isn't frantic Jane is gone, he might also suspect she ran away and hired Jack to find her first before the cops to save a scandal."

"Both good points," Riley said. "You can see why this case is complex. Now add in what looks like two murders, and we have a real mess on our hands. Are you sure you want to be involved, Cooper?"

Cooper yawned. "I like complex cases. What leads do you have so far?"

"Jane mentioned a boyfriend Liam so that's a lead to run down. She also mentioned in her journal a group called the Clovers she was pledging here at the school and some trouble with a girl she called N. It looked like there was some bullying. Jane's parents didn't know anything about that. Jane could have also been looking into Maddie's murder and got herself into trouble. I just need to dig in and start talking to people."

Cooper gave Luke a sideways glance, but he just shrugged. If Luke were being honest, the case interested him, too. He wasn't going to be able to stop Riley at this point so he might as well just join in.

Cooper teased, "Are you going to solve this before I even get up there?"

"Hardly, I'm already feeling overwhelmed by everything that needs to get done."

Riley and Luke finished the call. Hitting the end call button on the steering column, Luke asked, "What do you think about this case?"

Cooper adjusted himself in the passenger seat. "I think Riley is in further than she said she'd get and suddenly you don't seem to mind."

"I don't want to argue with her. As you said, Riley is passionate about what she does. I'm just trying to accept it. I took your advice for once. Don't make it a thing."

Cooper smiled. "That approach will save you grief in the long run."

"Cooper learned early how well arguing with a strong determined woman works for him," Adele said from the backseat. "He's right, Luke, you're not going to get Riley to change so you either love her for who she is or scrap the marriage before it even gets started."

Luke eyed her in the rearview mirror. "Nothing is being scrapped. Were you listening to Riley talk about the case?"

"I was, and she's right. It sounds complex. It also sounds interesting. I think you're both right though. I've seen kidnapping cases and this doesn't feel like a kidnapping. There are easier ways to take a kid other than her crowded dorm room at night. If I were a betting woman, I'd say something happened to her when she was looking into her friend's murder or pledging the Clovers. Nothing good comes from secret societies run by adolescent girls."

CHAPTER 15

"You look like ten miles of bad road," Liv said to me as I wandered into the kitchen after hanging up with Luke.

I still had on my pajamas and hadn't showered so my hair was a mess of auburn waves around my face. "Thanks for that. I was tired and slept late. I'm entitled to a lazy morning."

Liv looked me up and down. "You never sleep this late. What's going on?"

I brushed her off and headed to the fridge. I poured myself a glass of orange juice and leaned against the counter. "Nothing is going on. I was out late helping the detective on the case."

Liv dramatically raised her eyebrows. "That hot detective I saw on the news this morning? Miles something or other? He made a statement about the teacher's death."

"I wouldn't call him hot, but yeah, him." I sorted through the bread and other items on the counter until I found the cheese Danish I knew my mother bought. I cut myself a thick piece and sat down next to Liv.

"You're not fooling anyone, sister. Miles is hot, and more importantly, he's exactly the kind of guy you would have been crushing over before meeting Luke."

I shrugged noncommittally. Liv wasn't wrong. The fact that Miles was charming and probably a heartbreaker made him all the more appealing. Just admitting that though made me feel guilty. Nothing had happened last night. We finished dinner and he drove us back to the school. We did sit in his car talking for longer than I cared to admit. It turns out, we have a few old friends in common. He insisted I looked familiar, but I was fairly certain had I met him back then, I wouldn't have made it out of high school a virgin.

Liv snapped her fingers in front of my face. "Were you just daydreaming about kissing him?"

I swatted her hand away. "Don't be ridiculous. I'm about to get married."

"Maybe you just wanted one last fling. I can't blame you if you did. Don't get me wrong, I like him, but Luke is kind of boring." Liv got up and cut a slice of Danish for herself and offered me more.

As much as I wanted it, I declined. I have a dress to fit into. I scowled at my sister. "Luke isn't boring at all. You're confusing stable with boring." Liv had a poor track record with dating, generally choosing excitement over stability. The longest relationship she had was with my ex.

Liv shrugged. "He's boring for me. If you're not going after the hot detective, maybe I will. When is he coming over?"

"He's not and you need to stay away from him."

"Jealous?" Liv teased.

"Hardly, Miles is hard at work solving these cases."

"I bet he's hard all right." Liv winked at me.

Disgusted with my sister, I got up from the table and left. I didn't get far though. I did an about-face and went back into the kitchen. "Liv, what did Miles say about the teacher's death on the news?"

Liv looked up at me. "They hinted it was a suicide, but Miles called it suspicious."

That didn't surprise me. While I was standing there, I thought of something else. "You had friends who went to Austen Academy. Did any of them ever talk to you about the Clovers?"

Liv grabbed another piece of Danish and sat back down, taking sticky bites as she talked. "I had a friend who was a Clover. It's tough to get into."

"Did she ever talk to you about its purpose?" Sometimes it still surprised me how much of a wealth of information my sister could be. I needed to stop discounting her so easily.

"Purpose?" Liv asked, scrunching up her face at me. "I don't think they have much of a purpose other than being a secret society. They have a strong alumni core, and from what I heard, it's a foot in the door to an Ivy League college in addition to tons of connections for internships. Back then, my friend even said it might land her a rich husband."

I sat back down at the table. "Do they do any community service projects or volunteer?"

"No." Liv laughed sarcastically. "Are you kidding me? They don't do any charitable work or help improve the school or community in any way. You'll be lucky if you even get anyone to admit they exist. How did you even hear about them?"

"Jane's journal. She mentioned she was pledging them."

"Writing anything about them breaks the rules, too. It's not an easy society to get into. The pledging is extreme. One girl in my friend's pledge class ended up with a broken arm."

I didn't understand this at all. "How does that happen on a school campus? Aren't there teachers around?"

Liv shot me a look like I was an idiot. "There are teachers who are alumni of the Clovers. They know how it goes."

"You're telling me grown adult women allow students to harass other students?"

"They don't see it as harassment," Liv stressed. "They see it as a rite of passage. Don't turn your nose up at it, Riley. You didn't go to school there. It's prestigious to be a Clover. If I went there and was asked, I would have pledged in a heartbeat."

That was another major difference between Liv and me. She was a joiner. I was not. There was also no way I'd allow people to be mean or put me in physical danger just to join a group. I wasn't desperate for friends, power, or money. I narrowed my eyes at her. "If it's supposed to be so secret, why did your friend tell you about it?"

Liv shrugged. "I don't know. We were pretty close for a while. It's stressful. Maybe she just needed someone to talk to."

"Wait here." I ran upstairs and grabbed a pen and paper. I came back to the kitchen, caved in and cut myself more Danish, and sat down. "Tell me everything you know about them."

Liv sighed like she wanted to talk about anything else. "Okay, but don't tell anyone it was me who told you. My friend is an alumnus, and I don't want this getting back to her or negatively impacting her."

"I promise. Now spill."

"This is all from what my friend told me, mind you. None of it is confirmed so you'll have to take it with a grain of salt."

"Fine, just tell me," I urged, impatiently.

"The Clovers go back as far as the founding of the school. It was started by one of the girls in the original senior class. She got a small group of girls together and it blossomed from there. From what I know, the women came together because it still wasn't common for women to go to college. They used the power of the sisterhood to advance themselves and their issues."

"Sounds like early feminism."

Liv bounced her head back and forth. "I'd say a distorted view of it. Some of the women wanted to advance their studies. Others wanted to land husbands from rich and powerful families. My friend said that some classes of the Clovers even convinced the administration to remove teachers. Back in the 1920s, there is a legend that the Clovers overthrew the entire administration of the school and put in the people they wanted. They were very powerful, at least at one time. I don't know what the girls do now. Once my friend was in, she stopped talking to me."

"Did you have a falling out or something?"

"No. That's just how it goes with the Clovers. They close ranks. The girls are so absorbed their senior year with this society and other members, they are the only friends they have. Even other friendships at Austen are broken. The Clovers are friends among themselves and no one else. This is why I don't think you'll get any information."

"Jane wrote in her journal about being bullied. She was being harassed by members, one in particular."

"That's the process. There is a great test of loyalty."

"Jane wrote she wanted to quit but couldn't. Why not?"

Liv leaned across the table and said quietly, "No one quits the Clovers. My friend heard one girl tried back in the 1940s, and they killed her to keep the secret. That's probably just urban legend though. Once you're tapped and you accept, there's no getting out."

This all sounded like some bad horror movie. It couldn't be real. I said as much to my sister.

Liv threw her hands up frustrated with me. "You asked and I'm telling you what I know. It does sound like a bad horror movie, but once my friend made it through pledging, she acted as if she'd never met me before. It was like her old life ceased to exist." Liv got up and gathered her things to leave. She walked out of the kitchen without saying another word. When she got to the front door, she called back over her shoulder. "I'm coming back for dinner. You should invite the hot detective."

I exhaled. Not that I thought getting information about the Clovers would be easy, but I didn't think it would be impossible until now.

CHAPTER 16

I prepared myself for a long day of tracking down Jane's friends and interviewing them. The goal was to make more headway than Miles had achieved. Sometimes a private investigator was able to get further than the cops, but then again, the girls might not say a word to me. Right before I left, I called Jack, but he said he was busy running down leads and would get back to me as soon as he could. He said he was sure I could handle the interviews. I appreciated his vote of confidence, but it didn't do much to assure me I'd get what I needed.

I left and locked the door behind me. The news vans were back and each one had a cameraman focused on a news anchor talking to the camera. No one even noticed me. I caught a few words here and there. Most were talking about Erik Yates. Evidence, indicating it was murder, had been leaked by an unnamed source. A few news anchors mentioned possible division within the police ranks. Austen Academy had put out a statement adamant the police had told them no such thing. The school was calling for the police to put up their evidence or essentially shut up.

I approached the side entrance to the school, but cops, who flanked each side of the barricade, refused to let me pass. I had met one of them the day before, so he knew I was a private investigator. I suggested they call Det. Ward. When they balked, I told them maybe they needed to call Senator Crandall and explain why they were impeding the investigation to find his daughter.

"You are ruthless," Miles said sarcastically as he approached the barricade. He waved the cops off and let me through. "What brings you up here today?"

"I have Jane's friends to interview. I passed reporters on my way here. Someone leaked that Erik Yates was murdered?"

Miles didn't respond. He guided me by the arm until we were back in the middle of the quad. When he was sure no one else was around, Miles explained, "I leaked it to the press. Given what happened with Maddie, I wanted to get in front of this so there was no way it could be brushed under the rug. The school is furious, of course. They have had parents calling all day asking if their daughters are safe."

What Miles did was what Luke would have done. It was exactly the kind of move Luke has made before in cases. It impressed me. "Why not just make an official statement?"

"I'll do that soon," Miles assured, "but I'm getting push-back to rule it a suicide and close the case. Now that can't happen."

"Who wants you to call it a suicide?"

Miles looked around again and pulled me closer to him until his mouth was nearly touching my ear. I could feel his breath against it. "I'm getting some pressure to say it was suicide for the sake of the school's reputation. They pay a good deal of tax revenue to the city and their board of trustees is connected. If you grew up here, you know Troy politics. I needed to get out in front of this and put the message out there that it was likely murder before anything underhanded happens."

"Doesn't the medical examiner make the ultimate determination?"

Miles smirked. "He does, but what did he do with Maddie's case? Now he can't do the same without looking suspicious. Besides, I know it's murder. My crime scene techs told me there are no prints on the gun. Dead men can't wipe off their prints."

I was stunned by what he told me. It was absolutely murder, but as Miles spoke, his breath tickled my ear in a way that made me a little weak. I pulled out of his grasp and put some distance between us. "Won't your captain suspect it was you who leaked it to the media?"

Miles grinned devilishly. "I'm a by-the-book cop, which is why when I do things like this, no one suspects it's me. I have my connections with the local newspaper. They never give up a source."

Miles didn't know much about my background. "I was a journalist before I was an investigator. I've had sources like you before."

Miles smiled. "I can see you as a hard-hitting reporter, but I can see why you became an investigator, too."

"What's your plan for the day?" I asked, itching to get started.

"I don't know yet. The medical examiner should have his findings today. Even with political pressure, he can't deny the facts. I have a meeting later at the police station, and we'll probably come out with a formal statement tonight. Who are you interviewing?"

I pulled the list of girls' names from my pocket. "Lynn, Jane's mother, gave me a list of Jane's friends. I planned to start with them. I was also hoping to speak to Jane's roommate."

"The roommate won't know anything. She was gone when it happened."

What Miles said didn't surprise me. Sometimes cops were shortsighted. I explained, "I'm less interested in the night Jane disappeared and instead focused on what led up to it. I'm sure Jane left her room and the building of her own free will. What happened after is anyone's guess."

Miles read over the list and handed it back to me. "None of them would speak to me. I don't think you'll get very far."

"You've never seen me in action. I have powers of persuasion."

Miles stepped back appraising me. "I never said you didn't, but let me walk you into the administration building so you can get the girls' schedules and a campus pass. Otherwise, you're going to get booted out of here before you even begin."

"That's nice of you." I eyed him suspiciously as we walked back to the admin building. "Why are you helping me?"

"If you think you can get the girls to talk that's more than I could accomplish, but you have to tell me what you find out. Dinner tonight?"

I stopped. "I can't go on a date with you."

He laughed. "You're full of yourself. Nobody said anything about a date. You have to eat. I have to eat. We can share information away from here."

For a minute I thought I had misread some signals he had sent last night, but when I looked back at him, the grin I knew spelled trouble was written all over his face. "I'm serious! I'm an engaged woman."

"But you're not married yet."

I sighed. I'd kill Luke if he put himself in the same situation. "I'm all for sharing information so we should invite Jack along."

Miles stuck his hand out to shake mine. "A chaperone then."

I jerked my hand back. "I didn't say anything about needing a chaperone. If the purpose is sharing information, Jack should be there."

"You're used to always being in control, aren't you?" he teased.

"You're infuriating." I walked ahead of him to the admin building, leaving Miles to catch up with me. Thankfully, he didn't say another word as he guided me into the building and to the office of the person who gave me the schedules and a pass without so much as questioning or arguing with me. When we were done, Miles told me that he'd text me later about dinner, and then we went our separate ways.

The first girl on the list was Annie Summers. She and Jane had been roommates since they were freshmen. Right now, she was supposed to be in the English building having a free study period. At least, I had timed something right. I navigated into the building with ease and asked the first person I saw where the free study period was held. I found Annie alone in a cozy room with leather sofas, a fireplace that looked original, and walls stacked with books. She had her head buried in Shakespeare, which she read softly aloud. I cleared my throat to let her know I was there.

She picked her head up, clearly embarrassed. "Reading aloud makes it easier to get through," Annie explained.

Annie had square-framed glasses and a head full of shoulder-length dark curls. She looked like one of those fresh-faced pretty girls seen in makeup commercials, except Annie didn't look like she had on anything more than lip gloss.

I told her who I was and why I was there. She hesitated at first, explaining her father told her not to talk to anyone about Jane. I explained I wasn't the cops but was hired by Jane's father to find her. Annie relented quickly.

"Sit down," she said suddenly full of confidence, pointing to the seat across the table. "There are things you should know. I hope Jane is okay."

I didn't want to waste any time. I wasn't sure how long Annie had or would be willing to talk. "Do you think Jane ran away?"

Annie scrunched up her nose. "The last time I saw Jane was Thursday evening. I went to bed before her that night, and she was gone Friday morning when I got up. I left campus shortly after that. Jane was excited though. She told me at dinner Thursday night she had made significant progress on a project. By project, I knew she meant her search for Maddie's killer. So no, I don't think Jane ran away. I'm pretty sure whatever happened to Jane happened because she was close to naming Maddie's killer."

CHAPTER 17

The more I dug into Jane's disappearance, the more I believed what Annie said was true. I leaned on the table across from Annie. "Did you know Maddie well?"

"Maddie was Jane's best friend from home. The three of us spent a lot of time together." A tear formed in the corner of Annie's eye, and she quickly wiped it away. "Freshman year, I worried Jane and Maddie would be cliquey because they had known each other so long, but they weren't like that. They were both excited to make new friends, which is why they weren't roommates. They had the option, but they decided if they were roommates, they probably wouldn't talk to anyone else."

Annie had suffered two losses. I couldn't imagine how she was feeling. The worst thing that had happened when I was in high school was the deaths of older relatives. Annie was strong though. That much was obvious. She spoke with the confidence of a young woman much older than sixteen.

"Were you surprised by Maddie's death?"

Annie reached her hand across the table to touch my arm. She said seriously, "You have to know right now, no one believes Maddie killed herself. None of us girls anyway, and I know her parents don't. We can't say otherwise around teachers or our parents, but we talk with each other. Maddie wasn't suicidal."

Part of me wanted to refocus the conversation back to Jane, but I felt strongly in my gut learning more about Maddie was critical. I lowered my voice. "If you don't think Maddie killed herself, what do you think happened to her?"

"I don't know." Annie paused and took a few breaths. "I wish I did. We all do. Maddie was someone everyone loved. You couldn't help yourself. She was pretty, smart, funny, and charming. It didn't matter who you were, Maddie always had a smile for you. But that might have been her downfall."

This was the first time I had a clear picture of the type of person Maddie was, but I didn't understand what Annie meant. "If Maddie was so friendly, how could that be a downfall?"

Annie smiled sadly. "Do you not remember being in high school?"

"It's been a while," I admitted.

"While girls like Maddie may be popular, they aren't always well-liked. Girls were jealous of her. Everything seemed to come easily to Maddie, effortless really. She was a great athlete, excelled in school, was the lead in school plays, and had the attention of boys and even men quite easily. Maddie's downfall was that she was too nice and expected other people were too. She was far too trusting."

I understood what Annie was saying. I let the message sink in for a moment. It brought up far more questions than answers.

Before I could gather my thoughts, Annie added, "Jane used to say all the time the easiest way to make other people angry was to not care what they thought about you. That's a freedom that's both enviable and infuriating to some. Maddie didn't seem to notice when people didn't like her. She just went on being friendly. She came across like she didn't care what people thought. She just went right on living her life. There's no way she killed herself."

"Who do you think killed her?"

Annie shook her head. "I wish I knew. Jane was obsessed from the moment they found Maddie's body. The day they found Maddie's body we were locked into our rooms. Jane fumed with anger and was adamant Maddie hadn't killed herself. I agreed. We drew up a list that night of suspects. There were a lot of names on the list, both teachers and students. The person Jane focused on most was Natalie Gallo. She was a year ahead of us."

Annie got up and came around to my side of the table. She whispered in my ear. "Natalie was in the Clovers. She runs the whole thing now. It's why when Jane was tapped to join, she accepted. I also think it was why Natalie selected Jane. Natalie wanted to keep a better eye on her."

Annie went back and sat down. Because she whispered the name of the society, I wasn't going to say it aloud. I assumed Natalie was who Jane had written about in her journal.

"Tell me more about Natalie and why Jane suspected her."

Annie tapped at the table nervously. I could tell just talking about Natalie was uncomfortable for her, but I needed the information. Finally, Annie gathered some courage and said, "I don't know the full story. Something happened last spring semester between them. Maddie showed up to our room late, well past curfew. Her hair was a mess. She had been crying. Jane left with her and didn't return for two hours. When Jane came back, she said Maddie wouldn't tell her what had happened. I never heard anything more after that, but something happened between Natalie and Maddie. That much I knew for sure."

I knew Annie wasn't telling me the whole truth, but I didn't think I'd get it out of her right now. "Is there anyone else I should look into?"

Annie didn't answer. Instead, she grabbed a notebook and jotted down a note. She tore off the page and slid it to me. The note read: *Teacher Heidi Sykes. She hated Maddie and no one knew why.* I slipped the note in my pocket and didn't say a word about it.

Before I left Annie, I asked some questions about Jane and where she might have gone if she ran away. Annie didn't know. I nearly forgot about Jane's boyfriend. "Jane's mother found her journal. In it, she mentioned a boy named Liam. Do you know anything about him?"

It was the first time Annie smiled. "We met Liam at a school dance here last year. Jane and Liam connected right away. Later, he called her and they went out several times. Jane had a huge crush on him. I don't know his last name or much about him. I wouldn't say Jane was secretive, but she kept a lot to herself."

"Understood." I gave Annie an encouraging smile. "How have you been holding up?"

"I'm focused on getting out of here. There's a lot more here than meets the eye if you know what I mean. It's not quite as fun without Maddie and Jane so I'm trying to keep my head down, get my work done, and plan for college." Annie grabbed for her book.

I took that as a sign she didn't want to talk anymore. I gave her my number just in case she thought of anything. I said a few encouraging words and got up to leave. I had made it to the doorway when Annie called after me.

"I just remembered something," she said softly. "Jane kept a lot of stuff under her bed. Sometimes when she was down there getting something, I heard metal sounds. If I were you, I'd check the grate behind her bed."

I thanked her for the well-timed tip and was on my way. I checked my list and had six more girls who were good friends of Jane. I debated only for a second and shoved the list back in my pocket.

I was itching to see what was behind Jane's bed. There was no way I was going to wait. I left the building the way I had come in and stepped out into the glaring sunlight. I squinted my eyes and instinctively put my hand up to protect from the glare.

I made my way as quickly as possible to Jane's dorm. I climbed the stairs and navigated back down the hall towards her room. The halls were empty at this time of day with students in their classes. As I approached Jane's door, a woman yelled from behind me.

"You can't go in there," the woman said not once but three times.

I had heard her the first time, but she hadn't given me a chance to respond. I turned and came face to face with an older woman about my height. She had gray hair twisted up on the top of her head, glasses that rode low on the bridge of her nose, and deep-set wrinkles around her eyes.

I explained who I was and why I was there. I handed over my campus pass and identification. "I just spoke to Annie during her free time, and she suggested I take a look again through Jane's things. You can call the office or even Jane's parents. They are the ones who hired Jack Malone. I'm his partner."

She took a quick view of my credentials and handed them back to me. She sized me up. "Are you Karen Sullivan's daughter?"

I wasn't surprised. My mother knew everyone. "I am. How do you know my mother?"

"We go to church together. I'm Mary, the housemother here. I was the last person to see Jane as far as we know." Mary pointed to Jane's room and walked with me to the door, but she didn't step through. "I hope Jane is found quickly. If there is anything that I can do to help you, let me know."

CHAPTER 18

The room looked the same as it had the night before when I was with Jack and had met Senator Crandall and his wife, but the vibe today was distinctly different. I couldn't quite place what had changed, but maybe it was just being here in daylight. Looking around, the room was nicely decorated and comfortable. I could see Annie and Jane doing homework and sitting up late talking.

I went to Jane's desk first and pulled out drawers and flipped through notebooks and pads of paper for any notes or writing of interest. It all seemed like schoolwork to me. There were still smudge marks in the dust on the desktop where her laptop had sat. Jack had taken Jane's laptop and had an expert going through it to see if there was anything of interest. He said we'd have the results back in a day or two. Other than a lamp and a few pens, Jane had kept her desk spotless.

I went to her upright six-drawer dresser, which stood at the end of the bed against the far wall. I found nothing but clothes. I looked at Jane's twin bed wedged in the corner. The bed was covered in a medallion print in purple, pink, and turquoise blue. There were two throw pillows in similar shades that pulled the set together. I imagined Jane and her mother shopping for her school bedding and thought of my trips before I left for college. The time held so much promise.

If Annie was right and she heard metal scraping when Jane was under her bed, something could be hidden. I didn't have a flashlight or tools with me, and crawling under the bed didn't seem like the brightest of ideas. I went to the end of the bed and shoved the dresser down a few feet. I tugged at the twin frame and was excited when it slid easily across the floor. I glanced out of the door into the hallway and thought better of leaving the door open for all to see. I stopped what I was doing and closed it gently and then slid the lock in place for good measure.

I went back and moved furniture around until the bed was completely away from the wall. Under the bed, Jane had several bins of clothes and a box of personal items. I opened the lid and found scrapbooks from her childhood and one for her freshman and sophomore years. I thought kids did everything online now, so I was surprised to see printed photos. I dropped them back down in the box, planning to go through them later.

I crouched down low and then thought better of my creaking knees and plopped down on the ground completely. There was a return grate on the wall that had one screw loose. I didn't have a screwdriver with me to remove the grate. I slid around and rummaged through the items Jane had kept under her bed until I found a silver knife that would work just as well. I loosened each screw and removed the grate with ease. I had enough light to see inside. Sitting just back from the opening was a book. I pulled it out and flipped through it. It was another journal. It was without question Jane's writing.

I glanced behind me, and even with the door closed, it was too risky to sit here and read it. I took the journal and slipped it in the back waistband of my pants, pulling my shirt and sweater down on top of it. I'd read it first and then let Miles know if there was anything of importance. I placed the grate back in place and tightened the screws like no one had bothered with it at all.

While I was on the ground, I turned back to the pile of Jane's things. I searched through clothes and other personal items, but there was nothing suspicious or really of interest. I placed lids back on and moved to the box of scrapbooks. I started with sophomore year. The book was filled with memories, quotes, and photos of Jane and her friends. Annie had been right. Jane and Maddie had welcomed her into their little group, and the three of them were close. There were several other girls in the photos who I did not recognize. They were probably girls I'd soon be interviewing.

As I got to the second to last page of the book, a photo caught my eye. Jane stood in the middle of Maddie and Annie in front of the humanities building on a snowy day. They were smiling and fresh-faced. Around Jane's neck was a very similar purple scarf to the one I found outside of the teachers' cottages. I grabbed my phone and snapped a photo of the photo and another zoomed in on the scarf. I texted it to Miles.

I stood up and put everything in Jane's room back the way I found it. I took one last glance around the room to make sure nothing seemed disturbed and then opened the door to the hall. Mary stood on the other side. I wasn't sure if she had been there the whole time.

"Did you find anything?" she asked quietly.

The journal was wedged against my back. Unless Mary planned to pat me down, I was in the clear. I lied, "No, there were some nice photos Jane had in some scrapbooks under her bed, but nothing that tells me where she might be."

Mary nodded once and leaned in. Barely above a whisper, she said, "I think we should talk, but not here. Meet me tonight at eight." She slipped a piece of paper with an address into my hand and walked back down the hall without saying another word.

I put the paper in my pocket and navigated back out to the quad. I nearly walked into Miles a few feet from the building. My nerves ratcheted up knowing I had Jane's journal shoved in the back of my pants.

"You look like you're up to something," Miles teased.

"Oh, you know me, always getting into trouble." My voice squeaked, giving me away. Sneaking potential evidence out of Jane's room was proving more harrowing than I planned.

Miles raised his eyebrows. "I was just kidding, but now you have me curious."

I shrugged and walked past him, moving back to our spot near the bench in the middle of the quad. He walked in step next to me. I looked straight ahead. "It's nothing. This place is just different than I expected. The housemother, Mary, wants me to meet her tonight. She slipped me a note with an address before I left. I interviewed

Jane's roommate Annie. She's a sweet girl and had a lot to say. Neither seemed comfortable talking openly here on campus."

Miles shook his head. "I can't even get straight answers from the administration at this point. They are protecting themselves from liability."

"You'd think they might be more concerned with their missing student and finding a murderer running loose among them."

Miles reached out his hand to stop me. "What makes you say the murderer is among them?"

I turned to face him. "What makes you think the killer isn't here?"

"Erik Yates was murdered. I'll give you that much," Miles countered. "But he had a life outside of this school. You even said yourself, this campus is open. Erik could have had a visitor from outside of the school who killed him. I still have more security footage to go through. The school is making me get a warrant. You'd think they would have offered it up freely and not make me jump through a hundred hoops to get the info."

I looked away. Miles was right. Erik's killer could have been someone he knew from outside of the school, but that's not what I felt in my gut. I ran a strand of hair through my fingers and twisted it around. "I can't tell you that you're wrong, but it's not how it feels. If it was just Erik who was murdered, I might believe it. But Maddie last spring, too. Plus, Jane is missing. Annie told me from the moment they found Maddie's body, Jane was on a hunt for the truth. I can't look at all three separately. The cases are connected. I'm not sure how yet."

Miles rested his hands on his hips. He watched me carefully. "It's cute the way you play with your hair when you're lost in thought."

I let go of my hair. "I do not."

Miles reached out a hand to touch my hair, but I swatted it away. "I think you're trying to purposefully throw me off my game."

"How would I do that?" Miles feigned innocent.

"This flirting or whatever you want to call it."

Miles held his hands up in surrender. "I'm not flirting, but you better stop flirting with me. You're nearly a married woman remember."

I bit the inside of my cheek because I felt like screaming at him. "Let's just stick to the case." I pulled out my phone and pulled up the photo of Jane and her friends. I pointed. "Here, Jane is wearing what appears to be the purple scarf we found." I pulled up the second photo of just the scarf and showed him that, too. "I texted you both earlier."

Miles moved closer to me and peered down at the phone. "That does look like it. I have crime scene techs seeing if they can get DNA off the scarf we found. Even if it's Jane's, we won't know when the scarf was dropped. I can't even get anyone to tell me what Jane was wearing the last time she was seen. If you get anyone to talk, ask them that." Miles stepped back but not before bringing his face close to the top of my head and breathing in.

I elbowed him in the gut. "Knock it off."

"Stop smelling so good."

Aggravated, I shoved my phone back in my pocket and walked away without looking back.

CHAPTER 19

Luke tried to nap, but he just couldn't get comfortable in the passenger seat. Lunch, which they had eaten a few hours ago, sat like a rock in his stomach. Adele had complained of the same. They were all a little road weary and still had halfway to go. Cooper had taken over driving in the late afternoon. They planned to stop for dinner at eight, which meant Luke could get a couple of hours of sleep before dinner, and then, it would be his turn to drive again.

He took a few deep breaths and felt himself finally giving over to sleep when the phone rang through the Bluetooth.

"I don't recognize the number," Cooper said. "It looks international."

Luke sat up and told Cooper to answer it. "Hello. This is Det. Luke Morgan."

"The one marrying my daughter?" a man asked, his voice deep with a strong Irish brogue.

Cooper and Luke shared a look. It was Riley's father, Patrick Sullivan. The one she never talked about and hadn't seen in years. Luke stammered. "Yes, sir, that would be me."

"You may call me Sully. Everyone else does including my daughter who didn't even tell me she was getting married. Is Cooper there with you?"

Cooper's mouth dropped open and his eyes glanced toward Luke. "Yes, he's here. His girlfriend, Adele, is too, but she has headphones in."

"You must be wondering why I'm calling."

Luke regained his composure. "It's surprising for sure. Have you spoken to Riley recently?"

"Not in two years, but I know she's in New York with her mother right now so I wouldn't dare call her. I don't know how much you have been privy to my relationship with Riley, but suffice it to say, it's been strained."

Luke knew very little, snippets really about Riley's father and her relationship with him. Mostly, Luke knew he was absent from her life for most of it, and when he was around, they clashed. Riley wasn't on board with Sully's criminal activity. The Irish mob was the way Riley had described it. Luke didn't know what exactly the man did, and he didn't want to know. But now, Sully was bringing it right to his front door.

"Is there something you need from me?" Luke asked cautiously.

"I'm calling just to say congratulations and that Riley has made a good choice. I approve."

"Where are you calling from? Are you in the United States?"

Sully laughed. "I can't answer that."

Riley had told Luke more than once her father wasn't allowed in the United States. Luke had never taken it seriously. He thought she was exaggerating or being sarcastic. Now Luke believed she had been telling him the truth all along. Luke wanted to end the call as quickly as possible. "I appreciate you calling. I can certainly let Riley know you're sending your wishes on our marriage."

"I'd appreciate that," he said but didn't hang up. Sully breathed heavily on the other end.

"Is there something else?" Luke asked, glancing over at Cooper.

"Keep an eye on her, please. Some men wouldn't hesitate to take away those I cherish most."

The line went dead.

Luke sat there for a moment unsure of what to say or do, but the feeling of being watched was ever-present. Sully knew Riley was in New York. He knew Cooper and Luke were together at that very moment. Worst of all, Luke had no idea how the man had come by that information.

"What was that about?" Cooper asked, wide-eyed.

"I have no idea." Luke ran a hand over his bald head. "I'm not even sure if I should tell Riley he called."

"You have to tell her. You can't start your marriage with a secret like that," Adele said from the backseat.

Luke craned his neck to look at her. "I didn't realize you heard. I'm glad you did though. Has Riley ever told you much about her father?"

Adele shook her head. "She's never mentioned him once and I never asked. I assumed he was deceased. She's only ever spoken about her mother and sister."

"Riley doesn't talk about him much," Cooper said. "She's told me a little and it felt like pulling teeth to get her to tell me that much."

"We've talked about him," Luke said wearily. He took a couple of deep breaths and let them out slowly. Adele was right, he needed to tell Riley, especially if she was being watched. That wasn't something he could keep from her.

"What's his deal?" Adele asked, leaning forward in her seat.

Luke recounted the little he knew about Patrick Sullivan and his criminal empire. "Riley's mother, Karen, had no idea what Sully was all about when they were first married. He was here in the United States to go to college. Karen learned about his 'business dealings' soon after Riley was born, and she left him. He went back to Ireland, and sometime later, they rekindled. Riley's sister, Liv, was born, but they split again. That time for good. By all accounts, Sully went back to Ireland and wasn't very involved in the girls' lives. I don't know if that's because he stayed away or Karen kept him away. If Karen kept him away, it sounds like for good reason."

Cooper laughed. "Riley's mom has a whole arsenal of guns hidden in a safe in the upstairs hallway of the house. She told Luke and me last year that given Sully's connections, she wanted the added protection. I was shocked, to say the least."

"Gun-toting mama, I like her already," Adele hooted.

Luke explained, "She's not like that at all though. Karen is sweet but stern. When she told us about the guns and the reasons, I was speechless. But clearly, Karen felt a need to protect her girls from him."

Cooper changed lanes to move around a slow car. When he navigated safely over, he asked, "Don't you think it's creepy he knew where we all were?"

"More than creepy," Luke said. "I don't want to jump to conclusions. For all we know, he was just lying and talked to Riley earlier today. I doubt it, but thinking about the alternative that we have someone following us or he's had us under surveillance isn't anything I can think about right now."

"Do you think Riley is in danger, Luke?" Adele asked. "The last thing he said sounded like he might be worried Riley is in danger."

Luke nodded. "That's what it sounded like to me, too. But then again, it might just be an ongoing threat." Luke watched the road signs for the next exit. There were a few places to stop. "I know it's earlier than planned, but can we pull off here? I want to call Riley."

Cooper did as Luke asked and pulled off at the next exit. He navigated off the exit ramp and took a right at the intersection. No one was hungry yet, but they settled on a coffee shop. Cooper and Adele left Luke alone to call Riley.

He sat for a few minutes unsure of what to say. Luke worried her father calling might bring Riley added stress, which was the last thing he wanted to do. But Luke had to tell her.

The phone rang longer than he expected. Riley answered a bit out of breath. "I'm here. I'm here," she said.

"Are you okay?"

"Yeah, I'm fine. Sorry, I was running around with the dog in the backyard and didn't hear the phone."

Luke smiled. "I'm glad you're taking a break."

"I was over at the school nearly all day and have a meeting tonight. I'm trying to get some downtime in. How's the drive?"

"It's good. We are just past Bristol, Virginia with about halfway to go. I think we should be in by six or seven in the morning."

"I can't wait to see you. You sound stressed though. Is everything okay?"

Luke took a deep breath and said it quickly. "Your dad called me. I got off the phone with him about ten minutes ago. He knows you're in New York. He knew I was with Cooper. He wanted to send his well-wishes for the wedding. How does he know we're getting married?"

Riley didn't say anything for several moments. Her silence was more worrying to Luke than an outburst. Finally, she said, "Sully has his ways. I'm sorry he called you."

"You don't need to apologize. I'm not angry."

"Okay," Riley said slowly. "I'm not sure what to say. I haven't talked to him in a long time. It doesn't surprise me he's kept up with what I'm doing and where I am. That's how he's always been. By extension that would apply to you, too."

"I thought you'd be angry." Luke was taken aback. Riley didn't have the response he thought she'd have. She sounded far calmer than he anticipated.

Riley exhaled. "I learned a long time ago my father is going to do whatever he wants to do, and if I get angry every time he does, I'm going to spend a lot of time being angry. I'm still his daughter. I think no matter what, he does care what's going on in my life. Does he like you?"

"Yeah, he said you made a good choice."

"Good. Then we have nothing to worry about. Worry when Sully stops liking you."

Luke let out a nervous laugh. "You make it sound like I'm marrying into the mob."

"Kind of," Riley said sarcastically. When Luke didn't say anything, she added, "I'm teasing you. I've grown up with Sully and his quirks. It's new for you, and it will take time to adjust. Bottom line, he's not in my life so it's not a big deal."

Luke was going to tell Riley about what Sully said about keeping her safe but thought better of it. If Riley wasn't going to worry, then neither would he.

CHAPTER 20

My mother stood with her back to me as I walked through the kitchen door with Dusty in tow. His tongue hung out of his mouth waiting for me to fill his water bowl. I needed a glass of water, too. He wore me out. As I grabbed his water bowl and filled it at the sink, I said to my mother, "Luke just called me. Sully called him and freaked him out."

She raised her eyebrows. "Your father is getting brazen. What did he want?"

"Luke told me he wanted to send his best wishes for the wedding. Mind you, I didn't tell Sully I was getting married. Luke said Sully knew I was in New York and that he was with Cooper."

"He does that just to make sure Luke knows he's watching."

"I know, Mom. You don't think after all these years, I know how this works with him? It never changes. Have you heard anything about him being back here?"

Karen shook her head. "Not a thing, but I can reach out to some old connections and see if anyone has seen him. You know even if he's back, he keeps a low profile."

"I know, but it would be good to know if he's been seen." I finished my water and started down the hall so I could go up and take a shower. Before I reached the stairs, my mother called me back. I walked to the kitchen and leaned against the archway.

She pinned her eyes on me. "What exactly does Luke know about Sully? I want to make sure we are all on the same page."

"What we've always talked about telling people. You guys met, married, had me, and divorced when you found out he was in the Irish mob. He went back to Ireland, but he came back once, got you knocked up with Liv, and left again."

My mother frowned at me. "Don't say it like that. I didn't get 'knocked up', your sister was planned."

I shrugged. "I don't think I used those words anyway, but you understand. I stuck to the story."

"Good girl." My mother came over and kissed me on the cheek. "It's never been easy with your father, but I know you make the best of it."

I headed back upstairs. I was meeting with Mary and then had a late meeting after that with Miles and Jack. I needed a shower and some fresh clothes. I texted Luke a quick message, reinforcing how much I loved him, couldn't wait to marry him, and included kiss emojis at the end.

I finished getting ready and was downstairs and heading out the front door with ten minutes to spare. Although the address Mary gave me was only about a mile away, I drove. It was the same direction I would need to go to meet Miles and Jack later. I drove farther out Pawling Avenue and cut down one of the side streets near Sacred Heart Church. The house was a two-family with wide front porches upstairs and down. I parked out front and stood for a moment trying to figure out which door to knock on. Before I could, Mary opened the heavy wooden door.

She poked her head outside. "You alone?"

"Yeah, I came directly from home. I haven't been at Austen Academy for a few hours."

Mary stepped back and let me into the house. We walked right into a long front hallway that led into a wide living room. "This is my sister's place. I didn't want to talk on school grounds. There are ears everywhere."

"Sure, I understand." Mary guided me into the dining room directly connected to the living room. I took a seat. When she sat across from me, I asked, "What did you want to tell me?"

Mary still looked uncertain. She glanced down at her hands folded on the table and then back up at me. "Please don't judge me," she said, finally. "I've been a housemother at Austen going on thirty years. I love my job. I tried to retire a few years ago, but they convinced me to stay. It's too hard on me. I'm too old. Those girls today aren't like the girls twenty years ago."

"What do you mean?" I asked even though I knew the answer already.

"Some of these girls are brazen and disrespectful. They don't listen like girls years ago. Before, I could set rules, and the majority followed. Sure, we'd always get a rebel, but now, it's more than one. Most of the girls who come to Austen have parents who are powerful and have money. Many of them have been taught they don't need to follow the rules."

Mary paused and shook her head. "Now don't get me wrong. There are good girls. Maddie, Annie, and Jane and a few of their friends – all good girls, but they still skirt around the rules. Then others are more blatant about it."

"What kind of rules?"

"We have some standard rules at Austen Academy. Girls need to be in their rooms by eight and lights out at ten. Weekends there is more flexibility. It's always a process of rounding them up from the common room. The television is on. They are talking with their friends. These rules are broken all the time. All of us housemothers try to be flexible within reason. We do bed checks every night. It's my job to know where they are and that they are safe. Do you have any idea how hard it is to do at my age? I have twenty girls on my floor to keep track of night and day. Before it was a breeze. The girls came to me, confided in me. Not these girls. Now I'm just an obstacle to what they want."

"What is it that they want?"

"Freedom like they had at home. Many of them were raised by nannies. They were given the run of their houses, but here, there are rules. It's an adjustment for some, not all, but some for sure. Some girls are even sent here because they were out of control at home. They expect us to give them structure."

"What's the biggest challenge with them?"

"Boys from the fraternities in the neighborhood and other local high schools. You saw the campus. We don't have a problem with boys sneaking onto the grounds. The problem is girls sneaking off-campus. It's been a problem for a few years, but this isn't a reformatory school. They aren't under lock and key. I'm not a warden, and I'm too old to chase them down."

I felt like Mary had a point, but she was taking a long way around to get there. "Are you saying you think Jane snuck out to meet a boy?"

Mary looked away and then back at me. "She'd done it before. Most of the girls have at one time or another. I'm supposed to write up reports, get the administration involved, call parents, and such. In the last few years, I've let it slide with some of the girls."

Before I could comment, Mary held her hands up in defeat. "I admit I play favorites. Some girls are good most of the time, but they slip up occasionally. I don't see a reason to come crashing down on their heads. The other ones who flaunt the rules all the time, I come down on hard."

I wasn't exactly sure where Mary was going with this, but I figured the direct approach was best. "Are you trying to tell me when you did the bed check Friday night Jane wasn't in her room?"

Tears formed in Mary's eyes, and she sniffled. "That's exactly what I'm saying. Jane didn't sneak out very often. But she wasn't in her bed Friday night when I said she was. I had no idea she was in any danger or might have run away. You have to believe that. I didn't want to get in trouble for not sounding the alarm earlier. I thought I was protecting her and letting her have a little freedom. I didn't know it would lead to this."

I believed Mary meant no harm, but now, we had no timeline. We based everything on Jane being in her room at nine-thirty. Now that wasn't true. I rubbed my forehead. "When did you last see Jane on Friday?"

"She was in her room at seven. Jane went to dinner with some girls on the floor and then came back to her room. Jane looked like she had been crying so I asked her if she was okay."

"Did she tell you what was wrong?"

"No," Mary said softly. "I heard her the day before telling her friends she had been arguing with her boyfriend, Liam. I knew Jane had been struggling since she started pledging the Clovers, but it could have been any number of things. I asked. She said she was fine, and I didn't push. When I came around to make sure the girls were in their rooms at nine-thirty, Jane was gone. I assumed she was either with the Clovers or went to see her boyfriend."

The casual way Mary mentioned the Clovers made me suck in a breath. "You were aware Jane was pledging the Clovers? I didn't think that information was common knowledge."

"I knew because Jane was supposed to transfer to their residence hall, but she didn't want to so she stayed behind. They weren't going to allow it for long, but because of Maddie's death, they were giving her a break. Heidi Sykes, a teacher at Austen, is the housemother for that residence. She told me about Jane pledging because she needed to be out past curfew sometimes."

"I didn't realize any teachers were directly involved with the Clovers."

Mary raised her eyebrows. "Heidi is an alumnus. She went to college locally and lived as a housemother during those years. Her first teaching job was here. She's very entrenched at Austen Academy. Heidi has lived on campus for sixteen years. She started as a freshman. Nothing happens on this campus without her knowing about it." Mary leaned forward. "What are you going to do about what I told you?"

"I don't have a choice. I have to tell the detective."

"Let me retire first, please. This will disgrace all of my years of good service to the school. I plan to go in tomorrow morning and retire. Please let me do that first."

We didn't have time to wait, but I didn't want to hurt Mary in the process. "I'll do what I can. Thank you for telling me." I got up from the table. As I headed out, I encouraged Mary to call me if anything else came to mind. I got to the front door when I turned back to her. "What was Jane wearing the last time you saw her?"

Mary paused as if remembering. "Jeans and a sweater, I think. I don't remember exactly. It's not something you remember. All the girls dress similarly."

I understood. With my hand still on the door, I took a shot in the dark. "Do you think Maddie killed herself? You probably knew her better than most on the campus besides the girls."

Mary stepped toward me. "Maddie didn't kill herself. I'd stake my own life on it. But I understand why Erik Yates might have killed himself. He had a special bond with Maddie. Her death hit him hard."

It was the first anyone connected Erik Yates and Maddie. I stepped back into the hall. Mary and I had much more to talk about than I realized.

CHAPTER 21

Miles popped another French fry into his mouth as he listened to me explain in detail everything Mary told me. I had been more than an hour late meeting Miles and Jack, but with the information I had, it was worth the wait.

I took a bite of my burger and washed it down with some soda. "Jane was not in her room at nine-thirty, so our timeline is off. Mary last saw Jane around seven. You need to interview Heidi Sykes. Her name keeps coming up. Annie mentioned her and now Mary. She was the teacher I met creeping around those cottages the night we were out there."

"I talked to her already," Miles said. "She's been a teacher at Austen Academy for a long time. She worked as a housemother during college and was a student there in high school. The administration loves her. I think you're barking up the wrong tree. Plus, she was more than willing to answer my questions and didn't have anything to hide."

Jack and I shared a look. I had been texting him a lot earlier in the day. We both decided not to share with Miles that I had found Jane's other journal. I still hadn't had time to read through it, but even Jack agreed, the fewer people who knew about it right now the better.

Jack tapped at the table. "No disrespect, Miles, but I might run a background check on her. Riley, you should interview her if she's willing to talk."

"Do what you need to do," Miles said dismissively. "For me, what Mary said confirms Jane ran away. She had done it before and now again."

I shook my head. "Jane snuck off-campus before and came right back. This isn't the same. I said all along I thought Jane left her dormitory by her own will. We can't dismiss the idea that maybe something happened to her after that. If Jane just went to see her boyfriend, she would have come back by now. She's been gone for days. No money is missing from her account. She hasn't called anyone. This isn't like her at all."

"Drugs or unplanned pregnancy? Jane could be hiding out for a reason," Miles countered.

I looked up to the ceiling, frustrated. "Jane was an athlete. Nothing indicates anything related to drugs. I can't say there wasn't an unplanned pregnancy, but I still think we'd have heard from her by now – someone anyway. A friend, teacher, or her sister. There's been no word. I'm telling you something has happened to her."

"I tend to agree with Riley." Jack put his sandwich down and wiped his mouth with his napkin. "Mary said in the past Jane snuck off campus to see her boyfriend. There was never any indication she was gone for more than a few hours. She's never run away before. No, something more sinister is happening here."

"What did you find out today?" I asked Jack.

"Nothing," he said with frustration in his voice. "I sat down with Senator Crandall and his wife and went over every contact they have, including any threats there might be against him and his family. I called and interviewed other family members and family friends. I spoke to some of Crandall's staff. Senator Crandall has been very open with me. I went over the bank and credit card records, and there is no sign of Jane. Senator Crandall is well-respected and tough, but there haven't been any active threats."

"Luke said ransom requests come in early."

"That's true. That's why I think we can rule out kidnapping for ransom," Jack said definitively.

"I'm telling you, Jane ran away," Miles said again, obviously annoyed with us.

I ignored Miles and wouldn't even turn my head to look at him. "Jack, what are the next steps?"

"We're going to need to reestablish a timeline for who last saw Jane and go from there. Without establishing a true timeline, we are going to be spinning our wheels."

The server came over and cleared our plates. She asked if we wanted dessert and none of us did, but Jack ordered coffee to go.

When the server walked away, Miles explained, "We aren't officially calling Jane a runaway, but that's how it's being handled so investigating beyond that is on you two. Besides, now I have my hands full with the Erik Yates case." Miles pinned his eyes on me. "Did Mary say anything about Erik Yates?"

I wanted Miles to focus on Jane for more than five minutes, but it was obvious his mind was made up. "Maddie and Jane had Erik for history their sophomore year. Many of the girls had a crush on him. According to Mary, he didn't pay too much attention to it. He was a good-looking guy and was personable but seemed to do okay keeping good boundaries with the students, even living on campus. Maddie, though, he seemed to have a special bond with. From what Mary said, Maddie loved American history. She had a real passion for it, and that's how the two connected. Erik planned a few school trips to New York City and Boston, and Maddie always went. They talked about history together constantly. Mary said Erik had even come by Maddie's room a few times to leave her biographies about important figures in history."

"Any chance it was more inappropriate than that?" Jack asked.

"I didn't get any indication from Mary, but that's the worry, right? Whenever you hear a male teacher has a special interest in a young female student that's what comes to mind. I think we need to explore this more."

Miles shook his head. "There is no we. You focus on Jane. I'll focus on Erik."

I exhaled. "You just told me the other night you couldn't look into Maddie's death, so we'd have to do that. If she had a relationship of any kind with Erik, that's critical to know. What's changed?"

"We are officially going public tonight that Erik Yates was murdered." Miles checked his watch. "Actually, the chief is probably holding a press conference right now. He asked me to stay away. The less the media has my face, the easier I can do my job. There is going to be far more scrutiny on this case than before. I have to make sure I'm doing everything right."

"You need distance from us is what you're saying?" Jack asked.

"That's not what I'm saying. I'm saying that if any of us are going to dig around into the relationship Erik Yates had with Maddie, it should be me."

"What happens when no one tells you anything? You couldn't even get Annie to talk, and she was an open book with me," I countered.

Miles didn't say anything for several moments. "Then I'll call in reinforcements as long as you stay under the radar, but I have to have the first crack. It goes without saying, we never had this conversation. Even with you, Jack. You're still well-respected at the police department, but it won't stay that way if you compromise an open investigation."

Jack waved his hand at Miles like he was swatting away an annoying bug. "You do what you have to do. I'm not interested in the Erik Yates homicide unless we find it interconnects with Jane. Then you'll have me breathing down your neck."

"It does connect to Jane or at least it might," I reminded them. I pulled up the photo on my phone and showed it to Jack. I looked at Miles. "The scarf we found near the cottages. Did you confirm whether it's Jane's?"

"The crime scene lab has it and will see if they can pull any DNA." Miles bobbed his head to the side and admitted, "It does look like the same scarf that's in the photo you showed me. I called Lynn Crandall and sent her the photo. She said it looks familiar, but she can't be sure. There is probably enough to say it's Jane's unless the DNA comes back and says otherwise."

Jack groaned. "You said there's no connection between Jane and Erik, but now her scarf is found behind the cottages. How can you say there is no connection?"

"I don't have an answer for that yet. We don't even know how long the scarf has been there. Jane could have lost it last winter." Miles took a sip of his drink. He softened his tone. "I want us to work collaboratively. You have to believe I want Jane found as much as you do. The police department believes Jane ran away. I happen to believe the same based on the lack of evidence to suggest otherwise. If I'm wrong, I'm wrong. I won't stand in your way."

"I'm not looking to argue with you either," Jack said. He took a few deep breaths. "This meeting got a little off the rails. I think it's important we keep the lines of communication open if you're willing. Riley and I will run down leads on Jane, and we will stay clear of the Erik Yates case. If they intersect, we will come to you with anything we find."

Miles readily agreed to that. "I really am on your side here."

I leaned my arms on the table. "What do you want us to do if we come across evidence that might suggest Jane didn't run away?"

Miles raised his eyebrows. "Is this hypothetical or is this your way of telling me you found something?"

"Hypothetical. Annie and Mary were willing to speak to me and that might be true of the other girls. If we come across evidence while looking for Jane, I want to know right now what my obligation is to tell you."

"I'm hoping we continue to share information going forward. As I said, if I have a witness and I think you might get further speaking with them, I have no problem pulling you in as a consultant to interview them for me. We've done that before at the police department. I'm a guy in a school full of young girls whose parents told them not to talk to the cops. No one told them not to talk to you."

We wrapped up our meeting fairly uneventfully. I said goodbye to Jack who was going to check in with me in the morning. As I walked to my car, Miles followed.

"I didn't mean for that to be so tense," he said to my back.

I turned around and leaned on my car. "You were kind of a jerk, especially to Jack. We are just trying to help you. If it were up to me, I wouldn't have met you at all tonight. I'm trying to play by the rules this time."

"This time?" Miles asked with a curious glance.

I laughed. "You can ask Luke when you meet him. I don't always play by cop rules. I can go my own way sometimes."

Miles winked at me. "Luke might not like that about you, but I do. You should stick around. We'd make a good team."

CHAPTER 22

"It's like Miles was sent to give me one last test before I marry Luke." I pulled the blanket higher around me on the couch.

Liv shrugged. "If you don't want him, I said I'd take him off your hands for you."

After meeting with Miles and Jack, I came home to find my sister curled up on the couch in the living room watching television. My mother had left for Jack's house for the night. According to my sister, that was becoming more and more frequent. I was happy she was happy. It also made me feel better she wouldn't be home when Luke, Cooper, and Adele arrived in the morning. I didn't know what time they'd get in, and there was no point in all of us losing sleep.

Liv nudged me. "Are you tempted?"

"No, of course not. Miles is attractive and charming as I said, but no one compares to Luke. I just wish sometimes Luke had more fun with me and was a little less serious. Miles also likes that I'm an investigator. He seems to enjoy working with me. I wish I had that with Luke."

"You can't have everything." Liv pulled the end of my blanket to cover her. "If there were no Luke, would you have a fling with Miles?"

My cheeks grew warm, and I bit my lip. "I would, but don't you dare tell anyone."

Liv laughed. "I knew you would. He's your type."

Liv and I watched three episodes of *Modern Family* and then I went up to my room. She was spending the night. I knew Liv didn't like living on her own, but she was too stubborn to actually tell my mom that and come back home.

I found Dusty sprawled out on my bed. "You know, you're going to get in trouble for that."

Dusty picked his head up and looked at me as if to say he didn't care and then put it back down and closed his eyes. He knew I wasn't going to do anything. I grabbed Jane's journal from where I stashed it in my dresser earlier in the evening and snuggled into my favorite chair. My stomach churned a bit from anxiety about what I'd find. Hidden away, clearly, Jane didn't want anyone to read its contents.

I flipped open the first page, which was dated the day after they found Maddie's body. Jane expressed grief over losing her friend, but more than anything, she expressed her anger. Jane was sure Maddie did not kill herself. She vowed to find the killer.

Jane wrote entire pages dedicated to Maddie's behavior right up to the time she died.

It's hard for me to even sit here and write this. Maddie was like my sister. We did everything together, but in the months leading up to her death, Maddie changed. She wasn't happy and smiling all the time. I couldn't get her to go for walks or play soccer or lacrosse with me. She didn't want to eat. Two days straight Maddie said she wasn't feeling well and stayed in her room and didn't come out. The hardest part was I knew something was wrong, and she wouldn't tell me. We told each other everything!

I thought at first maybe Maddie fought with Davis, but I texted him and he said Maddie had been acting the same way with him. Maddie and Davis had only hung out a few times so I guess it wasn't that. I spent a lot of time in those few weeks trying to figure out what was wrong, but she wouldn't tell me. Maddie had a secret she was hiding from everyone even me.

Some girls wanted the school to hold a memorial service for Maddie, but they said under the circumstances they couldn't. I still don't know what that means, but we couldn't get them to change their minds. I know Maddie didn't kill herself, and I'm going to find out who killed her if it's the last thing I do at this school.

I read ten more pages like that where Jane's frustration leaped off the page. Jane's writing wasn't that of a schoolgirl in denial of a friend's suicide but of someone sure that isn't how it happened. Jane was articulate, well-reasoned, and brought to life a scene of those few weeks. Another passage caught my eye.

The weekend before Maddie died, she slept in my room. Annie had to go home for the weekend, and we got permission for Maddie to spend the weekend in our room. In the middle of the night, I woke up to hear Maddie crying. I went over to her bed and she was screaming that she was sorry, she wouldn't tell anyone what she saw. She said over and over again she wouldn't tell anyone. I shook her and woke her up, but Maddie said she didn't remember what she was dreaming about and that she was okay. I didn't believe her, but when I tried to talk about it, she just ignored me. I think this was important. I think this was a clue.

As the pages of the journal went on, it detailed the steps Jane took to find who killed her friend. Jane was convinced that it was someone at the school. There were notes about Jane's conversations with every one of Maddie's teachers that year. Many cautioned Jane to let it go and to move on with her life. An advisor with Austen Academy administration even told Jane she should seek some grief counseling to process what happened. Jane refused. The more staff and teachers at Austen Academy who told Jane to let it go, the more Jane's passion for finding the truth burned in her. Jane even wrote she didn't know who she could trust so she'd have to start flying a bit more under the radar with her investigation. That's what Jane called it – an investigation.

Close to the middle of the journal, I came to a page that featured Jane's suspect list. There were only three names on the page, and I wasn't the least bit surprised – Erik Yates, Heidi Sykes, and Natalie Gallo. Jane didn't list motives though.

My eyes grew heavy, but I wanted to keep reading. The next page after the suspect list gave more insight into Maddie's relationship with Erik Yates.

Maddie likes Mr. Yates, but I don't. I'm not sure what it is about him. At first, I liked him. He was a good teacher and didn't give too much homework. The class was interesting and he was fair. Maddie loves history. It's her favorite subject. I'm pretty sure she's going to be a history teacher. She talks about it all the time so it didn't surprise me when Mr. Yates took an interest in Maddie.

At first, I joked maybe her crush had a crush on her, too. Maddie said it wasn't like that though. All they talked about was history. He was impressed Maddie knew so much, but she told him even outside of class, she read a lot. Mr. Yates even brought Maddie books, which I thought was kind of weird, but Maddie read them faster than she read anything else. I knew she had a crush on him. A lot of the girls did. I hate to admit it but even I did for a while. I got over it fast because there is something about him I don't trust. I wish I knew what it was.

Dad says I should always trust my instinct. That's how he's gotten so far in politics. I'm doing that this time. I wish I had told Maddie to be careful more, especially the times she went to his cottage. Maddie said they talk late into the night. I asked her if it was just about history, and she admitted that it was about everything. She said that Erik (that's what she calls him when they are alone) is the first adult that has talked to her like an adult instead of a kid.

Maddie takes the hidden tunnel so no one sees her. The other girls think Maddie is going to meet Davis so they can hook up in his car. She's done that once or twice, but most times, she meets Mr. Yates. I followed her twice. Maddie never knew that. At least, she never told me she knew. There is a window at the back of his cottage and if you stand just right in the woods, you can see in, but they can't see you watching. I never saw anything though. They just sat in the living room talking. Mr. Yates never even touched her. I admit I thought Maddie was having sex with him, but she says she's still a virgin. That's why she fights with Davis so much. He wants more, and she's not ready.

After following Maddie, I kind of get why she likes him. I mean, I still don't trust him. Why does he let Maddie sneak to his cottage? Weird, right? But I can kind of understand because Maddie can have the kinds of conversations with him that boys our age don't have.

Maddie hadn't snuck out in a while. I wonder if something happened between them. That's why Mr. Yates is on my suspect list. There's something not right there, and I need to find out what it is.

I flipped through more pages to see if there was more Jane had found out, but there was nothing with any leads. The last quarter of the journal was blank. I closed the journal more convinced than ever Maddie's and Erik's murders and Jane's disappearance were connected. Jane was right. Even if the relationship wasn't sexual, it didn't sit well with me that Maddie, a sixteen-year-old sophomore, and Erik Yates, a man close to forty, would be spending time alone together in his cottage. I needed to get to the bottom of that, but I wasn't sure how since both of them were dead.

CHAPTER 23

Luke's eyes were barely open as he pulled his SUV into the driveway at Karen's house. The porch light gave just enough light for Luke to make his way up the steps and find the key Riley had hidden on the far side of the porch under a rug.

It was just after six in the morning. Cooper and Adele were both asleep in the car, and Luke was going to leave them there. There was no point waking them up. Riley had texted that Karen had stayed with Jack the night before so there was no one in the house other than Riley and her sister. Luke dragged himself to the front door and unlocked it. Dusty stood at the top of the stairs checking him out.

"It's just me. Good boy," Luke said as he climbed the stairs. At the landing, he gave Dusty a scratch behind the ears and rubbed him under the jaw the way he liked. Dusty followed him right into Riley's room. Luke let him in and then closed the door behind him. He stripped down to his boxers and climbed into bed next to Riley. As soon as he slipped his arm around her waist, she snuggled back into him.

"You're here," she said softly. "What time is it?"

"Just after six." Luke pulled Riley close so her bottom was right up against him and he could smell the sweet scent of her hair. "I can't keep my eyes open for much longer. Cooper and Adele are asleep in the car. I left the house door unlocked though so they can just walk in if they wake up. I figured that would be okay in this neighborhood."

"It is. Were there media vans out front?"

"No, I didn't see any." Luke yawned.

"How was the drive?"

Luke heard Riley's questions, but sleep pulled him under before he could give her an answer. He snuggled into her happier than he'd been in the last few days.

Hours later, the smell of coffee and baking bread woke Luke from his sleep. He reached for Riley but found nothing but the cold sheets on the empty side of her bed. Luke rolled onto his back and blinked his eyes adjusting to the daylight. He rubbed his forehead hoping that would erase the brain fog. He slapped at the nightstand for his phone to get a look at the time. It was just after eleven. Luke could easily roll back over and sleep for a few more hours, but the coffee smelled too good to keep him prone.

Luke got out of bed and cracked open the door. There didn't seem to be anyone up there with him. Each of the bedroom doors was open. He didn't bring in his luggage though. He walked down the hall and found the bathroom. Across from it was the room where Cooper and Adele were staying. Luke couldn't believe his luck when he spotted his suitcase sitting on the floor of the bedroom. He went quickly and rummaged through it until he found fresh clothes for the day.

As Luke stepped back into the hall, he slammed right into Liv. "I didn't know anyone was up here," he said quickly, embarrassed.

Liv laughed. "We're going to be family. I've seen men in their underwear before."

"You've never seen me in my underwear before, and I had been hoping to keep it that way. Where's your sister?"

"She's downstairs eating a late breakfast with Cooper and Adele. We saved you some." Liv walked into her bedroom and closed the door.

Luke walked to the bathroom, and just as he was about to step in, Liv popped her head back out of her bedroom door. She winked. "You need to lighten up. In this family, once Riley is done, it's my turn. I'm going to see you naked eventually."

Luke's mouth hung open and he had no retort. He stared at her blankly.

Liv laughed. "I'm teasing you, silly. You're so easy to rile up." She closed her bedroom door and left Luke standing in the hall.

This was only the second time meeting Liv, but Riley said she had a sarcastic sense of humor. A forced chuckle escaped him, but the fact that Liv had dated Riley's ex-husband was ever-present in his mind.

After a quick shower, Luke joined everyone in the kitchen. As he walked in, Riley came over immediately and wrapped her arms around him. "Do you want some breakfast?"

Luke embraced her. "I'm starving, but all I want right now is some coffee." As Riley went to fix him a cup, he sat down at the table with Cooper and Adele. "I think your sister just hit on me."

"Liv's a hoot," Adele said smiling. "She hit on Cooper right in front of me and then told me she hoped I shared. I don't, but still funny."

Riley set his cup down, grimacing. "What awful thing did Liv say to you?"

Luke took a sip. "Thanks, Cooper, for bringing in my suitcase. I was headed for the bathroom and found some fresh clothes. She saw me in my boxers and told me when you're done with me, she gets me."

"Liv is awful!" Riley hooted. "I'd say she's kidding, but she did date my ex-husband."

"That's exactly what I was thinking when she said it!" Luke laughed and pulled Riley onto his lap. He kissed her cheek. "I missed you."

"I missed you too." Riley got up and fixed Luke a plate of bacon, eggs, and toast. She set it down in front of him. "I was telling Cooper and Adele about the case before you came down. If you want me to tell you, I can, but if you don't want to talk about it, I won't."

Luke dug into his food, not realizing how hungry he was until he had the first bite. He took another sip of his coffee. "Tell me. I listened to talk radio most of the night, and that's all everyone talked about. I know I told you to stay away, but I'm completely hooked on the case."

Riley sat across from him. "That's good because we need your help." Riley gave him an overview of the case to date including the official statement from the police that Erik Yates was not a suicide but a homicide. She detailed some of the information she had found out about Jane, which surprised Luke. He had no idea an all-girls boarding school could have so much drama brewing.

"What about the parents?" Luke asked, popping a crispy piece of bacon in his mouth.

"Jack and I have spoken to both. Neither believed Jane ran away, but they don't seem particularly in touch with what their daughter was doing here at school. It could just be that Jane is a teenage girl and at boarding school, so they only know what she tells them."

"That's true," Adele said. "I didn't tell my parents much at that age, but I was at home, so they were right there hovering. I can imagine being far away there is a lot you can hide."

"Did Jane have a boyfriend?" Luke asked, finishing off the last of his breakfast.

"She did," Riley confirmed. "His name is Liam, but I haven't had much of a chance to get a lead on him. I don't know his last name. Jane's father didn't even think she had a boyfriend. Her mother and sister didn't know either. That's a lead we need to run down."

Luke rested his arms on the table. "No one knew Jane had a boyfriend?"

"People at school knew, but they don't know much about him. Her roommate, Annie, said that Jane met Liam at a school dance at Austen, but she didn't know his last name. I don't know how we find him."

Luke rubbed his temples and then he snapped his fingers. "I wonder if the school keeps any sort of log of what schools were invited to the dance. Someone has to know that. There might even be a record of the kids who attended. If not, we can check cellphone records."

"That's a great idea. Austen Academy is not the least bit happy we are on campus and investigating, but I think they won't shut us down because it's Senator Crandall's daughter. Imagine how bad it would look if they blocked an investigation to help find her. I think you should probably go with Jack though to get info from the school. As for the cellphone records, Jack was handling that, too."

Cooper asked, "What about the local cops? Have they given you any trouble digging around in their case?"

Riley shook her head. "Miles has been pretty collaborative."

"Miles?" Cooper shot Luke a look.

"What?" Riley said defensively.

"Nothing." Cooper took a sip of his juice. "You were saying…"

"Det. Ward is my age. He told me to call him Miles. He even called me one night to help him explore some of the tunnels. Miles thinks Jane ran away and is treating it as such. He's been consumed with the murder of the teacher. We have the freedom to do what we need to do."

"How can we help?" Cooper asked.

Riley stood and leaned against the kitchen counter. She white-knuckled her coffee mug so Luke knew she was feeling defensive. "I think Luke can work with Jack today and you can come with me to the school. I have students and a teacher I need to interview. Is that okay?"

Adele raised her hand. "Can I just stay here? As much as I love your adventures, I need more sleep, and I have a legal brief I need to finish preparing."

Riley laughed. "You can have the run of the house. You've already met Liv, but I think she will be heading back to her place soon. My mom should be back, too, but no one will bother you. Feel free to use the desk in my room."

Luke thought he'd be annoyed to jump right into work, but this didn't feel like work for him. Captain Meadows wasn't waiting for evidence. The mayor wasn't calling his desk demanding to know why a case wasn't solved. Not that he'd ever become a private investigator like Riley and Cooper, but he saw the appeal.

CHAPTER 24

"Where are we heading first?" Cooper asked as we stepped off the porch.

"We have to go into the administration building and get a pass for the day." I was happy to see even though it was near noon, the news vans still hadn't made an appearance. Cooper and I walked up the road and took a right onto the main road.

Pointing ahead, Cooper asked, "Is that the school?"

"It is. Where you see the trees and the wrought iron fencing. I told you I was close."

"This is practically next door."

"Liv and I both had friends who went to school there, which is the only reason why I got involved. I hope Luke wasn't too angry." I stepped off the sidewalk at the light and crossed to the other side of the street.

Cooper followed right next to me. "I think he was at first, but he seems okay now. What's up with you and the detective?"

"What do you mean?" My face grew hot.

"That right there, you're turning red." Cooper reached over and gave my cheek a playful pinch. "You did that in the kitchen when you were talking about him. Then you got all defensive. Don't think Luke didn't notice. So, I'll ask again, what's the deal with you and the detective?"

I bit my lip. "Miles has flirted with me a few times. I think it's harmless."

"You think?"

"It's harmless on my end."

"You've flirted back?" Cooper nudged my arm.

"No, I wouldn't say that. We have a certain chemistry between us though."

"You shouldn't have anything," Cooper scolded loudly.

I shushed him. "Miles knows I'm engaged and about to be married. At first, I thought he was just trying to throw me off my game by flirting with me. I think he might be serious though. I'm putting distance there, don't worry. It was just because Jack was handling some other things and Miles and I worked together a little. That's all."

Cooper reached out and grabbed my arm to stop me from walking. He looked down at me, his green eyes locked with mine. "You and Luke didn't have the best start. You got scared and bolted. You wrecked him for a couple of years there. You're back on track. Life is good. Don't mess it up. If you hurt him again, we won't be able to work together anymore."

I rolled my eyes at Cooper. "I have no intention of hurting Luke, but message heard." I walked quickly up the street and to the side entrance to the school. At this point, the cops standing guard knew me and waved me through even with Cooper.

I entered the administration building and held the door open for Cooper.

"This is a high school? It looks more like a college," he said, stepping into the building.

"You haven't seen anything yet." Cooper followed me down the hall and up the stairs to the office where I picked up the passes. The woman had them on her desk, and after checking Cooper's identification, she thrust them in my direction.

"We aren't happy you're on campus disturbing our students," the woman said.

"I think a murder and missing student might disturb the students more than people trying to help find their classmates." I looped the pass on the string around my neck.

The woman grunted at me, clearly displeased. "We've been told to give you full access so we are. I don't have to be happy about it though."

"Thanks. Do you happen to know where I can find Heidi Sykes?"

The woman slapped at the keyboard. She stared straight at the screen instead of looking at us. "Ms. Sykes should be in her classroom in the humanities building until three when she is done with classes for the day. She lives in Wells Hall. That's the building with the bell tower."

"Thank you." I started to leave the room, but Cooper tugged me back.

"Ma'am, I'm curious if y'all keep records here from school dances? What other schools attended or maybe even a student roster?"

The woman smiled for the first time. I couldn't believe how thick Cooper was laying on his southern accent, but it seemed to work like a charm.

"We do keep those records," she said, practically batting her eyelashes at him. "Would you like to see them?"

"That's great to hear, ma'am. I'm going to let our other investigator know, and he will be by soon. You have a great day." Cooper winked at her as he left the room.

I held in my laughter as we walked down the hall and back outside. "Where did that come from?"

Cooper shrugged. "Not many women can resist the accent. I thought I'd lay it on a little thicker. I'm going to text Luke and let him know they have those records. Riley, do you know when the dance was held?"

"I didn't even think to ask that when I spoke to Annie."

"It's okay. When do you think the dance was held?" Cooper asked.

"Sometime earlier this year."

Cooper said he'd be right back. He headed back into the building before I even had a chance to ask him if he wanted me to come. I pulled out my phone and went through several messages. I picked my head up and glanced back at the building, worried Cooper had sweet-talked himself into some trouble. My attention was diverted when Miles called my name.

"I'm surprised to see you here," he said, walking right up to me. "Didn't your fiancé get in this morning? I figured you'd be off the case."

"Luke is going with Jack today to run down a few leads. My investigative partner is here with me. He just went back inside to ask a question."

Miles hitched his jaw in the direction of the building. "Good luck to him. I can't get them to share anything. I've had to threaten them twice with legal action. I've never encountered such uncooperative people. I've tried several times to have a meeting with Headmistress Winslow. It's been rescheduled and rescheduled. Even when I show up at her office, she's not there or in another meeting. You'd think they would want us to catch whoever is responsible."

"Maybe they know it's someone on campus." I meant that. The more I learned, I was fairly certain the killer was among the staff, teachers, or even students at the school. I couldn't see any outsider causing all this violence.

Miles shrugged. "I guess we'll see. Where you headed today?"

"I need to talk to some of the girls." I left it vague on purpose. Miles wasn't interested in what we were doing so I no longer felt a need to share.

"Do you want to meet by our bench later and talk?" Miles asked hopefully.

I laughed. "We don't have a bench, so no."

"You're breaking my heart, Riley," Miles teased back.

From behind me, Cooper said, "Luke is going to break more than your heart."

"Cooper, he was kidding!" The last thing I needed was tension. I introduced them and they shook hands begrudgingly.

"You have a good day, Riley. Stay out of trouble." Miles walked away without looking back.

I turned to Cooper. "Did you have to do that? He's annoying but harmless. I don't want to be on his bad side though. He's given us complete access but could shut us down anytime. I'd rather stay on his good side."

Cooper ignored me but held up a piece of paper. "I got Liam's name."

I nearly hugged him. "How? I gave you hardly any information."

"Southern charm." Cooper winked at me. "I suggested there may be a reason for Jane to be missing not connected to any wrongdoing by the school. I hinted she may have run off with a boy and their records might have his name. Sure enough, there was a record of the school dance, which was held in early February for Valentine's Day. It listed only one school, La Salle Institute, whose students attended. She also had a list of all the students who attended. There was only one Liam on the list. His name is Liam Keller."

"That makes sense," I said, impressed. "La Salle is an all-boys high school. Text it to Luke so he and Jack can run it down. I'm sure Jack can pull the address."

Cooper texted the information and received confirmation back that Luke would run with the info. "Luke said he's on his way to meet Jack right now. Where are we headed?"

I pulled out the list I had from the other day with girls who I needed to interview. "I think we should start with Jane's friends."

As Cooper and I headed for the middle of campus, the feeling that someone was watching crept into my mind. Sure enough, as I turned to glance behind us, a woman was standing in the window of the administration building glaring right at us.

CHAPTER 25

I led Cooper through the maze of buildings on the campus until we reached the science center. Three of Jane's friends had a free study period in this building. A lunch period followed so I hoped we'd get lucky and speak to all three. I entered the building and the smell of formaldehyde knocked me back. I crinkled up my nose. "It smells like a high school biology class when we dissected frogs."

Cooper rubbed his nose. "I didn't realize they still do that. It feels like fifty years since I was in high school. But I never attended a school that looked like this."

We navigated up a set of steps and then turned right into a hall that held a row of classrooms. "They are in room 112. I think that's got to be at the end of this hall." Most of the doors were closed with classes in session. We walked nearly to the end and found room 112, the last door on the right.

"You go first." Cooper nudged me in the back. "I feel completely out of place here."

I craned my neck around. "You never feel out of place. What's wrong with you?"

"It's too snooty for my taste. Plus, it's all women. I haven't even seen a male teacher yet."

I pushed open the heavy wooden door to find a room much like Annie had been in the other day. There was a fireplace, floor to ceiling bookshelves, chairs, and couches along with several round tables where girls were studying. Glancing around, I counted sixteen girls. I hoped the three I needed were in the room, but there was no way we could talk here like I had with Annie. The space didn't offer any privacy.

"Excuse me," I said tentatively. "I'm looking for a few of Jane Crandall's friends. Zara, Cathy, and Willow."

When no one stood or identified themselves, I introduced myself and Cooper and explained why we were there. "I just have a few questions about Jane's disappearance. I want to speak to her friends to learn more about Jane, but if anyone knows anything that might help us find her, we'd appreciate it. Our only goal is to find Jane."

"My dad says she ran away," one girl said from the back.

Another girl turned to her and said, "She's dead. If they didn't find her within the first forty-eight hours, they never will."

"Ladies," I said sternly, commanding their attention. "We have no reason right now to believe that any harm has come to Jane. We just have a few questions."

Two girls, who identified themselves as Zara and Willow, stood up from the table and gathered their things.

The third girl, Cathy, said, "My father instructed me not to speak to anyone so I'm not. I don't know where Jane is, and even if I did, I wouldn't tell you."

Zara and Willow shared a look and rolled their eyes. They followed us into the hall. As the door closed behind them, I asked, "Is there a good place for us to speak privately?"

Zara pointed to a set of steps at the end of the hall. "There's empty classroom space upstairs we can use."

We followed her up the wide staircase until we reached the second landing. Willow and Zara briefly discussed which classroom would be the best and then led us down a hall. "There are some classrooms in use right now so I figured away from everyone else is probably best," Zara explained.

Our shoes squeaked on the recently polished floor. Zara led us into an open classroom and the girls took a seat at desks. Cooper and I sat down as well. I try to interview people separately, but it felt a bit silly now to ask one to wait in the hall.

"I understand you both were good friends of Jane." I moved my chair back slightly to be able to see each of them.

Willow nodded. "We all met freshman year. I was Maddie's roommate. Zara lived next to me."

"Cathy is my roommate," Zara offered. "It doesn't surprise me she won't speak to you. Her father is a lawyer and was up here from Washington D.C. on Sunday, cautioning all of us not to speak to anyone. My parents don't want me involved either, but I'm worried about Jane."

Cooper leaned forward, clasping his hands between his knees. "Is there a reason Cathy's father doesn't want any of you girls to talk to the police? If Jane was your friend, I think you'd want to do everything you can to help us find her."

"We do want to find her, but our parents don't want us getting caught up in any scandal," Willow admitted.

I narrowed my eyes, looking right at Willow. "Is there scandal to be caught up in?"

She looked away. I pushed a little harder. "There is a possibility we can keep what you tell us a secret. That's one of the benefits of being a private investigator. I don't always have to tell people where I got the information."

Willow and Zara shared a look. Zara spoke first. "We honestly don't know what happened to Jane, but the last time I saw her was in the hall on Friday night for dinner. We ate early about five and headed back up to our rooms around six-thirty."

I pulled up my phone and checked through some notes I had written. What Zara said checked with what Mary had told me, too. "We heard Jane might have been upset at dinner. Is that true?"

Zara hesitated, but I knew she had something more to say. I leaned forward. "Zara, if there is something else, please tell us. It might be the key to helping us find Jane."

"There were a few things, to be honest," Zara started, exhaling a breath she seemed to have been holding in. "Jane fought with her boyfriend Liam the day before. He was worried about her and wanted her to stop doing some of the things she was doing. Jane was having a rough time, and it was impacting every relationship she had, even with us. She told us about the fight at dinner and was thinking about breaking up with him."

"You said there were a few things," Cooper reminded her. "What were the others?"

When Zara didn't say anything, I asked, "What was Jane doing that upset Liam?"

Zara still didn't respond and neither did Willow. I crossed my legs and looked between them. "Let me make this a little easier for both of you. I already know about the Clovers."

"Don't say it so loudly," Willow scolded me, fear in her eyes. Zara had the same look. "We aren't involved with them, and we don't know who is pledging. You have to watch what you say."

"I'm not afraid of them," I assured them. "I know you think they probably wield a lot of power here at the school, and it's this great big secret, but they aren't as big a secret as you think. I know about them. Cooper knows about them. Even my sister knew about them back when we were younger. If the Clovers have something to do with Jane's disappearance, I need to know."

"I don't know if they do," Zara said, honestly. "Natalie, one of the Clovers, who is in charge of all the pledges, gave Jane a hard time."

"How?" I still didn't understand.

"To be a Clover, you have to conform. They close ranks around the girls who are chosen pretty quickly. To be one of them means to give total loyalty to them. Jane found that difficult. They are mean and cruel during the pledging process. They often leave school grounds and do all kinds of crazy rituals. I don't know what's true or not. I heard they might even sacrifice animals."

Cooper said, "Help me understand this group. What do they do exactly?"

Zara explained, "It's mostly for networking. Clover women are very well-connected in government and business. Clovers have added support when applying for colleges, calls made for them to their top schools, letters of recommendation, meetings with powerful people who help guide them into college and beyond. There could be more, but the group has been so secretive for so long, no one knows. It's hard to sort fact from fiction."

"That doesn't sound like something that would need that much secrecy," I countered.

"To become a Clover is to have access to a very powerful network that guarantees you entrance into any Ivy League college you want, even if your grades aren't up to par. It also later paves the way into whatever work you want, including beating out more worthy candidates," Zara said and then paused. She repositioned herself in her chair. "Let me explain it this way. Everyone knows wealth and power pave the way for more wealth and power. It's one thing to know that and another to see behind the scenes of who is pulling those strings."

I still thought there had to be more, but I didn't think pushing harder would help. "Are you telling me Jane was upset about pledging and fought with her boyfriend over it? That's it?"

Zara nodded her head, but Willow didn't look so sure.

"Is there something else?" I asked.

Willow crossed and uncrossed her legs and clasped her hands so tightly in her lap, the blood drained from them. "Dinner wasn't the last time I saw Jane that night. I saw her again right around seven-forty. I was walking to the bathroom and saw Jane headed down the hall, heading toward the stairs. She had a flashlight in her hand and was dressed like she was going out."

"What was she wearing?" I asked.

Willow looked up like she was trying to remember. "I just saw the back of her, but she had on jeans, boots she always wore, a hoodie and her favorite purple scarf. I don't know what she had on under the hoodie because I didn't see the front of her."

Cooper glanced at me and then back at Willow. He moved to the edge of his seat. "Do you know where Jane was going?"

Willow looked to Zara who nodded once at her friend. Turning back to us, Willow said, "She was going to confront Maddie's killer."

CHAPTER 26

"We're in luck. Liam Keller is home from school today," Jack said to Luke as he walked into the kitchen. "I pulled his address, and it's not far from here." Jack sat down across from Luke at the table.

After Riley left with Cooper, Luke had gone upstairs and finished getting ready for the day. He even unpacked a little and then checked on Adele, who was sound asleep. Luke went back down to the kitchen to wait for Jack. Soon after, Cooper had texted him the information about Liam, which he sent directly to Jack.

When Jack arrived a few minutes later, Luke said, "I hope you don't mind me tagging along. Riley told me about the case, and I spent a car ride listening to talk radio. It's all the media is covering." Luke took the last sip of his coffee.

"I'd love the help. I feel bad I haven't been able to work with Riley directly as much as I thought, but she has a way of running with things on her own." Jack poured some coffee into a silver Thermos.

"Don't feel bad about Riley. She does the same to me when we have a case that collides. She's amazing though at what she does."

"It's in her blood. I just hope she stays safe. I know I haven't been dating her mom long, but Riley and Liv are like my own."

"What do you mean investigating is in Riley's blood?" Luke stood and grabbed his wallet and keys to go.

Jack started to say something and then stopped himself, leaving Luke standing there even more confused. Finally, Jack said, "I think one of her grandfathers was a detective, but I can't remember now which one it was."

Luke had no idea. Riley had never talked much about her grandparents. He took it for what it was and followed Jack out of the house and slipped into the passenger seat. "Did you find out anything about Liam?"

Jack put the Thermos in the cup holder and started the car. As he backed out of the driveway, he explained, "I talked to one of the faculty at La Salle. Liam is a junior, will be seventeen in a week, and is a straight-A student. He plays baseball. A good kid all around. I saw nothing that indicates the kid is trouble or up to no good, but as you and I both know, that doesn't tell us much. Some of the kids I've arrested for the worst violent crimes were perfect angels to the outside world."

"That's true. I've seen the same, but I don't want to put him on the defensive right away."

Jack turned to look at him. "I'm with you there. How long you been a detective?"

"Just about twelve years. I joined the force out of college, but didn't stay a beat cop for long."

"How long you been in homicide?" Jack navigated out of the suburbs and onto a more rural road. He handled the curves with ease like he had been driving the road for all of his life, which Luke assumed he probably had.

"I've taken homicide cases for ten of those twelve years. At the time I was promoted to detective, the unit was thin. There was an opening as a sex crimes investigator and I took it. I hated those cases, but I met my partner who had been working them for years. We got handed a homicide case when all the other detectives had their hands full, and we solved it within two weeks. Captain Meadows was sure it would end up a cold case. We both were moved into the homicide unit. I've been there ever since. How about you?"

"I was a cop my whole life. I spent thirty years as a detective, almost all of that in homicide."

"That's impressive. I hope one day to have a career that long."

"It can take a toll on a marriage, but you might not have the same issues with Riley since she understands your work. I saw many of my fellow detectives not be able to hold the job while keeping their families together."

Luke nodded. "I see the same, but I've also seen the successes. I think Riley and I will be okay."

"I do too." Jack navigated further outside of Troy's city limits into a more rural part of the county.

Luke stared out the window, still surprised how much rural land there was in upstate New York. As a kid growing up, all he saw were pictures of New York City. He always wondered how people wanted to live with that much concrete around them. After meeting Riley and visiting her hometown, he learned his impressions of New York were all wrong.

After a few minutes, Jack pointed to a Cape Cod-style house. It sat back up on a hill without a neighbor in sight. There were no cars in the driveway. "Let's hope he's home." Jack pulled up the driveway and put the car in park. A dog barked loudly from inside the house.

As they made their way to the front door, a woman stood waiting for them. "Can I help you?" she asked casually, not a trace of suspicion in her voice.

Jack explained who they were and that they were there to speak to Liam about Jane Crandall's disappearance.

"I'm Brenda, Liam's mom." She stepped out of the way and let them into the house. "Liam is home from school today. He said he wasn't feeling well, but I think Jane's disappearance has hit him hard. I'm surprised you're here. Even the cops haven't spoken to Liam yet." Brenda went to the bottom of the stairs and called his name.

Luke shifted his eyes toward Jack who just shrugged. "You've met Jane?" Luke asked, surprised she knew about Jane. Luke assumed Liam's parents wouldn't have known about the relationship since none of Jane's friends even knew his last name and her parents had no idea Liam existed.

Brenda turned to Luke and smiled. "Of course, we knew. Jane's been here to the house a couple of times at the end of the last school year. The kids talked all summer." Brenda called Liam again, and this time a lanky kid with a head full of dark hair stood at the top of the stairs in shorts and a Boston Red Sox tee-shirt.

"Come down, there are two people who want to talk to you about Jane."

Liam hesitantly came down the steps, taking his time. He looked at both Jack and Luke apprehensively and then shook their hands. "Did you find Jane?"

"No, that's what we are here to talk to you about," Jack said. Looking at Brenda, he asked, "Is there someplace we can talk?"

"Please sit in the living room. Can I get you anything?"

Both Luke and Jack declined. Luke said quietly, "If you'd rather talk without your mom that's okay."

"It's fine, there isn't anything I'd say I wouldn't say in front of my parents." Liam sat at one end of the couch and Luke at the other. Jack took a straight-back chair across from them.

"Jack has some questions for you about Jane, but before that, can you help me understand why your parents know about Jane, but her parents didn't know. Her friends didn't even know your last name. That's why the cops haven't come talk to you. No one knew who you were."

Liam rubbed his hands down the front of his thighs. He looked crestfallen at that information. "I don't know what to say. Jane had a lot of secrets. I guess I was one of them."

Luke didn't mean to hurt the kid's feelings. "Liam, that isn't what I meant. Jane's friends knew you two were dating. You were important to Jane, but they didn't know much about you. I'm wondering why that is."

Liam nodded, the corners of his mouth turning up in a brief smile. "Jane didn't have a lot that was her own. Her dad was focused on his career. Her mom was involved in a lot of charity work. Jane always said her sister Abby was the favorite. At Austen Academy not much is private. Everyone kind of knows everything about everyone else. Jane liked to keep our relationship just for her. We have only hung out in person a few times. She doesn't get to leave campus much."

"We heard Jane snuck out a few times to meet you?"

Liam nodded. "We didn't do anything other than go get ice cream and talk. As my mom said, Jane came here a few times to watch movies, and then I'd drive her back."

Luke felt for the kids. He remembered high school crushes and even sneaking out. He couldn't fault the kid for that. "Did your parents know Jane was sneaking out when she came here?"

"No. If they did, they would have put a stop to it." Liam looked Luke right in the eyes. "I didn't realize no one knew my last name. I don't know where Jane is. I've been so worried about her."

"Do you think Jane ran away?" Jack asked, drawing Liam's attention to him.

"No, she would have texted me. She would have let me know she was okay. We talked every day for most of the day. She told me everything." Liam frowned and started to tear up. He quickly wiped his eyes on the back of his hand.

Jack waited for him to regain his composure. "Where were you on Friday night?"

"My brother had a football game in Albany, so I went with my parents. I met a few friends and we came back here and watched movies. I was here with my parents nearly the whole night. I didn't know Jane was missing until I saw it on the news."

"You said you talked to Jane all the time. Didn't you text her on Friday or even Saturday when you hadn't heard from her? I don't remember hearing anything about texts from you on Jane's phone."

"No," Liam said, again sniffling back tears. "Jane and I got into a huge argument on Thursday, and we hadn't spoken since. I feel awful about that now. Maybe I could have done something to protect her, but I was mad at her."

Luke raised his eyebrows. "What was the fight about?"

"The same thing it had been about since school started. Jane was going after the person she thought killed Maddie. She was looking for proof, and I was worried she was putting herself in danger." Liam opened his arms wide. "Now look at what happened. The killer got to Jane first."

CHAPTER 27

"We don't know that," Jack stressed. "It's important you tell us everything you know. We can find Jane if we have the information."

Liam didn't say anything for several moments. Brenda came into the living room and sat next to her son. She put her arms around him. "You have to tell them what you know. Finding Jane is the only thing that matters right now."

Liam took a breath. "You know her friend Maddie that died last May?"

Luke nodded. "We know most people don't believe Maddie killed herself. Jane was trying to find the killer. We know all that. What we don't know is what Jane found."

"Jane wasn't sure who the killer was. She suspected a lot of people at first, but she started to narrow it down recently. Jane thought it might be Erik Yates or Heidi Sykes, both teachers there, and she also suspected one of the students, Natalie Gallo." Liam stopped talking. He rubbed his hands together and looked away.

They sat in silence for several moments waiting for Liam to say more. When he didn't, Luke encouraged, "Liam, I know there is more. You said you feel bad you didn't protect Jane before. Now is your chance."

Liam exhaled loudly. "Jane told me she suspected Natalie because Maddie had caught her stealing tests from a teacher's office a couple of months before she died. Jane didn't know this directly though and was trying to confirm it. I guess Maddie said something to her roommate Willow after it happened. She didn't want to tell Jane."

Jack asked, "Why didn't she want Jane to know?"

"Because Jane would have told someone. Doing the right thing was important to her. Willow, Maddie's roommate, is the one who finally told Jane after Maddie died. That's what put Jane on the path thinking it was Natalie. Cheating is a big deal, but especially at that school. It would cause a huge scandal."

Pieces of information Riley told Luke earlier that morning were clicking into place. "Do you know the teacher whose office was broken into?"

"No, Jane didn't tell me much about it. She just gave me an overview. I know she wrote things down in a journal she kept hidden behind her bed."

"We found that," Luke said. "One of our other investigators is still going through it. Do you think Jane was scared because she felt threatened and maybe ran away?"

"Not without telling someone," Liam said, shaking his head. He looked up at Luke. "Do you know how powerful her father is? If Jane told him she was in danger, he would have done something about it. Jane wouldn't have needed to run away. Senator Crandall might not have been around a lot, but Jane knew she could always count on him or least she thought that sometimes. She did try to tell him Maddie was murdered, but he told her to let adults handle it. I know that made Jane angry a lot."

Jack was about to say something, but Luke held up a finger. "Liam, I believe you, but let's just say Jane ran away. Maybe she was so scared she couldn't tell anyone. Is there any place where she could be hiding out?"

Confusion blanketed Liam's face. "What do you mean?"

"Did Jane's parents have a vacation house? Did Senator Crandall have a hunting cabin?"

"Not that I know of. I don't think Jane would have run away."

Luke reached out and put an arm on his shoulder. "I know you don't think Jane ran away, but we have to explore every possibility. Is there any place Jane ever spoke about where she said she felt safe or she had access to far away from people where no one would find her?"

"I don't think so. Jane never talked about any place like that."

As Liam spoke, his mother's eyes got wide. She interrupted her son. "I don't know if this is important, but once when Jane was here, she saw a photo of our cabin at Brant Lake up in Adirondacks. Jane commented that it looked peaceful and might be nice if someone needed some time to think."

Jack perked up at that information. "When was this?"

"It was probably the last time Jane was here, which was right before school ended last year. It was a few weeks after they found Maddie."

"Did Jane ask you any questions about it at the time?"

Brenda sat quiet for a moment before saying, "Not really. She asked me if we had the cabin for long. I told her we went up there every summer since before Liam was born. She asked where it was since it looked so secluded. I told her the road name, but I can't imagine she'd be able to find it."

"Can you show me the photo Jane saw?" Jack asked, standing.

"Sure, follow me."

As Jack followed Brenda out of the living room, Luke was left sitting on the couch with Liam. By the look on Liam's face, Luke knew he had more to say. "Did Jane ever ask you questions about the cabin?"

"I didn't think to say anything because it didn't even occur to me, but Jane asked me about it a few times. Just last week she asked me about it and wanted to know how close it was to a town. You have to understand, when Jane asked, it was always in conversation like we were just talking about stuff. A couple of times I brought up the cabin as maybe a place we could sneak away to one weekend and just hang out. We hardly got to see each other."

"Could Jane have found it on her own with the information you gave her?"

"I gave her the address. I even told her how to get there. She said she looked on her GPS on her phone, but she couldn't find it. It's hard to find and out of the way up a dirt road. With the information I gave her, Jane could have found it though eventually. How would she have gotten up there? It's more than an hour away."

"It's not hard these days. She could have called an Uber or taken a taxi. Jane had snuck out of school before. She knew how to get off the school grounds undetected. But Jane hasn't used any money from her bank accounts. Do you know if she had cash on her?"

Liam smiled for the first time. "Jane kept a lot of cash under her bed. She always took out more money from her bank than she needed. Her parents gave her a good allowance for anything she needed at school. She took it out a little at a time and saved it. Jane probably had five thousand dollars in cash."

"I don't understand. Why would Jane take the money out if it was safe in the bank?"

"I don't know," Liam said honestly. "Jane was weird about money. She didn't like using her bank card. She said her mom would call her and ask about every expenditure. It was a way her parents kept tabs on her. Jane wasn't doing anything wrong, but I think taking out the cash and having it made her feel like she was independent. Like she could go out and do things without her mother asking her a million questions."

Luke raised his eyebrows. "She's in high school. That's kind of their job. Have you tried to call Jane since she went missing?"

Liam pulled his phone out of the pocket on his shorts. He handed it to Luke. "I've tried her at least fifty times. It all just goes straight to voice mail."

Luke didn't need to see Liam's phone, but he scanned through the calls anyway. Liam was right, he had called Jane fifty-two times since Saturday afternoon.

"You know, if Jane did run away, she knows how not to be found," Liam started.

"What do you mean?" Luke asked, handing him back the phone.

"Jane is smart enough to shut her phone off and disable the GPS tracking so you can't find her or get a ping off a tower."

"How would she know about that?"

"Cop shows, the internet…you know, normal stuff. That's not a secret."

Luke sat back and appraised him. "What I hear you saying is that even if you don't believe Jane ran away, it's possible, and she knew how to do it and not be found?"

Liam bit at his lip. "I guess that's exactly what I'm saying. Do you think Jane is at my parents' cabin?"

"I don't know, but Jack and I are going to need to take a ride up and see."

"I think that's exactly what we are going to need to do," Jack said from behind Luke on his way back into the room. "I have directions and the key. We should head up there now before it gets dark."

"Are you sure you don't want to wait for my husband?" Brenda asked, coming to stand by Liam.

"I can go with you if you want," Liam offered.

"No, we will be fine," Jack reassured. "It's better we go alone that way we don't spook her if Jane is hiding out up there. We need to make sure she knows she's not in any trouble, and figure out why she ran away. We should do that alone."

Luke and Jack said goodbye and thanked them both for the information. As they got into the car, Jack said, "It's a good thing Cooper found his last name. Brenda said the cabin is close enough to a store Jane could have bought food, but the cabin doesn't have a phone. It's close to the lake but still fairly remote."

"Liam confirmed the same. Jane has a spot to hide out, plenty of cash on hand, and she knows how to disable her cellphone to not be traced."

Jack raised his eyebrows in a question.

"I'll tell you about it as we drive." Luke grabbed his cellphone to call Riley.

CHAPTER 28

I hung up the phone with Luke slightly stunned. Willow hadn't told me anything about Maddie witnessing Natalie stealing a test. All she said was Jane suspected Natalie might have killed Maddie. When I asked Willow why Jane thought it was Natalie, she said she didn't know. Willow lied.

It made sense though. That must have been why Maddie was feeling so out of sorts in the last few months of her life. She held a secret. Jane said as much in her journal. The note Jane's roommate, Annie, passed me flashed in my mind. She said Heidi hated Maddie. If the theft had anything to do with the Clovers, and Heidi knew about it, then it would make sense Maddie might have also felt threatened by Heidi. The pieces were starting to fall into place.

I explained everything Luke just told me to Cooper and added in the details about Heidi. "They are heading up to Brant Lake right now. Luke will let us know what they find. We have to go confront Willow about what Luke just told me." I checked my phone and cursed at the time. "We're running late. I need to catch Heidi Sykes in her office before the end of the day."

"Why don't you go talk to Willow again, and I'll go talk to Heidi Sykes," Cooper offered. "You said you had a bit of confrontation with her outside of the cottages anyway. Maybe I should talk to her alone. I might get further."

I squinted up at him. "Do you feel like you know enough about the case to find out what you need?"

Cooper shrugged. "Do we know anything else beyond what you just told me?"

"Not really," I admitted. I gave Cooper directions to Heidi's office, and we went our separate ways.

I trudged back toward the building that housed the café. When we finished interviewing them, Zara and Willow said they were going to skip the main dining hall and have a light lunch in the café that was on campus for staff and teachers. I found the building with ease and marched up the steps with purpose. I didn't like that Willow had lied, and it was a waste of my time having to backtrack.

I spotted Willow at a table with Zara. I'm sure she could tell by my expression I wasn't happy because she said something to Zara and quickly got up from the table. She walked away, glancing over her shoulder to see if I was following.

I was hot on her heels. When I caught up to her in the hallway, I reached for her shoulder and gripped her tightly. "You lied to me."

She turned and the fear was evident in her eyes. Willow whispered, "I didn't lie. I can't talk about this."

Willow started to walk away again and I followed. She turned back to me twice and told me to leave her alone, but that wasn't going to happen. I knew I was close to getting the truth, and I wanted to hear it from the source.

I was right behind her and said to her back, "If something happens to Jane, this is going to haunt you for the rest of your life."

Willow turned to me finally, glancing around to make sure we were alone. "You're not going to stop, are you?"

"Not until I find Jane."

"Follow me," she said resigned.

I followed Willow down the hall and then down a flight of stairs. We wound our way through the basement corridor until we reached the door. Willow pulled it open and stepped inside. It was just a small closet with cleaning supplies. We stood toe to toe in the tiny space.

Willow tugged at her hair. "You shouldn't have come after me like that. I can't talk out in the open."

I gestured with my hand around the small cramped enclosed space. "We're alone now. Tell me the truth about Natalie and Maddie."

"I could get expelled for not doing anything about it."

"I don't work at the school. I don't need to tell anyone you told," I countered, aggravated she wouldn't just spit it out.

Willow wouldn't meet my eyes. She looked down at the dirty floor. "It started last March right before mid-terms. Maddie did some extra credit for Ms. Hodge, who teaches tenth and eleventh grade English. She read a few books and handed in book reports. Maddie needed to get her grade up. One night, she forgot the book she was reading back in the classroom, so Maddie left our room and went through the tunnel to the humanities building. She figured the classroom would be unlocked, and she would grab her book and come back quickly. When Maddie left the classroom, she saw someone at the end of the hall with a flashlight. She stood out of the way and watched Natalie go into Ms. Hodge's office. Natalie came back out with some papers."

Willow paused for far too long, so I pushed, "What did Maddie do then?"

"She hid, but she heard Natalie on the phone tell someone she got a copy of the mid-term. Maddie was almost in the clear, but she tripped and made a noise when she was leaving. Natalie found her. At first, Natalie offered Maddie the test questions, but Maddie said no. We are a year younger than Natalie so it wouldn't have been our mid-term anyway, but Maddie isn't a cheater regardless. Natalie pushed her up against the wall and then punched her. Told her not to tell anyone."

I raised my eyebrows. "Natalie got violent with her?"

Willow nodded. "Maddie came back with her shirt torn and blood on her face. She told everyone she got hurt playing soccer, but we all knew that wasn't true. A couple of people thought maybe it was her boyfriend, Davis, but Maddie denied that."

"Did Maddie tell Ms. Hodge what she saw?"

"Maddie was going to the next day, but when Maddie took a shower that morning, Natalie was waiting. When Maddie went into the shower stall, Natalie pulled open the curtain and snapped a photo of her naked. Natalie threatened to send it to everyone. Maddie decided right then she would keep quiet. But the longer it went on, the worse it got. Natalie threatened Maddie all the time."

"Maddie didn't tell anyone else the truth? What about Jane or Erik Yates?" I couldn't believe all this was going on right under the nose of teachers and school administrators.

"Maddie didn't want Jane to know. She worried Jane would make it worse. Jane would have told a teacher. She would have confronted Natalie. There was no way Jane wasn't going to protect Maddie. I don't know about Mr. Yates, but I doubt it. He would have done something."

"Was the only cheating incidence in March?"

Willow frowned. "No, I wish it was. Maybe it would have blown over. At first, Maddie promised Natalie not to tell anyone, but Natalie kept harassing her. Maddie didn't know what else to do. As much as she was afraid of Natalie, Maddie knew if she was going to tell now, she needed proof. Maddie figured if Natalie stole the mid-term maybe she was stealing other tests. Maddie left our room a lot at night between March and May. She finally caught Natalie stealing again from Ms. Hodge in May. This time Maddie got a video of it. She rushed back to our room and showed me. The video was dark, so Maddie stayed home from classes on Friday to work on making the video brighter. It was that Friday night Maddie went missing. She left to see Mr. Yates and never came back to our room. The next day, we found her dead in the tunnel."

"Where is the video now?"

"I don't know. A school administrator cleaned out Maddie's room and sent her stuff back to her parents. I don't know if Maddie had her phone on her or where it was, but I never saw or heard about the video again."

I shifted my weight from one foot to the other. The temperature was rising in the small space. "Did you tell anyone what happened?"

Willow bit at her fingernails. "Not at first. I was worried I would get expelled for knowing someone cheated and not telling or falsely accusing someone because I didn't have any proof. I tried telling my parents, but they told me to stay out of it."

I locked eyes with her. "You said not at first. Does that mean you did tell someone else later on?"

Willow sniffled back tears. "I did, but I wish now I hadn't. Maddie had always been close to Mr. Yates. He was so upset over

Maddie's death last spring. I knew he didn't think Maddie killed herself. I always wondered if she had told him about Natalie, so I approached him and asked. Mr. Yates asked me to tell him what I knew so I did. I don't know if he knew it before I told him or not. He never said. He didn't seem shocked or anything. He just told me he'd handle it." Tears rolled down her cheeks. "I'm afraid it got him killed just like Maddie."

I wanted to reach out and hug Willow, but I didn't. If her story was true, I felt for her. It was too much for a girl her age to take on. She had lied to me before though. "Did you tell Jane what happened?"

Willow nodded and wiped her tears away. "I told her over the summer while we were away from school. I think Natalie invited Jane to pledge the Clovers to figure out what she knew. I know that's why Jane accepted. She thought the whole thing was bigger than Natalie. She thought it was directly tied to the Clovers, but I don't have any proof of that."

I was ready to let Willow go but thought of something I hadn't asked. "Do you know much about Maddie's relationship with Mr. Yates?"

Willow shrugged. "I know we're not supposed to be friends with teachers, but Maddie and Mr. Yates were friends. She'd stop by his cottage after dinner some nights before curfew to talk to him. She kind of had to sneak down so other teachers didn't know, but Maddie thought of him as a big brother."

"Is there any chance Mr. Yates got the wrong idea or tried to make it more?"

Willow squinted at me. "You mean like sex?"

"Yes."

"No way. Mr. Yates wasn't like that at all. Mr. Yates was probably the best teacher we had, but he was also really strict. I was surprised he let Maddie go to his cottage like that, but all they ever did was talk. Maddie said she felt at home with him. She was happy whenever she'd get a chance to see him, but it was nothing more than that."

It was hard to believe, but based on Jane's journal the interaction between them was just friendship. Willow confirmed it. There was no evidence of anything else. The truth would die with Erik and Maddie. I thanked Willow and told her she could go.

Willow left. I stood there for a moment and texted Cooper the information. He'd need to see what Heidi Sykes knew given her connection to the Clovers and being in the same English department as Irene Hodge.

CHAPTER 29

Cooper grew more impatient by the second. He had been standing in the hallway outside of a classroom for the last twenty minutes, waiting for Heidi Sykes to finish speaking to a student. He had arrived at her free period only to find Heidi chatting with a student. Cooper had interrupted, introducing himself and explaining why he was there. Heidi tried to brush him off until another time, but Cooper said he'd wait. He had stepped back out into the hall and watched as she closed the door.

While speaking to the student, Heidi occasionally glanced through the square window in the wooden door to see if Cooper was still there. He wasn't giving up that easily. Riley at least had more success. He read over the text she sent about Natalie and digested the information about Heidi's potential connection.

Finally, when Cooper thought he couldn't wait another moment, the student pulled open the door and stepped into the hall. Cooper grabbed the door before it closed. "Ms. Sykes, it's important I speak to you."

Heidi stapled some papers together. "As I told you a few minutes ago, I don't have a lot of time. It was pointless for you to wait."

Cooper smiled and said softly, "If you're not willing to speak to me, that's okay, ma'am. I can just tell Senator Crandall you refused to help find his daughter. I'm not sure the school's administration will be happy with that though." Cooper turned to head back out the door.

"That isn't true," Heidi called to his back. "I'm not refusing. I just don't have a lot of time. You'll need to walk with me as we talk."

"That's fine with me." Cooper stepped out of the way to let her pass and then walked right next to her down the hall.

"You have lunch now, right?" Cooper asked.

Heidi turned her head up to look at him. "Do you know my whole schedule?"

"The school provided it. I believe they thought it was important we speak, otherwise, I doubt they would have given it to me."

Heidi pursed her lips together. "I don't know how I can help you. Jane was a very troubled girl. Before Jane ran away, she accused several people of killing her friend Maddie. If you don't know, Maddie's death was ruled a suicide. Poor Jane just couldn't accept it."

"I don't understand something," Cooper said, ensuring he sounded confused. "If Jane was so troubled, why would you allow her to pledge the Clovers?"

Heidi stopped in her tracks. She turned to him angrily. "How did you know about that? No one is supposed to know who is pledging the Clovers."

Cooper shrugged, knowing he had thrown her off her game, which is exactly what he had intended. "I thought it was fairly common knowledge. All the Clovers, including the pledges, live in Wells Hall and you're the housemother. You were a Clover yourself back when you went to school here. It's fairly common knowledge you have oversight. Was I provided incorrect information?"

Heidi toyed with her necklace. "It's correct. It's just not something that is known around the school and certainly not information available to the public. How did you find out about it?"

Cooper shook his head. "Like a journalist, I don't reveal my sources."

"You have to tell me right now," Heidi demanded.

Cooper could tell she was the kind of woman who was usually given what she wants, but not this time. Cooper glared down at her. "I don't have to tell you anything. It isn't how this works. So, I'll ask again, why would you allow Jane to pledge the Clovers if she was so troubled? That doesn't make a lot of sense. As her teacher, I'd think you'd want to help ensure Jane was as healthy and safe as possible."

Heidi didn't look away. She maintained intense eye contact. "I didn't know until she was pledging just how troubled she was. At that point, I figured it was better to keep an eye on her."

"Did you ever make a referral for counseling for Jane?"

"No," Heidi said slowly. "I didn't want to ruin Jane's reputation. If other people knew she was in counseling, it could be challenging for her." Heidi started walking again and Cooper kept right in step.

"You just said Jane was accusing people of killing Maddie. I'd think it was common knowledge how troubled Jane was. Are you saying Jane's reputation was more important than her mental health? Is that how things work at this school?"

Frustrated, Heidi said, "You're twisting my words."

"Well then," Cooper said slowly, "what do you mean?"

Heidi fumbled over her words, starting and stopping, and then finally just giving in and saying nothing.

Cooper tried again. "Curiously, I haven't heard from anyone else Jane was troubled. By all accounts, she was an athlete, straight-A student, and had many friends. Nothing indicates she was having a hard time other than dealing with some normal grief."

Heidi didn't address what Cooper said, and he didn't think she would. Instead, she said, "Jane was having a hard time accepting Maddie's suicide. That's why we let her continue living in her dormitory instead of moving her over to Wells like the other girls who are pledging. As you can see, by doing that, I was trying to help her."

"That was nice of you," Cooper said dryly. "Let me ask you this. You said Jane was accusing people of killing Maddie. Who did she accuse?"

Heidi hesitated for a moment and then resigned herself to answering. "Jane accused a couple of teachers and another student, but that doesn't have anything to do with her running away."

"How could you possibly know that? If Jane ran away, she didn't indicate one way or another why she was leaving."

Heidi stopped walking again and turned to him. "What exactly are you trying to do?"

"I'm trying to find Jane, but it's more complex than that. Her best friend died under what can only be described as mysterious circumstances and now you have a teacher who was murdered on the same night Jane disappeared." Cooper paused and let that sink in. He raked a hand through his hair and plastered his best charming smile on his face. "I've been an investigator for a long time, and I can tell you, those aren't coincidences. There is a common denominator to it all. I'm going to find it."

"You have no proof of anything."

Cooper smirked at her. "Who said we have no proof? You were surprised I knew about the Clovers. You have no idea what kind of information I have."

Heidi stopped walking and put her hands on her hips to face him. "If you had so much information, you wouldn't be here talking to me."

"Why wouldn't I talk to a suspect to see what she knows?"

Heidi took a step back and put her hand up to her mouth. "You think I'm a suspect?"

This isn't how Cooper wanted to do this, but Heidi was more combative than he had planned. "While you made me wait, I decided to do a little research on you. I snooped on your Facebook page and found some interesting things about you. You like to sail. The last two summers you were sailing with your family."

Heidi blinked rapidly. "What does that have to do with anything?"

Cooper couldn't tell if she was genuinely confused or if she was faking it. "I spoke to Maddie's parents. They sent me the police photos of Maddie's body. When she was found, she had a rope around her neck that was tied to a pipe. It was intended to look like Maddie hung herself. What was most interesting to me and Maddie's parents were the intricate knots on the rope. It was a clove hitch knot used often in sailing."

Heidi's eyes got wide. "You think that means I killed Maddie?"

"I think you're as good a suspect as any. I haven't searched the rest of the school to see who might have the same sailing knowledge so you could be one among a few."

"Maddie killed herself," Heidi said adamantly. "Knots don't prove anything."

"I disagree," Cooper said. "Funny though, it was a clove hitch knot. All roads seem to lead back to the Clovers. Was the person who killed Maddie trying to send a message?"

"You are completely speculating!" Heidi yelled. "You have no evidence to prove anything. Maddie killed herself. She was depressed and upset for the last couple of months of her life. Everyone knew that. The pressure of school or her boyfriend or whatever finally got to her and she killed herself. It's tragic, but it happens. The fact that you're trying to blame me, and tie it into a society that has done wonderful things for girls for generations is both clueless and wrong."

Cooper shrugged. "I just go where the evidence leads. Who was the student Jane accused?"

"I'm not telling you that. You're wildly speculating, and there is no evidence to suggest it was the student Jane accused. I'm not into wild speculation and ruining anyone's reputation for fun."

Cooper reached his arm out to stop her. He bore his eyes into hers. "You think I'm here for fun? There are two murdered people and a missing student. I think if you cared so much about reputations, you'd care what happens to this school. We know without a shadow of a doubt that it was someone from the inside. If it's not you, I'd watch your back."

"I don't…" Heidi started to respond angrily but then stopped herself. She just watched Cooper but had nothing more to say.

"That's what I thought." Cooper walked away from her without turning back.

CHAPTER 30

I stood in the middle of the quad unsure of my next move. Given what Willow just told me, I wanted to interview Irene Hodge to see if she knew about the theft. I also needed to interview Natalie Gallo, which I wasn't looking forward to. I checked my watch. It was going on three. There might be enough time to get to the administration building and access Irene's schedule. I walked quickly but stopped short when I saw Miles.

"Making any progress?" he asked as he closed the gap between us.

"I am actually, but I'm not sure you'd care about what I found out."

"Try me," Miles said, walking in the direction of the bench in the middle of the quad.

As we walked, I explained to Miles everything Willow had confided in me, including all of the harassment Natalie had doled out. I stressed, "Earlier this semester, Jane and Erik knew Natalie had cheated and was harassing Maddie in the months leading up to her death. The harassment was clearly why Maddie's mood changed. Do you know where Maddie's cellphone is now? It might still have the video on it."

"Because Maddie's death was ruled a suicide, everything was turned back over to her parents." Miles sat down on the bench and rubbed his temples. "Do you think a student could have killed Maddie and Erik? It doesn't seem possible to me."

"I have no idea, especially about Erik. I'm just telling you what I found out. Cooper is interviewing Heidi Sykes right now. I know you said you don't think she had any involvement, but she has connections through the Clovers to both Jane and Natalie. It was also brought to my attention Heidi hated Maddie. I can only assume it had something to do with Natalie's cheating, but I can't prove that."

Miles stared across the quad. "This is all a mess, you know. How could something like this happen on this campus?"

"How doesn't it happen more?" I countered. "You have young girls in high school away from home. You have a secret society. Mary, the housemother, said these girls today aren't like the girls when she first started working. They have more freedom and access to money. Look at Jane, and she was one of the good ones. She had access to large amounts of money, more so than any kid I knew in school."

Miles nodded. "It's true. I worked part-time during the summers in high school to pay for my first car and have a little spending money. I'm pretty sure I didn't even make enough to qualify to pay taxes."

"Exactly. This isn't our world. Sure, I grew up right down the street, but I came from a solidly middle-class family. I paid for my first car myself. I worked through school. I'm not saying money caused this. But these girls have access to a lot of power and wealth and sometimes there is a downside. Mary mentioned some of these girls felt very entitled. They wanted their freedom as they had back at home. Did you interview Natalie yet?"

"No, I wanted to. Her parents refused. Her father is a hedge fund manager in New York City and told her not to speak with me without an attorney present. He had some high-powered attorney call me and reinforce the message. He told me there was no way he was allowing Natalie to speak to me. I didn't press the issue, but then again, I didn't know all this at the time."

"Let me interview her and see what I get. If I get anything of interest, you can cut through all that red tape and sit down with her."

Miles looked around. "Your fiancé here with you?"

"No," I said hesitantly. I wasn't sure I wanted to tell Miles where Luke and Jack were headed.

Miles leveled a look at me. "Is something wrong?"

I shook my head, still stalling. Miles would probably find out anyway. It was probably better to be upfront now. "Jack and Luke found Liam Keller, Jane's boyfriend. They went to his house today to talk to him."

"Sounds like they made some progress. Does Liam know where Jane is?"

"Luke said the last time Liam spoke to Jane was by text on Thursday. They had been arguing because he was worried about Jane looking into Maddie's death. He didn't feel it was safe for her. Jane's friends confirm she had been upset on Friday about the argument. Liam also has a solid alibi for Friday night. He went to his brother's football game and was with his parents all night. Luke said Liam has no idea where Jane is and seemed quite upset by it all, especially because the last time they talked, they argued."

Miles folded his hands on his stomach and sat back on the bench. "It sounds like we can rule him out."

"Yes and no," I said hesitantly. "Luke and Jack are on their way up to Brant Lake right now. Liam's mother mentioned they have a cabin on the lake Jane knew about. Liam also confirmed Jane asked questions about the cabin and could find it if she wanted to. If she found out who killed Maddie or got herself in some trouble, I think Jane would be smart enough to get out of here. Have you checked taxis or rideshare to see if anyone picked up a girl Friday night?"

"It was one of the first things we did. No hits. Jane's photo has been all over the news, Riley. Don't you think if someone gave her a ride, they would have come forward?"

"I don't know." I sat quietly for a moment trying unsuccessfully to process everything I knew. "According to Liam, Jane kept cash under her bed. She had been stashing it away for a while and had more than five thousand dollars. Jane could have paid the driver not to say anything. She could have told them she was in trouble. You have no idea where she could have gone. Jane could have slipped across the Canadian border by now, or whoever killed Maddie could have gotten to her. Jane could be dead. We just don't know."

"When you started this, you were pretty adamant Jane didn't run away. Has that changed?" Miles gave me a look of both confusion and concern.

Frustrated, I clarified, "Given what Willow said about Natalie and Maddie, it's likely Jane felt threatened. If she did, then maybe she did run away. I can't explain why Jane wouldn't have told her parents though. I'm sure if Jane felt threatened, they would have helped her."

"I guess we will just have to wait and see what Luke and Jack find." Miles turned his head to me. "Will you text me later and let me know?"

"Sure. Are you making any progress on Erik's murder?" I felt myself starting to like Miles again. He could come on so strong, but when we were just sitting talking like now, I did like him.

"Not really anything that points to a suspect." Miles looked down at the ground. He seemed to want to tell me more. I stayed quiet hoping he'd talk. Finally, he said, "I really shouldn't tell you anything, but have you ever had a staged suicide case that looked sloppy?"

I raised my eyebrows. "Sloppy? What do you mean?"

"On the one hand, someone was smart enough to stage it like it was a suicide, but on the other hand, they left a lot of evidence behind. The missing prints on the gun. You'd think if they were smart enough to stage a suicide, they'd have just worn gloves. They had to know if you wipe all the prints off, we are going to suspect the guy didn't kill himself. It's clear whoever killed him knew him well. It was someone he trusted. No forced entry and no signs of a struggle."

I understood why it was bothering Miles. It wasn't a normal case. Someone didn't think about staging the scene all the way through. "Was the gun Erik's?"

"Yeah, it was, but he hadn't had it for very long. He just got his license to carry and bought it over the summer."

I rubbed my brow. I hated confusing cases. "Willow told me Erik didn't believe Maddie had killed herself. She said he had been asking questions last semester about her death. Willow said she felt really bad for him, which is why she finally told him about Natalie. But Willow also said Erik didn't act surprised at the news so maybe he already knew. Maybe Erik felt like he needed protection."

"He could have," Miles agreed, kicking a stone in front of his foot. "I haven't found anything indicating Erik liked to shoot or had been to a range. I spoke to the gun shop where Erik bought the gun. The guy remembered Erik and said he didn't seem like the typical gun owner. He was with a friend who was making most of the decisions. The guy said Erik didn't seem comfortable handling the gun at all and was quite nervous even making the purchase. If I had found his prints on the gun, I'd have chalked it up to the actions of a suicidal man or even an accident, but that's not the case. You can't wipe off prints after you're dead." Miles caught my eye. "I still have a dead teacher on what should be a safe campus and not even the hint of a suspect. None of it makes any sense."

CHAPTER 31

Miles was right. None of it added up. I sat with him for a few more minutes. I wanted to leave and go find Irene Hodge, but finding Erik's killer might also lead me to Jane. I thought through all the evidence and then settled on something I thought might be helpful.

I asked, "Is there any chance the person who killed Erik didn't plan on killing him so the scene ended up looking a bit frenzied?" Miles started to speak, but I asked him to wait while I continued with my thought. "Maybe the killer didn't think it all the way through because they didn't go to his place that night with the intent to kill him. It was a spur of the moment action."

Miles shrugged. "That would make some sense and could explain away the prints. They knew enough to wipe their own away, but never stopped to think we'd know he didn't kill himself if his prints weren't present on the gun."

There was another possibility. I got closer to him and said it quietly. "You only assumed that it was a suicide when you assessed the scene. It's easy at first glance to think it's suicide because there were no signs of a struggle so what else would you think. Given no prints on the gun, now you assume it was staged to look like a suicide, but what if it wasn't staged at all? It could be that's just how the murder happened. We don't know where Erik kept his gun. He could have had it out. Think about it this way. The person showed up and they argued. It doesn't take much to grab for the gun and shoot him. They could have wiped their prints and got out of there without even thinking."

Miles looked up to the sky and groaned in frustration. "The medical examiner said Erik was shot in the forehead, but the shot was angled up. It could have been the way he held the gun, but most suicides go for the temple not the forehead. But there was no struggle. I can't see him just letting someone shoot him and not even defending himself. How did they get the gun away from him?"

I countered, "Was he dating or involved with anyone?"

Miles looked at me. "Like a lover's spat gone wrong?"

"Exactly. A woman he'd been involved with came over to his place. He has his gun accessible for some reason, and after they argue, she took it and killed him."

"If they were arguing, don't you think there would be some kind of struggle? There were no signs of that at all."

"You heard Erik wasn't all that experienced or comfortable with the gun. Maybe he was just trying to talk whoever it was down instead of lunging for the gun. If it's someone he trusted, he probably didn't think they'd shoot him." Miles didn't comment so I continued. "I think what you're seeing is the frenzied aftermath, which is why it doesn't make a lot of sense. You're looking at it like it was planned out and staged, which the evidence doesn't fit. Suicide doesn't fit either."

Miles agreed it was possible. "I finally saw the camera feeds from Friday night. If Erik had a visitor, she would have been seen going back to her car, and there is no one unknown who parked at the school Friday night. We have some administration staff leaving, but it was a quiet night overall."

"If the killer lives on campus, she could have walked to his cottage."

Miles stood. "You think a teacher killed him then?"

I tilted my head up at him. "She could have easily killed Erik and then slipped right out the back door of his house and into the tunnel we found in the woods right behind his cottage."

"I want to ask you something, but I don't want you to get angry." Miles ran a hand down his face. He paused for several beats and then rushed it out in one breath. "Is there any chance Jane could have killed him?"

I gasped aloud. "Absolutely not. Jane had no motive to kill Erik." I thought back to Jane's journal. Erik was on the list of suspects who could have killed Maddie, but there was no way I thought she could have killed him. "I told you this before, but Erik spent a good deal of time with Maddie at his cottage. No one told me anything inappropriate happened between them. Willow said it was harmless. They were friends. Maddie wasn't there late at night, but right after dinner before curfew. It wasn't a secret to anyone they liked talking about history. Jane suspected it was more, but it was never confirmed. Plus, by all accounts, Erik was distraught after Maddie's death. Jane did suspect him though."

"Could Jane have confronted him about Maddie, lost her temper, and killed him?" Miles asked more insistent this time.

"I don't think so," I said, hoping that was true. "Besides, we just said it had to be someone Erik trusted. I've found no information that puts Erik and Jane together at all outside of the classroom. I can't see it happening."

"We found her scarf outside of his cottage," Miles argued. "She could have been watching him."

"Okay, that's a possibility," I said cautiously agreeing. "But Jane could have also dropped her scarf if she ran away. I'm sure she took the tunnel. Jane had to go through those woods to get to the back gate, which we know if she ran away that's how she left. There are many ways Jane could have dropped the scarf."

"Fair enough. I'm probably grasping at straws anyway." Miles checked his watch. "I need to get out of here for the night. I have an interview with one of Erik's friends."

I wanted to ask to go with him, but that would have been inappropriate on so many levels. "Let me know if he says anything about Jane."

"Will do and let me know what Luke and Jack find."

I told Miles I would and watched him walk across campus toward the parking lot. I turned to head between two buildings and take the path to the teachers' cottages when I saw Cooper off in the distance. He waved once and then jogged to catch up with me.

"Where are you headed?" Cooper asked when he finally reached me.

"I'm going to interview Irene Hodge before I wrap up for the day. If she's home, that is. Otherwise, I'll need to find her tomorrow. You want to come with me and tell me about your interview with Heidi?"

"Sure," Cooper said and walked in step with me.

We cut between the buildings and past the athletic center. When we reached the part of campus that opened up to the wide-open grassy area with woods on each side, Cooper remarked, "This campus is deceiving. You have no idea how big it is from the front."

"There used to be a back entrance, but it's fenced off now. It connects to a rural road." I remembered Cooper might be familiar with the area. "Do you remember the road Pinewoods Cemetery is on?"

Cooper shuddered. "That creepy one from the last time I was here?"

"That's the one. The back of campus goes back to that road."

"Let's avoid that if we can. This campus is creepy enough."

I turned my head to look up at him. "I like the campus, but it can be a little eerie at night. It's why I was trying to get out of here before dark, but that's not going to happen so I'm glad you're coming with me. What did Heidi have to say?"

"I don't trust her at all," Cooper said seriously. "She's hiding something. I didn't think I was going to have a hard time with her, but the tension started from the word go."

I laughed. "I guess your southern charms didn't work on her."

"Not even close. I tripped her up a few times. Heidi insists Jane was troubled after Maddie's death. She said Jane accused people of killing Maddie, which I know you said she had suspected a few people. I asked her why she'd allow Jane to pledge the Clovers if she was so troubled. That sent her over the edge."

"It's supposed to be a secret. Did she have an answer?"

Cooper shook his head. "Not a good one. I don't think we will get much more from her, but maybe you can try with a different angle."

"Maybe." I pointed down the hill to where the teachers' cottages sat on the left. "Irene Hodge has the cottage closest to us on the end. Erik Yates had the cottage farthest away from where we are now. Back in the woods behind them, there is an opening in the ground with stairs going down into the underground tunnel system, which gives someone access to any building on campus."

"That isn't exactly secure."

"I don't know how many people know about that tunnel. We found it by accident."

"We?" Cooper asked, peering down at me.

"Miles and I the night we searched the tunnels. I told you about that. I just spoke to him in the quad. He told me how frenzied the crime scene looked in Erik's cottage. I'm starting to suspect Erik's murder wasn't planned. He was killed with his own gun."

As we approached the cottage, it was obvious Irene wasn't home. There wasn't a light on in the place. I explained, "She was away the weekend Jane went missing and Erik was murdered. I wanted to talk to her about Natalie stealing tests from her office. It seems like that's what sparked this whole thing."

Cooper glanced around. "You'll have to catch her later. Do you know when she came back from her trip?"

"I have no idea. I ran into Heidi in those woods the night Miles and I were out here. She acted like Irene should have been back already."

Cooper watched the house for a moment longer. "Let's hope she's not missing, too."

CHAPTER 32

Luke and Jack had already stopped to ask for directions twice. They had reached the exit for Brant Lake on I-87 North but got lost almost immediately after turning off the interstate. The dark roads were difficult to navigate. Few were marked with road signs, and most were dirt paths that led farther into the woods.

Luke was sure they had traveled the same roads two and three times without realizing it. Finally, they gave up and asked for directions. The first directions only got them so far. They stopped again at a small corner store with a sign for bait and beer and tried again. The owner knew the Kellers so Luke was confident this time, they'd find the cabin.

While they were in the store, they showed the guy Jane's photo, but he shook his head and denied having seen her or anyone like her. He explained that this time of the season, the area was mostly locals. Someone new would probably stand out. The guy didn't make eye contact while he said it, so Luke left the store feeling like he might know more. He wasn't going to tell Luke though. That much was obvious.

Jack turned up one more dirt road, the high-beams giving the only illumination. Tall trees blocked out most of the light. The tires kicked rocks behind them as they climbed. Jack pounded the sterling wheel. "I hate there's no way we can do this with any element of surprise. If I didn't have these lights on, we'd be off the road in seconds."

"If she's up there, I don't know where she'd run to anyway. Where is the lake from here?"

"It should be right around here. Brenda said there is a short path through the woods to the lake from their cabin."

The car continued to climb the winding road until they hit the fork in the road the shop owner had told them about. Jack made the right as instructed and the car began a descent.

"There," Jack said, pointing up ahead. "I see the cabin. There are lights on."

Luke sat up a little straighter. Jack was right. The cabin lights were on, but there were no cars in the driveway. Jack cut off the lights as he pulled to the side of the road and parked.

"Let's go see who is here." Jack got out of the car first and Luke followed.

Luke instinctively reached his hand down to put it on his gun, which was common for him when walking into an unknown scene. There was nothing on his hip though. Luke had momentarily forgotten. It was weird rolling up to a scene unarmed. He looked over at Jack. "Do you have your gun on you?"

"Always, but I'm hoping we don't need it." Jack walked up the four wooden steps of the cabin to the front porch.

Luke followed right behind him. Instead of hitting rickety steps like he thought he might, his feet landed on a solid wood foundation. Once on the porch landing, Luke realized how wrong his perception of the place was. He had imagined a hunting cabin with tight quarters and sparse furniture. The place was more like a small log home. The porch had four wooden rocking chairs, two on each side of the door. There were pots for summer flowers, which were empty right now, and tables with outdoor candles. This wasn't an out of the way place the Kellers visited from time to time. It was a summer home. Brenda kept up the place in the same way she did her home.

Jack and Luke stood for a few moments at the door, hoping to hear someone inside, but there was no one. Luke thought he might have heard some faint rustling off in the distance, but it was probably just an animal. Jack knocked once and then twice, but no one responded. Jack called out, identifying himself, but again, no one responded. The lights remained on as if someone were inside.

"That's more than lights on a timer, right?" Jack asked. "It's too lit up for there to be no one home. No one is supposed to even be here. That's why Brenda gave me the key."

Luke reached out and turned the silver doorknob. It turned effortlessly, and the door inched open. "Looks like you won't need the key. Someone has been here."

Jack pushed open the door all the way, calling out for Jane. "We're just here to make sure you're okay, Jane," he called out once and then twice. "We're coming in."

With that, they stepped into the cabin and hit warmer air. The heat had recently been blowing, warming up the entire cabin. The living room was anchored by a large stone fireplace and comfortable-looking brown leather sofas in an L shape. The living room led right into a large eat-in kitchen that had updated appliances. Part of the kitchen was blocked off by an island and a row of four chairs sat in front of it. Off the kitchen was a hall. Luke looked up to see an open loft space above.

What Luke didn't see was any sign of someone staying there, at least from the neat appearance of the living room. Luke turned to Jack. "If you check upstairs, I'll check the kitchen and down the hall."

Jack agreed and headed for the stairs. Luke walked into the kitchen and around the island. The first thing he saw made him step back. A glass had been smashed on the tile floor. Just one glass like it had slipped from someone's hand. Luke stepped around the shattered pieces. He pulled open the fridge. Someone had recently gone shopping. He was sure the Kellers hadn't left food after the summer season. He checked the milk. Its expiration date was three days from now.

The bread on the counter was fresh. There were no dishes in the sink. When Luke pulled open the dishwasher door, water dripped from the top and steam billowed out, hitting Luke in the face. The racks were full of glasses, plates, and two pans. Luke closed the door and exhaled loudly.

He started down the hall when Jack called his name. "I'll be right there," Luke called back, pushing a door in the hall open. He stepped into the darkened room and found a light switch on the wall. A bed, positioned in the center of the far wall, was neatly made. The flower bedspread looked comfortable if not a bit outdated. Luke assumed the room functioned as the master given there was a small ensuite bathroom. The room had an empty feeling like it hadn't been used in a while. Luke shut the door and headed back into the living room. He headed up the stairs quickly, taking the steps two at a time.

"You find something?" he asked Jack when he hit the landing.

Jack waved him into one of the two bedrooms. "Someone has been staying here. I found girl's clothing. There are toiletries in the bathroom, too."

The bed had been made, but the comforter was askew. There were shirts and pants in piles on the dresser, tags still on most of them. A pair of sneakers sat on the floor in front of the dresser. Luke reached for a pair of pants to check the size. When he pulled them from the pile, a slip of paper dropped to the floor. Luke set the pants down and grabbed for the note. Simple handwriting in black ink detailed a grocery list.

Luke took a quick photo of the note with his phone and texted it to Riley, asking if this was Jane's handwriting. While he waited for a response, Luke said to Jack, "What do you think we are looking at here?"

"I have no idea. If this is Jane's stuff, I don't see any sign of a struggle."

"There's a glass broken on the kitchen floor."

Jack exhaled. "That could mean something or nothing. Maybe Jane got spooked when she saw the headlights and dropped a glass. If she took off, she's not safe out in the woods alone."

They decided to search further, hoping to find evidence of whose clothes they were. Luke went through the things in the bedroom while Jack headed back to the bathroom. The clothes were new and not name brand. The sole on the sneaker told Luke they were well-worn and probably a few years old. There was no identification or money or anything to identify who was staying there or where they had gone.

Luke's phone pinged with Riley's response. *I don't have Jane's journal in front of me, but it looks like her handwriting. Did you find her?*

Luke texted back they hadn't, but it seemed Jane might be staying at the cabin. He texted photos of some of her clothes and the sneakers to Riley. She responded nearly immediately letting Luke know the sneakers looked like ones Jane had been wearing in a photo she had seen earlier.

Luke walked to the upstairs bathroom, but Jack was nowhere in sight. "Jack," Luke called.

"I'm down here. You should come down," Jack said, his voice unsteady.

Luke went back to the hall and looked over the balcony. Jack stood near the doorway with his hands up. An older woman had a shotgun pointed directly at his chest.

CHAPTER 33

"Where's the girl?" the woman demanded, shoving the gun forward in Jack's direction. She spotted Luke as soon as he leaned over the balcony railing. "Get down here. I have no problem shooting perverts."

Luke raised his hands to show he was no threat. "I'm not sure who you think we are, but we don't mean anyone any harm."

"If you don't, then where is the girl?"

Luke carefully walked down the steps to join Jack. He needed to deescalate this calmly. He kept his voice even and steady. "We are investigators looking for Jane Crandall. I'm Det. Luke Morgan. I'm a homicide detective from Little Rock, Arkansas. Jack Malone is a retired homicide detective from Troy, New York. We don't mean you any harm."

"I tried telling you that. I can show you some identification if you just drop the gun and let me get it for you," Jack said dryly. It was clear he didn't like being on the other end of the gun.

The woman, who stood about five-eight, had a ruddy weathered face, gray hair pulled up in a bun, and thick strong hands that gripped the gun like an expert. Luke had no doubt she was a good shot, but he had no idea if she was a real threat.

Calmly, Luke said, "Brenda Keller gave us the key to check the cabin for Jane, but when we got here, it was empty. Do you know Jane?"

The woman twitched and pulled her back straighter. "You know the Kellers?"

Luke nodded. "We were just with them earlier tonight. If you want to call them, you can confirm who we are."

"You could also just look at our identification," Jack groused.

The woman moved her aim off Jack's chest, but she didn't lower the gun. "Give me your identification, slowly."

Jack lowered his hands and reached around to his back pocket for his wallet. Luke did the same. His badge, which he normally wore on a chain around his neck, was slipped into his other pocket. Jack and Luke held out their hands with their identifications. The woman took a tentative step toward them and glanced down. When she was satisfied with what she saw, she took a step back.

She appraised them again. Hitching her strong jaw toward Luke, she asked, "The girl who was staying here said her name was Jane, but how do I know you aren't after her? She said she was in danger."

Jack responded before Luke could. "I was hired by Jane's parents, Senator Thomas Crandall and his wife Lynn. Jane disappeared from Austen Academy for Girls last Friday night. We got a tip today she might be here at this cabin. Jane is friends with Liam Keller. We just want to bring her home safely."

"I don't know anything about a senator's kid. The girl who was here said she was in danger. Why would a senator's kid be in danger?" The woman still wouldn't drop the gun completely. She stood ready with her back straight and tension in her face ready to protect herself if needed.

Luke had no idea what to say to get her to relax. "Have you watched the news recently?"

"I don't have a television. Rots the mind."

Luke noticed the remote control on the living room coffee table. He hoped he could at least get a news channel. He pointed to the remote. "Let me turn on the television for you. It might help you understand why we are here."

"Go ahead, but move slowly. I can still shoot you from here."

Luke picked up the remote and clicked the on button. The screen jumped to life. He changed the channels until he found a national cable news network. The anchor discussed Jane's disappearance and the murder of Erik Yates.

The woman didn't drop her gun completely but held it down at her side. She stepped into the cabin, walked by Jack, and stood near Luke watching the screen. When they flashed a photo of Jane, she said, "That's her, but she cut off her hair and dyed it red. A box red, and she didn't do a good job. It's her though."

"I'm sorry I didn't catch your name," Luke said, sitting down on the couch and hoping to decrease the tension.

"Just call me Betty, everyone else does. It's Elizabeth really, but nobody calls me that." She sat down next to him and rested the gun at her feet.

Jack came over and sat in a nearby chair. "How did you meet Jane?"

"I live up here year-round," Betty explained. "There's not too many of us who do. I know the Kellers so I knew they had closed up for the fall and wouldn't be back until spring. When I saw the light on, I thought I should check it out. We get squatters up here sometimes. I figured I wouldn't waste the state police's time unless it was something serious. I startled her, but we got to talking, and I let her stay. I figured she'd be hungry and scared. But that wasn't the case. Jane had groceries and had even bought some clothes. Jane wouldn't say much about why she was here at first, and I didn't push. She seemed like a good kid."

"It was kind of you to let her stay," Luke said, reaching out his hand to touch her arm.

Betty finally smiled for the first time. "I didn't mean to hold the gun on you like that, but there was a car here earlier. Jane was supposed to be up to my place for dinner, but she didn't show. Then I saw your headlights. I worried something happened to her."

Jack perked up at that. "There was another car?"

"Probably about two hours before you got here before it turned dark. I heard the car before I saw it. You can't see my cabin now in the dark, but I'm just down the road. I can see the driveway and side of the Kellers' house in the daylight. It was an SUV of some kind. I'm pretty sure I heard a woman's voice. I thought maybe Jane had finally called her parents or someone she trusted. That's why I didn't think too much of it when she didn't show for dinner, but then I heard another car and the cabin light was on. I thought I'd better check it out."

"It's good you did," Luke said reassuring her. "Do you have any idea how Jane got up here? It's a trek from Troy."

"I asked her, but she said she caught a ride. I didn't know what she meant but didn't want to push." Betty scrunched up her face. "Sometimes kids her age get skittish if you ask too many questions. I wanted her to know she could trust me. You have to have patience with kids."

"You sound like you know what you're doing." Luke leaned forward and rested his hands on his knees. He shared a look with Jack. Luke was doing the same right now, using patience to draw out Betty's story. He didn't want to spook her either.

Betty looked between them. "I was a teacher for thirty years. You learn a thing or two. I had no idea Jane was a missing senator's kid or I would have called the cops. I thought about calling the cops anyway when she eventually told me why she ran away. But Jane said she didn't trust the cops. She insisted they had to be in on it."

"In on what exactly?" Jack asked.

Betty's eyes got wide. "You mean you don't know? I assumed you knew."

Luke shook his head. "No, Betty, we don't know much of anything. We weren't even sure until now Jane ran away. We just knew she was missing."

"Oh my," Betty said, her hand going to her chest. "I better explain. Jane said she witnessed a murder. She said she wanted to talk to her teacher, but when she got to his place, she heard a gunshot coming from inside his house. Jane told me she looked into a back window and saw him there dead. Jane said there was blood everywhere. She said she was so focused on the blood she almost missed the other person."

"The other person?" Jack asked.

"Yes, Jane told me she saw the back of someone, but they had their hood up so she never saw their face. Jane said she was so scared, she was sure she caused so much racket from the twigs underfoot they would know she was there. Jane said she took off and didn't look back."

Jack stood abruptly. "Why didn't Jane go to the cops or her parents?"

"I asked her that very thing. Jane said her friend Maddie had been killed earlier this year, and the cops said it was a suicide. Jane said she was sure then the cops had to be protecting whoever killed her friend. Now you know that's not the logic of adults, but Jane is young. I can understand why she'd feel that way. But she said the school didn't seem to care much either. Now with the teacher murdered, Jane was sure she was next."

"What about telling her parents?" Jack pressed. "They are incredibly worried about her. If you had a television, you'd have seen how frantic they are."

Betty slapped her leg. "I tried to get her parents' names out of her. No dice, but Jane said her parents didn't believe her about her friend's death and they probably wouldn't have believed her about this. No, Jane said, she'd have to sort it out on her own. That's what she was doing up here. Figuring out what she was going to do, but now she's gone. We best call the state police."

Jack pulled his phone from his pocket. "I'm calling the detective on the murder investigation right now."

Luke turned to Betty. "I'll call the state police with you. We need to start a search for Jane before it's too late."

Betty's eyes dropped to her lap. "I'll never forgive myself if something happens to her. I swear I was just trying to give her some time to get her head right. I didn't know what to do since Jane believed the cops were in on it. I was just trying to protect her."

CHAPTER 34

I had tried staying awake to hear about Luke's search up north, but I must have fallen asleep. I didn't hear Luke get home, but I woke when he slid into bed next to me. His body was damp from a shower, and the earthy smell of his body wash reminded me of home. I rolled over and put my head on his shoulder. "Did you find Jane?"

"No, not yet," Luke said, his voice tight. He snuggled into me, and I could feel how tense his muscles were.

I massaged his bicep with my fingers. "What time is it?"

Luke yawned. "It's close to three. I don't even know how I'm still awake."

I ran my cheek over his chest. "I'm so sorry. You deserve a break. Tomorrow, I'm telling Jack he's going to have to work with just Cooper because we quit."

Luke laced his fingers through my hair and massaged my scalp. Through yawns, he said, "I want to be involved. We both should be taking a break, but it's really important we find Jane. We got lucky today and pinned down some information. Jane told a woman up there she saw her teacher get killed. Jane's a smart girl. She got herself out of there and did everything she could to keep herself safe, including telling someone what happened. If Jane hadn't opened up to Betty, we'd never know anything."

"How did you leave it up there?"

"The state police brought in a search and rescue team with dogs. They traced Jane's scent to Betty's house, but we already knew Jane had gone there a few times. Otherwise, her scent stops at the road and then down at the lake. Jack and I think someone showed up, and there was a struggle. No idea what happened from there. I'll go back tomorrow if we don't hear anything."

Luke yawned and added sleepily, "Everyone across the state knows about the case, except for Betty who doesn't even own a television. Jack called that detective, Miles, I think is his name. They are going to dust the house for prints, too. They didn't have a choice but to take it seriously after what Betty told them."

"Thank God for nosey neighbors."

Luke trailed a finger over my back. "You find a troubled kid in a cabin by herself, you help. Betty mentioned she was a teacher for thirty years. She has a way with kids."

Luke's breathing became soft and even, and I snuggled into him. I worried Jane was now in more danger than she was before, but I was grateful she was alive. At least now it sounded like there were more resources than just Jack and I trying to find her. Luke wrapped his arm around me tighter in his sleep and I drifted off next to him.

I woke the next morning before nine and crept out of bed careful not to wake Luke. Dusty remained at the foot of the bed snoring peacefully. Luke could stay asleep until tomorrow for all I cared. He deserved the break.

Downstairs, my mother and sister sat in the living room on the couch curled up under a blanket. A fire roared in the fireplace, and an anchor from CNN talked through the recent developments in the Jane Crandall case.

I touched my mom on the shoulder. "You started a fire already?"

"We're supposed to get snow today, and the temperature is supposed to drop into the thirties. I figured I'd just keep it lit all day and conserve on the heater. Your friends are not used to this cold. Cooper and Adele needed another blanket last night."

I completely forgot about that. I had lived my life in the frigid weather of the Northeast. There's nothing quite like waiting for the bus in a Catholic school uniform in below zero weather next to a three-foot pile of snow. It made me worry about Jane though, potentially out in the cold alone.

"Where are Cooper and Adele?" I asked as I wandered off into the kitchen to grab some coffee. My sister followed me out.

"Still asleep," Liv said. She grabbed a mug and poured it three-fourths of the way full. Liv knew how much creamer I needed. Handing it to me, she said. "They are probably still tired from their drive." She grabbed a muffin and carried it back to the living room.

I picked through the boxes and tins of breakfast treats my mother had on the counter. She'd give me the side-eye if I chose anything too fattening, but I wasn't in the mood for a reminder today. I snagged a pumpkin muffin and a napkin and grabbed my coffee mug in the other hand. My mother and sister were too cozy under the blanket to be disturbed even though I wanted to snuggle right next to them. I grabbed the chair and kicked the ottoman out in front of me and planted my feet on it.

"Have you heard from Jack?" I asked my mother.

"He's asleep upstairs."

I nearly choked on my muffin. We were all adults, and clearly, I was sleeping with my fiancé, but the casual way my mother said it took me by surprise.

"What's with the face?" my mother snapped at me.

"No face," I lied. "Good muffin."

"Yes, that's going to look fabulous on your backside on your wedding day." My mother laughed and winked at me. She scolded, "Hush up and watch the news. Jack said he and Luke are heading back up to Brant Lake today to join in the search. I'm trying to catch up on the case. Jack doesn't tell me much."

I breathed in deeply and let myself sink back into the chair. It had been a long time since I sat in the living room with my mother and sister like this. I couldn't even recall the last time. Fall and winter had always been my favorites in this house.

My mother bumped up the volume of the television a notch when Miles appeared on the screen. He gave an overview of the case to date. Miles said a source came forward and alerted authorities Jane might be at a cabin up near Brant Lake. He acted as if the police acted immediately on the tip and were now heavily engaged in a search. It was a total fabrication of events.

What Miles left out was that it was Cooper who finally tracked down Liam's last name and Jack and Luke who had interviewed Liam in the first place. If not for them, Miles wouldn't have a clue. It galled me to no end, but I was sure someone a higher pay grade than Miles had instructed him what to say. I didn't realize I was muttering angrily until my sister snapped at me.

"I thought you liked him?" she said.

I crossed my legs at my ankles. "I don't like it when anyone takes credit for someone else's hard work."

Liv smirked at me. "It's too bad you're mad at your boyfriend. He's so cute. I was hoping to meet him."

"What's going on?" My mother's eyes were on me quickly.

I waved her off. "Liv's kidding. Miles has just been a little flirtatious, and I've put a stop to it. Don't make a big deal about it, especially in front of Luke."

My mother turned back to the television, and Liv laughed at me the way she did when we were kids and she'd tattle on me for something. I'm not saying Liv was the favorite child, but my mother let her get away with far more than I ever did.

"Has Senator Crandall given an interview?" I asked, sipping my coffee.

"It should be coming back up again," Liv said. "You'll probably be happier with his interview. He mentioned Jack and you and even Luke and Cooper. Jack talked to him last night and explained how it was a team effort. The local cops have to be pretty angry because Senator Crandall refuted what Miles said about how it went down."

I smiled from ear to ear without realizing it. Miles was only jumping on the case now because Jane was a potential witness for his murder investigation. We sat there watching the news a few minutes longer, but a sharp knock on the door made the three of us turn to look.

Liv jumped and went to the door. I heard the door pull open and my sister laugh. Miles' voice echoed in the front hallway. I cursed under my breath. Miles was the last person I wanted to see, especially since I hadn't showered and had on my favorite plaid pajama bottoms and a tee-shirt with no bra.

CHAPTER 35

"Is Riley here?" Miles said from the front hall.

"She's right in here," Liv said, guiding him into the room. She had a trace of amusement in her voice and an annoying smirk plastered across her face. She was failing to hold back her laughter at my embarrassment.

My mother stood and introduced herself. "Can I get you a cup of coffee, Det. Ward?"

"Thank you. I'd appreciate it. It's so early I didn't stop to get any yet." Miles offered up the charming smile I was sure won over everyone he met. My mother ate it up.

I got up from the chair and stood in place. My mother may be fixing him coffee like it was a social visit, but I didn't like him being at the house. I crossed my arms over my chest. "What are you doing here so early? Well really at all. You could have texted me."

Miles smirked at my pajamas or maybe it was because I was so fiercely trying to cover my chest with my arms. He dropped his voice an octave and said, "I knew you'd look this cute in the morning."

"Luke is right upstairs," I said sharply.

Miles took a step toward me and I stepped back. "I'm not worried about him. I owe him a thank you for finding the cabin. You all have done far more work on this case than we have." Miles raked a hand through his hair. "I'm embarrassed we didn't listen to you sooner."

"You should be," I said defiantly. "Senator Crandall wants us to stick with the case and find Jane. If you're here to call us off of it, I think you should take it up with him."

Miles shook his head. "It's not why I'm here. I found a lead, well I think it's a lead, but I can't make sense of it. I thought you might."

My mother chose that moment to bring Miles in his coffee. She also had a napkin with a muffin in her other hand. She set both down on the coffee table. "I'll leave you both to talk. If you need Jack, I can wake him up."

"Let him sleep," Miles said. "He might end up having another late night." He thanked my mother for the coffee and muffin and apologized for the intrusion.

My mother gave me a knowing look. "I'll be in the kitchen with your sister if you need anything."

"You have a full house here." Miles sat down on the couch and took a sip of the coffee. He glanced back up at me. "Sit down and talk to me. I promise not to bite."

I didn't join him on the couch but rather sat back in the chair. "What's the lead?"

Miles leaned back, bringing his coffee cup with him. "We found a set of prints at the cabin. They belong to Irene Hodge."

"The English teacher at Austen Academy?" I didn't think there would be another, but it was surprising.

"The very one," Miles said. "Any idea why she'd know Jane was at the cabin?"

"Did you ask her?"

"Can't reach her," Miles said with a tone in his voice I couldn't quite distinguish.

"You believe Irene Hodge is with Jane? She wasn't even around last Friday when Erik was killed or Jane went missing. I tried to interview her last night, but her cottage was dark. Why would she be with Jane?"

"That's the million-dollar question I hoped you could answer."

I repositioned on the chair, finally letting my arms fall loose at my sides. "Irene Hodge was the teacher who had her tests stolen by Natalie Gallo, which seems to have been the first domino to have fallen in this situation. The night you and I found the tunnel that led to the teachers' cottages, I met Heidi for the first time. She said she was out there looking for Irene. Heidi is the one who told me Irene was away for the weekend. She acted like Irene was supposed to be back though. I think we are going to have to ask the administration."

"I finally have a meeting scheduled for later this afternoon with Headmistress Winslow," Miles explained. "I want you there with me. You know more about what happened to Jane. Let Jack and Luke go back up north and search."

"I can do that." I had wanted a way in to speak to someone in the administration, but the response until now had been icy. "Do you think Irene is a danger to Jane?"

"I don't know," Miles said seriously. "She's a wild card in this right now. If she was rescuing Jane, I'd think we would have heard from her."

"What if they are hiding out together?" I asked. Miles looked at me blankly. I explained, "It was Irene who had tests stolen. Even if Maddie didn't tell her, I'm sure Jane did at some point once she found out. Erik Yates knew at the start of this school year. He is her neighbor and colleague. I'm sure he said something to her. It would have been odd if he hadn't. Maddie is dead. Erik is dead and Jane is missing. Irene could have felt threatened and taken off. She finds out Jane is missing, and they make contact. Maybe they are both on the run."

Miles seemed to roll the theory around in his head. He took another sip of coffee and popped a piece of muffin in his mouth. "I can't rule it out," he said finally. "What if Irene was in on the cheating? Let's suppose Erik tells her what he knows and he suspects someone killed Maddie to keep her quiet. Maybe Irene killed him to keep him quiet and is now after Jane?"

"If that's the case, why not just kill Jane at the cabin?" I asked, thinking it through as I said it. "We have no idea if anyone besides Betty up in Brant Lake had any idea Jane witnessed the murder. We don't know that whoever killed Erik saw her. Jane didn't tell anyone, not even her boyfriend."

"I don't know," Miles said, frustration evident in his voice. "There are too many variables at play. But we need to pinpoint a timeline first of where Irene was and when. We also need more information about her background."

I motioned my head towards the stairs. "Cooper is great at digging up background info. Once he's up, we can put him to work. He spoke to Heidi yesterday and said she was antagonistic, but she talked to him at least." I caught the look of relief on his face and asked, "Are you still not getting a lot of help on these cases?"

"No. We just don't have the manpower. There was a shooting last night at the north end of the city and a few other cases pending. We went into this thinking it was a runaway kid and a suicide. I don't think anyone had any idea this much was going on at the school." Miles finished off his coffee and stared over at me.

Heat rose in my cheeks. "Why are you staring at me like that?"

Miles pushed himself off the couch to stand. "No reason. I just feel like we've met before now, and I can't figure it out."

"I don't know," I said honestly.

Miles shrugged. "Either way, I wish we had met sooner."

There was a seriousness to his tone that far surpassed his normal flirting and teasing. It occurred to me he genuinely meant what he said. In a lot of ways, I wish we had as well. Not because I was romantically interested, but I genuinely liked him and thought despite challenges he was a good investigator. I looked up at him and smiled, not quite sure what to say.

Miles left without saying another word. I followed him and saw him out. I shut the door and turned to head into the kitchen, stopping in the living room briefly to grab my empty coffee cup.

As I entered the kitchen, Liv raised her eyes up from the cup she had halfway to her mouth. "The hot detective is making house calls now?"

I didn't respond and went about pouring myself some coffee, totally focused on why Irene Hodge's fingerprints might be at the cabin. The sinking feeling Jane was in far more danger than I had initially thought overwhelmed me. I didn't have time for my sister's teasing.

CHAPTER 36

"Did Riley seem off to you?" Luke asked Jack across the car. They were just a few miles from the Brant Lake exit and had made the drive mostly in silence.

"A little," Jack said, glancing over at Luke as he drove. "Maybe she's just stressed. A lot is going on. Are you nervous about getting married?"

"No, not at all. I can't wait to marry her, but Riley spooks easily."

Jack gripped the wheel tighter until blood drained from his fingers. He kept his eyes right on the road.

Luke knew Jack probably wasn't comfortable having this conversation, but he didn't have anyone else to talk to about this. Luke apologized. "I know I'm putting you in an awkward situation. I'm not asking you to tell me anything Karen might have said. I'm just worried."

Jack relaxed his posture. "There's nothing to tell. From what I hear, Riley is excited about the wedding. Karen said Riley looks beautiful in her dress and everything is going according to plan."

"But Riley did seem off." Luke turned to face him. "Are you sure there isn't anything?"

Jack sucked in a breath and coughed. "Det. Miles Ward."

"What about him?"

"He's been flirting with Riley. I think it's throwing her a little off her game."

A sinking feeling spread through Luke's gut. "Has she been flirting back?"

Jack laughed. "No! Riley has done nothing but give him a hard time at every turn, which has goaded him on. Miles is a nice guy. I trained him myself. I'm not sure if he's teasing her or is genuinely smitten with her, but Riley isn't having any part of it. You have nothing to worry about. Karen did say he stopped at the house this morning to talk to Riley about doing some interviews with him at the admin office." Jack took his eyes off the road for a few seconds. "Riley probably doesn't want to risk upsetting you right before the wedding."

Luke relaxed. "I haven't met him yet, but I probably should."

"You should." Jack navigated the car off the exit and through the small town of Brant Lake. Finding the cabin in daylight proved much easier than when they had arrived the night before. But this time, they couldn't get near the place. Cars lined the road for at least a half-mile in both directions. Many were state police vehicles, others Luke assumed belonged to the search volunteers, and then there was a smattering of news vans. The cops had been tightlipped and gave no interviews about the specific location of the cabin. What hit the news was all speculation, but clearly, they had found the place.

Jack drove past the cabin and down the road toward the lake. There were no other houses on the road except for the cabin and Betty's house. As they got closer, Luke noticed Betty standing on her front porch talking to a state police officer. When she saw them, Betty waved them into her driveway.

"I thought she might save us a spot," Jack said, inching down the road careful not to hit the cars on either side. He pulled into her driveway, and Betty stopped her conversation and walked over to them. She waited for them to get out of the car.

Impatiently, she said, "I've been waiting for you two to get back. This is the most action this area has seen in a dog's age. I don't know what they are expecting to find. I told them there was a car last night and then you two. I don't think they will find Jane in those woods though." Betty wrung her hands.

Luke reached his hand out and squeezed her shoulder. "Jane took off before. We believe there was a struggle at the cabin, but Jane has proved more resourceful than we thought. She could have taken off, and if she did, she's out there someplace. We are going to join the search. Better to rule it out quickly."

Betty put her hands on her ample hips. "What else are you doing?"

"We have it under control. I promise you," Jack said dismissively as he gathered some of his gear from the car for the search.

Luke understood Betty's worry a little better. It's what his own family went through when his sister was missing. Luke tried to reassure her. "While we are here, we have investigators back at the school interviewing people trying to find information. There were prints found in the cabin belonging to someone who has been identified. We have investigators running down those leads as well. This search is just a small part of what we are doing to help find Jane."

Betty didn't say anything. She searched Luke's face, probably to assess his truthfulness. She nodded once and turned and went back into her house.

"You're good at comforting people," Jack said with a hint of admiration in his voice. "It was never my skill set. I want to get the work done."

Jack wasn't unlike every old school detective Luke knew. Not that Luke's way was any better or worse, it was just different. But it was the only way he knew how to do his job. He told Jack as much as they found the table manned by a state police representative and signed-in to the search. The woman gave them an area to search down by the lake.

Jack and Luke walked side by side down to the lake. They were supposed to walk the shoreline for two miles down and back and check at least fifty yards back from the water. Jack took the area close to the water while Luke moved farther away closer to the tree line. Once they got past a small beach and swimming area, the terrain became a little more difficult to walk, but they managed. The search was slow and methodical. Periodically, they'd confirm with each other that nothing suspicious had been found. Every so often, a team of searchers could be seen through the tree line, but otherwise, there wasn't a soul in sight.

When they reached a little over a mile into their search, Luke spotted a large boulder off in the distance. It caught his eye because of a splash of hot pink, which peaked out over the edge enough to be seen.

Luke pointed up ahead. "Probably nothing, but I'm going to check it out." He headed for the large rock with his head down watching the area where he walked, searching the entire way. Once Luke reached the area, he had to climb over two boulders to reach the one he wanted. When he saw the writing, Luke nearly toppled over. Written in hot pink was a message.

They are trying to kill me. Help. Jane

The boulders had slick wet surfaces and were nearly impossible to balance on for too long. Luke had no idea what Jane might have used to write the words, but it appeared fresh. He pulled his cellphone from his pocket and snapped a few pictures.

"Jack, over here!" Luke yelled, moving off the boulders and down into the grassy area.

"What is it?" Jack asked when he reached Luke.

"A message from Jane. I think she might have gotten away from Irene Hodge last night, but there's no telling now where she went."

Jack moved to the boulders but didn't climb over them. Luke handed Jack his cellphone with one of the photos enlarged. Jack furrowed his brow. "She's running scared, but at least we know she's still alive."

"At least we hope she is. We have no idea if Irene Hodge caught up to her."

Jack nodded. "Jane isn't your average girl."

Both Jack and Luke spent a few more minutes searching the brush, moving twigs and leaves and tall blades of grass out of the way looking for any nugget of information that hinted at where Jane could have gone. When nothing else was found, Luke asked if Jack would stay there and wait while he ran back and got a crime scene tech. Luke was itching to question Betty again.

Jack agreed and Luke didn't waste any time. He took off in a jog toward the area they had signed-in for the search. When Luke made it back up the hill near Betty's house, he motioned for the woman behind the table.

"We found something," he said a little out of breath. "Jane left us a message on a rock. We need a crime scene tech down there to photograph and sample what she used to write the message. Jack is down there still. We checked the area but didn't see anything else."

The woman assured Luke she'd have someone there immediately, and before he even walked away in the direction of Betty's house, she had radioed in the message.

CHAPTER 37

"Aren't you going to tell me you're going to do all the talking?" I asked Miles as we stepped through the door into the Austen Academy's administration building five minutes before our appointment with Headmistress Marybeth Winslow. She had mentioned in her message to Miles she might have the school's legal counsel and public relations department chair in on the meeting.

"I don't want to do all the talking. You have a better way with people than I do." Miles navigated down the hall and up two flights of stairs.

When we reached the landing, I asked, "Do you think they will tell us anything or stonewall us again?"

"I don't know. I've tried to speak to this woman at least six other times. She constantly sends me to speak to her underlings. I'm surprised she even agreed to the meeting, but after some of those news conferences with Senator Crandall, she's feeling the heat."

I followed Miles into the office. Her secretary, Roseline, sat ramrod straight at her desk. She glanced up at us. "You're here to see Headmistress Winslow, I presume?"

Miles flashed his badge and gave our names. Roseline didn't respond. She simply got up from her desk, maintaining the same ridged posture she had while sitting, and escorted us into the office.

Miles walked in first and I followed behind him. The room had rich cherry wood paneling and a hardwood floor. There was no rug to cushion our footfalls. Winslow sat behind a desk that appeared far too big for her small frame. It surprised me how young she appeared. She had her dark hair cut in a severe bob, wore a tailored business suit, and had just enough makeup to highlight her blue eyes, high cheekbones, and full lips. If I had to guess, I wouldn't have put her any older than fifty. I had imagined we were meeting someone much older. I also thought there would be other people in the meeting, but Headmistress Winslow was alone.

"Please have a seat," she said crisply, pointing to the two chairs in front of her desk.

The way she said it brought up the same feeling as being called to the principal's office, only you're not sure exactly what you did wrong. We did as we were told. As he sat, Miles began to explain the reason for the visit, but Winslow cut him off.

She peered at us over her desk. "You might be surprised I don't have other staff here with me. Our legal counsel forbade me to speak to you alone and our public relations chair cautioned the same, but I don't have time for either of them interrupting me and getting in the way. We don't have anything to hide. I've been at this school for three years. I'm the youngest headmistress Austen Academy has had. In that time, we have had a series of tragedies. It's been unfortunate but more a sign of the times than any wrongdoing on our part. I'll speak with you and answer your questions to the best of my ability, but I don't play games. You need to be direct and clear and brief."

Miles glanced at me and then turned back to Headmistress Winslow. Evenly, he explained, "We have reason to believe Irene Hodge has something to do with Jane Crandall's disappearance, which might also tie into the murder of Erik Yates."

In one sentence, Miles knocked all the bluster out of her. Winslow blinked rapidly and sat there without saying a word. Finally, recovering, she asked, "What evidence do you have?"

"I can't get into that right now. Jane Crandall is believed to have been hiding at a cabin up north. We have reason to believe Irene Hodge was also at the cabin within the last day or so. Can you tell me where Irene Hodge is right now?"

Winslow picked up the phone on her desk and placed a call. The person on the other end answered quickly. They spoke for a few moments. After Winslow finished the call, she dropped the phone back in its cradle and stared at us smugly. "Irene Hodge is at home in New Jersey with her sick mother. She left the school last Thursday and was supposed to be back this weekend, but she called late Sunday night to explain her mother was sicker than she realized and needed the week off. Are you satisfied?"

"Not by a long shot," Miles said, narrowing his eyes at her. "What's her mother's name and phone number?"

Winslow pursed her lips. "Not necessary. I have her cellphone number right here. We can call and take care of this right now."

"Go right ahead."

Winslow clicked a few keys on her keyboard and traced a finger down her screen until she found what she needed. She punched in the numbers and picked up the phone.

"Put it on speakerphone, please," Miles instructed. While his words were polite, his tone indicated it was more than a request. Winslow complied, but it didn't even ring. It went straight to Irene Hodge's voicemail. Before Winslow could say anything, Miles left a message instructing Irene to call his cellphone immediately.

Winslow dropped the phone down after the call ended, clearly not happy with his actions. "I could have left the message, Detective."

"Who is Irene's emergency contact?"

"No, I absolutely cannot give out her information like that." Winslow sat back in her chair and folded her arms across her chest in defiance.

Miles stood. "You're under the impression I'll take no for an answer. Let me make myself clear. Irene Hodge is currently a suspect in the disappearance of Jane Crandall. If you don't cooperate, I'll give a statement to the press that you're refusing to aid us in finding a student. Then I'll get a search warrant and access any information I want."

Headmistress Winslow held firm, but she shifted uncomfortably in her chair. I could tell she wasn't sure of her decision.

I locked eyes with her. "Headmistress Winslow, you obviously want to be helpful, otherwise you would have just shoved us off to your lawyer and public relations person. Our only goal is to find Jane. It's to your benefit to help us do that. If we can clear Irene quickly as a suspect, that's all the better. If not, it's going to look very bad for the school."

Begrudgingly, Headmistress Winslow jerked forward and slapped at the keys on her computer. "Irene's emergency contact is her sister, Regina." Winslow rattled off the number, and this time, Miles placed the call on his cell. Someone answered right away.

Miles walked to the far corner of Winslow's office and had a brief conversation. I didn't know exactly what the person on the other line said, but it wasn't good. His voice was filled with confusion and concern and then all-out anger. He ended the call and turned to us. "Regina hasn't heard from Irene in a few weeks. She is also sure Irene is not with their mother."

Winslow turned her head towards him. "How is she sure of that?"

"Because their mother moved in with Regina last year, and neither of them has seen Irene in at least six months. Their mother is old and frail but otherwise in perfect health."

He leveled a look at Winslow. "It seems your staff is lying to you."

"My staff doesn't lie. There must be some logical explanation." Winslow looked at him. "You got what you wanted. You can go now."

"We aren't done yet," Miles said, sitting back down. He shot a look at me, indicating I should ask my questions.

I brought it back to the very beginning. "What do you know about Natalie Gallo stealing Irene Hodge's tests?"

"I don't see how this has to do with anything," Winslow said firmly, barely looking at us.

Miles snapped, "We think it does so just answer the question."

Winslow cast her eyes toward him and gave Miles a dirty look. She didn't like him one bit. To me, she responded, "There was never any proof it happened. We take cheating very seriously here. If a student is found cheating, they are immediately expelled."

I asked, "You'd say then, their entire academic career could be in jeopardy?"

"Very much so. If they were to be expelled, the mark would sit on their transcript. Even if they left and went to a public high school, the stain of cheating would carry. Their chance of gaining admittance into an Ivy League or top tier college, which is the goal of many girls here, would be nearly impossible."

Miles asked what I had been thinking. "What you're saying is if a girl was cheating, she'd have great motivation to ensure no one found out?"

"Yes, I'd say that's true," Winslow said slowly. "I'm not sure why it's important. We have no proof anyone cheated."

"Who told you that?" I asked, not sure where she was coming by the assumption, which is what it was.

Winslow explained evenly, "One of our teachers spoke to Natalie when the rumors surfaced. Natalie denied it, and this teacher thought Natalie was credible. Since the student making the accusation killed herself, we had nothing more and the situation ended."

"Let me guess," I said sarcastically, "the teacher was Heidi Sykes."

Winslow said stiffly, "Well yes, but I'm not sure why it would matter. Heidi is an alumnus of the school and has been a long-term staff member here. She has the most direct contact with Natalie and would have the best understanding of whether she's telling the truth or not."

"She also has the most incentive to lie." Miles pounded his fist into his open hand. "Here's what I think happened. Maddie caught Natalie stealing tests. Natalie found out and tried to harass and humiliate Maddie into keeping quiet, but it didn't work. Maddie told people, and by all accounts, she was planning to come forward with proof. But before Maddie did that someone silenced her. Erik Yates knew at the start of the school year about the entire cheating scandal and never believed Maddie killed herself and neither did Jane. Now Erik is dead and Jane is missing. Irene Hodge, the teacher who had the tests stolen, is also missing."

Miles stood and stepped toward Winslow's desk. "You and this school are in a whole heap of trouble, and you better start helping us to sort it out because if anything happens to Jane, I'm holding you accountable. You know more than you are letting on. I'll arrest you right now for obstruction of justice so if I were you, I'd get to talking."

All the color drained from Headmistress Winslow's face. She sank back in her chair but didn't say a word. Miles had shocked both of us into silence.

CHAPTER 38

Cooper was supposed to be back at the house doing research, but his poor interview with Heidi yesterday left a lot of questions on the table. Now he was on a mission, and he wasn't going to fail this time. He didn't care how much Heidi dodged him. He hurried across campus, yanked open the door to the humanities building, and reached her office door in record time. He was about to pull open her classroom door when he realized Heidi wasn't alone. At first, Cooper thought she might be teaching a class, but after listening for a few minutes, he realized Heidi was in the room with a student. Not just any student – Natalie Gallo.

Riley had told him Natalie refused to speak to the police. Her father had even gone so far as to get her a lawyer, who also refused to let Natalie speak. Riley hadn't even bothered trying to interview Natalie yet. Cooper debated the merits of waiting until Heidi was alone to speak to her again, but decided he'd forge ahead and maybe get Natalie to speak as well.

Cooper crouched low and snuck up closer to the door to hear what they were saying. He had no idea what excuse he'd use if a teacher or student came upon him in the hall. Cooper couldn't make out too many words because they were speaking in hushed tones, but Cooper heard Natalie's name again and then Heidi told her she didn't have to worry because it was being handled. Cooper had no idea what *it* was. A lull in conversation was the opening Cooper needed.

He stepped back, took a deep breath, and knocked once loudly on the door. Heidi pulled it open, her face contorted like she was going to yell at a student, but seeing Cooper, she softened her expression a little too quickly for Cooper's liking. It revealed a fakeness about her Cooper had thought was just below the surface.

"How can I help you today?" Heidi said, holding back her annoyance.

"We've made some progress in the search for Jane, but I need to run a few things by you."

"You found Jane?" Natalie asked from across the classroom.

Cooper pulled the door open wider and stepped around Heidi into the classroom. He extended his hand and introduced himself. She did the same. Cooper was surprised by how strong the girl's grip was. Natalie stood about five-foot-nine, had an athletic build, and straight shoulder-length dark hair. Her brown eyes widened as Cooper explained why he was there.

"We haven't found Jane per se, but we believe we are close. Natalie, I'm glad you're here. I needed to speak to you as well."

Heidi went to the girl and took her by the arm. "Remember, Natalie, your father doesn't want you to speak to the police. You should go."

"I'm not the cops," Cooper reminded her. "You also shouldn't encourage your students to avoid telling the truth."

"What truth?" Natalie asked sternly. "I don't know what you've heard, but it's not true."

"Natalie, please do as I say and go," Heidi cautioned her again. Turning to Cooper, "You can't speak to a student without parental permission."

The corners of Cooper's mouth turned up in a sly smile. "What you said would be true if Natalie were a child, but since she turned eighteen two weeks ago, she's legally an adult and can make that decision herself." Cooper had taken it upon himself to do a little research on Natalie as well. He never went in unprepared.

"She is still in high school!" Heidi persisted.

Cooper shrugged. "It's up to you then, Natalie. Everyone is making you out to be the bad person here. If it were me, I'd want a chance to defend myself."

"What are they saying about me?" Natalie asked, planting her hands on her narrow hips.

Cooper caught her eye. "I think you know."

Heidi nudged Natalie again. "He's just trying to manipulate you."

"No, I'm not. I'm giving you a chance to tell the truth." Cooper knew he needed to take a different approach. He grabbed a chair from one of the students' desks and sat down. He leaned forward and clasped his hands together like he had all the time in the world. "What did you say to Maddie the night she saw you steal those tests?"

Ire sparked in the girl's eyes. "I didn't steal any tests," she denied. "Maddie made it all up."

"Why would she do something like that?" Cooper asked curiously.

"Why do girls do anything? She was jealous and wanted to get me in trouble. I'm the victim here," Natalie said, holding her hands out to her side emphasizing her point.

Cooper shook his head. "What you're saying doesn't make any sense at all. From what I hear, Maddie didn't run and tell a teacher to get you into trouble. She didn't do anything at all for a couple of months until she saw you do it again. Even then, she was quite conflicted as to what she should do."

Natalie didn't respond to Cooper's statement. Instead, she doubled down. "Maddie was jealous of me and my friends. We have more money than her family. I heard she was even here on financial aid."

Cooper smirked; flashes of his poor childhood flashed in his mind. "Does it bother you, Natalie, having to go to school with girls whose families aren't as wealthy as yours?"

She stood defiantly. "If they can't afford it, they shouldn't be here."

"Why is that?" Cooper pressed.

Heidi tried again to intervene, but the girl shook her free. "Because they take the spots of girls who deserve to be here."

Cooper didn't know if what he was about to say was technically true or not, but he took a swing in the dark. "I saw both of your transcripts. Maddie had better grades than you did. She had every right to be here, more so than you even. You're not the student she was."

Natalie shook her head. "This school is for girls who come from the best families, and it should stay that way." It came as a shock to Cooper when Natalie turned to Heidi and asked, "You feel the same, right? You said some girls just don't belong here. They didn't get in on their own."

Heidi took a step back as if distancing from the remark, but Cooper believed she had said it. Heidi had probably reinforced it as head of the Clovers.

Cooper hitched his jaw toward Heidi. "Is that what you believe? Only girls from wealthy families deserve a solid education? Merit and skill mean nothing as long as the bank account is full?"

Heidi went to speak, but there was nothing she could say in her defense. She tried and faltered. Cooper wasn't having any of it. Maybe it was because he grew up poor or didn't have a normal family life. None of these things even applied to Maddie. Her family had more money than most. They might not have been as wealthy as Natalie's family or even Jane's, and they might have needed some financial aid to pay tuition and room and board, but none of it took away from Maddie's accomplishments.

Cooper pushed himself up from the chair and stepped toward Natalie. "Is that why you didn't like Maddie? Because you didn't think she belonged here?"

"She wasn't one of us, and she was never going to be," Natalie said firmly. "I gave her every chance to stop what she was doing, but she didn't. Maddie had no right to do what she did."

Cooper knew they were right on the brink. "What was that, Natalie? What is it Maddie did so wrong?"

"Maddie got involved in something that was none of her business," she spat.

Cooper pushed harder. "Could it be Maddie saw another student cheating, and based on the honor code here, thought she would tell someone?" Cooper's tone had an edge he hadn't intended with a girl still in high school, but at that moment he didn't care.

Natalie's face grew red. "Maddie had no right to spy on me. She had no right to be in the humanities building that night. If she had just stayed in her room where she belonged, none of this would have happened. We have special privileges and she doesn't. That's why she was so mad."

"Who is *we*?"

"Us," Natalie said, pointing between herself and Heidi. "The chosen girls on this campus. We were chosen for a reason. It means we are better than all the other girls. We will succeed no matter what we have to do to get there."

Cooper bore his eyes into her. "Let's be clear, Natalie. Are you admitting you cheated or that you murdered Maddie to keep her quiet? Maybe both?"

"That's enough!" Heidi yelled, now trying to physically shove Natalie out of her classroom, but given Heidi's small height and stature, the girl barely registered the shove.

Natalie cast her eyes up toward him, a light going off in them finally indicating she knew she had outed herself. "It's not what I meant," she said. "I didn't admit to anything."

"If it isn't what you meant, what did Maddie need to mind her own business about?"

Natalie didn't say anything. She turned toward her teacher, but Heidi offered nothing because it was clear all Heidi wanted was to get her to leave.

Finally, Natalie said, "It wasn't just me."

"It wasn't just you, what? I'm not understanding," Cooper said sternly.

"It was something I had to do," Natalie said, faltering some in her speech for the first time.

Cooper wondered if the gravity of the situation had finally hit her. "Someone made you steal the tests?"

"It was my task," Natalie said annoyance in her voice. "If I'm going to get in trouble for it, then everyone else should, too."

"Who is everyone else, Natalie?" Cooper pushed again, even though he was fairly sure of the answer.

Natalie didn't respond. She cast her eyes between Heidi and Cooper.

"Natalie, did you steal the tests as an initiation into the Clovers?"

Natalie's eyes grew wide. "How do you even know about us? It's all supposed to be a secret."

"Everyone knows, Natalie. It's not a secret."

Natalie shook her head, looking confused now. She stumbled over her words. "It wasn't an initiation. I had gone through that the previous fall semester. This was different."

"Natalie, don't say another word!" Heidi physically put herself between Natalie and Cooper and shoved the girl backward toward the door. "I've had enough of this. Go, get out of here. I will handle this."

"This is your last chance," Cooper said above Heidi's yelling.

Natalie got to the door and looked back at Cooper. She said confidently, "The Clovers are for life. They are my sisters. This is why Maddie would have never been one of us. She wasn't loyal, and she paid the price."

CHAPTER 39

After Heidi shut the door to her classroom, she turned on Cooper. Taking several steps toward him, she pointed her finger at him angrily. "How dare you manipulate a student like that? I'm calling security and having you removed from this school immediately." Heidi moved to her desk and dug through her purse for her phone. She held it in her hands but hesitated. Heidi didn't make the call. She stood there with her phone in her hands.

Cooper smirked at her. "I thought you were calling security?"

Heidi didn't move or say anything. She watched him intensely.

Cooper sauntered back over to the chair and sat down. He leaned forward on the desk. "I don't think you're calling anyone. You're up to your eyeballs in this, and we are going to get to the bottom of this right now. You have one chance to save yourself."

"I never told those girls to steal tests," Heidi said seriously, setting the phone on the desk.

Cooper raised his eyebrows. "But you knew they tested each other's loyalty. You were a Clover. You knew what they were up to."

"All girls do it," Heidi began to justify. "It's not just here. It's boarding schools across the country. These societies give girls a huge advantage going into college and later in life. As Natalie said, only a few who are worthy are chosen."

"I don't get it. Breaking into a teacher's office and stealing is a crime. Cheating goes against every moral code this school has."

Heidi tried to explain it away. "The girls go through silly stuff for initiation in the fall semester. In the spring, before they take their oath, there is a loyalty test."

"Is it always criminal?"

"No, of course not. It was never supposed to be criminal." Heidi wrung her hands.

Cooper locked eyes with her. "What was yours?"

"What do you mean?"

"You're a Clover. What was your loyalty test? You must have had one, too."

Heidi shook her head. "I can't tell you that."

"You won't tell me is more like it."

Heidi held firm and didn't say a word. Cooper knew he wasn't going to get her to talk about her time in the Clovers so he paused for a beat and mulled over other questions he needed answers to. He knocked his fist on the desk. "Did Irene Hodge know Natalie stole tests from her?"

"No, of course not," Heidi said and then paused. She narrowed her eyes at Cooper and he knew he had her. Heidi had just inadvertently admitted she knew Natalie stole the tests.

Cooper didn't press her on it. Not yet anyway. "Irene had to know at some point though."

"I'm not aware of that."

Cooper moved his body so he faced her more directly. "When did you know?"

Heidi sighed. "Later, weeks after it happened. The girls came to me and told me Maddie might have proof Natalie stole some tests and planned to tell the administration. I tried to speak to Maddie about it."

Cooper narrowed his gaze at her. "You're telling me you confronted Maddie about what she saw?"

Heidi shook her head and looked away. "I wouldn't say confront. I went to Maddie and told her if she had proof Natalie stole those tests, she needed to hand it over to me. I was going to handle it."

"What did Maddie do?" Cooper asked, knowing Heidi wasn't giving him the full truth, but it was enough for him to get an idea about how it played out.

"She refused," Heidi said angrily.

Cooper looked at her, skepticism written all over his face. "A student refused to give a teacher proof that another student was cheating. Why? Maddie had to have a reason."

"She told me she didn't have any. Maddie refused to speak to me about it at all."

"You didn't find it odd?" Cooper asked.

"I assumed Maddie didn't have any proof, and I thought that would be the end of the matter." Heidi held herself upright a little more confidently than she had been before.

"You didn't think you should go to the administration?"

"Of course not. Natalie would have been expelled over a little prank. It wasn't anything. The girls tested her loyalty and she passed. It would have been the end of it if Natalie hadn't gotten caught. No one would have ever known."

"That doesn't excuse it," Cooper said. He pointed at her. "You had a responsibility to go to the administration with what you found."

Heidi grew angrier now. "You don't understand how things work around here. I had no proof anything occurred. When I was asked, that's what I said."

Cooper glared back at her. "You lied to the administration then is what you're saying? Natalie admitted it to you. What more proof did you need?" Cooper paused so she could answer, but she didn't. He started to speak but a buzzing in his pants pocket called his attention. He pulled the phone out and read a text from Riley.

"Who is that?" Heidi asked.

Cooper didn't respond to the text and slid the phone back in his pocket. "Nothing you need to worry about. Where were we?" Cooper ran the conversation in his head until he remembered what he was going to say before the interruption. He narrowed his eyes at her. "I think you went to Maddie to find out what she knew, and she was too smart to tell you. Maddie was too smart to hand over the evidence she had. I only have one question. Did you believe Maddie when she told you she didn't have proof?"

Heidi glared at him, but she didn't confirm or deny.

Cooper leaned back and stared at her. He shrugged. "I guess you're not going to help me out at all. I'll tell you then. I don't think you believed Maddie. I think you conspired with the girls to harass her until she gave it up, but Maddie was stronger than that. The only question I'm left with is did you kill Maddie or did Natalie?"

Heidi gasped, stumbled back, and put her hand up to her mouth. "We didn't kill her. I swear to you."

Cooper stood. "Someone did."

"Maddie killed herself," Heidi insisted.

Cooper took a step toward her. "No, she didn't. Those girls harassed and bullied her. But Maddie didn't give in. The night before she died, she was about to take the whole thing to the administration, video and all."

Heidi shook her head, growing more upset by the second. "That's not true."

"It is true. Maddie had a video of Natalie stealing tests from Irene Hodge's office. Where is she, Heidi? Where is Irene right now?"

Confused, Heidi asked, "What do you mean where is she? She took time off to be with her mother."

"Nope, she didn't. The other investigators working on the case checked out her story. Irene is not with her mother and hasn't been in at least six months. Want to try your answer again?"

"I don't have to sit here and listen to this." Heidi walked to the door.

"It's okay," Cooper said coolly. "Det. Ward is going to have some questions for you anyway. I was giving you an opportunity to get your story straight. I figured I could save you the embarrassment of formal questioning."

Heidi's hand stayed firm on the door, but she didn't open it. She turned her body halfway around to look at him. "What would I be formally questioned about?"

"Any number of things." Cooper held out his hand and counted down his fingers. "Failure to report a break-in and then covering it up. The suspicious deaths of Maddie and Erik. Not to mention Jane is still missing."

This time Heidi let go of the door and turned around to face him. "You can't possibly think that's all connected to me?"

"Doesn't matter what I think." Cooper headed toward the door. "It only matters what the cops think, and right now, they think you're a person of interest." Cooper reached in his pocket and pulled out his phone. He lied, "The text I received while we were talking was from Det. Ward wanting to know if I was with you because he wants to formally question you. I don't know about you, but something like that can't be good for your reputation."

Heidi took a deep breath and exhaled with her whole body. She slumped against the door and rubbed at her temples. "This has all gotten so out of hand."

"I'd say so," Cooper said, appraising her. Heidi remained slumped against the door, which was the only exit out. He didn't know if she'd give up any more, but he considered it a win. He had gained far more this second time speaking to her than the first. Having Heidi admit she knew about Natalie stealing the tests and had even questioned Maddie about it herself was huge as far as Cooper was concerned.

Cooper shoved his hands in his pockets. "I don't think there's much else I can do for you since you refuse to tell me the truth. Could you move out of the way? I have some other people to speak to today."

Heidi didn't move. She just stared up at him. Biting her lip and starting to cry, she asked, "Can you put a good word in for me with Det. Ward? I didn't do anything wrong."

"Why would I put a good word in for you? You lied to me, dodged my questions, and haven't been the least bit helpful. I don't have anything good about you to say."

Heidi opened her eyes wide and pulled her bottom lip through her teeth. She pushed herself off of the door and moved like a cat over to Cooper. She reached her hand up and traced a finger down from his chest to the top of his pants. She dared to drop it lower, but Cooper caught her hand in his. She purred, "I can make your help worthwhile."

Cooper gripped her shoulders and moved her out of the way. "That's not going to happen, but thanks for showing me exactly how manipulative you are. I'll be sure to pass the information on to Det. Ward." Cooper walked out of the classroom and left Heidi fuming with anger.

Cooper left the classroom, slightly more shook up by the whole encounter than he let on. He made it down the hall and was halfway out of the building when a young woman appeared from a classroom.

"Are you an investigator?" she asked quietly.

Startled, Cooper stopped and walked over to where she stood. He dropped his voice to almost a whisper. "Yes, is there something you need?"

She nodded. "I think you'll want to hear what I have to say. Meet me tonight by the tunnel entrance near the teachers' cottages. Don't tell anyone."

CHAPTER 40

Luke knocked hard on Betty's front door. The woman appeared nearly immediately with a pan in one hand and dishtowel in the other. "Why are you banging like that? I'm right here."

"Sorry," Luke said as he stepped inside of her house, "I didn't know if you'd hear me. I need to speak with you again."

"Did you find Jane?"

"No, but we found a message from Jane."

"Doesn't surprise me. Jane struck me as smart and resourceful." Betty went into her kitchen and dropped the pan and the dishtowel on the counter. She wiped her hands on her pants as she came back into the living room. "Don't just stand there. Take a seat and ask me what you need to know."

Luke did as she asked. He sat down on the couch and propped his arms on his knees as he leaned forward to speak to her. "Tell me again what Jane told you about the murder."

Betty stayed quiet a moment as if thinking through the details. When she spoke, her voice was even and strong. "Jane didn't provide me any details, and no matter how much I tried, I couldn't get them out of her. She said she had snuck out of her residence Friday evening because she needed to speak to a teacher. Before she could get to his door, she heard gunshots. Jane saw someone, but as I said before, their back was turned to her. All she saw was a hood up. As she walked back from the window, Jane fell. She said she took off after that. The last thing she wanted to do was give herself away."

"I know you said you don't know how she got up here, but did Jane say anything that might have given you a clue? It's quite a distance from school, and Jane isn't from this area. She only knew about the cabin because it's her boyfriend's parents' place."

Betty sighed. "I wish I had pushed harder for information, but you have to understand, I didn't want to spook her into running away from here. I thought she was at least safe. I was giving her some breathing space." Betty shifted in her seat and gestured with her hand. "You have to understand kids Jane's age. If she had run away from home, normally it's because things at home aren't working out or there are too many rules and such. The last thing I wanted to be was one more adult hassling her."

Luke understood, and he couldn't judge Betty for the choices she made. "Did you have any concerns when you first found Jane in the cabin?"

"Sure, at first, I did," Betty said seriously. "You saw how I approached it with you. I wasn't like that the night I confronted Jane, but I was direct. When I saw nothing was broken in the cabin and realized Jane had a key, I figured the Kellers wouldn't mind. I was going to keep an eye on her anyway. Since Jane used the key to get in, I also assumed that maybe Jane knew one of the Kellers' kids." Betty looked at Luke, her eyes dropping down. "All I was trying to do was give her some time. My goal was to get her to tell me what was going on, and then I was going to call for help. I had no idea Jane was a senator's daughter. After Jane told me she witnessed a murder, then I was worried about her safety. I figured up here was better than anywhere."

Luke took a deep breath. He believed Betty had told them everything she knew, but there had to be more – something they were both missing. The one part of the story that didn't make sense to Luke was if Jane ran away only after witnessing the murder – why did she have money for groceries and clothes with her. He asked Betty if she knew.

"You don't know much, do you, Det. Morgan?" The question was rhetorical. "I asked Jane where she got the money for the food and the clothing. Jane told me she had it with her because she took cash to her teacher's house. She was going to try to convince him to hire a private investigator. Jane had done some research and figured that would be the only way to find out who killed her friend. She needed an adult to sign the contract. Jane figured if her teacher was willing to help her, then he'd be off her suspect list. If he refused, she'd be one step closer to finding the truth based on his reaction."

Luke sighed heavily. "You're right. She is smarter than we thought." The information didn't get him any closer to finding her, but it hadn't occurred to Luke until that moment just how much Jane reminded him of Riley. She was smart beyond her years and more logical than most he had come across. If Jane wanted to disappear, she could.

Luke decided right then to level with Betty. Standing up and going to the window to see what was going on down near the waterline, Luke explained, "We found a note from Jane down on some boulders. She wrote she needed help because people were after her. She said they, not him or her, but they. We think Jane got away from the woman who came to get her, but we have no idea where she is now." Luke turned to face Betty. "Do you?"

"Not a clue, Detective. Jane didn't say anything to me about knowing anyone else up here. She didn't act like she knew the area very well at all. I don't have any idea where she could have gone. I swear I would tell you. Are you sure someone didn't snatch her?"

"I'm positive," Luke said seriously. "The note she painted on the boulders was fresh. I'm still waiting for the techs to tell me what Jane used to write it, but it couldn't have been more than a day or two old."

"A kid with money is going to be able to get far. She could be up into Canada by now," Betty said thoughtfully. "How can I help?"

Luke ran a hand over his bald head. "If you think of anything Jane said at all that might give us some clue as to where she went, let us know. Otherwise, we are going to have to keep searching. We are going to put her photos on the local stations here in the hopes someone will alert us."

Betty shook her head. "I doubt that will happen."

"What do you mean?"

"Folks up here stick to themselves. They will help a kid in trouble, but good luck getting them to call the police."

It didn't make any sense to Luke. "Even if the kid is in trouble?"

Betty nodded. "It depends on what she tells them. As soon as Jane told me her story, I gave her more time. I thought it was the right thing for her, especially because she said she didn't trust the police. Now, I know I should have called then, but why would I bring more trouble down on Jane if what she was saying was true? I wanted to help her not hurt her more. People up here handle our own."

After a beat, Betty stood and walked over to Luke. "If you're going to make an appeal to find Jane, you'll need more than a photo. You are going to have to get on the news and appeal to people that all you want is to protect Jane. You're going to have to tell them she has to come in for her protection. Then you might get someplace."

Luke hadn't thought of it before and he should have. Jane needed someone she could trust. Jane ran because she didn't know where to go to feel safe and protected. That was no place to leave a kid. Luke thanked Betty and headed for the door.

Luke stood on Betty's front stoop for a few minutes considering the best course of action. His mind spun with all the options in front of him. Someone needed to make a public appeal to Jane. He wasn't the right one to do it. Neither was Jack. Riley could do it though. She could hit the right tone of concern, understanding, and protection needed to possibly bring Jane in. Not only could Riley strike the right tone, but she was also a private investigator licensed in New York. She could publicly offer Jane the help she had been seeking with Erik Yates on the night of his murder. If anyone could do it, it would be Riley.

Luke pulled his phone from his pocket and sent Riley a quick text. She didn't respond right away so Luke headed back down to the water to see Jack. As Luke grew closer to the spot, his heart thumped in his chest. There were so many cops and crime scene techs around, Luke worried they might have found something more than Jane's note.

Luke took off in a run, closing the rest of the distance quickly. "What's going on, Jack?" Luke asked with concern in his voice as soon as he reached him.

"When you sounded the alarm bells, they all came running," Jack explained. He pointed to a place in the woods back from the shoreline. "The dogs traced Jane's scent back there, but they still haven't found anything."

"I don't think they will." Luke recounted what Betty had told him about Jane's quest to hire a private investigator and the cash she had on hand. "As Betty said, if Jane wanted, she could be in Canada by now. The locals, if they come across her, aren't going to rat her out."

Jack gave him a skeptical look. "What do you suggest we do then? We can't just leave Jane out here."

Luke explained his idea about Riley giving a press conference and speaking directly to Jane.

"Do you think Jane will believe her or just think it's a trap?" Jack asked.

Luke shrugged. "She has to trust someone sooner or later. Hopefully, whatever went down with Irene Hodge was enough to convince Jane she can't do this alone."

Jack furrowed his brow. "If Jane's alive, that is."

CHAPTER 41

"I can't believe you browbeat Headmistress Winslow into telling you she knew about the cheating." I sat next to Miles on the bench in the middle of the quad. Cooper stood in front of us. We met as soon as both of our interviews were done.

Miles smiled like a Cheshire cat. "Yeah, but she didn't do anything about it. Winslow heard the information and decided there was no proof – of course, the only witness was then deceased. She did nothing. She didn't even launch an internal investigation. Winslow swept it under the rug like everything else here."

"This place," Cooper said with disgust as he toed the grass in front of him, "it's so pretty on the outside, but once you start peeling back the layers, it's not what it seems. I wouldn't send my kid here."

I understood how Cooper felt. "It's a moment in time," I reminded him. "Think about how many young women have passed through this school who might not have had an opportunity for education otherwise. Throughout its history, Austen Academy has done far more good than bad. We've just hit a moment in time where there are some students and staff who aren't the most ethical."

"That's a nice way of saying someone is a deranged killer," Miles said. He looked up at Cooper. "What was your impression of Heidi?"

Cooper smirked. "Before or after she tried to get into my pants?"

"Are you serious?" I asked, not completely shocked by what Cooper said. Heidi had given off a vibe that she wasn't as innocent as she might appear.

Miles feigned insult. "She didn't hit on me."

Cooper shrugged. "Maybe you're not her type. It was towards the end of the interview. Heidi wanted me to put in a good word with you, Miles. I told her you'd be coming to interrogate her. She knows far more than what she's letting on. I'm sure of it. If Heidi had flat out told me she murdered Maddie, I wouldn't have been surprised."

I raised an eyebrow. "Did you give in to her advances? I might need to rat you out to Adele."

Cooper shifted his eyes between Miles and me. "You'd rat *me* out?" I caught his meaning without him saying another word. Then he laughed. "Of course, I didn't give in. Not even on the wildest drunken night in my twenties would I have given in to her. She has hot mess written all over her."

Cooper gave us a short overview of his interaction with Heidi and the information she told him about Maddie and Natalie and the cheating. "Heidi brushed it off," he explained. "She said it was just a loyalty test. Not a big deal."

"I'll have to go talk to her again. She didn't tell me much of anything the first time." Miles stood up next to Cooper. He shook his hand. "Good job. I didn't think Heidi had much to tell."

I rolled my eyes at him. "Because you didn't think anything was happening here. You saw a pretty face and fell for her hook, line, and sinker."

"I don't think she's pretty." Miles locked eyes with me. "She's not my type."

"Regardless, you didn't do your job," I said, my tone a little meaner than I intended.

"Ouch." Miles rubbed a spot near his heart as if I had shot him. "You're right though. My whole department didn't give this the seriousness it warranted upfront so now we are playing catch up."

"There's something else," Cooper said, refocusing our attention. When our eyes were on him, he said, "As I left Heidi's classroom, a girl poked her head out of a classroom down the hall. She told me she had some information and wanted to meet tonight by the tunnel entrance behind the teachers' cottages. Riley, I want you to go with me. Miles, it would probably be better without the cops. I'm sure there isn't anyone on this campus who doesn't know who you are by now. If she had wanted to seek out the police, she would have done so, but she saw me and asked."

Miles nodded. "You've been hired to do a job so I can't stand in your way. You guys have a way of getting the students and staff talking. Anything we can do to find Jane is fine by me. Of course, if you get anything on Erik's murder, pass it along promptly."

Cooper agreed. "Riley, have you heard any news from Luke lately?"

"I haven't checked my phone. It's been on silent." I pulled my phone from my pocket and clicked on the screen. I had missed a call from my mother and had a text from Luke. I read it over slowly and then read it again. I wasn't as confident as Luke that I'd be the one to draw Jane out, but I was willing to do anything he thought might help.

"Luke and Jack are on their way back," I explained, setting the phone down next to me. "Luke thinks it would be helpful for me to give a media interview, telling Jane I'm a private investigator willing to help her."

Cooper and Miles both shared the same look. "How would that help?" Cooper asked.

"I'm not sure exactly. Luke said he'd explain more when he gets here. Luke texted me right before he left, which was about forty minutes ago. He should be home soon."

Cooper asked, "You want to go back to the house and wait? I don't have much else to do here until tonight."

I turned to Miles. "Do you want to come back with us? I'm not sure how you feel about us giving a statement, but Luke is usually on target. He must have found something out we don't know yet."

Miles checked his phone and frowned. "My crime scene techs just came back with several print matches from inside Erik's cottage. Irene Hodge's prints are there."

"She was his neighbor. Wouldn't you expect to find her prints there?" I stood to join them.

Miles nodded. "If her prints weren't also found at the cabin, I'd be less suspicious. Jane tells the woman up there she witnessed Erik's murder. Irene was clearly up at the cabin doing who knows what, and now her prints are at Erik's. She's not where she told the school. Irene's a person of interest at this point. I'm going to get a search warrant for her place."

Cooper glanced at him. "You going public with that?"

"Not yet. A few teachers said they'd be available for interviews after class. Now that Winslow has capitulated a little, she's greasing some wheels for me and encouraging her faculty to speak to me. I'm going to stick around campus and see what more I can find out before I name Irene as a suspect. The sooner I can find some leads, the better it will be for both cases."

"When you're done, head over to my mother's house," I suggested. "You have to eat at some point, and you said you wanted to meet Luke. Plus, I think it would be good to have you in on the discussion about the interview I'll give."

Miles agreed. He said goodbye to both of us and headed toward the science building on the far side of campus. When he was out of sight, I turned to Cooper, "I can't believe Heidi tried to seduce you."

Cooper blushed. "I thought she was going to drop to her knees right in front of me. It was insane. I've never had something like that happen in the middle of an investigation."

"Some women…" I said, leaving the rest unspoken between us.

"Do you trust Miles?" Cooper asked quietly.

"I do. Why?"

"It just doesn't seem like he took Jane's disappearance seriously from the start. I've been trying to assess Miles' motivation and angle."

"He's been a straight shooter with me." Miles had, for good, bad and completely inappropriate, given it to me straight since we met. But I understood what Cooper was feeling. "You're feeling the same frustration I had at the start. Everyone treated Jane as a typical runaway. While it's clear now she did run away, there's much more to it."

With his voice hushed lower than normal, Cooper said, "I didn't tell you something back there because I think it should stay between us for now."

"Let's wait until we get off campus."

CHAPTER 42

When we reached my porch, I said, "I think we're clear here. What did you find?"

We both sat down on comfortable wicker chairs with thick cushions on the seat and back. Cooper settled in. "I talked to Natalie. It wasn't planned, but she was in the classroom when I went to speak to Heidi."

"Miles said her father told her not to speak to anyone. Their lawyer called Miles and said she was off-limits. I hadn't even bothered trying. How did you manage it?"

Cooper kicked his feet up on the porch railing and leaned back. "Right place, right time. Natalie is a real piece of work. She didn't believe Maddie deserved to be at Austen Academy because she came from a family who wasn't as affluent as hers. For Natalie, Maddie's scholarship meant she didn't deserve to be there. She wasn't the *right* kind of girl to attend Austen."

I sighed. "Maddie went in with a disadvantage. It was one of many reasons I hadn't wanted to go to Austen. My mother could have never afforded the school fee, which was over $50,000 for tuition and room and board. I didn't even pay close to that much for undergrad for all four years at my state college."

He whistled. "That's a hefty price tag."

I kicked my legs out in front of me. "None of us could have afforded to go there. I assumed there was some snobbery, but if Natalie is saying it outright to a stranger, I can't imagine what she's saying with her friends. It just provides another reason Maddie might have been reluctant to tell. I know she was trying to gain proof. She must have wanted something rock solid no one could dispute."

Cooper countered, "It doesn't seem like it was hidden all that well. Heidi made excuses for it. By what you and Miles said, Headmistress Winslow knew, too."

I corrected him. "Winslow claimed she knew after Maddie's body was found. I'm not sure what to believe. If only Heidi and some of the Clovers knew, it could be easily hidden from the administration. Maddie wasn't telling anyone, not even Jane. Even when the harassment got bad, Maddie kept quiet. But I see your point. No one did anything even when they found out."

"Heidi protected Natalie, which makes me wonder if Irene was in on the cheating, too. Given it seems connected to the Clovers, maybe teachers just looked the other way when they pulled these stunts."

"It's not a stunt though. Natalie stole tests for exams for a class she was in."

Cooper nodded. "That's true. I guess it does add a different spin if she wasn't taking the class at the time. Do you think Heidi told Irene?"

"I don't know. I can't figure out where Irene fits in to all of this. She's a wild card for me. Heidi had a motive to protect the Clovers, and Natalie didn't like Maddie. We know Erik Yates knew earlier this semester. Maybe someone killed him to keep him quiet."

Cooper eyed me. "You think Heidi or Natalie could have killed Erik Yates?"

I speculated, "I don't know. Maybe Natalie distracted him and Heidi pulled the trigger."

"That's a huge stretch for me. Natalie just barely turned eighteen. She's a snob and entitled, but it's a far stretch to cold-blooded killer."

Cooper wasn't wrong. We needed definitive evidence, and we just didn't have it. "Have you heard anything about Erik?"

"What do you mean?"

"Erik was close to Maddie, closer than teachers normally are," I explained, sitting up more in my chair. "I know there is no evidence to suggest anything more than friendship was going on, but Maddie was on scholarship. It meant a great deal to her to be here. What if Erik took advantage of that? What if it wasn't as innocent as it appeared? What if he assaulted her? Maybe Erik worried Maddie would tell someone. He could have killed her to keep her quiet."

Cooper rubbed at his head. "It seems like it would be the most obvious answer, but then who killed him?"

"Maybe Maddie wasn't the only one."

"You're right. Another girl could have been jealous or she feared for her safety after Maddie was killed. Maybe she got to him first." Cooper looked over at me with eyebrows raised. "Jane?"

"I haven't seen anything to indicate that, and she told the woman up north she had witnessed a murder."

"Do you think Jane would tell her she had just killed someone?"

I exhaled. "Probably not."

Just then Luke and Jack rounded the corner from Pawling and headed toward the driveway. We had plenty to speculate about, but I hoped Luke had something solid for us. We waited as they got out of the SUV and made their way onto the porch. I got up and Luke wrapped his arms around me as he planted a kiss on the top of my head.

"We have a glitch in your statement to the media," he said softly.

Jack held up his phone. "Miles just called me. The police aren't so keen on you giving a statement. I have a call into Senator Crandall to discuss."

Cooper and I shared a look. I stepped back from Luke. "We just left Miles, and he didn't seem to have any problem with it."

"He has a problem now," Luke said, annoyance in his voice.

Jack interrupted. "We don't know if it's Miles or the higher-ups. Either way, they want to wait until they have more solid information on Irene Hodge before we say publicly that she was at the cabin."

"I had no intention of doing that. I thought the point was to appeal to Jane to let her know I'm willing to help her if she wants the help."

"I know," Jack said, shrugging. "I can't make decisions for them. Miles has been great about not blocking our access, and the last thing we should do is cause trouble for him. He didn't tell us you couldn't give a statement. Miles said we need to wait."

"Fine," I said annoyed, but it wasn't fine at all. Jane may not have time. She could be hiding out and every second wasted could be another second Irene was closer to harming Jane, if that's what she was doing. I reached my hand out and brushed Luke's arm to get his attention. "What did you find today? You didn't tell me much in text."

Luke leaned against the porch railing. He told us about the search earlier in the day and finding the note Jane left. "She said they, which I think is important. Jane didn't name a person and, clearly, she thinks it's more than one."

It didn't surprise me. "How did Jane get away from Irene?"

"We aren't exactly sure," Jack explained. "Jane is cleverer than we thought. She could have easily taken off from the cabin and hid until dark. She's had a few days to know the terrain. It would have been hard for Irene to find her up there last night. From the boulders where Jane wrote the note, the dogs picked up her scent going back from the shoreline into the woods. They lost her scent after about a mile. Those woods are dense. She could have picked up a trail near Schroon River and gotten herself back out to I-87."

"Is there any chance the note was written before Irene came up there?"

Luke shook his head. "I don't think so. There'd be no point. Jane was safe in the cabin. Betty said she was pretty content. She was working through a plan. Betty explained to me Jane had cash on her for a private investigator. She was going to Erik's that night looking for help. She couldn't sign a contract so she was going to ask Erik to do it for her. If he agreed, Betty said Jane would believe he had nothing to do with Maddie's death, but if he refused, he'd still be a suspect."

Cooper smiled. "Pretty smart girl. But she's right, no private investigator is going to take money from a kid. She'd need an adult."

"Cooper and I were just going over the potential suspect list." I explained to them Cooper's conversation with Heidi and Natalie and how Miles was able to get Headmistress Winslow to admit she knew about Natalie stealing the tests. After I was done and no one had anything to add, I asked, "Don't think I'm crazy, but is there any way you think Jane could have killed Erik?"

Jack and Luke both started to say no, but I held up my hand. "There is one factor at play here we don't know much about because it hasn't been our focus. Erik Yates had an unusual relationship with Maddie. It was closer than a normal teacher. Now the only two people who know what went on between them are dead. The relationship is the reason Jane thought he might be a suspect."

"Right," Luke said, "but Jane was seeking out his help."

"According to what Jane told Betty. Jane had every reason to lie to look sympathetic." I saw their skeptical looks but pressed on anyway. "I'm not saying Jane went there with the intent to kill Erik. She could have gone to ask for his help. What if he said no? There is the possibility that the relationship between him and Maddie wasn't as innocent as everyone thought. What if Erik threatened Jane or tried something inappropriate with her? You said Jane is cleverer than we thought. She could have been defending herself. She could have gotten the gun away from him, shot him, and made it look like he did it himself and took off."

I watched the three of them as they ran the scenario over in their heads. Cooper seemed to be debating it more than the others. Jack appeared on the fence, but I could tell from Luke's expression, he was a definite no.

"There's one problem in your theory," Luke said, "if that's how it went down, then where does Irene Hodge fit into the mix? She lied about where she was going before Erik was murdered and Jane went missing. Why lie?"

He was right. Irene was still the wild card I had no answer for.

CHAPTER 43

After dinner, Luke convinced Riley to go up to her bedroom with him before she headed out to interview the student Cooper encountered earlier in the day. Luke changed out of his jeans and put on shorts. Riley stripped down to her panties and slipped into bed next to him. They snuggled under the covers, and he ran his fingers through her hair. "I wanted a chance to reconnect a little. It's been a crazy week."

"It has," she agreed. "I don't feel like we have had much of a chance to talk at all."

Luke pulled her closer. "Call me crazy, but I'm a little worried maybe you don't want to get married, or maybe we just didn't give ourselves enough engagement time."

Riley pulled back and fear in her voice, she asked, "Is that what you want? More time? Are you second-guessing your proposal?"

Luke laughed and kissed her. "Absolutely not! I would have already married you if it were up to me. I just wondered if you had reservations."

"I don't have reservations at all," Riley said seriously, but her tone implied there was something.

"I know something has been bothering you," Luke ran his fingers over her arm, tickling her sweetly.

"I just…" Riley started and then stopped. She took a breath and expelled it with a sigh. "Det. Ward has been flirting with me. I didn't think he was serious at first, but now, I'm not so sure."

"Flirting is harmless, Riley."

She got wide-eyed. "You flirt with other women when I'm not around?"

"No, I don't flirt," Luke said laughing, pinching her side. "You are more than I can handle. If you did, I'm not going to be mad. It's common right before you get married to have some second thoughts. Flirting with Det. Ward might be a way of avoiding some fear about getting married."

Riley laid her hands on both sides of Luke's face and kissed him. Pulling back, she looked him in the eyes. "It's sweet of you to think I might be that complex. I'm not. I had an attractive man flirt with me, and I was surprised and flattered. I was probably too flattered, but I've put a stop to it."

Relief washed over him. Luke would rather hear the truth all day, every day than be placated with a lie. He teased, "Do I need to do that tough fiancé thing and put him in his place?"

Riley giggled. "No, please don't. Cooper already did it for you – a few times."

Cooper always had Luke's back. It didn't matter what it was. They had been friends since their freshman year in college. "Did Cooper hit him?"

Riley playfully pushed Luke back. "What's with you guys? Of course, Cooper didn't hit him. I would have raised a fit if he had."

"We can act like cavemen sometimes." Luke lowered his eyes at her. "I thought you like that tough side of me."

Riley kissed him again, teasing his tongue with hers. She broke the kiss to say, "I like this softer side much better." She kissed him again more passionately and Luke grew aroused.

He was the one who pulled back this time. "We can't do this here."

"Why not?" Riley said, trailing a hand down his stomach.

Luke caught her hand before she reached her primary destination. "It's your mom's house, in your childhood room, and there is a houseful of people. There's no way I can do this here."

Riley rolled over on her back and stared up at the ceiling. "Please tell me you aren't going to make me wait until our wedding night."

Luke turned over and looked at her. Riley looked so pretty lying there completely frustrated. He hated to tell her, but it was exactly what he was going to do only because there was no way he could make love to her in her mother's house full of people. Luke didn't say anything, but Riley turned her head and caught his look.

"You're killing me," she said exasperated.

"I'm the guy! It's supposed to be me who can't wait." Luke pinched her playfully on the side.

"I know. The wedding just feels so far away. If I had known this is what you were planning, I would have just stayed at a hotel," Riley whined uncharacteristically. She rolled over to face him and bobbed her eyebrows up and down. "Are you sure there isn't a way I can entice you?"

"There's always a way you can…" Luke didn't finish his thought because Jack called from the floor below. Luke frowned. "Duty calls." He got out of bed but had to wait to make himself decent and then he opened the door and stepped out into the hall. Riley groaned loudly as he left.

"What's up, Jack?" Luke said as he reached the top of the stairs.

Jack's face flushed. "I didn't mean to bother you guys. I got a call from Sharon Yates, Erik's sister. She wants to speak to us."

Luke raised his eyebrows. "The cops don't mind?"

"She refuses to speak to them. Sharon got my name from the interview Senator Crandall did with the media. She is insisting on only speaking to me. I called her back and told her we'd meet her."

"Let me throw on pants, and I'll be right down."

Luke went back into the room. Riley was sitting up in bed staring at her phone. She glanced up when he walked him. "What did Jack want?"

Luke explained about meeting Sharon Yates. "Jack said she wouldn't speak to the police."

"I'm sure that's going to go over well," Riley said sarcastically. "Cooper and I need to go back up to Austen Academy in an hour. I don't know how late I'll be."

Luke finished dressing and kissed her on the cheek before he left. "Be safe up there."

Riley nodded as he walked out the door. Luke bounded down the steps and met Jack at the front door. Together they walked to Jack's ride. In fifteen minutes, they were in downtown Troy pulling up in front of a brownstone. Jack explained, "The sister isn't from here. Sharon lives in New Hampshire. She came all the way here to collect her brother's things and is staying with a friend of a friend. She insisted she has information to help solve his murder."

Luke reached for the door handle. "Is there a reason she didn't want to talk to Det. Ward?"

"Sharon said it was delicate and she didn't want to give the cops the wrong idea about her brother."

"Fair enough," Luke said as they exited the SUV. Luke followed Jack up the few steps to the front door. The sidewalk was slick from rain earlier in the evening and night had fallen. The wrought-iron lampposts dotted the street every few feet. Downtown Troy had beautiful architecture with many original brownstones from the late 1880s. The one Sharon was staying in didn't disappoint.

Before they could knock, a petite woman wrapped in an oversized cardigan sweater answered the door. Sharon introduced herself and ushered them into the living room. "I can get you coffee if you'd like something warm to drink."

They declined. As they all sat in the living room, Jack started, "You said on the phone you didn't want to talk to the cops. I'd be happy to hear what you have to say, but we aren't investigating your brother's murder. We'd need to pass the information on to the detective."

Sharon nodded in understanding as she tightened her ponytail and brushed strands of hair out of her eyes. She pulled her legs up on the couch and tucked them under her. "I understand. I'm hoping what I tell you might be helpful, but I don't know if it will lead to finding his killer or not. My goal was for you to evaluate, and if we need to take it to the detective, we can."

"Sounds reasonable," Jack said.

Sharon exhaled a breath, explaining more. "I've worked with cops before. I know they can take innocuous information and run with it like a dog with a bone. I'm just trying to protect my brother's reputation."

Luke leaned forward on the couch with his arms resting on his legs. "I'm sorry for your loss. I understand wanting to protect Erik's reputation so we will help in any way we can. Why don't you just start wherever is most comfortable for you. We can ask questions when you're done."

Sharon didn't look them in the eyes, but rather, stared at the floor between them as she spoke. Her grief was like a blanket around her. Luke wanted to tell her it would get better, but sometimes he didn't think it did. He still mourned for his sister in little ways every day.

"Erik loved teaching history," Sharon started, "and he loved teaching at Austen Academy for the most part. He had many offers, but he chose here. Erik enjoyed the city and the campus, but it wasn't always easy for him. There aren't many male teachers on campus. Some of the students and the teachers were flirtatious. It made him intensely uncomfortable. Erik was always cognizant of how he was perceived. He'd seen the scandals of male teachers at all-girls boarding schools. He kept his distance until he met Maddie."

Luke knew he had promised to wait, but Sharon paused so he asked, "You knew about your brother's relationship with Maddie?"

Sharon frowned. "Relationship isn't the word I'd use. Friendship, maybe. Maddie reminded him of my daughter. She was inquisitive and loved history as much as Erik did. Their friendship would have been fine had it not been for a few of the other students."

Luke and Jack shared a look. "Who?" Jack asked.

"Some group called the Clovers. They were the ones trying to seduce Erik."

CHAPTER 44

"Seduce?" Luke asked, leveling a look at Sharon. He wasn't sure he had heard correctly.

"Seduce," she said again with emphasis. "I know it might seem like a strong word, especially in the context of adolescent girls, but it was the word Erik used. In January, a few of the girls in the Clovers started visiting Erik after hours at his cottage. The first time, the group of girls said they were out for a walk and stopped by to say hello. Erik didn't think much of it. The girls roamed around campus all the time. The visits became more frequent though. Many times, he'd just shut off his lights and pretend he wasn't home."

"All the same girls or different ones?" Jack asked.

"The same ones. There were three of them — Cara, Ginny, and Natalie." Sharon reached across the couch and grabbed for a small journal and opened it up on her lap. She glanced down at it, read for a moment, and then looked back up at them. "I wrote some things down so I'd remember. I only have their first names, unfortunately. Erik didn't tell me much about who they were. He just said they were part of a secret society no one was supposed to know about, but everyone knew anyway. Erik said the girls received special attention and privileges the other girls didn't receive. They were a real force on campus. Erik told me they had secret rituals and ceremonies, but he didn't give me specifics about that. It all seemed a bit strange to have a secret society everyone knew about. It was like they were flaunting it."

"That seems to be the consensus about them," Luke agreed. "Did Erik tell you anything else about the girls who were visiting him?"

Sharon nodded and brushed hair away from her face. "Erik said the girls all came from wealthy powerful families, and he worried about angering them. Erik said he tried to speak to the school administration about their visits, but he was encouraged to be friendly and supportive of the girls. He didn't want to make too big of a deal about it because he tried to just fly under the radar."

Luke shook his head not understanding. He asked what he thought was an obvious question. "Erik went to someone in the school administration and told them these girls were trying to seduce him, and he was told to placate them and be nice?"

"Sorry for the confusion," Sharon said. "I don't believe Erik told anyone in the administration about the girls flirting with him. Erik wanted someone in the administration to know these girls were visiting his cottage in the evening, showing up to chat with him in his classroom even though they didn't have a class with him, and were going out of their way to spend time with him. Erik wanted it on record this wasn't something he was encouraging or participating in and wasn't comfortable with. Erik's biggest fear was someone accusing him of being inappropriate with one of these girls."

Jack sat forward on his chair. "Is there a reason he had such a fear? I'm asking basically if it was grounded in something that happened to him?"

"No, nothing like that," Sharon assured. "A few years ago, a friend of Erik's, a fellow teacher, was teaching at a boarding school in New Hampshire. He was accused of having a sexual relationship with a seventeen-year-old student. The girl later recanted her story, but it destroyed his reputation. He left teaching for good and said he'd never go back."

"Was any part of the allegation true?" Luke asked. He saw the confused look on Sharon's face so he rephrased. "It's rare that women and girls make up stories about sexual assault. It doesn't happen often, but it does happen for a variety of reasons. Just because the student recanted her story doesn't mean it wasn't true."

Sharon nodded in understanding. "Well, that's kind of the point Erik made. He never knew for sure if the allegations were true or not, but this drove home the point for him that once someone is accused, the suspicion sticks – even with people who once completely trusted them. Erik made sure no one could ever even hint at impropriety going on in his life with his students."

It was Luke's turn to not understand. Skeptically, he asked, "If that were true, why would Erik let himself get so close to Maddie? It seems like the relationship could raise the same kind of concerns."

Sharon smiled sadly. "I asked Erik the same question, but he said Maddie was different. In a lot of ways, she was as out of place as he was there. Maddie looked up to him. It might have crossed from teacher to friendship, in a mentorship sort of way, but nothing more. Erik had no worries Maddie had any interest in him and he kept fairly firm boundaries even though he was friendly with her."

Luke understood, sort of. It wasn't something he'd ever do but understood how it could happen. Luke refocused the conversation. "What did Erik do about the Clovers? You said they were trying to seduce him so there has to be more than stopping by his cottage and flirting."

"There is more," Sharon said, an edge of fear and regret in her voice. "It escalated in March. It started one Saturday night. Natalie showed up alone at his cottage close to ten at night. It was well past the time she was supposed to be in her dormitory. Erik told me Natalie was crying and upset. He didn't ask her in, but she brushed past him and sat on his couch. As soon as Natalie got inside his cottage, her mood changed. She started flirting with him. She straight out asked him if he thought she was pretty. Erik said he didn't respond. Natalie then got up and came over to him and tried to kiss him. He said he pushed her back and immediately called her housemother, another teacher."

"Erik didn't kick her out of his house?" Jack asked.

"Erik couldn't. Natalie was a student breaking curfew. While the campus was safe at night, he'd be responsible if something happened to her so Erik called another teacher to come and get her."

Luke looked at her. He knew the answer before he asked. "Heidi Sykes?"

"Yes, her. Erik said she came down immediately and got Natalie. She apologized and said she'd handle it. Erik wasn't comfortable with that. He wanted to speak to Headmistress Winslow, but Heidi told him Natalie was going through a really hard time and assured him it wouldn't happen again."

This story was getting worse by the second. If it went down the way Sharon was describing, Luke understood Erik's discomfort. He asked, "It didn't stop?"

Sharon shook her head. "It happened three more times. Not quite the same way. The final incident was when Erik came back from class to find Natalie and Cara sitting in his living room. He had no idea how they got in. Erik picked up the phone to call Headmistress Winslow directly, but Cara said she'd tell everyone he tried to have sex with her. Erik said he put the phone down and asked what they wanted. He said it was clear they had an agenda that had nothing to do with sex."

"What was that?" Jack asked.

Sharon smirked. "They wanted Erik to stop spending time with Maddie. They were jealous. Erik called Cara's bluff. He called Headmistress Winslow and they all ended up in her office. Erik told Headmistress Winslow about Cara's threat before the meeting. Of course, Cara denied she ever said it. Nothing came of the whole debacle. The girls were free to continue harassing him, but it stopped. Two days later Maddie was dead. I've never seen my brother so distraught. He thought about not going back to the school."

Sharon paused and took a deep breath. "I wish he hadn't gone back. He'd be alive now."

Luke dropped his eyes to the floor and cursed. The pieces started to come together. When he spoke again, Luke's voice was strained. "They weren't jealous," he explained. "They were worried Maddie told Erik about Natalie stealing tests from another teacher. They were harassing Maddie from March to May. I bet this was an attempt to isolate Maddie further."

Sharon teared up. "The poor kid. I knew Erik was looking into what happened to Maddie. I think that's what got him killed."

Luke winced. "Did he ever mention a student named Jane to you?"

"Once or twice. Erik said she had asked about his relationship with Maddie. He said Jane was concerned the relationship had been inappropriate. Erik told me Jane believed him. He hadn't said that much else about her. Is she the girl who's missing?"

Jack nodded. "Not only is Jane missing, but we have reason to believe she might have witnessed your brother's murder."

Sharon sniffed back a sob. "Do you think you'll be able to find her?"

"We hope," Luke said. "You mentioned Heidi Sykes, but did Erik ever mention Irene Hodge to you?"

"His neighbor, right?" Sharon asked. Jack confirmed, and she picked up her journal again and thumbed through it. She stopped on a page and read the content. "The only thing I noted in here is Erik said Irene was attractive and they had a few things in common. It wasn't a name he brought up much."

Jack leaned forward. "Did Erik mention anything about Irene's relationship with Jane?"

"Nothing. Jane and Irene were not my brother's focus of concern."

Jack looked at Luke. "You have anything else to ask?"

Luke clasped his hands together. "Who do you believe killed your brother?"

Sharon put the book to the side and remained quiet for several moments.

Luke wondered if she wasn't sure or was just measuring her words carefully.

She finally said quietly, "I keep coming back to the same person over and over again. Heidi Sykes. She protected those girls. I never got a good feeling when Erik talked about her." She locked eyes with Luke. "I can't say for certain, of course, but I'm very suspicious of her." Sharon paused a beat too long. "If not Heidi, I thought it might be the mystery woman my brother was dating."

Luke leaned forward not sure he had heard correctly. "We didn't know Erik was dating anyone."

"Erik refused to tell me anything about her. There's only one person who knew and that's his friend, Steve. I asked him recently, but he wouldn't break Erik's confidence. Maybe you can get him to tell you." Sharon rattled off an address and phone number.

CHAPTER 45

Cooper and I walked back to Austen Academy about fifteen minutes before we were supposed to meet the student. The air had turned so chilly Cooper borrowed a scarf from my sister before we left the house. If Liv had something besides fluffy knitted hot pink mittens, he might have borrowed those, too.

"I forgot how cold it can get here," Cooper said as we walked on up the side entrance of the school and waved to the cop who was still sitting at the blocked off entrance. "Is Det. Ward still on campus?" I asked him.

"Haven't seen him in a few hours," the young cop responded. "Are you going to be long tonight?"

I shrugged. "It's just an interview. It shouldn't take too long." I hadn't wanted to tell him the student was sneaking out of her dorm to meet us. She was technically supposed to be in for curfew at nine, but she wasn't meeting us until nine-thirty. Earlier when I had mentioned it to Cooper, he said he hadn't known. It was the time she had picked.

The cop waved us through and didn't even say a word when we went left toward the athletic center instead of straight to the main part of campus.

Cooper shivered. "I'm glad he knows you. It wouldn't be much fun standing around here getting hassled. I hope she's there on time and is quick with information."

I agreed with him. I was used to the cold, but the air had a bite about it tonight. "How's Adele doing? I haven't seen her much since you arrived."

"Adele is great. She loves your mom. They have been chatting while they are both at the house. I think Adele is exhausted and is using this trip as a break from life. It's been a lot for her in the last year. Finally solving her sister's murder last year and the move to Little Rock and all that entailed. She's been busy getting her new law firm up and running. It's all great stuff, don't get me wrong. Adele is just beat – mentally and physically."

I completely understood. Too many life changes all at once can have that effect. "I'm glad she's finding some rest at the house then. My mom has a way of making everyone feel at home." It was one of the things I liked best about my childhood home. No one ever felt like a guest. It was cozy and comfortable and laid back. I was happy my friends were enjoying it now.

We walked past the athletic field and down the hill toward the teachers' cottages. With Erik deceased and Irene on the run, the area was desolate and more than a little creepy. It set my teeth on edge. I hated the feeling that washed over me when I traveled to this part of the campus. We cut back behind Irene's cottage and entered into the woods. Twigs snapped and leaves crunched under our feet. The sounds magnified against the silence.

Cooper spotted her before I did. He pointed her out sitting on a tree stump off to our right. His eyes were much better than mine. The trees, although most had lost their leaves, were dense the closer we got to the tunnel entrance.

Cooper said hello and introduced us. "Riley is the one who has been investigating this longer. Jane's father, Senator Crandall, is the one who hired Riley and Jack. I'm just helping out, but we'd be happy to hear what you have to say. Can we get your name?"

"Deanna," she said slowly, giving us her name but nothing else. Her hair had been pulled up in a high ponytail with wisps of bangs across her forehead. With her bulky coat and scarf, it was hard to tell much about her shape. She, like many of the girls, looked older than her years.

"Is there something you wanted to tell us about Jane?" I asked.

"It's not about Jane," she started and then stopped. "It might be about Jane. I don't know. I just know something I think might be helpful."

Cooper nodded. "Is there a reason we can't talk inside the school?"

"I don't want anyone to know this information came from me. Nobody would ever suspect I'd break anyone's loyalty, and I want to keep it that way." Deanna glanced past us.

"I get it. We can keep this confidential between us." I wanted to sit and listen, but there was nowhere to do that. Standing among the leaves was the only option. The wind whipped my hair around and the biting cold stung my face. I wanted Deanna to hurry up and spill it, but I knew better than to push someone willing to talk.

I encouraged, "Just take your time and tell us what you think is important."

Deanna took a breath. "First, you need to know I'm a senior and a Clover. I was in Natalie's pledge class, and there isn't much we don't know about our members." She leveled a look at us. "Meaning, what I'm telling you is firsthand information. It's not something I heard from someone who heard it from someone else. What I know I saw and heard myself."

"Good to know," Cooper said, his tone level and serious.

Deanna pushed her backside back on the tree stump so her legs dangled and her coat bunched up around her middle. "You probably think this started with Natalie stealing some tests. It didn't. It started when Heidi Sykes took over the Clovers a few years ago. Since then, the pledging has been harder, the loyalty tests more dangerous, and the bullying out of control. My oldest sister went here the year Heidi took over. I'm a legacy. All five of my sisters have been Clovers. I'm the youngest. I didn't want to be a Clover. I thought it was pretty lame, but it's a family thing so I did it."

I appreciated Deanna giving us the context. She knew how to tell a story. I could tell right off we were dealing with an intelligent girl. Maybe an angry girl, too. "What role does Heidi play in the Clovers?"

Deanna smiled. "That's the thing. She's not supposed to play any role. Sure, she's an alumnus of the school and the Clovers, a teacher and our housemother, but there has never been a teacher who was hands-on within the Clovers. The seniors are supposed to run the society and then we network with alumni. Heidi, though, couldn't let go of the control. As soon as she started as a teacher here, she was directly involved." Deanna spoke with her hands emphasizing her point. "I mean with everything – what girls were tapped to join, what happened during pledging, choosing each girl's loyalty tests, and all the activities. None of us girls had any say whatsoever. We are supposed to vote who gets a bid to join. That hasn't been my experience."

I had questions, but I wanted her to keep going so I tucked them away for later. Cooper appeared to do the same.

Deanna watched us carefully, and when we didn't comment, she went on. "Heidi had a real rivalry with Ms. Hodge. I don't know why. I didn't understand it, and I don't think Ms. Hodge even knew about it. Heidi is the kind of woman jealous of everyone – really territorial and controlling. Later, after we finished pledging, it was Heidi who chose our loyalty tests."

With eyebrows raised, I asked, "It was Heidi who told Natalie to steal the tests from Irene Hodge?"

"Yes. When one of the other girls asked Heidi why and reminded her it was against the ethics code and probably a crime to break into her office, Heidi brushed us off. She said we wouldn't get in any trouble so nothing to worry about."

Deanna paused again waiting to see if we had anything to say. When we didn't, she continued, "Natalie told Heidi that Maddie saw her that night. Heidi goaded Natalie into harassing Maddie, but it didn't take much. Natalie is just like Heidi, two peas in a pod. They both teamed up to give Maddie a hard time. Maddie was such a sweet girl. I don't even think she was going to tell anyone. If Natalie had just dropped it, Maddie might have as well. But it didn't happen. In some ways, I think they pushed Maddie to tell, and right before she could, she was dead. It wasn't a suicide. No one on this campus believes that."

Cooper stepped towards her. "Do you know who killed Maddie?"

Deanna held up her hand. "Before I get to that, you should know something else. Heidi and Natalie didn't like Maddie's relationship with Mr. Yates. They worried Maddie would tell him. They hatched a plot to make it look like Mr. Yates was being flirtatious with his students to try to get him fired, but he didn't take the bait."

Cooper asked about the plan, and Deanna detailed for us the many trips Natalie and a few of the girls took to his cottage late at night, the flirtatious conversations they tried to engage him in, and even the few times they outright hit on him, which failed to produce even mild interest.

"Mr. Yates wasn't giving in. Of course, from what we know now, he also had no idea what was going on with Maddie. She never told him. I heard it was her roommate who finally told Mr. Yates in September. It didn't matter though if he knew or not. Natalie was jealous of the attention he paid Maddie anyway. They wanted him disgraced and fired and wanted Maddie too scared to tell anyone."

Deanna got quiet, so I asked, "Now can you tell us who killed Maddie?"

"I wish I knew for sure, but I don't," Deanna said dryly. "The last time anyone saw Maddie was Friday night around eight. Her body was found the next day. Nobody could find Heidi that Friday night, which was unusual because she was normally right there with us night and day. The only relief we got was class time. I also heard the knots that were used were clove hitch knots. Heidi took us all sailing. She showed us how to make those knots. Heidi told Natalie she was going to take care of the problem one way or the other and not to worry. She said that in front of all of us. Heidi said no one was going to mess with the Clovers. A week after that conversation, Maddie was dead."

Cooper and I shared a look. Neither of us was surprised. She had been my prime suspect the entire time. From the first time I saw her, I knew something was off.

Deanna hopped off the tree stump. "I'll tell you something else, too. Heidi took us all to a gun range once. She said if we were going to be out there in the world, we had to know how to defend ourselves. If I were the cops, I'd be looking at her for Mr. Yates' murder, too."

CHAPTER 46

Deanna didn't have much else to share. We asked a few follow up questions for clarification, but there were no more bombshells. She didn't know where Jane went or why she was missing. The only thing Deanna said about Jane was that Heidi purposefully asked her to join the Clovers to keep an eye on her, but Jane proved to be more difficult to manage than Maddie and Erik combined. Deanna and some of the Clovers had speculated Jane's disappearance had something to do with the murders, but no one knew for sure.

After Deanna left, Cooper and I stood among the trees and talked about what she had just told us. "Do you think she's credible?" Cooper asked.

"I do. She had no reason to tell us all that. Deanna also doesn't seem like she has a real tie to the Clovers in the same way the other girls do."

"We have to tell Det. Ward," Cooper said as we started our walk out of the woods. "I'm not sure how he'll take it. Even when I had suspicions about Heidi, he didn't seem to take it very seriously. How are we going to share the information and still protect Deanna?"

"I don't know, but we have to. Let me worry about Miles. He only occasionally pays attention to what I have to say, but maybe I can convince him."

I stared off in the direction of the school as we walked through the woods, but in my periphery, I caught the flicker of light off to my left. I tugged on the back of Cooper's shirt and pointed. Quietly, I whispered, "There's someone over there."

Cooper followed my finger with his eyes. "Looks like a flashlight. Let's go check it out."

The biggest challenge was walking quietly through the blanket of twigs and leaves. We managed, but it wasn't easy. As we got closer to the light, we realized it was coming from inside Erik Yates' cottage. There was someone inside.

"Do you think it's a cop?" Cooper asked.

"No. The cottage has electricity. Why would a cop come sneaking around in the dark?" We inched closer to the cottage but still couldn't see anything other than the light from the flashlight through the window.

I waited back at the edge of the woods while Cooper crept up to the window in the back of Erik's place. It was probably the same window Jane had been looking in the night of the murder. Cooper stayed there crouched low for several minutes. Then he turned and waved me back farther into the woods. When I didn't move fast enough, he got up and grabbed me by the arm and dragged me with him as he went. "There's someone in there," he whispered.

"Can you see who it is?"

"No. It looks like they are searching for something." Cooper pulled me behind the trunk of a thick tree. "Do you have your phone?"

I pulled it from my pocket. "You think I should call Det. Ward?"

"We are catching someone in the act of breaking into a crime scene. If this doesn't jolt him to action nothing will."

I stepped farther into the woods, hopefully out of earshot of the person in the house. It rang right through to voicemail. I hung up and tried again. Miles finally answered, sounding groggy like he'd been sleeping.

"Miles, I need you. I'm at the Austen Academy in the woods behind Erik Yates' cottage. There is someone inside with a flashlight searching around. You need to come now or send someone down here."

"I'm on it," he said, fully awake now. He clicked off before saying anything else. As I made my way back to where Cooper stood,

I received a text from Miles, letting me know the cops at the front gate were on their way down. He told me to make sure the person didn't get away. I wasn't sure what I was supposed to do. I wasn't exactly going to tackle them.

"Watch the house," I said to Cooper as I finished reading the text. "Miles is sending cops down, but we need to make sure whoever is in the cottage doesn't leave. We are going to need to confront them if we have to."

Cooper nodded and shoved his hands in his pockets. "I'm too cold to get physical with anyone, but I'm going to hope I don't have to."

I cursed louder than I meant to as I watched the light bounce toward the door. "Looks like you're going to have to. The person is leaving, and the cops aren't here yet." I glanced up the hill toward the main part of campus but didn't see any cops on their way down. I didn't even wait for Cooper. I took off in a run towards the cottage. I knew Cooper was following and would catch up to me quickly. I wasn't a runner by any stretch. But I made it to the front door just as the person exited.

"What are you doing?" I said to the hooded figure as they stepped out onto the tiny front stoop.

The person turned to me and I stepped back, completely shocked. Words caught in my throat. "Headmistress Winslow? What are you doing sneaking around in the dark?"

Her eyes caught mine, and for a second, I thought she might run. She glanced over my shoulder and saw Cooper. She let go of the door and tugged off the hood from her head.

Cooper asked, "If you needed something in the cottage, why not just tell the cops?"

Winslow didn't respond. "I'm leaving," she said and turned to do just that. She came face to face with the cop who had waved me onto the school grounds earlier that night.

"What's going on?" he asked, looking between us.

"I'm not sure. I was hoping Headmistress Winslow could explain why she's sneaking around a closed crime scene at night."

The cop nodded, clearly wanting to know the same thing. Winslow didn't explain. The cop hesitated not sure what to do. "Det. Ward only told me to stop whoever it was. He didn't say to detain them."

"I'm going then," Winslow said. She stepped off the porch, but I wasn't letting it go. I was hot on her heels behind her.

"You can't walk away that easily," I said to her back. She didn't even turn around to look at me so I continued to follow her to the top of the hill, past the athletic building, and into the driveway entrance. "Det. Ward will be here any minute and will want to speak to you."

Winslow stopped in her tracks and spun around to face me. "What exactly do you think you're doing here this late?"

"I had permission to be here. There was a witness who wanted to speak to me."

Winslow took a few steps and was right in my face. "Who?"

"Confidential," I responded. She started to argue, and I held up my hand. "I don't have to tell you. The witness had information she thought was pertinent and she shared it. What you might want to be concerned about is why this person felt they had to sneak around to tell me instead of just going to the police."

Winslow contorted her face like she had been slapped. "I'd never stop anyone from speaking to the police."

"I didn't say the witness was afraid of you, but you have allowed dysfunction to grow here at the school like cancer. Now, it's impacting everything."

Winslow blinked rapidly. "I don't know what you're talking about."

"Don't you?" I let the question hang.

She swallowed hard but didn't respond. At this point, I knew silence was Winslow's defense mechanism. She didn't ramble like many witnesses. She just shut down and didn't say anything. Whether it gave her time to think or she thought it made her look tough, I wasn't sure. It made me think she had something to hide.

Winslow was about to walk away again when bright headlights pushed us both out of the road. Miles pulled his SUV to a stop a few feet from us. He cut the lights and got out of the car.

"What's going on, Riley? Why aren't you back down at the cottages?" he asked stepping towards me. His tone had the edge he used with Winslow before.

I explained about the cop refusing to detain her and then following Winslow as she left. "I wasn't sure what you wanted me to do."

Miles stepped back to his car and reached inside. He slammed the door shut and returned with handcuffs. He started reading Winslow her rights.

"Hold on. Hold on," Winslow screeched, interrupting him. "I have every right to be in the cottage. It's a staff residence. I don't need anyone's permission!"

"It's an active crime scene. You need my permission." Miles reached for her wrists and clamped the handcuffs on. He hadn't cuffed her behind her back though. I thought that was probably a gesture of goodwill.

Miles nudged her toward his car. "If you want to talk, you can do it down at the station."

It was the first time I saw fear in Winslow's eyes. "I'll talk right now." She thrust her handcuffed hands toward Miles. "Take these ridiculous things off me, and I'll talk right now."

Miles held on for a few moments longer, letting the tension rise. Finally, he looked at her. "You are going to tell me everything right now. If not, I'll put them back on and take you down to the station. The morning newspaper's headlines can tell the whole city how you interfered with a crime scene."

Winslow exhaled a breath. "I'll tell you what you want to know."

Miles undid the cuffs and stepped back. "You've said that. Now talk."

Winslow rubbed her right wrist. "I thought there might be some evidence of Erik being with his students in an inappropriate way that might be important to recover to protect his reputation."

Miles wasn't buying it. "To protect Erik's reputation or protect the school?"

"Erik...okay the school, too," Winslow admitted slowly. "A teacher had come to me with some concerns awhile back. I didn't think anything of it at the time, but now this happens. It makes you think."

I pinned my eyes on her. "Wasn't Erik the teacher who came to you with concerns when girls in the Clovers were acting inappropriately towards him?" Miles glanced at me surprised. When Winslow didn't respond, I said, "If I recall from a witness statement, your advice to Erik was to placate the girls. You left Erik vulnerable while he was pleading for your help."

"It was his fault," Winslow barked. "He never knew how to play by the rules here. Those girls were just being young and foolish, but I had reason to believe he took advantage of that."

"Let me guess – from Heidi Sykes?" I asked sarcastically.

"Yes!" Winslow said. "Right before Erik died Heidi convinced me it was too much risk to have Erik around the girls. I had planned to fire him."

"Did Erik know this?" Miles asked.

"No, I had only just decided."

"Heidi lied," I interjected. "Heidi planned to get Erik fired because she was afraid Maddie had told him about the cheating. She's the one who sent those girls to Erik's cottage. She's the one who instructed Natalie to steal the tests. She's the one who orchestrated this whole thing."

"No..." Winslow said adamantly. Then she stepped back as realization fell over her face.

"I think I need to bring in Heidi Sykes for questioning," Miles said.

"Finally," I responded dryly.

CHAPTER 47

It was later than Luke had planned to be out. He and Jack had gone to Steve's house only a few blocks over from where they had met Sharon. At first, they thought it might be better to wait until the next day given the approaching eleven o'clock hour, but Steve wasn't even home. They had hoped to interview him about Erik Yates' girlfriend.

As they were walking away from Steve's door, a neighbor taking out the trash told them Steve was at a bar a few streets over. The neighbor hadn't given the name of the bar, but Jack said he knew where he was going. He didn't. Once they walked a few blocks, Jack realized just how many new bars and restaurants dotted the streets of downtown Troy. Most were closed at that late hour, but a few were still open. They walked in and out of a few hoping to find him. No luck.

It was in the last bar on the street where they found Steve and one other guy sitting on barstools talking about football. Steve introduced himself before he realized who they were. When Jack told him, he slid a twenty on the bar and started to leave.

"Wait," Luke called after him. "Erik's not in any trouble. We were just hoping you might know who Erik's girlfriend was."

Steve turned, his face red both from the beer he drank and his rising anger. "My friend is dead because of that place. Do you think I'm going to help you ruin his reputation? Fat chance of that!"

"You don't get it," Jack said calmly. "We talked to Erik's sister. We know all about what they were doing to Erik. We are on your side here. I'm just trying to find a missing girl before she ends up the same as Erik – dead."

Steve scratched his head. "The girl that's missing. You think she's connected to Erik?"

Luke stuck his hand out and introduced himself to Steve. "We just want to find Jane. We have reason to believe she witnessed Erik's murder, which is why she's on the run. But someone is after her."

Steve narrowed his eyes. "You think the person who killed Erik might be after the girl?"

"We have reason to believe so," Jack said. "We just need to know what you know because it might just save a life."

Steve nodded once and turned around. "Come back to my place. We can talk there."

Jack and Luke followed Steve back to his house. Once inside, they sat in the sparse living room. "Can I get you anything?" Steve asked, pouring himself a glass of water and popping two aspirin.

Jack and Luke declined as Steve plopped down on a chair across from them. "Where do you want me to start?"

Luke tried to recall if he had heard Riley mention Steve's name or said anything about him at all. He didn't recall a thing. "Any cops been down to speak to you since Erik's murder?"

Steve kicked his legs out in front of him. "Nope and that's how I want it. They talked to a few other friends but not me. According to Erik, no one at the school or the cops are to be trusted. They hide the truth, according to Erik." He looked over at Luke and Jack and appraised them. "What do you want to know?"

Jack explained, "Sharon caught us up to speed about the girls coming by Erik's place, and the school administration who wouldn't stop them. We had no idea Erik was even dating anyone. Did you see Erik often?"

"A few times a week. Some weekends, he even signed off-campus like he was going out of town, and he'd just crash here. He needed the break."

Luke inched forward on the couch. "I know you said Erik didn't trust the school or the cops. I assume then Erik confided in you about what's been going on since last school term?"

"He did," Steve said. "Erik told me someone at the school killed Maddie, a student he had a close relationship with, earlier this year. He was trying to find out who killed her. He said the cops and school brushed it under the rug like it was a suicide. I told him to let it go, but Erik couldn't. It's most likely what got him killed."

Luke couldn't disagree with him. "Did Erik make any progress figuring out the killer?"

"Not that I'm aware of. At least he never told me he had." Steve took a sip of his drink. His eyes looked tired. Luke assumed maybe he hadn't been sleeping, given his friend's death. Steve took another drink and then set down the water glass. "Erik was going to apply for other jobs this year so he wouldn't have to go back to Austen Academy next year. He told me he was tired of teaching girls. He was going to try an all-boys boarding school next. He said it hadn't been a very good experience for him there."

No one, not even Sharon, had mentioned that to them, but Luke wasn't surprised. "Do you know if Erik got another job already?"

"No, he was just looking around to see what schools are out there. I don't think Erik could apply to anything until Spring."

"Understood," Jack said. He clasped his hands in front of himself. "I think what we most want to know is who Erik was dating and how that might factor into everything that's happened."

"How do you not know? I figured everyone up there knew."

Luke shook his head. "No one has said anything about Erik having a girlfriend. It was a surprise to us."

Steve nodded. "It was a fellow teacher. He lived near her so I told him it wasn't a good idea to date someone he worked with and lived practically right on top of, but he said she seemed nice – at first. Supportive, even."

Luke raised his eyebrows. "Irene Hodge?"

"That's her," Steve confirmed.

Jack asked, "You said at first Irene seemed nice. Did that change?"

"Yeah, she got all worked up earlier this year about his friendship with Maddie and those other girls who were stopping by his place. He tried to talk to Irene about it, but when the administration didn't do anything to help Erik out, Irene assumed he must have done something wrong."

"Did she break up with him?" Jack asked.

"Worse, she started getting psycho and controlling. She wanted him home at a certain time and for him to check-in at all hours. Irene wanted his relationship with Maddie to end. They fought about it all the time. Erik couldn't make her understand it was harmless. Irene told him he had to choose her or Maddie. Ridiculous, right?"

Luke had no idea what to make of the whole situation. "Did Erik choose?"

Steve looked down. "The decision was made for him. Maddie was dead within two weeks of that conversation."

Luke sat back defeated. For such a young girl, Maddie had made so many enemies doing nothing other than being a good kid. He looked over at Steve. "Did Erik suspect Irene might have had something to do with Maddie's death?"

"Not at first," Steve said, taking a sip of his water. "Irene swooped in and acted like she never even had the other conversation with him. She was back to being her super supportive self, but it never felt right to Erik. He started pulling away from Irene even more, which made her even crazier. But Erik couldn't escape her. He figured out what I said at the start – you don't have a relationship with someone you work with and live right near. There was no escaping it. That's part of the other reason Erik was looking for a new job."

"Did Erik live at the school over the summer or did he leave?" Luke asked.

"He left. Some summers he stayed, but this past one, he left. He stayed with his sister and then stayed here at my place. I offered to let him live with me this school semester, but he declined. Erik said he couldn't find the answers he needed about Maddie's death if he was removed from the campus. He wanted to live there and dig around for some answers."

"Erik was actively investigating Maddie's death?" Jack asked.

Steve nodded. "He talked to the cops and everything, but they told him to back off, too. He spoke to her parents a few times, but nothing came of it. They had no idea either."

Luke wanted a timeline of Erik's death in the days and hours leading up to it. It was one thing, among many, missing for Luke. "When was the last time you spoke to him?"

Steve cleared his throat and paused for a beat. "The night he died – about an hour before. That's how I knew Erik didn't kill himself. He seemed perfectly fine on the phone, and we had made plans for the next day. There was nothing to indicate he would have killed himself."

Luke stood and stretched. It was easier for Luke to think standing up. Although he didn't do it often because it could make witnesses nervous. Luke didn't think he'd have that problem with Steve. "What was Erik doing on the day leading up to the murder?"

Steve shrugged. "Regular school stuff. I've gone over this a thousand times and nothing seems out of place for me. Irene was giving him the same hard time she always gave him, but she had plans to be out of town that weekend. It was a welcome relief for Erik – a chance to breathe. He had a meeting with the headmistress of the school earlier on Friday, but he never mentioned the details of the meeting."

"What was Erik doing that night?"

"Nothing, we had spoken on the phone and then he was watching television. He didn't have plans. He said all was quiet." Steve glanced up at Luke. "I swear there was nothing out of the ordinary that indicated my friend would end up dead that night. I would have done something."

Luke believed him. There was something that had been bothering Luke though. "It seems odd to me that a teacher living on an all-girls school campus would need a gun. Has Erik always had a gun?"

Steve chuckled. "Erik hated guns. I have two legally registered and he didn't even like to see them. After Maddie was killed, he feared for his safety. He went and got a gun. I took him to the shooting range a few times so he'd be familiar with it."

"Did anyone else know Erik had bought a gun?" Luke asked.

"Not that I know of," Steve started, but then he paused. "Maybe he had to disclose it to the school administration. I'm not sure."

Luke and Jack looked at each other. Luke wasn't sure what other questions Jack might have. When Jack didn't say anything, Luke asked his final question. "Do you have any idea who killed Erik?"

"No, man, I don't. If I did, I'd have already gone public. I would have made it known until someone did something about it."

CHAPTER 48

The next morning, we gathered around my mother's kitchen table. She had made a French toast bake and had bought cinnamon rolls from a bakery down the street. The smell of freshly brewed coffee filled the air while Liv rambled about a coffee of the month club she had joined. Even though I was exhausted from the events of the previous evening, I smiled listening to my sister. Living in Little Rock, it was easy to forget how much I loved and missed my mother and sister.

Luke and I had tried to compare notes last night, but we didn't get far. Both of us fell asleep. I wasn't even sure who had been talking and who was supposed to be listening because sleep took over both of us at nearly the same time. We woke in a jumbled heap of blankets and limbs to sounds of chatter in the kitchen.

Over breakfast, Jack and Luke spent time telling us about everything that happened the night before, including surprising us all with the revelation that Erik and Irene had been dating. I had seen photos of them both. It was an odd pairing, to say the least.

Hearing what Erik's sister said about Heidi confirmed everything Deanna had told Cooper and me. I reminded them about seeing Heidi the night I was out with Miles. "What if Heidi wasn't down there to see Irene as she said. What if she was there because she killed Erik and wanted to make sure she hadn't left any evidence behind?"

"That's certainly a possibility," Jack said. He turned to Cooper. "What did your student witness have to say?"

Cooper spent a few minutes explaining what Deanna had told us the night before. He finished by saying, "If we believe Deanna, and I think she's credible, then we have to believe not only did Heidi know students were cheating, she is the one who had them steal the tests."

"Why steal from Irene though? Aren't they in the same department?" Luke asked.

"I didn't even think to ask that," I admitted.

Luke raised his eyebrows. "Could it have been over Erik? Irene was dating him, and by what Steve said, she was the jealous type. Maybe Heidi wanted him too or Irene knew she was sending the Clovers down there to his place. It seems like there was tension either way."

"That's as good a theory as any."

"What else did the student say?" Luke asked.

I went over our conversation in my head until I remembered what I thought was the most significant. "We all know Maddie was killed with the rope, which was tied with clove hitch knots. Deanna said Heidi had taken them all out sailing and taught them those knots. Any one of the Clovers could have known how to tie them. That wasn't all. She also took the girls to a gun range to have them practice shooting."

Luke nearly dropped his glass in surprise. "That doesn't seem like a normal activity of an all-girls school in upstate New York. I thought you all hated guns?"

I expected that kind of comment from Cooper but not from Luke. It was funny all the same – and weirdly true. Not that New Yorkers didn't have guns. My mother had a whole cache of them hidden upstairs. But Luke was right. Between all the Clovers learning how to shoot and Erik having a gun, it was a lot for an all-girls boarding school.

Jack's cellphone rang and he looked at the screen. "Senator Crandall," he said before excusing himself from the table.

Cooper got up and poured himself another glass of juice. He held the pitcher out to all of us. As Adele held up her glass, she said,

"I'm sorry I haven't been helpful at all. I've been trying to catch up with work and sleep."

I looked over at her and smiled. "You're fine. Relax all you want. This is the messiest case I've ever been involved in."

My mother, who had joined midway in the conversation, looked over the top of her glasses. "Are you any closer to figuring out what happened?"

"No," I said defeated. "Det. Ward is supposed to be interviewing Heidi this morning. Maybe we will get lucky and she'll confess to it all."

"I don't think there's a chance of Heidi confessing," Cooper said. "I tried every trick in the book to get information from her, but she wasn't giving it up."

Adele sipped her juice. "Have you ruled out the students?"

"I don't know that we've ruled anyone out," I admitted. "But I have trouble thinking high school girls killed their friend and shot their teacher."

Right now, Heidi and Irene were looking like the best suspects to me. They each had means, motive, and opportunity. Deanna said Natalie was just like Heidi, but I wasn't sure I could see her being a killer.

Jack finished his call and walked back into the kitchen. Before he sat down, there was a loud knock on the front door. He turned and answered it. From where I sat at the table, I could see it was Miles at the door. The heat rose in my face. Miles and Luke hadn't met yet, and I wasn't sure what to expect.

Jack walked Miles into the kitchen and introduced him. Luke locked eyes with me and smirked. He stood and shook Miles' hand. "Nice to meet you, Det. Ward. I hope you've enjoyed the time you've spent with Riley. She's told me about your adventures."

Miles coughed. "You have an incredible fiancé. She's an excellent investigator."

Adele smacked my leg under the table on one side and my sister nudged my knee on the other.

My mother stood, clearing some room at the table. "Let me get you some coffee and breakfast."

"Just coffee would be great." Miles stood against the wall, but Luke moved his chair over so Miles could sit next to him. A nervous laugh nearly escaped, but I kept my composure.

My mother poured coffee and carried it over to the table along with a cinnamon bun whether Miles wanted it or not. "Try it," she said. "I'm sure once you start eating, you'll realize you're hungry."

Miles thanked her and fixed his coffee from the cream and sugar on the table. When he was done, he took a sip and pulled off a piece of the pastry. "You're right, this is delicious," Miles said, winking at my mom.

"Did you have a reason for stopping by?" I asked.

"Riley, be nice to our guest," my mother scolded.

I thought I was being nice. "I'm just wondering what's up with the morning visit."

Miles smiled at me across the table. "I came to talk to Luke."

Luke looked at me surprised and back at Miles. "Okay," he said hesitantly.

Miles took another sip of his coffee. He set the cup down and said regretfully, "I spent the morning interviewing Heidi and didn't get anywhere. I couldn't even get her to admit to the things we know are true like her going to Winslow to lodge a concern Erik might be behaving inappropriately with students. She adamantly denied it."

"Are you sure Winslow isn't lying?"

Miles nodded. "Reasonably so. Based on the information Riley and Cooper obtained from the student they interviewed it was common knowledge among the Clovers Heidi was trying to get Erik fired. Unless this student and Winslow are cooking up some story to make Heidi look bad, it's Heidi who is lying."

"Understood," Luke said. "So, what do you need from me?"

Miles gave me a sheepish look. "I told the chief you were in town. Of course, everyone knows the great work you did catching the serial killer. I asked the chief if he'd allow you to officially interview Heidi and see if you can get anywhere with her. She hasn't lawyered up yet. The chief was fine with it as long as I was there. Would you be willing?"

It surprised me Miles would set aside his pride and ask Luke for help, but Luke's interview skills were some of the best I'd ever seen. If there was any detective who could get Heidi to confess, it would be Luke. Even Jack nodded his head, agreeing it was a good plan.

"Sure," Luke said. "I'd be happy to. What's the plan?"

"We are going to have to go back to the school to interview her. There's no way unless I arrest her that I'm getting Heidi back down to the station. When can you be ready to go?"

"Just let me shower and I'll be ready. It shouldn't take me more than twenty minutes." Luke got up from the table and went upstairs.

"I'm glad you're here, Miles, there's something else we need to address." Jack pointed to his phone. "Right before you came in Senator Crandall called me. He's very upset Riley hadn't given a statement on the news last night. He's insisting it happens today. He said he'd call the media himself and have them come here, which I know we don't want."

"I don't have the go-ahead if that's what you're asking me," Miles explained.

"I'm not asking you," Jack said sternly. "I'm telling you the interview with Riley is happening today. As long as she's on board with it."

I felt bad for Miles because he was stuck in the middle, but we had already waited too long and we hadn't made any significant headway. Jane could be dead by now for all we knew. "I'm in. Miles, I'm sorry, but we really can't delay it anymore. There's no point. Time is critical."

Miles nodded and then looked at Cooper. "I have one more favor to ask. Would you be willing to do some surveillance on Headmistress Winslow? I tried to get a team together, but my chief wouldn't authorize it. He said there's no way we are following her around. He practically ruled her out as a suspect even though after last night I'm starting to have my doubts. I just need someone to keep an eye on her while I'm handling some interviews."

"I'm in," Cooper said without even the hint of an argument.

Miles looked at me. "I'm really glad you're all here to help. I'm probably going to get fired for not keeping you all at bay, but the department is stretched thin and this isn't a one-man job."

CHAPTER 49

The first thing I needed to do before the massive press conference Senator Crandall had scheduled was speak to Natalie. I had no idea if she'd be willing to talk to me, but I hoped to catch her off guard enough she'd give in. The plan was for me to do that while Miles and Luke were interviewing Heidi. This way they couldn't collaborate as they had with Cooper yesterday.

After showering and getting ready for the day, I walked back over to campus. I worried I might have to fight through a crowd of media but most of them left me alone. Of course, they didn't know who I was yet, but they would later today when I made the statement.

As I walked to the school, I crafted exactly what I should say to the media. The goal was to let Jane know I was on her side. I also needed to convey I had the power to not only protect her, but I had to convince her I was willing to help. There was a balance that would take some finessing, especially because we didn't technically have the support of the police to make the statement. When I figured out exactly what I'd say, I refocused on the task at hand.

Finding Natalie today was going to be a challenge. We decided we didn't want to tip her off, so I had to locate her on the campus on my own instead of getting her class schedule. I had anticipated a morning of walking through halls and peeking in classrooms. I still had my pass from yesterday even though I was supposed to hand it in at the end of the day and sign in again. At this point, I hoped I was at least a familiar face on campus and no one would question me.

As I came through the side entrance, I waved to my cop buddy and then found myself in the middle of the quad looking at the buildings, wondering which one Natalie was in. I turned to the building where I knew history classes were taught, but then I heard my name. I spun around but couldn't figure out where it was coming from. Then I saw Annie jogging toward me, a stack of books in her arms.

"Have you heard anything about Jane?" she asked as she approached. Annie shifted the books to get a better grasp of them. I reached out and took a couple so she could situate herself a little better.

"Why are you carrying all these around?" I thought kids did everything on the internet.

"I have a paper to write and didn't want to do it in the library, so I'm headed back to my dorm," Annie explained. "About Jane – have you heard anything?"

"Mostly what you've seen on the news. We believe Jane is still alive, but we haven't found her yet."

Annie gave a hopeful nod. "People around here have been talking about Ms. Hodge being with Jane."

"The cops believe Ms. Hodge was at the cabin where Jane had been hiding out, but we don't know how she's involved in all of this, if at all. There are still a lot of unknowns."

Annie looked past me and then stepped closer to me. With her voice low, she said, "Ms. Hodge came looking for Jane last week before Jane went missing. I don't know if they ever got a chance to talk though."

"Ms. Hodge came to your dorm?"

"Yes, a few times in the evening, but Jane was never there. I told Jane to call her, but I don't think Jane ever did."

"Did Ms. Hodge ever tell you why she was looking for Jane?"

Annie furrowed her brow. "Ms. Hodge said she was worried about Jane and that she might be getting involved in things she wouldn't be able to handle. She said she could protect Jane so she needed to connect with her as soon as possible."

"When was the last time Ms. Hodge came looking for Jane?"

"It was Friday during dinner. I stayed back in my dorm and I saw Ms. Hodge in the hall. She seemed pretty surprised to see me, but I didn't think anything of it until later when I heard she was absent from school that day because she was going on a trip. But to be honest, I thought maybe she was going to leave for her trip that night. I didn't know people thought she had already left campus."

Miles would want to know. This was the first confirmation we had that Irene Hodge was on campus in the hours leading up to Erik's death. I reached out and put my hand on Annie's shoulder. "Would it be okay if I have Det. Ward call you? I'll tell him, but he might want to follow up with you."

"Sure, I didn't know if it was important or not," Annie said. The books slipped a little in her hands. She giggled, trying to juggle them. "I should get back to my dorm before I drop everything."

"Do you want some help?" It was out of my way, but Annie had just unknowingly provided critical information.

"Thanks, that would be great. Where you headed?"

"I'm trying to find Natalie Gallo. You don't happen to know where she is, do you?"

"She's at the pool or at least she was. I saw her there a little while ago before I went to the library."

I followed Annie back to her building. She chatted about school and some of her classes. I was happy she was able to find a little peace while she was still at the school. I wouldn't have wanted to stay, but it was a testament to how focused on her studies she was that Annie pressed on.

As I handed the books back to her at the front door, I reminded her, "Definitely call me if you need anything, Annie. Even if it's just to talk."

She promised she would and I waited while she disappeared into the building. I cut through the narrow walkway between the buildings to the back part of the school. I walked along the narrow walkway until I reached the athletic building. It was a quiet morning on campus. There wasn't a soul in sight. I pulled open the large glass door and stepped into the wide lobby. I made my way to the pool door entrance. I could hear the faint splash of water as soon as the chlorine smell hit my nose.

I stepped through to find an empty room and one lone swimmer. All I could make out were long lean limbs slicing gracefully through the water. It was hard to tell who it was, but I walked to the edge of the pool to get a better look. I saw the girl's dark hair and goggle strap. I still wasn't positive it was Natalie. "Excuse me!" I yelled loudly hoping she'd hear me. "Natalie!"

The swimmer slowed her pace and came to a stop in the middle of the pool. She planted her feet on the bottom and peeled off her goggles. She turned to face me. "You broke my concentration. What do you want?" she barked.

"Natalie, I was hoping to speak to you about Maddie and Jane."

"I don't know anything." Natalie reached her hand up to pull her goggles back over her eyes.

"That's not what I've been told. I'm here to make sure you're not in trouble for something someone else did."

Natalie blinked a few times, her face growing uncertain. "What do you mean?"

I sat down on the edge tucking my feet under me. "Natalie, you have to know people suspect you of hurting Maddie and maybe even Mr. Yates. I don't think you did that. You come from a good family. You wouldn't need to hurt anyone to get what you wanted. But that's not what other people think so given you were harassing Maddie they might blame you for her death."

Natalie shook her head. "I wasn't harassing her."

I held my hand up. "Poor choice of words. I know taking those tests wasn't about cheating. Heidi had you do it as a loyalty test for the Clovers, right?"

Natalie didn't say anything, but she moved closer to me in the water. "How do you know that?"

"People talk, Natalie. I also know it was Heidi who told you to make sure Maddie didn't tell. It sounds to me like the whole thing just got out of hand."

I waited a beat and when she didn't say anything I continued. "People are blaming you. Right now, my fiancé, who is a detective, is with Det. Ward talking to Heidi. Do you think she's going to take the blame and risk her career for you? She's not, Natalie, she's going to blame you. All the evidence points to you."

"I didn't do anything wrong." Natalie's face gave away her uncertainty.

"Right, I know. I just need you to talk to me to help me sort this out so I can convince the detectives it wasn't you."

Natalie didn't even hesitate. She moved quickly in the water to the edge of the pool and pulled herself up each ladder rung. "Let me change my clothes and we can talk. I'll tell you what I know."

CHAPTER 50

Luke and Miles found Heidi in the back part of the library, which was primarily used by teachers for research. She sat at a round table with her head bent over a book. Miles and Luke waited at the door for a moment, whispering over a plan of action and then proceeded into the room.

Heidi's head popped up as soon as she heard Miles' voice. "Heidi, I need to speak to you again. I have some follow up questions from last night."

Heidi sighed. "As you can see, I'm quite busy."

"This won't take long," Miles said and pulled out a chair from the table. Luke grabbed a chair as well. "This is Det. Luke Morgan. He is a detective from Little Rock helping to find Jane."

Heidi asked angrily, "Why would you be here from Little Rock? This doesn't have anything to do with you."

Luke rested his palms down on the table. "I think you spoke to Cooper, who I'm working with. There's a retired detective from Troy who was hired by Senator Crandall to find Jane. We are all helping him out."

"I see," Heidi said sternly. "Well as you know, I have no idea where Jane is. She refused to live in the dormitory where I'm the housemother so I don't know where she is. If Jane had made some better decisions, maybe this could have all been avoided."

"What questionable decisions has Jane made?" Luke asked.

Heidi closed her book and rested her hands on top of it. "She's a very troubled girl, Detective. I don't think she was getting the help she needed after her friend's suicide. I told this to Cooper though. I'm sorry, but I can't be of help to you. Now, I need to get back to my research."

Luke didn't get up. "What was your relationship like with Irene Hodge?"

"What does that have to do with anything?"

Luke smiled. "Irene is a person of interest in Jane's disappearance. She's also quickly becoming a suspect in the death of Mr. Yates. You know they were dating, right?"

Heidi faltered for the first time, seemingly unsure of what to say. Finally, she smiled. "I have better things to do than get involved in the campus gossip, but I had heard they were dating. Are you saying his death was a lover's spat?"

"That's what we are trying to figure out. That's why we asked how well you know her." Luke locked eyes on her. "You must have known her fairly well. She was the head of the English department and you taught a similar curriculum. I heard you were even working on a project for your students together."

"We did not have a project together," Heidi corrected him.

"Isn't that what you told us the night we found you at Irene's cottage late in the evening?" Miles asked, sitting back in his chair.

"Oh, right, well that..." Heidi stumbled. "I wasn't thinking of that because it had only been talked about. It wasn't something we ever got off the ground. I thought you meant something we were already doing together."

"You don't seem to like Irene much." Luke tapped on the table.

Heidi bit her lip, stalling for time. "Not really," she finally admitted, waving her hand dismissively. "I don't have to like everyone I work with. That isn't a job requirement."

"No, of course not," Luke said smugly. "Is your dislike for Irene the reason you had Natalie steal tests from her?"

"I did no such thing," Heidi said, red rising in her face.

Luke tapped on the table. "Yes, you did. I have a few witnesses from the Clovers who are willing to say that you did. Not just stealing tests, Heidi, but a whole host of other things you've put those girls through." Luke watched as her face fell. "What is wrong with you? You're the girls' teacher. You're supposed to be a role model. Instead, you're abusing them."

"I never abused those girls," Heidi argued. "I may have put them through exactly what I went through to join the Clovers. If you're going to be a part of a prestigious group, you have to prove your worth. You have to prove your loyalty. That's all I was doing – making sure the Clovers remained an exclusive society only joined by the worthiest."

"No, Heidi, you used those girls like your pawns," Luke countered. He slid back in his chair. "Was it your idea to kill Maddie when you couldn't shut her up? Did you do it yourself or did you have some of the girls do it for you?"

"You're disgusting. I didn't kill Maddie. I would never kill a student, and I certainly would never have young girls kill anyone."

Luke smirked. "But you'd kill another teacher?"

"That isn't what I meant. I wouldn't kill anyone."

Miles leaned forward. "I just don't think that's true, Heidi. Right now, I have officers searching your residence. When we find evidence that you killed Maddie and Erik, I'm going to bring you in and see that you spend the rest of your life in prison."

"I don't think you'll be able to boss around those prison ladies like you do your students," Luke said, nudging Miles. "What do you think? You think those ladies will take well to Heidi coming in there and telling them what to do?"

Miles shook his head. "They are going to eat her for lunch."

"I didn't kill anyone!" Heidi shouted.

Luke narrowed his eyes at her. "You took the Clovers sailing and taught them the clove hitch knot and then you took them to a gun range. Now, we have a student who ends up strangled with a clove hitch knot in the rope and a teacher who has been shot. You expect us to believe this was all a coincidence?"

Heidi didn't say anything. She tried to stare them down, but she was no match for Luke or Miles. When neither budged, Heidi's icy demeanor collapsed. Fear sparked in her eyes. "I swear to you, I didn't kill anyone. Search my place, search my computer, my phone – anything you want. You're not going to find evidence of anything."

Her pleas didn't mean anything to Luke. He had seen hardened criminals offer up the same thing because they knew, or at least believed, they had gotten rid of all the evidence and were smarter than the cops.

Acting bored, Luke rolled his eyes. "Heidi, I've heard this before. It means nothing to us. Your only hope is to cooperate. Trust me, we have investigators talking to each of the Clovers right now. Someone is going to roll on you. You think after everything you've put them through, one of those sweet girls isn't going to take her shot at taking you down? You can loyalty test them all you want, but when prison is involved, loyalty fades."

Heidi swallowed hard. "I don't know what more I can say. I didn't kill anyone. If Maddie didn't kill herself then I don't know what happened. I certainly didn't kill Erik either."

"But you did try to get him fired," Miles said. "Headmistress Winslow already confirmed it was you trying to have Erik fired."

Heidi tossed her hair around and held her head high. "I felt Erik was inappropriate with some of the girls. It's my job to protect them."

Luke laughed. "That's why you sent Natalie and a few of the other girls down to his house to flirt and try to seduce him. How far did you tell them to go? We can get you on charges right there."

Miles looked at Luke. "Sex trafficking, maybe?"

"Possibly, but there are a few other charges that might stick."

Heidi shook her head. "Those girls were eighteen. Adults in the eyes of the law."

"Not all of them," Miles said.

Heidi had fallen for the trap they set perfectly. Luke smiled. "You admit you tried to set up Erik?"

"Someone had to do something," Heidi admitted indignantly. "We all knew he had been spending too much time with Maddie. Something more had to be going on there. We had to catch him in the act."

"You used your students as bait," Miles said with disgust in his voice.

Heidi sat back but didn't say a word.

Luke pointed at her. "Erik wasn't doing anything. He was a mentor and friend to Maddie. That's all."

"There was more to it. You can't tell me different. I'm not stupid. Erik got what he deserved." Heidi crossed her arms over her chest.

"Did Maddie get what she deserved, too?" Miles asked.

Heidi looked at both of them. "I want my lawyer. I'm done talking."

Luke stood but Miles remained seated. He glared at her across the table. "You get a lawyer, but I'm still going to arrest you for murder and make sure you spend the rest of your life behind bars where you belong." Miles shoved his chair back with such force it fell over as he stood.

Neither of them said another word until they were out of the building, across the quad, and standing at the main entrance. Luke slapped Miles on the back. "That was some performance at the end."

Miles laughed. "You like that? I thought I'd leave a lasting impression. Do you think Heidi killed Erik?"

"I don't know. Usually, my gut gives me a good read one way or the other. I couldn't tell with Heidi. What would be her motive? Keeping Erik quiet about those tests being stolen?"

Miles didn't respond right away. He didn't seem to be sure either. Finally, he said, "I don't know if Heidi would do it just over the tests, but maybe he was getting wise to how she was setting him up. Maybe he confronted her and she got the gun away from him and shot him."

Luke thought that was possible. Since Steve had told him Erik wasn't a regular gun owner, the idea that someone had taken the gun from him and shot him seemed like a plausible scenario. He told Miles as much.

"You know Steve said Erik met with Headmistress Winslow earlier on Friday. Steve didn't know about what. Erik just said it wasn't a big deal. Do you have any idea why?"

Miles turned to Luke with his mouth slightly open in surprise. "No, I don't. Winslow said she was considering firing Erik but hadn't met with him yet. She mentioned nothing about meeting with him that day."

"I think you need to figure out why they met." Luke turned back to the administration building. "Want to try her now?"

"We might as well," Miles said, and they both walked back to the administration building.

CHAPTER 51

After Natalie pulled herself out of the water, I sat down on a bench at the far end of the pool and waited for her to shower and change her clothes. It took longer than expected so I was antsy, wondering if she had called her father to ask permission to speak to me. I worried I'd be shut out before I even got started.

By the time Natalie came out of the locker room dressed in jeans and a sweater, I had convinced myself the interview wasn't going to happen. It surprised me when Natalie dropped her gym bag near my feet and took a seat next to me. Her hair was still damp and she wore no makeup.

"What do you want to know?" Natalie asked, her voice strained and uncertain.

"I want to know the truth about what happened to Maddie."

Natalie nodded. "Can I really go to jail?"

I couldn't promise her anything because I had no idea what she had done, but I told her what I knew to be true. "Natalie, I don't think anyone wants to send you or anyone else your age to prison. You need to tell someone the truth."

Natalie reached for my arm. "I don't want to talk to Det. Ward. You've been a lot nicer to me than he has."

I smiled, thinking about how cocky Miles could come across and how it could look intimidating to a young girl. "Det. Ward is nice, but we are fine talking." I turned my body to face hers. "I know Maddie didn't kill herself. I also know you stole tests. I know you harassed Maddie, and I know Heidi put you up to it. I need to know what happened that night down in those tunnels."

Natalie looked down at her hands in her lap. She didn't make eye contact with me as she recounted what happened with her and Maddie on the lead up to that night. Nothing she told me was new. I had heard the information from everyone before. I let her talk though. Natalie had a story to tell and my only job right then was to listen without outward judgment. I cringed on the inside about how insidious and terrible adolescent girls could be to each other, but I couldn't let it show. Natalie had to believe I was on her side.

When Natalie got right up to the day of the murder, she stopped. I prodded her along. "It's okay, Natalie. You can tell me anything. I can't protect you if I don't know the truth."

"Heidi was really angry that Friday, but no one was sure why," Natalie started, finally exhaling a breath she had been holding in. "I think it had something to do with Headmistress Winslow not firing Erik Yates as she wanted."

I wanted her to focus on Maddie, so I said, "Tell me about when you first saw Maddie that day."

"I saw her twice actually. I passed by her when we were in the tunnels. I was heading back to my room after dinner and Maddie was headed in the opposite direction toward Mr. Yates' cottage. We all knew she took the tunnels when she'd go there and see him. I saw her later on her way back, too." Natalie sniffled.

I glanced over just as Natalie wiped her eyes with her hands. I hadn't even thought to bring tissues. Based on what I had heard about her, Natalie didn't strike me as a crier. "What happened when you saw Maddie later?"

"After I saw Maddie the first time, I went back and told Heidi. She was furious, even angrier than she had been earlier in the day. I didn't think it was a big deal. Maddie always went to see Mr. Yates, and I didn't think she had told him about stealing those tests because if she had, I would have been in trouble already. But Heidi was angrier than I had ever seen her. She told me to go confront Maddie on the way back and scare her."

"Scare her how?" I asked, hating where this was heading.

"You know, just yell at her and threaten to beat her up. We just wanted her to stay afraid of us. Heidi said to make it good." Natalie glanced over at me. Her big brown eyes rimmed in tears. "I didn't want to. I was sick of doing it. Maddie was an easy target. She didn't even fight back."

"What happened when you saw Maddie?"

"I waited for her in the tunnel. I knew she usually came back right before curfew. I could tell she was scared. People don't hang out in those tunnels. I think she sensed right away I was there for her. She asked what I wanted and I shoved her. Maddie fell back on the ground and promised me she hadn't told anyone and she wasn't going to. She said a few times she didn't want any trouble."

"What did you say?" I asked. I didn't want to listen to this. The flat unemotional way Natalie told me the story conveyed more than her actual words. She may have tears in her eyes, but I began to doubt she was sorry for anything.

"I told Maddie we had a problem with her even if she didn't have a problem with us. I was supposed to scare her. Maddie tried to stand up and I shoved her back down again. That's when Heidi showed up."

"Heidi was down in the tunnels with you?" I interrupted.

"Yeah. I was surprised to see her. The other times she told us to do things like this, Heidi stayed hands off, but this time she was there. Heidi told me to leave, that she would handle it."

"You left Heidi and Maddie alone in the tunnel?"

"Yeah," Natalie said seemingly surprised I asked. "She's a teacher. She told me to leave so I left."

"What happened after you left?"

"I went back to my room. It was probably about an hour or so before Heidi came back upstairs. We asked her what happened. She just said Maddie wouldn't be bothering us anymore and to stop asking questions. She went into her bedroom." Natalie sniffled again. "I swear I didn't know anything had happened to Maddie until the next day."

The hair on the back of my neck stood on end. I didn't believe a word Natalie said, but I played along. "Was Maddie found in the same place in the tunnels where you had shoved her?"

Natalie looked over at me finally making eye contact. "The very same spot. I knew at that point Heidi had done something to Maddie. We all knew she didn't kill herself, especially when we found out about the knots."

"How did you know clove hitch knots were used? That information wasn't public."

Natalie shrugged. "Headmistress Winslow gathered us all together the day after and told us. She wanted to know the last time each of us had seen Maddie. But Heidi told us not to say anything. I think Headmistress Winslow knew we were lying."

The implications of the entire thing were starting to paint a clear picture of what had happened, but I knew parts of it weren't right. I knew Natalie hadn't told me the full truth. "Are you sorry Maddie is dead?"

"Not really, if I'm being honest. Maddie betrayed us and that's just what happens sometimes. It's nobody's fault."

I swallowed hard. I was certain then I was sitting beside Maddie's killer. I didn't need to know the full details to know in my gut Natalie had killed her. I kept my tone steady and asked a few more questions, pushing at points and backing off. When I was certain I wasn't going to get Natalie to confess, I thanked her and told her I needed to go.

As we stood, Natalie reached her arm for me and I nearly flinched. She caught my look though. "Are you okay?" she asked suspiciously.

"I'm fine," I lied. "I think I'm just a little dizzy from the chlorine smell."

"Oh yeah, that happens sometimes." Natalie paused and waited, but when I didn't say anything, she asked, "You're going to make sure I don't get in any trouble, right?"

I smiled as best I could. "I need to talk to Det. Ward, but I'm going to tell him the good job you did in helping me."

"Good. That's important." Natalie stood there as I started to walk away. I was just to the door when she called after me. "You didn't even ask about Mr. Yates."

I pushed open the door to the hallway and held on to it tightly, fighting the urge to run. Turning back to her, I asked, "Did you know something about his death?"

Natalie didn't walk towards me. She just yelled from across the pool. "Heidi went to see Mr. Yates that night. She was very upset when she got back, but she didn't tell us what happened. When we found out he was murdered, we all thought it was her who killed him."

"I'll tell Det. Ward," I said and then I pushed open the hallway door and sprinted towards the main entrance of the athletic center. I wasn't a runner by any stretch, but Natalie scared me like I hadn't been scared in a long time. I didn't stop running until I hit the side entrance of the school. I slowed my pace to walk not to seem frantic or arouse suspicion, but once I hit the sidewalk, I jogged all the way to my front door and then bolted it shut once I was inside.

CHAPTER 52

"What is wrong with you running into the house like that, Riley? You scared me half to death," my mother barked at me from the couch.

"I just had a terrible interview with a student who I'm fairly sure killed Maddie," I groaned from the hall. I kicked off my shoes and left them in the front hall near the door. It was broiling hot in my mother's house. I pulled my sweater over my head and tossed it on the banister, leaving just a tee-shirt underneath. I went into the living room to find my mother, sister, and Adele sitting on the couch in front of a fire watching the news.

"Are you serious?" Liv asked as I sat down on the couch in between my mother and sister.

I swallowed hard and my mother handed me her glass of water. I took several sips, promising to refill her glass. When I felt better, I explained, "Natalie told me her teacher killed Maddie, but I'm pretty sure she did it. She confronted Maddie in the tunnels that night with the intent to scare her, and I think it got out of hand. I think it went too far. I don't know if she went there to kill Maddie, but it happened."

"She'd have to have the rope with her," Adele said.

"The rope could have been from anywhere. There are supply closets all over the place."

Adele leaned forward to look at me. "Is Natalie physically capable of it? I assume it would take a lot of physical strength to get Maddie tied up like that."

I spun through the possibilities. "The independent autopsy showed Maddie died of strangulation. Natalie could have strangled her with her hands and then tied her up like that to make it look like a suicide. I don't know for certain, but I'm sure Natalie played a part in it. I didn't believe her story at all. She had no affect when she told the story. It was like talking to a sociopath."

Liv scrunched up her face. "Do you think Natalie planned it all by herself ahead of time?"

"I have no idea," I said honestly. "I can't make heads or tails how it happened. I believed Natalie when she said she knew Maddie went to see Erik Yates that night. I also believed her when she said she confronted Maddie in the tunnel on her way back. When Natalie said Heidi showed up and told her to leave, I knew she was lying. I don't know if Heidi played a part, but I'd bet money Natalie was there."

"You're down to two suspects then," Liv said encouragingly.

My mother glanced over at me. "You have to get ready for the interview. Jack just texted me and said he needs you to meet him and Senator Crandall in the front of the school in an hour."

I sighed. The last thing I wanted to do right then was give a media interview. I pulled myself off the couch and headed upstairs to get ready.

Later, with twenty minutes to spare, I headed out of the house and walked the distance to the school. The press conference was being held right out front so the media could pull up into the circular drive. As I walked up to the front of the school, I wasn't able to see Jack or Senator Crandall through the media crowd. After moving through them, I finally saw Jack.

"You ready, kid?" Jack asked as I approached.

"As ready as I'm ever going to get."

Jack handed me a slip of paper with a cellphone number. "Give this number out for Jane to call. I didn't want to use the police station or the tip hotline we set up. It's easier if she knows she's calling directly." Jack pulled a phone out of his pocket and went to hand it to me, but Senator Crandall interrupted.

"Do you have a prepared statement?" he asked, moving to stand right in front of me.

"I thought about what I'm going to say if that's what you're asking. I don't want to read anything so I didn't write it down. It must come across sincere and natural."

"That's not acceptable," Senator Crandall scolded. "I need to approve what you say ahead of time. This can't be some amateur attempt at a media statement. I need something professional. My reputation is at stake."

"Are you kidding me?" I asked more sarcastically than I meant. Jack cringed as the words came out of my mouth.

Senator Crandall looked as if I'd slapped him. "I'm most definitely not kidding. If you're not prepared then you will not give the statement. I'll give it myself."

"You're the reason your daughter ran away," I said through gritted teeth. Once the dam broke, it all came flooding out. "I have been out here with Jack helping to find your daughter who ran away because she didn't trust you and your wife to believe her and keep her safe. Your daughter ran away to avoid telling you she was in danger. I'm less than a week to my wedding and my friends and I have put our lives on hold to help find Jane, and in the process, try to solve two homicides. You're going to stand there and tell me you need to review my statement to help your daughter know she is safe to come home? I don't think so." I walked away and didn't even care.

I didn't make it far though. The hot lights of the cameras had suddenly turned on me and reporters shouted questions. I swallowed hard and turned back around with a fake smile plastered across my face. I walked back past Senator Crandall whose mouth was shut. Jack stifled a smile.

I held up one hand to the reporters and smoothed my skirt down with the other. "Let me just give the statement and then I will answer questions when I'm done." I waited for the media to quiet down before I began. I spoke directly to Jane.

"Jane, my name is Riley Sullivan and I'm a private investigator. I've been trying to find you. You have a whole team of investigators standing behind you ready to help. We know you wanted to hire an investigator to help find who killed your friend Maddie. We've been investigating it, Jane. We know Maddie was murdered. We know why you ran away, too. We found where you were staying. We spoke to Betty. She was a big help to us. We found what you wrote on the rock. It was smart of you to leave us a message. The most important thing for you to know right now, Jane, is that I believe you and can help you. All you have to do is tell me where you are, and I'll come find you. My team can keep you safe, Jane. My fiancé is a detective from Little Rock. He believes you. We all do. Just give me a call and I can make sure you're safe." I wrapped up the statement with the special cellphone number Jack had provided me.

As soon as I was done, reporters shouted questions at me. I called on a reporter off to my left. She said, "You said in the statement you found where Jane was hiding out. Does that mean she definitely ran away?"

"Yes, she did." I didn't say anything more. This was the game with the media. Only give them enough, but don't give them more than needed.

Another reporter asked, "Can you tell us where she went?"

"No, we aren't disclosing that information for now."

The same reporter pressed, "The state police put out a photo of Jane and are asking residents to be on the lookout for her up near Brant Lake. The local police won't comment. Was Jane found to be in that region?"

This was a delicate balance for me. I didn't want to step on toes. "We had reason to believe Jane might have been in the area at one point. I can tell you honestly at this time we don't know where she is."

I fielded a few more questions and then wrapped the interview. A reporter asked Senator Crandall for an additional statement, but he waved them off. I wasn't going to stick around and have him berate me. I was going to leave the cleanup for Jack. I headed back to where Jack stood and reached my hand out for the phone.

Jack eyed me and placed it in my hand. "Good job on both accounts."

"You know you're going to have to play nice for me," I said quietly.

"I have no intention of doing that. You didn't say anything that didn't need to be said. Senator Crandall doesn't like it, he can fire us."

The more time I spent with Jack the more I liked him. "I'm going back to the house to wait for Jane's call." I left without saying a word to Senator Crandall. He watched me as I passed. I could feel the heat of his anger rise off of him like steam through a grate, but he didn't say a word.

CHAPTER 53

Luke and Miles were seated outside of Headmistress Winslow's office. Her secretary told them Winslow was on a call and should be done soon. They both took seats in the hallway while they waited. That was nearly ninety minutes ago.

"You think she's stalling?" Luke asked, checking his phone again for the time.

"She's been stalling this whole time so it wouldn't surprise me."

Luke liked Miles more than he thought he would. Miles was a good detective and had done his best with limited means on this case. They waited in silence for several more minutes until the secretary popped her head into the hall and called them back.

"Headmistress Winslow doesn't have very much time. She needs to head out to a donor meeting. You have about ten minutes with her."

Neither Luke nor Miles responded. Luke wanted to remind her that Miles was a cop trying to solve a homicide on campus and donors could wait, but since Miles didn't say anything, he kept quiet, too.

Winslow sat behind her desk, looking a bit more frazzled than Luke expected.

"We have a few more questions," Miles said as they took a seat in front of her desk.

Winslow looked up. "I don't have a lot of time. As you can imagine, our donors are pretty upset by everything that's happened at the school. I'm heading to a meeting where I have to do a bit of damage control so I can't be late."

Luke sat back and folded his arms. "You're going to have a lot more damage control to handle if you prevent Det. Ward from doing his job."

Luke knew Winslow wanted to intimidate. That was the reason for her large desk, which put considerable space between her and whoever sat in these chairs. Her office didn't offer a meeting table or comfortable couches even though there was more than enough space for it. Winslow was all about the bottom line.

"Be that as it may, I still can't be late, so get on with it." Winslow pursed her lips and peered at them.

"You met with Erik Yates on the Friday he was murdered. What was the meeting about?"

Winslow didn't falter. "I didn't meet with him. I told you already I put off firing him."

Miles was undeterred. "We have a witness who is willing to state on the record you met with Erik earlier that day. Now, unless something happened at this meeting you don't want us to know about, I can't see why you'd lie."

"I'm not lying," Winslow said calmly. "Your witness is mistaken." She reached for her phone and hit a button. "Roseline, please bring me my schedule. There are some questions these detectives have."

A moment later, Winslow's secretary came into the office with both a book and her iPad. "What's the date in question?" she asked standing next to Winslow's desk. Winslow told her the date and Roseline flipped open the book to the correct date and pulled it up on her iPad.

"Read me all of my meetings for that day," Winslow instructed.

Roseline went down the list of her boss' activities for the day, starting at seven in the morning and wrapping at six in the evening when Winslow left for a donor dinner with her husband.

"You can check with my husband, but I believe we came home around ten that evening. Roseline, you can leave."

"Roseline," Miles said, holding out his hand to stop her, "do you remember a meeting with Eric Yates on Friday the day of his death?"

She hesitated, but looked at Luke and held his gaze. "There was nothing on the schedule. As you can see from what I just read, nothing indicates Eric Yates had been here. We have to stick to the schedule. It can get very hectic without it." With that, Roseline left the room and closed the door as she exited.

Winslow sat behind her desk with a smug grin plastered on her face. "You heard for yourself. Erik Yates wasn't here. Your source is wrong." Before she could say anything else, her phone rang. She looked at the screen and answered, immediately asking the caller to hold. Winslow looked back up at Miles and Luke. "You'll need to leave now. This is a private call, and I need to take it."

Miles and Luke shared a look and then got up and left. They both nodded goodbye to Roseline and headed out into the hallway. Miles stopped to say something to Luke and then thought better of it and continued to walk down the hall. Before they hit the stairwell, someone called out from behind them.

"Excuse me." It was Roseline. She had left the office and was walking towards them. She handed Luke a small slip of paper. "You dropped this on your way out. I thought it might be important."

"Thank you. I appreciate it," Luke said, putting the paper in his pocket. He turned and followed Miles down the stairs and out of the administration building. Once outside and away from the building, Luke pulled out the slip of paper and read it. He wasn't surprised. Roseline had indicated she wanted to speak with him privately after Headmistress Winslow left for the day. She suggested down by the teachers' cottages in twenty minutes. He told Miles.

"What do you think she wants?" Miles asked.

Luke was surprised Miles hadn't picked up what he had heard. "She wants to tell us about the meeting between Winslow and Erik."

Miles furrowed his brow. "I don't get it. Roseline very specifically said Erik didn't have a meeting with Winslow on the day in question."

Luke held up his finger. "No, what Roseline said was that the meeting wasn't scheduled. She never said they didn't meet." Luke handed him the note. "There was a meeting Winslow doesn't want us to know about."

Miles took the note and read it. He looked at Luke with amazement. "You picked that up in there?"

"You just have to listen to the words Roseline used to answer your question. You asked if there had been a meeting and Roseline didn't say no. She said there wasn't one on the schedule."

"Same thing," Miles said, still not getting it. He shrugged. "Well, anyway, we better head down and meet her."

Luke texted Cooper that Winslow would be leaving soon and to keep on her. As they stood there talking to a few of the other cops, Winslow walked out of the building and headed for the staff parking lot. Luke sent another text. Cooper assured him he was set and ready to go. He'd tail the woman all night.

"Cooper is on Winslow," Luke told Miles. "Let's go find out what her secretary knows."

As they headed to the back of the campus, Miles received a text from the crime scene techs who had been going through Heidi Sykes' belongings. He explained to Luke one of the more eager techs found a rope that looked similar to the rope they knew had been used in Maddie's murder.

"I don't think you can use that to make anything stick," Luke said.

"No, definitely not. I looked through the report last night and it's a common rope found at any hardware store. Heidi having a similar rope this many months later doesn't mean a thing. Interesting though."

Luke and Miles walked the rest of the way down to the cottages. A few minutes later, Roseline appeared at the top of the hill. She moved swiftly and with purpose until she stood right in front of them.

"I don't have a lot of time," Roseline started, glancing behind her. "Headmistress Winslow met with Erik Yates the day of the murder."

"Are you sure it was the same day?" Luke asked.

"I am. She suggested I take a long lunch, which she never does. Most days, she's upset if I take too long eating my lunch at my desk. I left though and went to the parking lot to leave, but realized once I got to my car, I had left my keys at my desk so I went back to grab them. When I opened the door, I heard Headmistress Winslow. At first, I thought she was talking on the phone, but then, I heard a man arguing back with her. I stood there longer than I should have, but I thought it was important to stay."

Luke raised his eyebrows. "Why is that?"

Roseline lowered her voice, nearly to a whisper. "Headmistress Winslow offered Erik a bribe. He said he knew who killed Maddie and he was going to the police with the information. Erik wanted her support. Headmistress Winslow said Erik would never have her support and instead offered him one-hundred-thousand dollars to keep quiet. He stormed out after that."

Miles shifted from one foot to the other. "What did you do?"

"There was nothing I could do. Erik walked right past me. He knew I was there but didn't say anything to me. He stormed out. I got out of there right after him. To my knowledge, Winslow never saw me."

"Is there a reason you haven't come forward with this information until now?" Miles asked.

"I didn't know it was important until you asked today," Roseline said, surprise evident in her voice. "Erik never said who he suspected of killing Maddie. I thought the cops ruled her death a suicide. I didn't know what he was talking about. Winslow offering him a bribe was certainly out of character, but I knew she was thinking of firing him. I wondered if she was testing him."

As crazy as it sounded, Luke believed her. Roseline was coming forward now. That's all that mattered. "Do you happen to have a copy of her schedule for that evening?"

Roseline pulled out a folded piece of paper from her pocket and handed it to Luke. "I figured you'd want it. Headmistress Winslow and her husband were supposed to meet donors that night for dinner. I've provided you the name of the restaurant and phone number but more importantly the name of the donors and their contact information. I wouldn't talk to Winslow's husband."

"Why not?" Luke asked.

Roseline locked her eyes on Luke. "Winslow runs the house. If she told him to lie, he'd lie."

Luke nodded. "One last question before you go. If Winslow was serious about bribing Erik, where would she have gotten that kind of money?"

Roseline smiled. "I guess you don't recognize the name. The Winslow family is quite prominent in Saratoga. Racehorses and such.

She has the money or she could take it from the school. Headmistress Winslow has access to millions from our donors. The one thing I know to be true more than anything else - she'd do whatever it took to keep up the school's stellar reputation. She's ruthless in defending it."

CHAPTER 54

After Roseline left, Luke turned to Miles. "Is Winslow ruthless enough to kill to keep the school's reputation intact?"

Miles took the slip of paper Roseline had given him out of Luke's hand. "Let's make a couple of calls and find out." Miles called the donor listed on the paper first. After a few rings, someone answer. Miles explained who he was and why he was calling. He spoke for several minutes, but Luke couldn't quite make out the conversation from Miles' side of the call.

When he was done, Miles hung up. "Winslow cut the dinner short. She claimed she had a terrible headache and left. Her husband stayed playing nicely with the couple, but they thought it was very strange, particularly because Winslow's husband had to take a cab home. The donor said Winslow seemed out of sorts that evening. She was short-tempered and distracted. Nothing like they had ever seen before. They haven't donated yet because of the way she acted."

"Winslow has no alibi then," Luke said evenly.

"I don't know. I'm calling Winslow's husband next. Roseline provided their home information as well. If he lies, he lies, but I still need to ask." Miles called and someone answered quickly. All Luke could make out was Winslow's husband's name was Robert. But Robert wasn't who Miles was speaking to. Miles didn't say much on the call at all. Asked a few questions but that was it. He looked down at the ground as he took in the information.

When the call ended, Miles explained. "I just spoke to Winslow's live-in housekeeper. Winslow never came home that Friday night until late, well after eleven. Robert was home before his wife who supposedly was too sick to stay at dinner. She could have easily made it back here in time to kill Erik." Miles toed the dirt in front of him. "I never checked her alibi."

"She wasn't a suspect before." Luke looked back up at the school. "What do you want to do now?"

"Let's go back and check on Riley and Jack to see if she's heard anything on Jane. The crime scene techs are nearly done processing Heidi's room and will call me when they are done. Cooper has his eyes on Winslow. Let's see what other evidence we can gather first before I bring her in."

The two walked back to the house surprised by the lack of media on the street. Miles suggested they might all be on a dinner break. Luke hoped someone had cooked because his stomach growled at the suggestion of food.

Luke wasn't disappointed. Once back at Karen's house, Luke and Miles found them all, minus Cooper, sitting down to dinner. Karen had made chicken parmesan, Italian bread, and salad. As Luke sat down at the table, he asked Riley how the news conference went. He hadn't even had a chance to see it.

"It went well enough," Riley said in between bites. "We haven't heard from Jane yet. The national and local news stations keep replaying it, so hopefully, Jane will make contact. I hope she can get to a phone."

"If she was able to escape from the school and Irene Hodge, I'm sure Jane can get herself to a phone," Jack said. "How did the interview go with Heidi?"

Miles filled them in while Luke ate. Most weren't surprised by what Heidi had to say, but once Miles told them about their interview with Winslow and her lack of alibi the night Erik was killed, they perked up.

"Has anyone considered Winslow a suspect before?" Jack asked, taking a bite and washing it down with his drink.

"I didn't until now," Miles said. "Other than being aloof, she seemed genuinely surprised when we found out Irene wasn't with her family. I didn't like that she was looking through Erik's cottage late at night, but I believed her when she said she was looking for proof of misconduct. It made sense. Winslow has never denied us access to the school other than making us get a search warrant for the video surveillance. We've been all over that campus searching everything and everywhere. Winslow could have limited us or made it more difficult, but she hasn't. Not exactly the actions of a guilty person."

"Speaking to Winslow's secretary changed things for me," Luke said, sitting back. "Winslow has no alibi the night of the murder and she tried to bribe Erik. I bet that's why she didn't fire him."

Luke ran through a scenario in his head before he suggested it to the others. "What if Winslow knows who killed Maddie, and she's protecting them? Erik figures out who the killer is and goes to Winslow with his suspicion. If she fires him, Erik is going to spill that information to the police without question. Instead of firing him, Winslow tries to bribe him. What if she killed him because he refused to take the bribe?"

Riley followed the same train of thought. "That could be possible. It was a spur of the moment crime with Erik's gun. Winslow could have gone to his place to try to convince him, and if they got into an argument, she could have shot him to keep him quiet."

"It's also possible Winslow told Maddie's killer that Erik knew and then they went to silence him," Jack suggested.

Miles sighed and looked around the table. "That brings us right back to figuring out who killed Maddie."

Riley put down her fork. "I think I might know who killed Maddie." She explained about her earlier interview with Natalie and finished by saying, "I can't say for certain whether Natalie acted alone, but she was involved."

Miles exhaled. "I can't officially get Natalie in to interview her. Her father has a lawyer who refuses to let Natalie speak. Heidi won't crack and insists she didn't kill anyone. Winslow is lying to us. Irene Hodge is after Jane and the only witness I have is on the run. There is no forensic evidence tying anyone to either crime. I feel like I'm trying to run through quicksand."

"We have to find Jane," Riley said. "It's the only break we are going to get unless Winslow slips up when Cooper is watching her."

Miles reached in his pocket to grab his ringing phone and stepped away from the table to answer it. Riley leaned across the table to Luke. "Did everything go okay today?"

Luke smiled at her and teased, "You mean did I punch him in the face for trying to steal my fiancé?"

Riley's eyes grew wide. "Umm, yes, that."

"We're good," Luke reassured.

They all remained fairly quiet finishing dinner until Miles came back into the room. "Crime techs didn't find anything except the rope, which doesn't mean anything. I have nothing of substance on Heidi unless we are bringing her in on conspiracy to commit theft for stealing those tests. That's weak at best."

Luke didn't disagree. It was a rare occasion when he couldn't make heads or tails on a case. The more information they found, the more they seemed to stall.

Karen stood from her seat and carried her plate over to the sink. "You'll have a break. I can feel it. It just takes a little patience."

"You'll have to bring Winslow in for formal questioning," Jack said to Miles. "No one is going to like that. You might even get some push-back from the mayor's office, but it has to be done."

Miles gritted his teeth and pointed to the phone. "It wasn't the crime scene techs who called to tell me about Heidi. It was my chief. I'm already getting push-back. After my conversation with Winslow today, she called the chief and then the mayor. She told them we were harassing her. She told them we cannot speak to her again without her attorney present and she wants the investigation wrapped up now."

"It means we are getting close," Riley said.

"That's exactly what it means," Luke echoed, hoping Miles understood him. "This isn't the time to give up."

They started cleaning up after dinner. Karen said she had dessert in the fridge but no one wanted any. Jack made a call to his New York State Police contact to see if any progress had been made in the ongoing searches for Jane. They hadn't found her so far. Just as everyone settled into the house for the evening, unsure of what to do next, the phone Jack had given Riley rang.

"It might be Jane," she said nervously, looking at the screen.

Karen lowered the sound on the television and they all remained quiet.

"Hello, this is Riley," she said. The corners of her mouth immediately turned up in a surprised smile. She pointed to the phone indicating it was Jane. Riley listened, asked a few questions, and then said, "Stay put, Jane. I'll be there to get you. It will take me about an hour to get there, but I'm on my way." Riley ended the call.

"We need to go," she said, standing and rushing to get her things together to leave.

"Where is she?" Luke asked, right behind her.

"Jane is at a motel in Lake George. It's an older motel and she said the guy at the desk didn't ask any questions. She said she doesn't feel safe. She went out into the village to get something to eat and spotted Irene. I don't know how Jane has managed to dodge the state police but she has. We need to go now."

Miles stood to come with them, but Riley shook her head. "Jane said to come without the police. Let Luke and I go get her and we'll see what she has to say and convince her to come back."

"I really should be there," Miles insisted.

"I don't want anything to mess this up. She has probably seen you on television and knows you're a cop. I need her to trust me."

"Riley is right, Miles. Let us bring her to you." Luke slapped him on the back. "Trust me, we have this. It will be okay. As soon as we get her to tell us who killed Erik, you'll be here to bring them in."

"Do you want me to come with you?" Jack asked.

Riley considered and said, "Why don't you stay here, too. You can deal with Senator Crandall when we know more."

Jack agreed.

Luke grabbed his keys and they sprinted to the car.

CHAPTER 55

Cooper had been tailing Headmistress Winslow for so long now he was sure he was going to get made at any minute. That's what happens with a lot of stop and go surveillance. Winslow first went to her donor dinner. She sat sipping drinks at a high-end restaurant in Albany, and then later, joined her guest for dinner. They sat smiling and laughing as the server brought them appetizers and the main course. The meeting seemed to have gone well. Winslow left with a check in hand and a smile plastered on her face.

Cooper had sat at the bar and watched her from a distance. It was tricky getting out of the restaurant at the same time to follow her, but thankfully, traffic had been a bit heavy so it was stop and go for her. It allowed Cooper the time to catch up. Next Winslow stopped at a grocery store and pharmacy. It looked like she was headed home after that, but she turned quickly in the opposite direction and got on I-87 going north.

As they traveled north farther away from Albany, Cooper started seeing signs for Saratoga. Cooper had no idea where they were headed but pulled off the same exit as Winslow. These weren't roads he was familiar with, and the winding nature of them made keeping the tail a challenge. Winslow pulled into Congress Park.

Cooper gave her space but followed. When Winslow pulled into the parking lot, Cooper pulled in too, leaving several cars between them. He cut his lights and didn't move. It was so quiet he heard the gravel crunch as Winslow walked across the parking lot. Cooper wasn't sure what to do. If he sat there, he'd never see what Winslow was up to, but if she spotted him, he wouldn't be able to continue to follow her. He sat still with his hand on the door handle for several moments, debating his best plan of action.

Finally, he just went for it. Cooper pulled the door handle and stepped out into the night. Cooper took two steps and ducked behind his car. Winslow was right across the parking lot, talking to a man. He was too far away to hear what they were saying, but it was obvious they knew each other. Cooper peeked his head around the back bumper just time to see him hand her a slip of paper. She pulled a thick envelope from her purse and gave it to him.

Cooper popped back down again and moved over to the car door as Winslow turned and walked back to her car. They were on the move again. He let Winslow leave the lot first. He had no idea where the guy she had been talking to went.

Cooper let Winslow go until she was nearly out of sight down the road and then he tore out of the parking lot to give chase. When she took the I-87 North off-ramp, they lost two cars in between them so it was slightly easier for Cooper to keep up. He kept his foot on the accelerator and checked his speed – 70. Cooper wasn't even sure of the speed limit. He thought maybe he'd seen a sign for Speed 65, but he couldn't be sure. Cooper eased off the gas as he cruised up behind her. Luckily, Winslow wasn't as crazy a driver as some he had to follow. She at least obeyed traffic rules.

When Cooper's heart stopped racing and he sat comfortably a car behind Winslow in the fast lane, he called Riley using the car's Bluetooth. He explained what he had witnessed and read off the next exit sign.

"It sounds like you're headed north toward Lake George or back up to where Jane had been in Brant Lake," Riley explained. "Just keep on her. We aren't too far behind you."

Riley gave Cooper the address of the hotel and room number where Jane was hiding out. "I don't know where Winslow is going," she said, "but if she goes anywhere near that hotel, Jane is in danger. Keep an eye out for Irene Hodge, too. I'll text you her photo."

Surveillance was second nature for Cooper. It was what he was made to do, even more so than interviewing and forensic work. This time was different. He wasn't armed. He had no idea where Winslow was headed. There were other suspects at play, and the life of a young girl hung in the balance.

Cooper's heart rate jumped a notch when Winslow put on her turn signal and followed the exit for Lake George. This couldn't be a coincidence. Cooper continued to follow closely behind. At this point, it didn't matter if she realized she was being followed or not, Cooper wasn't letting her out of his sight.

Winslow made a quick turn into a large hotel parking lot. Cooper pulled in right behind her but backed into his spot so he'd have greater mobility and line of sight. He double-checked the address Riley had given him. At least this wasn't the place where Jane was staying. Cooper's sigh of relief lasted only a moment.

A disheveled woman burst out of the front door of the lobby of the hotel, the door nearly slamming into the wall behind it. She headed right for Winslow's car. The parking lot had plenty of light for Cooper to see her clearly. He pulled up the photo Riley had sent of Irene Hodge. It was a match for the woman. She had seen better days, but Cooper had no doubt it was her.

Irene's hair flew around her face. She had scratches across her cheek and her shirt was torn in two spots. The woman had the appearance of someone who fought off a grizzly bear and had lived to tell the tale. Cooper opened the door to go confront them both, but before he could, Irene got in Winslow's car. As soon as the passenger door slammed shut, Winslow took off again, squealing her tires out of the parking lot.

Cooper cursed and jammed the SUV into drive. They took a left out of the parking lot and drove through the small downtown streets of Lake George Village. The streets were lined with shops and restaurants but few people seemed to be out so late in the season. Winslow drove down the road for several minutes passing larger hotels. The road then gave way to smaller motels and motor courts, establishments that had seen their heyday decades ago.

At the far end of the road, nearly as they were navigating out of the main drag in Lake George, Winslow turned left into a motel. The place had a gravel drive and two rows of rooms on each side. A pool and deck area sat in the middle. There were only two cars in the lot and no one even visible in the small front office. Most of the lights that hung at each of the doors had been burned out, no one bothering to replace them. If Cooper had driven by at any other time, he'd have assumed the place had long ago gone out of business. It was the perfect place to hide.

Cooper didn't see a sign anywhere naming the place, but he was sure this was the place Riley had told him. He cut his lights and pulled right in and parked. Winslow drove down one side of the row of rooms and came to a stop in front of the second to the last.

With his eye on the car, he texted Riley and explained what was happening. Her response was straight to the point: *We are about fifteen minutes away. Don't let them anywhere near Jane!*

Cooper strained his eyes to check the room numbers, which hung unevenly, some missing completely next to the doors. Even-numbered rooms, where Jane was, were on the opposite of the courtyard from where they were.

Minutes ticked by. The only sound in the SUV was Cooper's uneven breaths. His heartbeat pounded in his ears. When Winslow finally made a move to open her car door, Cooper didn't even hesitate. He flung open his door and his feet hit the gravel. He didn't stop running until he stood toe to toe with Winslow.

Startled at first by Cooper's presence, she asked, "Do you work here?"

Cooper realized Winslow didn't recognize him. "No, the woman with you," he pointed inside the car, "she's wanted by the police."

Winslow got right up to him and then recognition took hold. "You have no right to be here. I don't have time for this. She hasn't done anything wrong. It's all a misunderstanding."

Cooper glared down at her unmoving. "What are you doing here?"

Winslow backed up an inch, assessing him. Cooper didn't give her any latitude. He stood with his hands on his hips, blocking her way. Finally, Winslow explained, "I'm here to retrieve Jane. We found her, and she's in danger."

"Jane isn't going anywhere with you." Cooper didn't budge and neither did Winslow. As he pinned his eyes on hers, he caught a flash of movement on the other side of the car. Irene Hodge made a break for it and ran around the car and straight toward Jane's room. Cooper had no choice but to go after her. He wasn't prepared for what happened next.

"Don't move or I'll shoot you!" Winslow yelled as Cooper had nearly caught up with Irene.

Cooper stopped and turned, his hands at his sides. "If you're here to make sure Jane is safe, why do you need a gun?"

Winslow took a few steps towards him. "I will not let anyone, especially not some snot-nose little brat, destroy all I've worked for. Get out of my way!"

Cooper backed up, but Winslow gained ground on him. He had no idea if she'd shoot, but Cooper wasn't taking any chances. If he were dead or injured, he couldn't help Jane. Cooper took off running, zig-zagging in case she fired off a shot. He had to get to Jane first.

CHAPTER 56

We pulled into the parking lot just as two women entered a room and the door closed behind them. I pointed in their direction. "Luke, I think that's Jane's room."

He pulled the car right up to the door. I grabbed for my phone and double-checked the number. "We have to get in there!"

"Where is Cooper?" Luke asked, getting out of the SUV.

I shut the door on the passenger side and took a step towards the door. Luke waved me back. "You don't know if she's armed. You can't just go charging in there."

The motel was barren, not a soul in sight. I couldn't believe this was the place Jane had picked to come. I understood why she'd assume no one would rat her out, but at the same time, anyone could get to her. She had no protection. I stood mere feet from her, but Luke was right. I couldn't just go charging in there. I didn't have a gun. Luke did though.

I spun around and looked for Cooper. The car he was driving was there but not him. "I'm worried, Luke. Cooper wouldn't just abandon this. I'm going in."

Luke handed me his gun, but I waved him off. "Let me try to get Jane out of there first. If you go in and Winslow does have a gun, someone is going to get hit in the crossfire. Just cover me."

Luke opened his mouth to argue, but I pleaded with a look and he backed off. I smiled at him before turning and knocking once on the door. "Help me!" a young girl yelled from behind the door.

I turned the knob, but it was locked. I pounded on it again and then tried to kick it in. It wouldn't budge. I waved Luke back to go to the office to get the key and some help. He didn't want to leave me, but we didn't have a choice.

"Jane, it's Riley! I'm here! Winslow, I know you're in there with her. Open the door!"

Before Luke could get back, the door slowly creaked open. I nudged it with my foot. "Jane, come out."

"She's coming with me," Winslow said, showing herself in the room for the first time. She had one arm around Jane's neck and the gun pointed at the girl's head.

I had seen photos of Jane before, but in the last few days, I had created an image of her as someone bigger and stronger than she was. Jane in Winslow's grip was young and scared. She shook and seemed to be trying not to cry. A streak of dirt crossed one of her cheeks. Her hands had been recently bloodied and nails broken off. Irene Hodge stood off to the side.

Winslow spat. "Listen, Riley, I don't have time for this. I have to get Jane back to the school. She's been running and causing trouble for far too long. I have a plan and you're messing it up."

"I'm not letting you leave."

Winslow looked up to the ceiling and exhaled a breath. "The other guy couldn't stop me and neither can you. I have a job to do. Now move!"

I sucked in a breath. She must have been referring to Cooper. I hoped he was okay. I locked eyes with Jane. "Tell me what happened, Jane. Who killed Mr. Yates? Was it Headmistress Winslow or Irene?"

"Don't be crazy. It was neither of us!" Irene said. "We are just trying to get the truth from Jane. That's all I've wanted from her and she just won't give it to me!"

Jane pinned her eyes on me. She didn't tell me who killed him, but she told me her story. "I was just trying to talk to Mr. Yates about helping me find Maddie's killer. I came through the tunnel and once I got close, I heard yelling. I couldn't understand what they were saying. All of sudden, there was a gunshot."

Jane started to cry. "I got up close to the window. There was so much blood. There wasn't anything I could do. That's when I saw the other person. I was about to scream when there was a hand over my mouth. Ms. Hodge pulled me back from the window. She told me we had to get out of there. She grabbed me and we ran to her car parked on the back road so we had to sneak through the fence. I thought she was going to drive us to the police station or call the police, but she didn't. I told Ms. Hodge we had to go to the police, but she said no. She wouldn't take me there. She wanted to know who I saw. I told her to take me to the cops. I didn't understand what she was doing, but she was acting crazy. She was crying and screaming at me. All she wanted was to know who I saw. I thought maybe she was involved. Ms. Hodge was crazy, swerving all over the place. When she had to stop at a red light, I saw my chance. I ran for it."

"Were you involved?" I asked, looking at Irene.

She shook her head. "I wanted to know who killed Erik. I just wanted to know!"

"Why didn't you take Jane to the cops?"

Irene yelled through sobs, "The cops don't do anything. I was going to kill whoever killed Erik. I loved him!"

I didn't understand. "Irene, you took a vacation day Friday. You were supposed to be gone and away from campus. What were you even still doing there?"

"We don't have time for this!" Winslow yelled and jerked Jane toward the door.

I put my hands up. "You're not going anywhere." Looking past her, I asked again, "Irene, why were you there?"

"I thought Erik might be cheating on me. I figured if he thought I was gone I'd catch whoever was going to his place. Then I saw Jane. I figured maybe the rumor was true about Erik. Maybe he was taking advantage of his students."

"How did you see Jane from your place? It's too far from Erik's."

"I was in the woods, waiting," Irene admitted. "I was so focused on Jane, I guess I didn't see the other person go into Erik's. Then I heard the gunshot and grabbed Jane to get out of there."

"What did you do when Jane got away from you?"

Irene didn't answer, but Winslow did. "She called me, like all my teachers do, to clean up the mess. That's what I do, Riley. I keep everything running smoothly. I keep all the secrets." Winslow shoved Jane forward. "Now, I need to get Jane back to school!"

I shook my head. "No, Winslow. No one is buying that. Why do you have a gun to Jane's head if you're just trying to get her back to school?"

Winslow didn't say a word.

Irene shouted, "She won't tell us what we want to know! We need to know who killed Erik!"

I exhaled and said calmly, "Jane, what did you do once you got away from Irene?"

"I ran and kept on running. There was a guy at a gas station. He looked like a dad. He had kids' stickers on the back of his SUV. I asked him for a ride up north. He wanted to take me to the cops, and I should have, but I thought maybe Ms. Hodge went there looking for me. I got thinking, too, the cops didn't help before. Maybe they wouldn't believe me or help me now. Irene knew I saw someone kill Mr. Yates. I worried about who she might tell. I needed to find a place to be safe until I could figure it all out. That's when I remembered my boyfriend's parents' cabin. I had the man drive me up north to Saratoga. I told him I had to get to a friend's house and had him drop me off at another gas station. I told him my friend would get me from there. I ditched my phone because I know that's how they track people. I found a trucker to drive me the rest of the way."

"Why didn't you call your parents or your sister?" I asked, trying to figure out how to get Jane away from Winslow without either of us getting shot. Winslow was running out of patience. I could tell by how she jerked Jane back and forth, but she had to get past me to get to the door and that wasn't going to happen.

"I just didn't trust anyone. Nobody did anything when Maddie was killed. Why would they help me?" Tears spilled down Jane's face.

"I'm here, Jane. I'm going to help you."

Winslow laughed. "You can't even help yourself. We are getting out of here!" Winslow shoved Jane forward, but I stood my ground. I didn't know if I could stop her, but I was going to try.

That's when I felt a hand on my back at the same time that I saw Cooper's face in the bathroom doorway. I turned to see Luke with his gun pointed at Winslow.

"We have you surrounded, Winslow. Give up before someone gets hurt," he commanded.

"I have a job to do! I have a school to protect," Winslow yelled. Her voice faltered though. She hadn't planned for any of this.

I locked eyes with Jane. "Now is your chance. Tell us. Who killed Mr. Yates?"

Jane closed her eyes and said quietly, "Headmistress Winslow."

"No! What?" Irene shrieked. "That can't be true."

Winslow turned to her. "It was Heidi. They are all lying! Don't be so stupid, Irene."

"But she…" Irene seemed to be processing something. Then all of a sudden, she launched herself forward onto Winslow's back as I reached for Jane's arm and jerked her free. I pulled her out the door as Luke shielded us. As we hit the gravel, a gunshot rang out and I stopped cold. Luke's face flashed in my mind. I couldn't lose him.

Pushing Jane farther into the parking lot, nearly making her stumble and fall, I turned back. I got to the door in time to see Irene slumped against the wall holding her arm, blood running from it. I didn't know if it was Winslow or Luke who had shot her. It didn't matter. Cooper and Luke had Winslow pinned to the ground. They were safe.

CHAPTER 57

Two hours later, we were still standing around the parking lot of the motel. Jane had been seen by a paramedic. She had some mild dehydration and some cuts and bruises that needed some tending to, but otherwise, she was okay. She was giving an account to a state police detective who had jurisdiction in the area.

Irene had been treated for her gunshot wound. The shot grazed her more than anything. She was sitting in the back of one cop car while Headmistress Winslow was cuffed and in the back of another. Luke and Cooper were giving their statements to the state police. I had already given mine right after calling Miles. We were waiting for him now.

Soon after Jane called me and we left, Miles got a call from Heidi. She had a confession of her own to make. I couldn't wait to hear what Miles had to say. I hoped it was an answer to who killed Maddie. When Luke finished with the detective, he came over to me as I sat on the curb outside of Jane's room.

He smiled down at me. "It's nice to be able to bring Jane home before we celebrate."

I pulled Luke down next to me. "I was terrified you had been hurt or killed. I feel so bad I just shoved Jane toward the parking lot. I had to get to you."

Luke reached over and laced his fingers through mine. "All I worried about was getting you out of there."

I moved closer to him and rested my head on his shoulder until Miles arrived. Luke gave me a quick kiss and stood up. "I'm going to let you and Miles talk and drive Jane home. You started this case together so you should finish it."

"Are you sure?" I asked, looking up at him.

Luke reached his hand down and pulled me up. "I'm positive. Besides, I'm exhausted. There's a lot of sleep I want to catch up on before I marry you." He pointed over to Cooper who was leaning against an ambulance. "I want to get Cooper home, too. He tore up his hands and his stomach crawling through that bathroom window. He's not hurting now because of the adrenaline running through him, but once it wears off, he's going to be miserable."

I nodded. I hadn't even stopped to consider how Cooper had gotten into the room. He was just there. I hugged Luke goodbye just as Miles walked over. Luke explained he was leaving and asked Miles if he wouldn't mind driving me home. Miles readily agreed.

Miles and I watched Luke walk off and go to Cooper. Together, they left a few minutes later. He turned to me. "Heidi called me and wanted to talk. I guess her conscience finally got the better of her. She wanted to cut a deal."

"She killed Maddie?"

"No, it was Natalie, but Heidi goaded her into it even if that's not what she meant to do." Miles paused and shook his head in disgust. "Heidi said she never thought Natalie could do something like that. Natalie confronted Maddie in the tunnel and it escalated. She ended up strangling Maddie with her hands. Natalie panicked and came to Heidi, who didn't know what to do so she called Headmistress Winslow. Together, the three of them went back down into the tunnels and found Maddie. Winslow decided it would be better to make it look like Maddie had killed herself so they tied her up to the pipe. As we suspected, Heidi tied the knots. She said she didn't even think about the kind of knots she tied. She had no idea she was leaving a clue pointing right at her."

I wasn't sure what to say. There was so much running through my mind. Finally, I asked the obvious. "How could Heidi and Winslow protect Natalie like that? How do you just let a killer go?"

"It's disgusting, but Heidi said she knew if she went to the police, the blame would come back to her. Natalie's parents are major donors for the school. Headmistress Winslow just cared about the money. After all, Maddie was just a scholarship kid."

I sighed. "How did Erik Yates fit into all of this?"

"Heidi needed some way to divert attention because she worried Erik would figure it out. Headmistress Winslow wasn't worried about Erik at first, but she thought firing him would push him to keep digging and expose them all. Heidi kept trying to set a trap, but Erik wouldn't take the bait. Eventually, Erik figured out Natalie killed Maddie. He went to Winslow demanding she do something about it or he would. He didn't have enough proof though. As we know, Winslow tried to bribe him and when that didn't work, she went to his place that night to try again. According to Heidi, they struggled and Winslow shot him. Heidi wasn't sure how Irene was involved."

The whole thing made me sick to my stomach. "Irene had no idea about any of it. She seemed to trust Winslow completely. But I don't understand. Why, if Natalie killed Maddie, would they ever invite Jane into the Clovers?"

"Heidi thought it would show Jane it wasn't them. She figured if they were able to get Jane in their good graces, it would throw off suspicion."

"What's going to happen to Heidi now?"

"The district attorney's office had to give her immunity for her cooperation. They didn't like doing it, but we'd never know all of this without her finally coming forward." Miles ran a hand down his face. "Of course, she only did it to save herself. We have Natalie in custody. As you can imagine, her parents are furious. She was seventeen when the murder happened, but I'm fairly certain she will be tried as an adult."

Miles looked over at the cars with Irene and Winslow. "Heidi said Winslow hired someone to track down Jane. It seems when they got a lead on the cabin, Winslow must have told Irene, who got there before Winslow could. Probably a good thing given Winslow showed up here with a gun."

I glanced over at Jane who sat on a curb giving the state police detective her statement. She would need counseling to process all of it. I hoped she'd find her way out of Austen Academy and some peace in her life.

Miles followed my eyes and then turned back to me. "It's funny, of all the places Jane could choose to hide out, it's here."

I glanced at him curiously. "What do you mean?"

He looked at me wide-eyed. "Do you not know where we are?" When I didn't respond, he said, "Cedarhurst Motel."

Could he be right? I glanced around the motel and took it in for the first time. I envisioned the building freshly painted, the area lit up and pool in use with chairs around it. Miles was right. Seniors in high school often came to Lake George for Memorial Weekend. I didn't know when the tradition started, but when I was a senior, I came with my friends. The Cedarhurst was where we had stayed. That weekend, the motel was filled with friends from my high school. Other motels and hotels were filled with seniors from other schools. I remember lots of drinking but not much else. We might have walked into Lake George Village for food and to find other friends, but mostly I remember drinking and partying with my friends here.

Miles pointed to the pool deck. "We met for the first time right there."

I stepped back. "We met before?"

Miles grinned at me. "Not only did we meet, but I kissed you right there."

"You kissed me?" I asked laughing, searching my memory of that weekend until I landed on the memory of kissing a guy from another school. I had no idea it was Miles though. I looked at his face and tried to envision him twenty years younger. I don't know how I didn't see it before, but it was him. "Did you know it was me when we met on this case?"

"No, it didn't come to me until the other night. I told you I thought we had met, but I couldn't place it. When I remembered, I wanted to text and tell you, but I had already made such a fool of myself and you were already so angry with me. I figured it was better not to tell you."

I didn't know what to say. I had liked Miles back then. The more I thought about that night, the more came back. Some Troy High kids had come to see friends and Miles was among them. I offered him a beer and we got talking. We sat on chairs by the pool for hours, drinking, talking, and laughing. Then he kissed me. It was a crush I had carried into college, but I never saw him again after that weekend. For a long time, I wondered what had happened to him.

I reached out my hand to him. "I guess it's good to reconnect with old friends. Let's not let another twenty years go by before we catch up again."

"Agreed." Miles smiled down at me. "Let's bring Jane home."

Epilogue

I stood in front of the full-length mirror in my suite at the hotel in Lake Placid. The wedding gown fit every curve of my body. The ivory lace played off my skin tone perfectly. My long auburn hair had been twisted into a chignon at the nape of my neck and adorned with a simple flower. I wore a simple diamond bracelet my mother had given me earlier in the day. Everything had come together exactly how I had planned. I could barely believe how happy I felt.

What was more unbelievable was my lack of nerves I figured I'd have on this day. I simply couldn't wait to be Luke's wife. There was no fear and no anxiety about making this commitment. All I had was pure joy about starting this next phase of life together.

"You look gorgeous," Liv said from behind me.

I turned around to face her. "I kind of do, don't I?"

"You really do. Ready?" she asked.

It was just Liv and I walking down the stairs together to the main lobby and out to the lake. Luke and I didn't want a big bridal party. Liv would stand up for me and Cooper for him. Our wedding was small, just immediate family and those who meant the most to us. My mother and Jack, Luke's parents, Cooper and Adele, Emma and Joe, Captain Meadows and his wife, and Det. Bill Tyler and his wife.

The October day had warmed just enough we decided that morning to have the very short ceremony down near the lake instead of the room we had reserved. The hotel had been more than accommodating. A wooden pier jutting out into the lake would be the perfect spot for pictures. The fall foliage gave us a magnificent blanket of color.

"Is Luke nervous?" I asked.

"Not in the least. He can't wait to see you," Liv said, and then she laughed. "I think Cooper is nervous you're going to trip down the stairs or do something equally clumsy."

I giggled. "I'm worried about that, too."

"Don't worry, I'll hold your hand," Liv said.

I teared up a little but tried to hold it back to avoid ruining my makeup. I had said the very same thing to my sister time after time growing up. Now, here she was doing the same for me.

"Don't start crying now," Liv scolded. "It will make me cry, and I'm the only single one here. I'm hoping to pick up a guy in the hotel after dinner." She held out her arms. "This is too much sexy to go to waste."

I raised my eyebrows at her in a question, but she just laughed. "Let's go," she urged, handing me my simple bouquet of fall flowers.

I made it down the stairs to the main lobby with Liv's help and through the room where our ceremony would have been held. As I stepped out the door to the back of the hotel, a beam of sunlight warmed my face. Liv and I walked arm and arm across the grass and down to the lake. As soon as I crested the hill, there was Luke and the rest of our family and friends. Luke wore a simple gray suit and white shirt and tie. His smile was as bright as the sun. From the first moment I met him, our connection and chemistry overwhelmed me. It hadn't been an easy road for us to get here, but even the struggles made this moment worth it. We had survived storms together.

"You forgot the music," Liv said quietly.

"No, I didn't. This is exactly how I planned it."

"We need music. I'm going to sing," Liv said, poking me in the side and making me laugh.

"Don't you dare."

Liv walked me right into Luke's arms. I glanced at my mother and all of my friends. Happiness radiated from each of them. Liv took my bouquet and Luke took my hands.

"You are so beautiful," he said, tears forming in his eyes. I knew Luke would cry at our wedding. He was the softie, and I loved him even more for it.

Our officiant stepped forward and started the ceremony. It was a blur for me. My eyes were gazing into Luke's and all I could see was the beautiful life in front of us. Vows and promises were made. I dos uttered and rings slipped on. Finally, I was in Luke's arms and his lips were on mine. There were cheers and clapping around us and peace and happiness poured through me. There was no greater feeling than knowing in a pivotal moment in my life I was surrounded by people who genuinely loved me and wanted nothing but the best for me.

As Luke and I turned to face our family and friends for the first time as husband and wife, it wasn't my mother or my sister or even Emma who caught my attention, but rather, the man standing at the top of the hill. I caught sight of him for only the briefest of seconds and then he was gone in a flash. I blinked, looked to my mother, and back again at the top of the hill.

"Riley?" my mother asked, stepping toward me, her confusion evident.

I forced a smile even as my brain tried to make sense of who I just saw. Luke noticed the shift in me, too.

"Babe, you okay?" Luke leaned down and whispered in my ear.

"I'm fine," I lied. "I'm just happy and a little overwhelmed."

"Me too," he said, kissing my cheek. He squeezed my hand tighter.

We moved together into the circle of our family and friends. I knew they were talking to me, but I couldn't process their words. I smiled. I kissed their cheeks. I said all the right things. My thoughts remained on that man. I was fairly certain it was my father, but it couldn't be. I forced the image out of my mind. Nothing would ruin this day and so I didn't let it. The rest of the day went by in a blissful blur. Photos and dinner and more laughter than any day had ever held. None of it mattered more than knowing Luke was at my side.

"I love you so much," I said later that evening as he unzipped my dress.

"You couldn't possibly love me as much as I love you." Luke kissed my shoulder.

I turned and faced him, smiling up at him and slipping his hands in mine. We would step into the future together, hand in hand – no matter what came our way.

READ THE NEXT
RILEY SULLIVAN MYSTERY

BOSTON UNDERGROUND

Have you read them all?

Riley Sullivan Mystery Series

Deadly Sins
The Bone Harvest
Missing Time Murders
We Last Saw Jane
Boston Underground

Harper & Hattie Magical Mystery Series

Saints & Sinners Ball
Secrets to Tell
Rule of Three
The Forever Curse

FBI Agent Kate Walsh Thriller Series

The Curators
The Founders

Access the Free Mystery Readers' Club Starter Library

Riley Sullivan Mystery Series novella "The 1922 Club Murder"
FBI Agent Kate Walsh Thriller Series novella "The Curators"
Harper & Hattie Mystery Series novella "Harper's Folly"

Sign up for the starter library along with exclusive launch-day pricing, special behind the scenes access, and extra content not available anywhere else.

Hit subscribe at

http://www.stacymjones.com/

Follow Stacy M. Jones for exclusive information on book signings, events, fan giveaways, and her next novel.

Facebook: StacyMJonesWriter
Twitter: @SMJonesWriter
Goodreads: StacyMJonesWriter

Please leave a review for We Last Saw Jane!
Thank you!
Amazon
BookBub
Goodreads

Made in the USA
Monee, IL
22 November 2024

70842408R00167